ACID BUBBLES

ACID BUBBLES

PAUL H ROUND

Copyright © 2015 Paul H Round

The moral right of the author has been asserted.

Apart from any fair dealing for the purposes of research or private study, or criticism or review, as permitted under the Copyright, Designs and Patents Act 1988, this publication may only be reproduced, stored or transmitted, in any form or by any means, with the prior permission in writing of the publishers, or in the case of reprographic reproduction in accordance with the terms of licences issued by the Copyright Licensing Agency. Enquiries concerning reproduction outside those terms should be sent to the publishers.

Matador
9 Priory Business Park
Kibworth Beauchamp
Leicestershire LE8 0RX, UK
Tel: (+44) 116 279 2299
Fax: (+44) 116 279 2277
Email: books@troubador.co.uk
Web: www.troubador.co.uk/matador

ISBN 978 1784621 995

British Library Cataloguing in Publication Data.
A catalogue record for this book is available from the British Library.

Printed and bound in the UK by TJ International, Padstow, Cornwall
Typeset in Adobe Garamond Pro by Troubador Publishing Ltd

Matador is an imprint of Troubador Publishing Ltd

To Heather who persuaded me I could do this…

To the glorious brightness of the morning dew, to Weetabix for breakfast, to my moorland inspiration, to Irish eyes, to one million strides all in identical shoes, to Liverpool football club, and to the Big Fella who never tells me I shouldn't drink the last one – bastard! Not forgotten – the myriad of incredible others that pushed me, shoved me, inspired me, and helped on this journey into a strange land…

Special thanks to Madge and Gina… Vicious old sisters who have inspired many ideas during our long walks.

CHAPTER 1

Today, right here right now. Hunting for the perfect day.

Perfect day, strange idea, does it exist? I don't think it does. I will tell you why. The very idea of a perfect day from dawn until dusk is impossible. To find perfection in every single passing moment or for just one minute would be too much to ask. Suppose it existed, everything in those wakeful hours on that fabulous day just perfect. The weather, all the people you encounter, every single aspect of the day working in harmony for every passing minute. This is where cynicism casts its dark shadow.

Nothing could stay that perfect for every single minute. A crying child distracts you, a meal less than perfect, or some lager-fuelled angry yobbo swearing at the sky. Anything could discolour the specialness of our own perspective of the perfect. Assume that during this magical day every moment gives fabulous satisfaction. Sometime towards the end of this impossible day, a realisation for a mere second darkens your soul; on a subliminal level you know your shining day will be followed by a duller tomorrow.

At this point the argument falls flat. No day can be true perfection when the knowledge of an inferior tomorrow taints the day. To think for only the briefest moment of a grey tomorrow breaks the perfection. A pessimistic view and you're probably right.

Eternal optimist... normally I am always the optimist imagining the outcome to dire situations will be good, but the perfect day idea is something else. Some perfect moments, yes, but the perfect day? Who are you kidding?

I always spoil my best moments thinking of tomorrow. "Enjoy the now" that's what they say, and I'm trying to master the art of enjoying each moment. One day, of course, will be my last day, and if this is an almost perfect day what could be better? Now I sound almost optimistic, suggesting it would be possible to experience the almost perfect. That's a step forward!

Death's cold grip closes its cruel hand around some unfortunate soul, and my day gets so much better! This man's death is the unexpected bonus…

I saw him go into the abyss in front of me! Feet wearing snow boots disappearing over the precipice. His death plunge obscured by blinding white late afternoon sunshine. An act not done to surprise the entire *après* ski crowd, or to give them some bar talk down in Marbella. To my mind it was carried out with a cold deliberation and produced for me a strange dramatic image. I'll admit it now, somewhere inside I laughed, it cheered me.

Only one outcome was possible after he'd plunged from the terrace. Jagged rocks and sharp cold fingers of ice waited to convert his velocity into death six hundred feet below. Anyone who witnessed the fall knew this man's death was certain. This vivid disturbing image came at the end of my extra special day. See! I still cannot say perfect. My day was not tainted by the constant creeping insistence of tomorrow, but – enhanced – by a brutal suicide, a final act to silence a tortured and tormented mind.

This will sound strange, but witnessing that tortured soul's death, almost turned an extra special day into a nearly perfect day. See, the cynic in me is softening!

Only twelve short hours earlier, my day had started with the horrible tyranny of the 5am alarm call. I was destined to suffer pain before the strident alarm had brought me rudely back to wakefulness. After watching a Tarantino war film until well after midnight with some beers, I was in for a beating before I awoke. So any chance of perfection was tainted by the day before! I hate alarm clocks, and no matter how early I go to bed, sleep is almost always disturbed by my internal brain-ghost stamping around waiting for the insidious vile alarm.

The mere act of setting the clock attacks the perfect day attempt. Beyond 4am I wake every ten minutes in expectation of its cutting insistent tones. This brings the inevitable early liquid breakfast. I rise and stumble, head buzzing, to the kitchen at 4.30am. Coffee, this is what I need, lots and black. For me a great day would start with a languid awakening by beautiful maidens sometime around midday. This God-awful early-morning stuff doesn't remind me of the lotus eater. My foolish indulgence means I am awakened in the cold ice grip of winter – inside my apartment! Now I'll have to talk about discounting!

Discounting time, discounting the rotten, discounting the uncomfortable, discounting anything unacceptable before the start of your quest. I will explain.

I love the sheer thrill of skiing. I'm going to the snow and the day starts at this odd one hour before the godforsaken. The preamble is all discounted time, not until I climb skis in hand on to the cable car does the clock start ticking on the quest for perfect moments. To achieve eight great hours in this unrealistic pursuit for nirvana would be an optimist's goal, the pessimist's miracle. Unhelpful pessimistic thoughts are beginning to consider the crush inside the cable car. So, to this end, I discount all the painful preambles until I push my feet hard into the ski bindings. Click, click! Let the day begin!

The physical pleasure of speed, ice crystals flying up from the hard edges of your skis, this is what it's all about! The glorious sensation of being alive on those amazing ice-white mountains, this is why I discount the early starts. The pleasure far outweighs the pain, and on the balance of things I'm on to a winner.

It's Monday morning. The slopes will be less hectic than the weekend. The few snowboarders falling on their arses every time they climb off the chairlift will not generate huge tedious queues. More space on the slopes to dodge those baggy trousers-wearing youths. In reality I'm jealous of their youthful vigour and their bodies seemingly made of rubber. It's never quiet during the season, even on weekdays, and it makes you wonder where all the people find time not to work. It's February, it snowed yesterday, the temperatures are low, and the sun is brilliant in an azure sky.

Every element is combining to give that once a year day, the prospect of perfect conditions. A great day was building in front of me, I could sense something special deep in my bones, and this day was to become far, far better than any I'd ever experienced. With strange events, a death included, bringing me close to the perfect day. If not perfect, then pretty dam near!

Skiing is something I came to quite late in life, only taking it up when everyone told me I was too old to pursue any ambitions to ski. This was the turning point, obstinacy taking over when they say, whoever they are, you shouldn't learn to ski at your age! I decided to learn to ski because this counted the flat people who'd lost their internal fire and wanted you to live in their ash grey world, desperate for you to share their lack of youthful spirit. They wouldn't step up and attempt anything. You were expected to step down into their mire of resentment of youthful vigour.

Confession time. I undertook hours of one-to-one instruction with a talented and very beautiful young instructor. I was distressed to discover I was a natural at skiing. A natural in business would have been a blessing, but my luck was to be a natural in an expensive niche sport. Three years have taken me away from the laughing children on the nursery slope's, to the steepest slopes, and with the passing of time to the very blackest of blacks.

On this day I had my master plan: start on the blue run to get the eye in. Shake out the rust, then on to the quieter red pistes to carve a few wild curves, and throw some ice around. I like watching the vaporous dancing shadows cast by the crystals in the low morning sunshine. Today I'm skiing free, looking for my special moments. I will ski alone, planning my day on the move, a selfish pursuit with no tyranny from others. Today, I could sense, would be different, possibly nearly perfect.

I cannot ski all day, I need to eat. It was during my snack break that I encountered a skiing group over from London. We fell into conversation and within minutes were getting on well, a sharp banter honed by the British north-south rivalry. So I skied with the group for an hour or so, having to push myself out of my comfort zone to stay with the best of them. I don't have to stay with the expert skiers, do I? I followed them hard and fast down two black runs without falls.

Some of these guys don't wear helmets and are very gung-ho. I always wear all the kit, but I'm still pushing myself into dangerous areas. With danger I hold a love-hate relationship. On the one hand if things are too easy, too comfortable, I feel life is passing me by. On the other, too much adrenaline makes me think I'm stupid to push so hard at the edges of the possible.

I am an adventurous coward afraid of missing something tenuous, and when amongst the action afraid of hitting something solid. Over the years I've learnt how to make internal compromises, a calculated balance of the risks, pushing to get the thrills, but not going too far. My instructor says I have natural balance, but I don't think we mean the same thing.

The guys Michael and Tony were on holiday and wanted to stop for more beers. After the discounted start and the hours of driving I didn't want to waste skiing time. It was beautiful soft almost perfect snow, so it couldn't be ignored even for a minute. I bid my farewells taking the usual and often never followed up email addresses. "We must catch up again," but we never do!

Twice emboldened by the London boys (not the band) I have stupid falls pushing the technique, and once a full hundred metre snow, sky, snow, sky, shoulder, head and bottom bruising moment. This leaves me winded for a minute or so, cursing my own stupidity at pushing the envelope. I lay in the snow recovering my breath. Gentle hands help me to my feet, assisting me by recovering my lost skis from thirty metres up the slope. I assure my helper that I'm okay, nothing permanently damaged, I'm only winded for a minute, and so I reflect on my sense of self-preservation and balance. How much thrill can I give myself without too much of this fear thing? I ease back... a little!

This truly lovely day passed as all things special; too quick for a man wanting more. A final consolation was visiting my favourite terrace bar for the lingering *après* ski. It was crowded, so as normal I share a table. You look more social that way. I do have friends but sadly none of them were foolish enough to learn to ski. Some were foolish taking up sub-aqua with all that rubber and cold water. Then again, rubber and cold water might be your thing!

I find a spare chair on the terrace and enquire if it's free. Yes, I think he said, and if he did it was the only word spoken, no others. He didn't look at me. It was as if I wasn't there, a passing shadow. The man at my side could have been me. Similar age, Northern European looks, hair colour more or less mine, but I think he had a little less, and definitely thinner. The big difference between us is in our demeanours. I'm taking the rays, slowly drinking my only pint of beer – I've got to drive. Eating my tapas and people watching, not exactly people, a more accurate term would be watching beauty. Today there are some spectacular forms on display in very tight ski pants, an excellent day all round, powder snow and a vintage day of *après* ski beauties. On the other end of the table, my compatriot's drinking his seventh or eighth strong bottled lager. I know this because the bar is too busy for the overstretched staff to clear tables and the dead bottles line up, testament to his insatiable thirst.

He's never without the bottle in his hand, pouring the stuff down at one hell of a rate. I suppose he's staying at one of the hotels in the ski resort. I hope to god he's not driving off the mountain tonight, or he may just drive into a waiting chasm. His gaze comes back time and again to the beer bottle as if he fears finding it empty.

All this time his concentration is devoted to listening. The object of his rapt attention is a small digital voice recorder. It's the type you see journalists using on the television news whilst trying to catch a damning sound bite from some hapless politico who's about to have the full support of the Prime Minister behind him and leave politics. His drinking and intent listening lead me to believe that he may be just that, a newshound reviewing prime sound bites, relaxing heavily, journalistic style.

Time passes as do more *après* ski visions on that bright, and for me, exceptional day. Though we have not spoken and are not facing each other, a tension existed between us. Sitting almost shoulder to shoulder my feeling was of an old festering argument. I don't know if I saw this or sensed it but I had the impression he'd finished with his listening. I see him, but he doesn't register me at all, he's staring into empty space, eyes not focusing on this world. He wrapped the recorder into its little papoose using the earpiece cables. His actions are slow, heavy and made with an unnerving deliberation. Why I'm having a bad vibe I have no idea, but the intense set of his body as he carries out these movements give me a disturbing cold sensation up my spine.

To my great surprise he places the machine down in front of me centred between my tapas and beer. It sits there abandoned. I look at the recorder and to my compatriot, our eyes will never meet. I return my gaze to the machine placed with deliberation in front of me. I start to ask a question; no words leave my lips.

For now this is the moment my story ends and his begins…

With sudden almost robotic abruptness of movement, he stands and stagger strolls across the terrace, weaving a drunken path between the tables. He bumps one or two tables hard with his loose moving body and receives loud complaints, all ignored. Spilt drinks, stained clothing, and scattered food. People are roused from their conversations, watching this swaying figure make his clumsy exit from the terrace. It's not too easy to watch him blinded by the low sunshine. A hint of nightfall comes with a sudden chill or is that something else about this moment I imagined?

I'm shielding my eyes watching or trying to watch what he's going to do. I hear a single shrill cry from a woman nearby, then the gasp from my left, a whole wave of sound moves across the crowded terrace. Everyone turns from conversation and food. Rapt attention has taken over the entire eating area. Everything is moving in slow motion focused on the one single figure I now see swaying on the stone balustrade topped with an ornate iron lamp post; used as an aid to climb up there. At that moment he was gripping it with a white knuckled clench, and I thought that he might address the terrace for some strange reason and make a speech against conspicuous consumption. No, he looks down into the void, and at that moment slumps as if all the weight in the world was inside him.

It's difficult to describe how he fell. It's hard to say what an outsider would have seen. To me the way his body crumpled would suggest weight pushing him down, or the abyss somehow pulled on his body like a magnetic force attracting human flesh. One second standing there, the next he was over the edge and gone. The sun was trying to burn the eyes from my head, but I couldn't tear my gaze away from the spot where moments before he'd been standing. His silhouette was burnt onto my eyeballs; seconds after he'd gone he would be dead. His image still alive in my eyes after his eyes could no longer see.

I'd been damaging my eyes picturing this man damage himself for the final time. The rock would take him, there was no soft option waiting below. The bulk of the crowd would rush forward in its morbid desire to see someone else's demise, perhaps to be glad that the horror of death was not theirs today. For some the nightmares would follow, possibly for months or even years. For others with harder souls it would be one hell of a pub story, and, for some, digital phone gold to post online. In the next five minutes a relation in hot Mumbai could watch cold death.

At this moment all the eyes were fixed towards the sun silhouetting the balustrade, not on me. So what do I do next? Pick up the voice recorder like it's my own, and place it in my pocket. Nobody else on the terrace sees this apparent theft. I have no desire to look over the precipice to see the image that was already burnt into my mind. I knew the fate awaiting anyone who plunged from that balustrade. There was no point looking into the abyss, I knew what was down there.

I placed money for my beer on the table. I didn't think my compatriot had paid. Yes he had! Without any hesitation I made my way to the car through the rapidly chilling day and joined the usual fume-filled snail-crawl of cars off the mountain into Granada. On the way down I listened to easy music, and took a Bluetooth phone call. Only when I reach the free moving, night time motorway does my fascination overcome me. It's time to listen to the story trapped inside the voice recorder.

I plug into the central system of my BMW coupe. When the digital machine started I thought I might gain some insight and understanding from a dead man's words. I drove at a steady pace staying on a longer motorway only route so I could listen without the interruptions associated with travel on crowded roads.

I hoped to hear it all in one sitting. My day had started at 4:30am, and twelve unique hours later it had ended with the 4:30pm death plunge. The machine was running and for the first few seconds, silence. Had he wiped it? Then a cough, then silence, then another cough, *Oh, get on with it*. Finally, the words came…

This is an accurate account of the words inside that digital memory.

The live digital confession of a man who no longer exists!

CHAPTER 2

Right here right now, reasons to be cheerful.

The recording machine's digital memory was decoded, producing words in a stranger's voice. This is what he said:

"How can I start my story?" (He paused at this point for several seconds then continued.)

"To be more accurate this is a confession! I have discovered after many years of wilful ignorance I've done things that you would describe as bad, very bad. This term is grossly understating some of the horrors I have been party too. As for committing murder, my personal jury is still out on that one. Evidence doesn't always tell the truth, does it?

"I'm also struggling to come to terms with strange and incredible events outside of the normal world, in a mysterious universe full of strange creatures. As I journeyed through this fantastic place I was shown the truths that lead to this confession. I was taken there, I lived there, and it's burnt into my psyche. I am tortured by the beauty...

"The wrongs I've committed were not always with malicious intent and sometimes with little understanding of the final horror my actions would bring. The damage to other people's lives, the problems I have brought to other people's doors, and the cold end I've given to some are all in this confession. I will start with the mundane, my name and age. The construction could be looked upon, I suppose, as a curriculum vitae of taking the wrong path and slipping into evil.

"I now call myself Peter Henry Jackson. That's my current surname, for all my life it's been Peter. The Henry Jackson bit was a gift from a fellow Nazi, not that I follow Nazi doctrine. I was given the name in a previous life, a time when I mixed with a heartless man. I'll come to that part later. I'm now in my fifth decade, though I don't believe it. In fact I feel about twenty-five-years-old and full of spirit. I suspect the girls I look at think I'm an old pervert and don't see the younger soul inside me. Time is difficult isn't it?

"Vanity makes me fight insidious age. I do a lot of cycling, don't smoke or drink too much. Okay, sometimes I push the bottle a bit. However, people still think that my true age is about forty-eight or so. That's what my friends tell me – Liars! Soon I will be sixty, and now, physically, I look good, too bloody good.

"The ironic thing about this last statement is that I have battled cancer, and during this illness I began to understand my lost history and it's horrors that lead to this very unusual confession. I know I'm going to die but it doesn't show to the world in the accepted stereotypical ways of baldness, terrible skin, and a horrible greyness. That manifestation of the cancerous me has gone, I have passed through that terrible dark stage. I no longer remind people of a victim of famine and plague. I am now robust for the world to see, and not robust in any way at all behind the facade!

"The fact is people I meet in the street say how good I look. This is another irony not lost on me. A few years ago I got super fit and people used to tell me how very ill I looked. Now people I meet in the street without prompting or knowledge of my cancer say things like, 'You're looking good, you must have found somebody'. My experience of finding somebody is usually very draining, so what do they mean? Love lifts you up where you belong. Am I quoting song lyrics?

"So back to this confession of a life less good. I had prostate cancer, quite young for it, though that doesn't give me any cheer as if I'd achieve something by doing it quite young. I suffered from secondary tumours, and these cancers unchecked usually metastasise into far more deadly bone cancer. How can something be more deadly than something that's deadly? I had an operation a few months ago. Going into theatre you've signed all these papers allowing them to do what is necessary to save your life, not the quality of your life.

"A very worrying thought when what is necessary to save your miserable life could leave you with no muscular control in your lower body and, the biggest horror of all, permanent double incontinence. You have no choice, you've signed all the papers and you're floating down hospital corridors on a trolley drugged out of your mind. You're away with the fairies, and you don't care.

"They've performed all the tests but nothing is certain until they go in there and have a dig around. What a horrible expression, 'to dig around'. Inside your body digging around among your organs like being on a treasure hunt! It's only after the knife has cut away deceased flesh you discover how much of a winner you've been in this lottery of bleakness.

"Frankly I came out of it with more intact than I really deserve. I walk okay and I'm in control of my own farts! On the second day after the operation, the sensation of a fart building up was a bit of a joy. The knowledge that you can actually feel your bowels filling with gas gives you the belief that you will be able to control them. I deliberately farted. It was a fart and not a vile mess. The best smelling fart in my entire life was full of strange delight. This milestone had me laughing out loud for several minutes. You might think a strange thing to laugh at? Not at all, the knowledge that you won't be shitting yourself for the rest of your days is something worth laughing over, a joy!

"In the first months after the operation, I had the penis of a five-year-old. The thing shrunk to the size it was before my post-puberty fumbling and by all accounts might never fully recover. Things did improve a lot with help from my friends. I'll get to that later on, much later on!

"Pissing my pants was another indignity following surgery. A year or two could see the end of this problem. At first I was using five nappies a day. I'm dry at night when I lie down. I discuss this with the doctor and I sound like a bloody toddler who's got knowledge beyond his years. 'Oh, he's dry at night'. Great!

"Then, of course, there's the chemotherapy, a poison in the bloodstream eradicating the cancerous cells and destroying many of the good cells in the same holocaust of the blood. It clears your system of almost everything including, on bad days, your will to go on. Days into weeks, these become long months, and the shadows grow across your face, a reflection of the poisons travelling inside you. Vomiting becomes so commonplace you can excuse yourself almost like you're going to cough.

"Do you mind if I vomit for a minute? Ah, that's better! Bit of a conversation stopper. Time and pain harden you against other people's sensibilities. Sympathetic eyes at the bedside drive you to want to claw at them, so I've slapped a face or two. Be cheerful, I'm trying to be!

"Then there's the radiotherapy. It burns. Invading your body slowly, the first few sessions are very innocuous making you believe it's ineffective. At first the whole thing seems as innocent as someone shining a torch on you. It isn't! If I'm going to burn in hell; I started to cook behind that foot thick lead door.

"Tests are not over and I still do not know if they've got it all. None of this now matters. During the nightmare months I discovered much of my terrible past, and in the last few days revelations have revealed the full scope of my evilness.

"I've not come to terms with my odious history and start this confession at a moment when physically I might fully recover. Do I deserve to, and do I want to? **No!**

"The following confession will tell you why."

CHAPTER 3

August 1971.

On this day my raging hormones triggered events that would change the course of my life forever. These were the moments I took the first step down a dangerous road, out of the world of adolescence and into the heavy footfalls of adulthood. I had no clue then, but that night was to be my last family meal around the old farmhouse table.

I'll try to be accurate in my remembrance of what was said during these times, and the way the words were spoken.

"What the hell is that smell?"

"It's Brut for men, it drives the girls wild," I said. (Even then I was exuding vile odours.)

Leaning in the doorway and grinning at me was Jane, my sister. Her eyes had a mischievous glint.

"Brutal for women don't you mean? The smell is sickening. . It smells worse than the bloody farmyard," she said.

"What do you know about seventeen-year-old girls?" I said in response.

"It may have passed your notice but I am a twenty-one-year-old girl, and I know what girls like."

I looked her up and down. Jane was dressed head to foot in black leather, wild dark hair was everywhere. I suppose if she hadn't been my sister, Jane would've been quite attractive. Of course I'd never tell her that, she would always be the older sister who tormented the five-year-old me in the farmyard. Her games invariably had something to do with accidents and animal waste. So no matter how attractive she was, I could never tell her, brothers never do.

"You're not a girl, you're a biker" I said. What a feeble response.

"I'm a girl that rides a motorbike! That so-called perfume is disgusting," she said.

"It's not perfume, its aftershave. If you were a proper girl you would know it's irresistible."

"If I was a sow I might find it slightly attractive," she said.

There was no arguing with her. I could never win. You never win against big sisters, and if you score a few points feminine guile will score revenge points ten times over.

"What the hell are you doing watching me anyway?" I said.

Her response was to tell me that dinner was ready down in the farmhouse kitchen. I always attempted, without success, to avoid the tension zoo around the family table. I dragged my disappointing face away from the mirror. Why do you always develop an enormous spot on a Friday night, never on Monday or Tuesday? I'd prodded at the pustule without hope. Reluctantly I plodded down the stairs of our 1960s farmhouse into the grand communal kitchen. With the assembled family waiting, I regarded this as entering the lion's cage in the circus ring.

Tonight dinner would be a special torture for me. I had to force it down onto a nervous stomach. This was a fact of life for me. Every time I faced crisis my stomach churns forcing me either to dry heave or rush to the toilet. Tonight would be no exception because I was out on the town with my best mate Bob Wilson.

Better than that, tonight we would be grooving (sounded good in 71) at a small intimate party. We were told we'd meet a girl or girls who were easy. Tonight of all nights might be the big moment, the time when we would become men. We were convinced that tonight we'd lose our virginities.

This is nothing new. Several times in the last year we'd ventured out on similar missions that ended in fruitless snogging sessions. Sometimes we gratified base desires touching drunken girls in the most intimate of places. What these girls thought of us we never ever found out. Most of the time we never saw them again, and if we did we were ignored with passion. It was more than obvious our techniques were not that of experienced lovers. The only wildness we were arousing in these girls was the animal instinct to run. Friday night facial eruptions never helped either!

Smiggy had arranged the small party tonight because Smiggy had connections. A couple of years older than us he could always be found down at our favourite pub, The Cauldron. How we got to know this little twisted work of art I don't remember, but he was one of the slimiest little maggots you could ever wish to meet. Not that we knew this at that time, though I think we sensed it, but we ignored it because we thought he could arrange things. This was Friday night and when we'd bumped into him on the Wednesday he'd told us he'd fixed it. "The girl really loves it. She's always gagging for some dick, can't leave it alone," was the charming way Smiggy had described this teenage girl.

Crude in hindsight, but in our defence we were seventeen-year-olds driven by too many wild hormones. He assured us that during our intimate party we would score with the girl or girls. Sex was a sure thing. I had my best friend Bob for moral support.

Bob Wilson looked like George Best. He was a perfect copy, and as handsome as George. This was the end of the good news and where it all started to go wrong for Bob. The problem was he had 100% less style, no style at all. He wore great clothes and succeeded in transcending any advantage they gave him. His twitchy, nervous style of speaking combined with a God-given gift for the inappropriate never let him down. Without fail he could offend the mildest teenage girl, always picking the wrong topic. He suffered slaps across the face or total indifference. We were a great team, Bob with his good looks and no class, with me hiding behind loud clothes and louder perfume – sorry aftershave!

All this fake machismo made me feel more nervous than I'd ever been in my life. Going sober to a party with a sure thing was daunting. The first move tonight would be to down a few pints in the pub before we ventured off on the road to our manhood. My stomach was very nervous and I dry retched my way down the stairs.

Running the gauntlet of the family dinner table was always a torture when the aunties were over from the old cottage. In the old days the cottage was the main farmhouse, but now occupied rent-free by my opinionated scrounging aunties, both closet Nazis. The old cottage was over a rise out of sight from the farmhouse, so if you were lucky you didn't have to see the old girls. Sadly it was too close, and they would invite themselves over for a free dinner on a regular basis, a far too regular basis.

The modern kitchen was dominated by an old Victorian farmhouse table. Around this expanse of wood were gathered the oddest assortment of mismatched chairs. Each of the chairs had arrived as if by magic and reflected the personality of its occupant. Where they came from nobody seemed to know, but these chairs will always be etched in my memory. Most had been standing mismatched around the table all my life. I can never remember a tablecloth and always the oddest place settings scattered around, never anything formal.

I was the last in the house to join the happy throng. Being the youngest wasn't good news, I'd be easy prey for my auntie's attentions.

The aunties, Beatrice and Violet, took over all conversations, and were dominating and more solidly Victorian than the table. Both war widows with sad and different stories, they shared a common hatred of everything German. Nazi Germany had taken their beloved Sidney and Joe away from them. They had a mint imperial smelling bitterness, unbroken after more than two decades alone.

My aunties formed an evil alliance as bad as any evil axis. These old ladies were my fascists. Anything, and I mean anything, I could do was never good enough. I was the big disappointment because I wasn't going into the family business. It was the livestock that I hated so much, finding the hideous-smelling crowded pens uninteresting. It was always bitterly cold at 5am no matter what time of the year. This wasn't the life for me. I was going to be a dentist or at worst a dental technician with a clean laboratory, more money and fewer hours. Best of all, no mountains of shit, I loathed animal waste, steaming piles of shit. You could keep farming!

"These modern girls showing their bottoms and fat legs get no respect from men!" Beattie boomed, showing the open page of a magazine to make her point to anybody who was interested. The picture featured a smart girl wearing a dress two inches above her knee, all very disturbing I didn't think.

"I think I would have worn a dress like that if I'd been eighteen now. I wish Jane would dress a little bit more feminine," Violet said, looking across in the direction of Beattie, her thin high vinegar voice cutting through the air. Beattie couldn't have heard above the sound of the pressure cooker, though the suggestion that somebody should wear such a disgusting item would have shocked her older sister.

"You only say that because you've got good legs. Big legs like mine aren't suited to that style. I was very lucky when I was eighteen, meeting Sidney," Beattie boomed. She had very good hearing when she decided to use it. When my mother asked for help her deafness was almost profound. She without any conscience expounded values she always failed miserably to demonstrate.

"We all covered up when I was eighteen," Violet said, "but if I were eighteen now I'd show my knickers."

"I didn't know you had such a wild side, Violet," Jane said in surprise.

"I haven't got a wild side, I'm jealous of you young girls. And you, young lady, don't make the best of yourself with all that leather," Violet responded.

"Looks like a boy, a ruffian, a ne'er-do-well!" Beattie boomed. My sister looked back uninterested and uncaring.

The evil axis legs debate had now finished. It was time to attack fresh prey, namely me!

"My God, what the hell is that smell?" Beattie said. She watched me with gimlet eyes whilst building her next bout of criticism. I always promised myself one day I would get revenge. Was my day ever going to come?

"Yes, what is that smell? It's really sickly like vanilla and chocolate but worse," Violet added.

"Look at your hair, it's just too long. You look more like a girl than a boy. Those shoes, they're higher than good girls wore in my day. Bad girls wore shoes like that," Beattie boomed at me.

"I'm not a bad girl, Auntie, I'm a boy," I exclaimed.

"You're wearing high-heeled shoes and sailors' trousers, flares I think you call them, and that hair. A common girl would dress like that for a night out with soldiers," Beattie said, and then buried her head in the magazine. She'd had the last word.

"This is 1971, the world has changed and I'm changing with it. This is new and wild," I said. Beattie and Violet snorted with derision.

"I think Peter looks nice. He's only seventeen he's allowed to make a few mistakes." My mother, Iris, voiced this over the sound from the pressure cooker, the steam making her ghostlike in the room. A comment I couldn't decide on. What was she saying?

"Dinner is ready. All sit down and stop arguing," My mother said. This carried weight, everyone was quiet. My mother's words always held a quiet authority. She'd been snatched away from the middle classes. Her grandfather was a gentleman farmer, and my father, John, a hard-working farm boy who had first seen my mother at a country fair. I think my mother wanted to escape the constraints of the family home. My very grand grandmother always schemed for her to marry someone from the right circle. She fell in love with John and I never heard my parents argue. I cannot recall a single harsh word between them.

Tough as my father was, my mother had quiet well-spoken strength. Through the haze of steam I could see her move towards a switch next to the door. It sounded bells in the farm buildings, and only at lambing time could we ignore the call for a family dinner around the large Victorian table. John my father and George my studious, quiet, twenty-three-year-old brother would be at the table within two minutes.

My father said little after the hard labour of his fourteen-hour-day. George would hardly speak to me. He thought I was letting the family down by not helping with the farm. He'd studied hard at agricultural college, and was always talking about modern agricultural methods. One day he would be the boss, and it would be like working for Hitler, a dictator, a fascist.

The chairs around that table were a mismatched broken bunch, and the people around that table were as strange and different as each chair they sat upon. The chairs were held by their usefulness around that table. What was holding us together, blood bonds?

"Dad, will you run me into town later?" I asked, halfway through the pudding. There was a heavy atmosphere in the room that night as if a storm was building. I didn't know at the time, but it was.

My father removed a rag from a pocket in the overalls he always seemed to wear. He threw this soiled cloth at me and my clean clothes. The piece of material wasn't dirty, but the force of my father's action and his words shocked me.

"I do fourteen hours, you do nothing! You can walk and wipe the muck from your own stupid shoes. Help me some time and I might help you!" my father said. There was finality in this statement that indicated I should remain quiet. I didn't!

"Dad…"

"Shut up now or you won't be going out!"

This was the end of my last family meal around the big table. My mismatched chair was about to be used for firewood.

My father and I were set on a hard path. Bitter arguments would fill the twisted future I would walk into tonight.

CHAPTER 4

A very short time before the now. One step beyond.

Shortly after I was diagnosed with cancer something quite extraordinary happened, and it happened in the dark shadows of the night. It started as a nightmare. No ordinary nightmare, a special kind of nightmare. Dreams are dreams, everybody has them. Sometimes they are vivid, sometimes vague. I think everybody in the world, and I mean everybody, knows what dreams are.

I thought I did until one night several months ago. This night was the first step on the road to revelation and discovery. In fact this very first strange step would lead me in the end to the truth, all the truths about my past. That first infant stumbling along this road wasn't an easy lesson. It was a journey that gave me a wretched awakening in terror.

Let me explain. It was just an ordinary night and I was inside a jumble of mundane dreams. These dreams were ordinary from me, many to be forgotten even before waking. It was during one of these dreams in the depths of night that I first discovered the crack, a small fissure into a different reality. Dreams are dreams and will always remain so. This is what I thought. Until I put my hand on the door handle…

After I'd walked through the door my whole perception of the real and the non-real changed forever. You see, I was in a passageway in a vague and very normal dreamlike state. When I grabbed a door handle at the end of this random corridor, it was cold to the touch, very cold. Straightaway something out of the ordinary was happening. The sensation of cold was like touching a shelf in an ice box. At first I thought I'd woken up and knocked over my glass of water. No, this was not the thing at all. The sensations were spreading and not only confined to my hand. My whole body was receiving new stimuli, a new world was opening. I could now feel it along my arm. More than that, I could perceive every hair on it, every sinew and every molecule making that part of my body, all with a stunning crystal clear intensity. It was with the joy of enlightenment more than fear of what lies ahead that I stepped up. After a moment's hesitation I decided my next move. Yes, inside what I thought was a dream I calculated what I was about to do.

I turned the door handle and I could feel the mechanism inside, not a simple sensation like when you're awake, but every single piece of metal touching every other piece of metal. Parts ground in the opening action of the door. The door creaked open, and I could feel the dryness in the hinges as they needed oiling. The wind hit me, and to my surprise it was a cold, damp night. The corridor had been null, dreamlike. Now my whole body, every molecule, was awake. It was ten times more real than any real I've ever known. It was like plunging your face into a bowl of icy cold water, a sensation of being far more awake than ever in any normal existence. I'd walked or been propelled into a new dimension, a world somewhere else other than here.

This was no nightmare, this was super reality. I wanted to discover more about this new found vital space. I stepped into the wet, dark cobbled street. It was lit by yellow, dull almost Victorian lighting. At first I thought it was a Victorian dream but no, there were modern signs, people in the strangest clothing, but not from any remembered past. A bone-chilling light drizzle was falling. I could smell everything that night, the rain, the dirt, food, even at a distance and the most disturbing part of all, the people. This is when a hint of agitation started to disturb me. It was the stench of the people. They smelt dangerous. I was overwhelmed by the smell of aggression. I had developed super senses and I was fascinated. At the same time somewhere in the back of what I assume was my own mind I was very frightened.

Then it struck me. The revelation came to me like a thunderbolt, and I knew without doubt what this strange dimension was. This other reality was a manifestation of my battle with cancer, my fear of a lingering painful death. This was a cancer experience with groups of dark shadowy foe characters hanging round in doorways, under lights, smoking and mumbling. All these dangerous smelling characters represented tumours in near human form. All were malicious-looking, the type always to be cast as bad guys in the movies. The problem was tonight I was inside the movie and these bad guys were very real.

I can only tell you this in hindsight because at the time things were very different for me. At that moment I could not tell if I was awake or not. It would be a complete lie to say I had any knowledge our universe existed. At that moment on that damp night I was alive. Dream did not exist, all my past was gone, and this was living reality in a cold damp street, with every sense in my body on fire. I could hear the locks turning behind me as if someone was forcing me into the alleyway. This made it impossible for any retreat back into soft option dreaming. By then it wasn't important, I'd already forgotten its existence. I turned to face a danger behind me, face down whoever was closing the door. I was shocked to discover no one behind me, the only thing there a graffiti scrawled brick wall. I turned and looked around that dingy disturbing street, discovering only one escape route.

The street was cobbled as if to take heavy traffic, but it didn't seem to be a through road of any kind. It was accessed by one solitary alleyway, narrow and darkly shadowed, off to my left. I could see into this disturbing alleyway from where I was standing. It was dark and wet. In every corner its shadows pulsed with the movement of cockroaches and rats. Beyond I could see a brightly lit street. I ran!

My running was a revelation. As I accelerated every tendon in my legs, every single muscle, and every fibre of my being worked in harmony. I could control my velocity, the drain on my energy, everything including a colossal top speed. Each footfall came with the knowledge of my toes contacting the ground. I could feel the type of stone the cobbles were made of. The sensation was one of slow motion though by now I must have been doing thirty miles an hour. I was faster than the fastest men in the world, and it seemed slow. Where could I push this to? The sticky, damp light rain started to sting my face such was the speed I was travelling. As my arms pumped I could feel the wind rushing between my fingertips. This was the most scintillating experience of velocity and power I think any living man has ever experienced. This was fabulous. I was escaping in epic style.

Fabulous, that is, until I could smell danger bubbling up behind me. They were moving very fast, possessing similar powers to me and were charging after me like a herd of stampeding cattle. It wasn't like one of those dreams where you can't run any faster no matter how hard you try, it wasn't like that at all. I was faster than the wind, moving well beyond the dreams of any Olympic athlete. No, the experience wasn't dreamlike, it was super reality!

I was going fast, very fast. In seconds I was through the dark infested alleyway, clear of all the dangers of the filth-smelling menace. I thought I was away and free, but things in this life weren't simple. I was now moving at speeds impossible in a normal dimension. Grave danger could be heard running behind me moving with increased urgency. It seemed to push its odour of vile stench ahead of it, then I realised the murderous mob were all gaining on me. They had more experience in this world than I had!

The brightness of the street had been an illusion made by looking through the dark infested tunnel of the alleyway. The lights themselves were large and high above the street, but they threw out a terrible sickly yellow light turning everything in that wide thoroughfare into a veiled malevolent threat. The whole street was thronged with dark people offering no safe haven. I was now surrounded by hundreds of cancerous figures all wanting to invade my body. I was in plain view for all to see, and the larger lights on that street made me no safer as they illuminated fresh meat for the mob. I was a magnet for their evil. I was the attraction they all wanted to devour!

At this point I finally realised the predicament I was running into. Panic took over and I pushed my body even harder. The sensation of feeling everything could be described as slow motion, but I wasn't running in slow motion as everything was happening in real time. I understood everything. I'd reached maximum velocity, and at that moment felt more alive than I'd ever done in all my life. This wasn't a dreamlike state, this was living in a place I never been before. It was the most exhilarating thing I'd ever experienced, and I was alive for the first time. The big problem with this crystal bright total sensual experience was, it wasn't going to last. It was life in the fast lane, the fast lane to a painful death as hunted prey.

Everybody I passed on this wide boulevard was dark wearing disgusting, shapeless, greasy clothes with expressions void of anything but maliciousness. Were my stalkers male or female? I could not tell, most seemed to be rat like in their movements and androgynous. They varied in size and colour, some quite tall and thin, others stocky with obvious latent power. The absolute impression this crowd of moving horror gave me was of a mudslide of evil dark flesh running, oozing along the alleyways and streets.

It wasn't the awfulness of their appearance that made them terrifying, it was their unwillingness to slow down, and their constant building stench as they closed in on me with every stride. The rain was now coming down hard beating at my face, and at forty miles an hour felt as if it was going to penetrate my eyes. This would have been a consideration under normal circumstances but I couldn't slow down, not for one second. Where I was running to I hadn't a clue, but I wasn't going to slow.

They were gaining on me stride by stride by stride. My lungs filling with the cold damp air were about to burst, this wet vapour of acrid water drowning me with each forced breath. I forced it out in a fine spray only for this to be followed a second later with the urge to feel that raw coldness fill my chest once again. I knew I could only keep this pace up for another few seconds, a handful of yards gained in front of the poisonous onslaught. The mob would never stop until its cancer consumed the cells of my body.

If there was somewhere to run and hide, a safe haven in this sickly yellow city, I didn't know where to look. Everything was new to me, all the sensations and all the horror. I was looking with the fever of a desperate man for a way out, a bright glass door, the golden door or a subway sign for *Tranquil Place*... None of this materialised. I found not a single friendly face, and with stinging eyes I looked for any possible escape. My eyes searched through the passengers travelling on the filthy blood-red convoys of double-decker buses, but I found no sanctuary. I couldn't see anywhere to go, and everybody in that city knew why I was there. They all wanted a share of my cells.

The first indication of my doom was the weight of rancid breath blowing on the back of my neck, the mob so close I could smell the stench of their breath from broken rotten teeth. A few seconds later I had the sensation of someone touching the back of my neck with fingers made of bone covered with a cold, tissue thin, greasy yellow skin. These horrible hands succeeded in gripping the back of my neck, clawing at it with a frantic desire. I could feel the long yellow nails with their blackened tips digging deep into my neck, gouging out bits of the flesh to be sucked into that horrible mouth with relish, as if this creature had found a fine delicacy.

In my state of total awareness the pain was beyond intense. I was being pulled apart bit by bit by the long talons of not just one but several of my pursuers. All possessed the ability to suck on my flesh and blood as they ran. The pain was unbearable in this heightened state and I could feel cell being ripped from cell, and the intensity of the agony was equal to the intensity of the experience. I had to fight to survive, I wasn't going to stop, and I wasn't going to die, not there, on that damp, yellow, slime-covered cobbled street. With so many pursuers chasing it seemed impossible I would survive the night, or the next three terrible minutes.

Hundreds were clawing at me, not just the original group from the alleyway, everybody in that wide thoroughfare wanted to eat me alive. I was flagging, my breath was coming in ragged lumps and now I couldn't make myself go faster. Without warning they were on me, and my legs losing all their strength buckled beneath me. I was forced hard down onto the sticky, wet cobbled street. I was on the cold and hard floor without hope. The mob piled on top of me and I could feel every sensation of pain as knees and elbows and teeth dug into my body. As dozens piled on top of me forcing my flesh against the harsh stone of the roadway my super senses never abated, bruises forming as capillaries ruptured under the weight of the attacking horde. This was a minor disturbance because they then started to eat me alive.

Every fraction of a second I could feel claws and teeth ripping at my super sensitive flesh. The next sensation was one of the most horrible things I've ever experienced in my life. I could feel fingers penetrating my chest cavity after which these creatures grabbed my intestines in their clawed hands, tugging and sucking as the red-black bloody tubes were ripped out from my body. Other thin skinned yellow hands clawed inside my chest driving their fingers tight around my pumping heart deep inside. More claw hands moved beyond my heart. They grabbed at my spine raising the agony in my brain beyond intolerable. These hands started to tug at my vertebrae with a fevered intensity attempting to rip me into two, three or one hundred pieces. The agony was unbearable, and then more filthy legs gathered around to invade my fading senses and to inflict more agony by stamping on my diminishing body.

Did I wake up? Not for about another minute. During this minute I was diminished until I was barely a skull with a fragment of brain and one eyeball. Then it all faded. This was the longest minute of my entire life, an almost infinite minute of blinding white agony. Shit, it hurt!

I woke from this incredible experience screaming in pain. The bedclothes were soaked with a sickly, sweet-smelling sweat. The bed was so wet I thought I'd involuntary urinated, or worse still soiled the sheets. I suffered the sensation that my whole body had been ripped apart and was soaking its visceral fluids into the linen on the bed. I was convinced everything would be covered in blood and ravaged warm flesh. My eyes told me different. The bed was sodden with sweat. It was so wet you could have physically wrung the sheets out, or I could have canoed out of there! I didn't believe it was possible somebody could sweat so much. My parched dry throat told the truth begging my thirst to be sated.

And the screaming! Screaming at such forced intensity, so loud, it hurt my chest. Perhaps all the time that I was running with my chest rasping with the effort I'd been screaming. I was thankful nobody was in the room to witness my terrors. A few minutes later I'd calmed down after realising I was back in my cancer filled real life. One thing I decided in those few minutes was I never wanted to ever experience anything like that again, though something about those incredible sensations were beginning to haunt me.

The full crystal clarity of the dream was beguiling, it had been very frightening, something to be wary of. Within an hour of waking I knew that I wanted more of this experience. Not the vicious experience of the cancer demons ripping at and consuming my body, I wanted more of the intense power of life this wondrous reality had given me. It was an addictive opiate, one experience and somewhere inside a craving for more was secretly growing. At that moment I was not strong enough to survive the terrors another visit might bring.

Fear was building inside me because I would tire through the day and tonight I would have to sleep. The knowledge that I could be in the same disgusting alleyway again was a terrifying prospect. The secret addiction had started its insidious creeping into my psyche. With my weakened broken body, the power I'd felt during the dream was irresistible. Already after a few short hours the pain was becoming a forgotten mist, and trapped in my ravaged body what I wanted now was more experiences of vital strength and sublime sensation.

Would I ever have another dream like this? Whilst I had cancer I feared this could be the first of many cancer demon-filled experiences. Could I stay awake for several months until I was cured or dead? No, impossible. I would have to face the demons regardless… I had discovered something special, but what? Was I to repeat that desperate flight over and over?

Moments later I was asleep once more…

CHAPTER 5

A warm summer's night. August 1971.

Mushbies were killed by the onset of the nerds! Let me explain. Mushbies existed long before the nerd, but are essentially the same weird creature. Mushbies are socially ostracised misfits, strange people who dwell on the arcane, the minutiae of detail, who live in another world of numbers and strange facts. They are nerds before the invention of the home computer.

The modern nerd exists and prospers because computers exist and prosper. The nerd is the tool that breathes life into modern technology. Before this dedicated lunacy they had no part in society. They were outcasts in every way, dreading every single boring day at school, and continuing beyond the classroom to become outcasts in so-called "normal" society.

They developed through the years into a group of twenty-something men who could not place themselves socially, continuing to live with their unfortunate mothers. The uniform was greasy hair and always ill-fitting, charity shop clothes, or at least the look was ill-fitting and second-hand. In the age before the modern electronic revolution, society had no place to put these people. The consequence of this was a job well below their academic ability. You know the guy, a school janitor who reads Sartre in the original French, or devours complex works in Latin and can multiply six-figure numbers in his head. This man only seemed to communicate with the strange kids, or were they the smart ones?

In 1971 mushbies hovered in corners in pubs, and in dark alcoves near the bar in nightclubs. Women could never be attained, it was not possible to drink enough courage beer to be able to walk and talk. By the time you had the courage you didn't have the legs. The worst thing about the mushbie was the choice of record on the jukebox. It couldn't be a bit of Rod Stewart or the Rolling Stones. No, it had to be Ray Stevens or Dawn. What was wrong with a bit of Redbone or The Doors? This was a vital clue. If you went into a pub and something totally shit was playing on the jukebox then be afraid. If this was followed by something equally bad you knew somewhere at a quiet table in a corner would be an infestation of mushbies.

Bob Wilson, my best friend, the one who looked like ersatz George Best, he was a mushbie!

He openly loathed all mushbies. The problem for Bob was apart from looking like an internationally famous sex symbol, he was, through and through in his manner and choice of music, a mushbie. In his defence he was never going to be the entire mushbie. He wasn't that smart. He had all the attributes, only hampered by good looks and a normal IQ. The secret side of me, the side you couldn't see staring at a reflection in the mirror, might also have hints of the godforsaken mushbie. But at least I was going to put Curved Hair or Carole King on the jukebox. Was Tapestry a good choice or verging towards forbidden territory?

Bob was waiting for me at the bus stop. He lived in a new estate on the edge of town. This was slightly strange as Bob's house was on the far side of the town. He'd taken a bus through the town centre and out to where I lived to meet me. He wanted reassurance as well as a large dose of joint Dutch courage. It was only a mile ride to the heart of the disheartening metropolis that was our small industrial town. This bus ride took me away from a stinking farm into a grubby odorous town centre. The economy of this so-called centre existed solely of travel agents, charity shops, estate agents, banks and pubs. Most of these were pretty dire, others were far worse. The pubs that is, not the banks, they started their downward path in the eighties.

The Cauldron was the place to be if you were young and out on the town, other than that it was not a town full of interesting nightspots. The only reason it was the centre of attention for the town's youth rested squarely on the shoulders of the very stout landlord, Billy. His eyesight must have been appalling and his business brain keyed in to the disposable income of the underage punter. Billy Jones was somewhere beyond his sixties and, according to him, even policemen look like sixteen-year-olds. A good excuse.

It was no surprise to anybody then that everybody in the pub looked old enough to be a policeman, therefore old enough to be served. This boosted Billy's economy no end, a respectable adult would never be seen dead in such grubby, loud dive. I think if you pushed a pram in there with a pound note pinned to the blanket the baby would get a drink. What made you a customer was money. There was one golden rule – no credit!

We were dressed in the gear and we thought we were cool. Other teenagers seeing us with the latest gear on probably thought we were cool too, but to anybody else we no doubt looked like a pair of fashion victims. Obvious seventeen-year-olds in killer clothes, killer perfume, we were the unstoppable force in the game of love.

The Cauldron in all its glory of peeling paint and mouldy brickwork was built in the early post-war period, constructed during a time when every estate needed a massive pub. I don't know if this time ever existed or the breweries thought it might come with future prosperity. The television killed going out and most of the big pubs. The upshot was every town in England seems to possess several of these massive crumbling pubs, usually at prime spots on the corner of busy crossroads.

These were eyesores, and The Cauldron was no exception. You've all been there at some time, a smoke-filled, yellow-walled games room. At the better end some even possessed a snooker room with its darkness only broken by shafts of smoke-filled light illuminating the baize. Then the usual bar with lounge bar and, for the appreciative of smoke-filled quiet, the snug. The Cauldron always had a pervading smell of stale cigarettes and stale beer topped off with a distinct whiff of old heating oil. The carpets once possessed some dark red floral pattern, now they were almost shiny black everywhere that mattered. Of course to the hardened customer the only thing they were there for was the beer. The fact that the beer was good and cheap made the place a winner. For the underage teenager the bonus was Billy became blind!

I walked up to Bob who was shuffling and fidgeting in his usual display of nervous tension. He was casting dancing shadows like a bizarre marionette shadow act under the street light at the bus stop. My stomach was doing its own dancing act, but at least I kept it on the inside unless, of course, I vomited.

"How's it going, Bob?" I said.

"Not bad, Pete, not bad, Pete. You loaded?" This was Bob's opener.

"Loaded? What's that supposed to mean?" I said.

"You know, johnnys (condoms), and cash for booze," he replied.

"I got money, no johnnies," I said.

"No johnnies! What you going to do if we score?"

"They sell them in a machine in the pub toilet," I said. I was acting cool, acting. Inside I was a ball of nerves.

I'd practised with a condom but never put one on in front of a woman. I imagined a woman pulling it down my erect penis, helping me with it. Jesus Christ that was an even scarier thought! I would become so nervous the whole thing could end in soft disaster. The more I thought about the mechanics of sex and some woman staring at my teenage body the more terrifying the experience ahead of me became. I couldn't imagine any form of success with all this tension. What I needed now was beer, lots of beer!

The conversation carried on like this all the way to the pub. Bob wanted to tick all the boxes and cross all the Ts before we got a sniff. He was nervous as hell, because this could be the magic night we both lose it. The more Bob banged on about different aspects of it the more my stomach started to react against me. It wanted to run and vomit. I wanted to be cool. No way was I going to vomit and no way was I as calm as I pretended to be.

I was playing it cool for Bob. I was playing a game of bullshit poker with my friend because he was breaking down into a display of open nervousness. If I went to pieces Bob would just drink nine pints then spend the rest of the evening throwing up in some alleyway. I would get no support, nobody to back me up. Next day he would blame me for spoiling it.

As we entered the brightly lit bar the jukebox was belting out 'Rose Garden'. I instantly knew that the bar full of odour and the crush of young bodies had been invaded by the mushbie. As we pushed through the crush towards the bar we ran smack bang into Lenny the Helmet. He was a character.

"Hello, tossers!" was Lenny's greeting.

"Alright, Lenny, you prize wanker?" was our stock response to this standard greeting. If we had said these words with malice it would have been something quite different. Lenny was a bit of a hardcase. Mates were mates, and if you weren't a mate then you were an enemy. Lenny was very black and white on most things.

Lenny the Helmet did not carry this title because he was a big, shambling, long-haired, greasy git who always walked around with a crash helmet under his arm. No, Lenny had the Helmet nickname because he possessed a very big penis, and at the slightest provocation would demonstrate its size, never failing to point out how splendid it was at the business end. It only took about four pints for Lenny to get into his amazing demonstration mode. This actually worked with some girls, to our surprise, and had us at times dumbfounded. Lenny was a special case. He was a man for whom the rules were made to be broken. *Etiquette* was a strange French word that didn't exist in the world of

Lenny. The only person who understood how very special Lenny was, of course, was Lenny.

He also had something we did not – money. Lots of money, and nobody we ever met knew where he worked or what he did. Somewhere disgusting like the abattoir would be where Lenny worked, you could tell this by his demeanour. An animal crudeness and everything about him spoke of filth and violence. Many rumours abounded that Lenny was the man to see if you wanted LSD; the very powerful hallucinogenic drug taken by weirdos and hippies. I would never be interested in anything so tainted, so mind destroying! Lenny never told us what he did. He was a monster and we were frightened children playing men. We didn't dare ask.

"Smiggy tells me you're going to break your cherry (lose your virginity) tonight with some sluts at a small party. Is that right?" Lenny asked.

We were about to reply when the man himself, Smiggy, weaselled his way through the crowd towards us. Small and spidery he wound his oily way between the crowds in the bar. If you watched him closely he always said "Excuse me" to all the men he forced his way between, all the while rubbing himself as hard as possible against the girls. If a girl was wearing a short skirt and no tights he would make certain his hand would be trailing down by his side. This would force him to rub it against her thighs at which he would pull a thin, cold smile.

"Hello, tossers!" He was in agreement with Lenny.

"It takes one," Lenny said.

I was about to say hello to this hideous creature. At this time in my history Smiggy didn't seem so bad, but as the years roll by I can see him in all his awfulness. I was going to say something but Bob jumped in.

"Hey, Smiggy, is the party still on tonight?"

"Of course it is, and you two spotty herberts will probably finally bust your sad cherries!" His reply was through cigarette-stained teeth clenched in a tight rictus smile.

My stomach took a turn at this news. The news that it was ON grabbed my intestines and twisted them. I was in need of a drink to calm my nerves. Downing a drink or three was definitely on the cards, after which, no doubt, I go to the toilet to buy condoms, and at the same time calm my stomach by vomiting. The driving force in my life that night was the sexual lust of a seventeen-year-old tired of playing with himself too much. I was desperate in my illusion that having sex would make me a man, after which I would probably masturbate more remembering the event.

The respect between us all continued unabated, with our conversation in that noisy bar dominated by bad jukebox choices. Benny Hill was playing at one time, and I think I wanted to burn the jukebox. Shooting the mushbie who'd selected H7 would be more productive for mankind. Conversation between the four of us continued along the lines of tosses, wankers and all the other usual robust pub insults.

Banter is the name of the game. That night the real game was macho bullshit bollocks. We were playing this hard, though on the inside we were soft strawberry jellies.

The beer flowed, pints being washed down at a swift rate. The worst feature in that bar was the snail speed you were served at – murderously slow. On Friday night it was double murder. They employed four staff, two of them very attractive cynical university students who possessed no skill with a beer pump. This was the only brake on the amount of beer we could drink. It took longer to get served than to drink a pint. Smiggy wanted all his beer for free. His reasoning being he'd organised the little party we were going to, and for this we should be eternally grateful. This little rat's idea of grateful would be buying him beer for the rest of his miserable life, and I didn't want to buy him beer for the rest of the miserable evening, unless it turned out to be a special night.

We didn't know too much about Smiggy. He wanted to drink enough to forget that he was only nineteen, married and the proud father of one. If his young wife wasn't lying he was about to be the proud father of two. He'd told us that skinny bitch of his was always lying. He didn't know if she was up the duff or not. The other thought he shared about his young wife was she was very hot in bed, always wanting it. This translated in his mind that she was probably shagging the milkman and God knows who else.

With this in mind the greasy little rat was always looking for a bit of outside action. He liked to spread it about. How he managed to get it was more of a mystery than Lenny the Helmet's sexual successes. God knows what Smiggy called action. He would have shagged anything including the milkman. His values were very skewed, but then I don't think our hormone driven values were too noble that night either!

Lenny said he might come along for a laugh, and see if any of the little girls could cope with a real man. We thought all this was bullshit designed to make us nervous, and he was succeeding. What we also thought secretly, and on some level knew, was Lenny knew what to do with a woman. We weren't going to admit this to ourselves but we were clueless, desperate, and, without a doubt, moving into unknown territory. When it came to fantasising about our short-term prospects we wanted to know too much to be cool. Lenny, if he did come along with us, would have intimidated us into a flaccid catatonic daze. We were useless and he would have magnified it!

It wasn't going to be like that tonight. Nobody was coming with us. Lenny was drinking like a champion, downing the beer like it was his last night on the planet. We were downing it like also-rans, amateurs in the world of beer drinking. After four or five pints were downed things started to move into the surreal. The smoke was getting thicker and our heads were becoming so thick with drink we didn't know why we were there. Smiggy was starting to get very graphic about all aspects of his sexual prowess and the animal desires of the girls we were going to meet. The whole thing got so explicit that I felt like throwing in the towel and calling the whole thing off. It would've been a good move.

The location of the small party was finally given to us. We sort of knew the street, and with luck we'd find the house, listening for the loud party music. Then we would meet the girls who were not from our school. We couldn't imagine meeting women old enough to have left school. If this was the case that thought alone would have scared us back to our own beds, safe in our own hands.

We were going to get the deed done, and once that was over with we could chat to any girl with confidence. There was no way we weren't going to go to this organised party. Our sole aim was to lose the burden of virginity and gain the knowledge of real sexual pleasure. Were we going to do it? Oh fucking yes we were!

"How many we 'ad?" I asked.

"Not a north," Bob said, or tried to.

"One more then, just get us right," I said.

"Least one more. I'm losing nerves," Bob said.

Two more it was then. I'm not sure even to this day if the two more was one each. I had no idea how much I'd consumed by the time we left, or what time we left at. The destination for our virginity mission was a mystery to me because I couldn't remember where the hell we were supposed to be going. In fact I was so pissed I think I'd forgotten the mission. I don't know where Bob was, but I was in a twilight world between drunk and unconscious.

When I asked Bob where we were going I think he said something like this:

"Shagging women…fucking shagging women. Tonight will be special, we won't forget it." I think that's what Bob said, or something equally profound.

"Scum on den," I said.

We left through the battered side door of the pub pushing against the dirt encrusted cracked paintwork, and working hard against dry hinges to force our way into the night air which was surprisingly cool after the choking, smoky heat inside the pub.

The handle had turned in my hand, and the cool breeze met my alcohol-fuelled body. We were stepping boldly into a new world of real men, or some such shit! I can't remember what we were talking about. It must have been rubbish. God we were pissed!

In the pub at this very moment, a mushbie was selecting 'Knock Three Times' by Dawn, another shit life choice.

We weren't making shit life choices were we?

CHAPTER 6

1971. Bright and early?

The sun! God, the sun! Where in the hell was I? I closed my burning, single opened eye as tight as humanly possible. I was warm and uncomfortable, lying beneath an untidy heap of blankets on some small folding bed. I was sweating, my whole body felt slick with water pumping out of every pore. I was far too hot. I squeezed my eyes tight, but the pain permeated every fibre of my conscious thought. Everything inside my skull was agony. The sensations of the heavy morning after went further than that. My whole body felt like it was glued immovably to this strange bed. Incapable of moving, I was unable to think of anything but my wretchedness. God we were pissed last night. I wondered where Bob was sleeping.

The nausea and the migraine dialogue continued for half an hour or so, but how was I to know how long? I was trapped in a dark sea of head pain. I'd thrown myself into this sea of post-drunken misery without a lifeboat, but nobody deserves a hangover this violent.

I started very slowly, almost imperceptible at first, to feel at some level more human. I was in the process of considering moving. You know the hangover? Do I move? Do I drink? Do I just lie here until I die? At this point I was in the "God I need a piss" moment. The one certain option I had was either to force myself to my feet and go to the toilet, or lay in a pool of my own making. Getting up was the thing. Small miracles start somewhere, I attempted with great success the eye opening task, one eye at least. My pupil reacted to the brilliant sunlight-filled space.

Then it struck me. The room, where I was being roasted alive under the blankets, I'd never seen before!

If I had been here before, at that moment, I couldn't remember whose house it was. I was slumped in a sweaty sad heap on a folding camp bed in a sunlit lounge. The rising sun was burning through the east-facing window melting me alive. This wasn't Bob's house. This wasn't Smiggy's grotty flat. It was a modern quality home, good furniture, big room, nice fireplace, but still I was lying in a house I'd never seen. Where the hell was I? Through the pain in my head not a single clue came to mind. This was followed by an even bigger more pressing worry… Where's the bloody toilet?

Where's the kitchen for a glass of water? I was desperate to get it out at one end and equally desperate to force some liquid into my dehydrated body from the other. Now up and about I remained in a torpor not moving any faster than my very best snail pace. This is when I considered the option that Bob and I had met somebody last night, and this was their house or their parent's home. I was considering, well, not really considering much, I didn't have enough active brain cells turned on for consideration. Just loose thoughts about this and that were passing through what was left of my brain. The lounge door opened. I would've jumped in surprise if that part of my body had been turned on.

"Hello, Peter," she said.

"Oh! Hi, hello," I replied. My response had been witless, I didn't have a clue who I was greeting.

"You look a bit worse for wear," she continued, in her sunny bright voice.

I was speechless, and the main reason for this was the obvious familiarity with which she addressed me. An indication she knew me quite well. I was perplexed. Here I was sleeping in what was probably her lounge and I didn't have a clue as to who the hell she was!

"Would you like a cup of tea, Peter," she asked.

"Oh, uuuuurrrrm, yes," was all I could manage.

My eyes were beginning to focus. I wasn't yet in full eagle eye mode, if indeed I ever achieved that. I was, however, breaking through the fog and taking in my surroundings. Then I noticed she was wearing a very attractive and almost diaphanous nightgown. She was probably somebody's mother, quite old, definitely old, about thirty-six or seven. For her age she was not bad, better than not bad. She was quite attractive. The sun was helping my impression by silhouetting her body. She was very fit. Nice thick, shiny hair tumbled across her shoulders. Best of all she possessed a lovely smile. It was this smile that had me wrong-footed. I didn't know who she was and it was obvious she knew me well. This in itself was a deep and disturbing mystery.

"I'll make you a cup of tea, Peter. I think you need it," she continued,

"Go upstairs and get yourself comfortable in my bed. It's much cooler up there."

It might have been my startled look, I don't really know. This woman wants me to go upstairs and get comfortable in her bed. She then added:

"I'm up now, and the bed is much cooler and more comfortable than that thing. You look like you could do with some more sleep." With this she walked off in what I assumed was to be the direction of the kitchen.

To this very day I don't quite know why I obeyed her. Some internal instinct, previous knowledge, genetic programming, not that that genetics existed in 1971, they were invented in the early 80s!

I'd dragged myself from a strange bed and had been confronted by this unknown woman. Everything in my life was strange and so out of focus I didn't realise I was standing naked in front of her, but I wasn't! I was wearing a pair of underpants except they weren't my underpants! She'd stopped halfway across the room and was looking me up and down. She smiled at me, a glowing, lustrous smile.

I felt embarrassed standing there in my underpants or not my underpants in front of this strange woman. She just smiled back as if she knew and understood something. Moments later she turned away and continued towards what I assumed to be the kitchen. I was assuming one hell of a lot, but I didn't know anything. She had gone out of the room, so I was going to get out of the lounge and up the stairs pretty damn quick. The thought of her return was filling me with teenage angst. The last thing I wanted was to be standing on display in underpants in front of this old woman. They still weren't my underpants! The style was all wrong.

What in hell's name had I done last night? Different underpants, a strange house and this woman asking me if I'd like to use her bed. It was all so strange that my fuddled brain couldn't think of any answers. I obeyed and plodded up the stairs, harbouring too much of a killer headache to care. I hauled myself step by step up into the house concentrating on my feet. These were made of wilful disobedience lead, not obeying the slightest instruction.

Where was the bedroom? This is the point where I found a bit of luck. Reaching the top of the stairs I was confronted by a large pair of double doors. Both doors were open, and the bed turned back on one side, and for some reason, which remains a vague sensation, I assumed correctly this was her bed.

Everything looked very comfortable and I could feel a coolness coming from the room. They had air conditioning. I didn't know anybody who had air conditioning, so obviously now I did. I found to my surprise a bathroom accessed directly from the bedroom. It was almost like a hotel. I peed like a horse and it seemed to last for two minutes. Afterwards I dragged my weary body towards the bed. I was asleep in a matter of seconds, and awake what seemed to be seconds later when Sam entered the bedroom. Sam was not the family dog. Sam was not even a man. Sam was this quite attractive older woman holding the cup of tea. How did I know her name was Sam? I didn't, that would come later!

"I'm off to get changed." That's all she said as she placed the cup of tea and some biscuits on the bedside table next to me. I was contemplating if anybody else was in the house. She was getting changed to go out somewhere and I didn't have the energy to leave the bed. Would I have to get up if she was leaving, and could I manage this without exposing my semi-naked teenage body to her all embracing gaze yet again? She seemed quite amused by my awkwardness.

I didn't know it was Sam until about half a cup and five minutes later when I discovered something important. I was lying there taking refreshing sips of my tea. She had disappeared some minutes earlier into what I knew to be a joint bathroom and dressing room. By this time I was feeling almost, and I have to stress, *almost*, human. What was starting to creep into my clearing head was that since the night before in The Cauldron something about me had changed. At first I couldn't put my finger on it. Then it struck me. I appeared to have become fatter, or was I just bloated by the beer? It was a feeling more than anything else. I felt full, and somehow weighty. I don't know, I couldn't make the thought connect. Had I eaten all the pies in the pub? I don't know, it must have been gas.

The radio was playing somewhere. It was Radio One but I didn't recognise the DJ's voice. Today they were playing none of the usual rubbish. They'd trawled the bottom of the music industry and were playing some new mushbie music. Somebody was singing something about tying a yellow ribbon around something followed by a dirge welcoming somebody home. The only reason I knew it was Radio One were the announcements suggesting it was the only radio worth listening to. In 1971 it was the only radio you could listen to! Apart from this I didn't recognise anything being played. Some band were wailing their guitars and singing about crazy horses. This was followed by something I quite liked: 'This Flight Tonight'. It later became a favourite that would often ignite forgotten memories.

I was contemplating my change of physical state peering under the bedclothes to look at my stomach which appeared to be larger than I remembered. My entire body, every part of me appeared to be larger. I must have damaged my eyes or my brain! Nothing in my world seemed remotely connected to last night in the pub. Try as I might, two and two were not going together. I was in the middle of this hazy contemplation when the door from the bathroom opened.

"Fucking… hell!" I think that's what I said.

"Peter, don't you want your little Sam this morning?" she whispered.

My little Sam? Was that what she said? She wore only high-heeled shoes with a bright red lipstick smile.

My hangover disappeared. More accurate, was forgotten in panic. I was frozen like a rabbit in the rush of headlights. The first thing that came into my head was a truth. This strange woman, who called herself Sam, was "my little Sam". I didn't even know her! I had never laid eyes on this woman in all my life and now through some trickery she was trying to convince me that I was more than a friend. I was a seventeen-year-old virgin, unsure about everything in the world. I could swagger but it was only swagger. My lips moved and made words without any connection to a thought process making her laugh.

"I don't know who you are, or what you want from me," I said.

"Oh, you don't know who I am? Are you going to play one of your games with me this morning?" she replied.

Moments passed, more moments passed. I was thinking of these games of mine, games I knew nothing about. I finally stuttered out the unthinkable.

"I'm a seventeen-year-old virgin and I don't know you are!" I said this and it was the best I could manage. My tongue was in knots, as was my stomach. I could barely speak I was so afraid. This comment kicked Sam into action starting with that lovely smile beaming at me. Then she approached the bed and put both hands on my shoulders pushing me down into the pillow.

"My naughty Peter. So this is the game you want to play this morning. This is a new one from you,"

I was terrified and fascinated. Her nipples were right in front of my face, full, large, dark and frightening. I didn't know whether to touch something, scream or run. All the options raced through my mind without answer, or I could lie there in panic. I was performing the small animal trapped by dazzling lights manoeuvre, and she kissed me wetly with a very full investigating tongue. I was trapped in delight and terror. I wanted to know much more about what was going to happen. I was frightened to know, God, I didn't know what I wanted! She stopped kissing me. Instead of continuing she pressed down on my shoulders, staring into my eyes.

"What are you?" she asked.

I wanted to be this older woman's lover, I wanted to run, I wanted a huge erection, and I was frightened that I might not get one at all. God I wanted her, God I wanted to run. Best plan, lie still, see what happens. That's not a plan, that's the rabbit waiting to be crushed under the wheels. My mind was frozen solid, not a single useful thought came into my head. Then I was saved, my penis was interested. I waited to be run over.

"What are you?" she asked again.

"I don't know you. I'm a seventeen-year-old virgin." I spoke the truth.

"You're sticking with that! I'm going to make you suffer," she responded. All I could see was her red smile. This looked delicious, like an advert in a glossy magazine.

If in doubt do nothing. All I did was smile back, too terrified to say another word. My smile might have come out as a little bit rigid. Other things were getting rigid and tension was gripping every muscle in my body.

The next thing she did took my breath away, and most of my erection. Sam moved back onto her feet rising from the edge of the bed. In this movement she threw the bedclothes back and, in one deft sweep of the arm, revealed my nakedness by removing with expert movement my unfamiliar underpants. I don't think I breathed for about thirty seconds. By this time she was back on the bed sitting across my stomach, both hands on my shoulders and kissing me with renewed passion. I could feel her wetness on my stomach. I could also feel my penis hard against the back of her soft buttocks.

"A seventeen-year-old virgin you said? Some parts of you aren't too shy," she said.

Then, to my shock, her hands released my shoulders. Instead she pressed my chest down with one hand and with the other behind her back starting to massage my testicles and erection. I was trying to concentrate on anything but what was happening, trying to control the hair trigger teenager inside me. Somebody on the radio was belting out something about canning the can. I tried to concentrate on the music. It didn't work.

"Ohmigod!" was what I said. As I came in a flood all up her arm and across her left buttock. She laughed, giggling like a teenage girl.

"You're playing this really well, Peter." She said this with what appeared to be some amusement.

I was stunned, bloody speechless, bloody embarrassed by my twenty-second performance. She just laughed some more and moved to lie completely on top of me, holding my neck and performing very sensuous gentle nibbling kisses to my ear.

"So, you're a seventeen-year-old virgin who knows nothing?" she continued.

"And I'm not very good at sex," I said. I was telling the truth.

"Not good at sex, you lying bastard? I'm going to teach you everything you taught me." She said this as almost a threat, a soft lapping threat, but to me I was going head first into the unknown. Within minutes, trapped beneath her hot beautiful body, life was returning, lust was returning.

One hour and forty-five minutes later, I'd gone from a totally inexperienced virgin to a rampant stud. The learning curve was so rapid that it had me worried. Something was not right. The music played on and I didn't recognise a single song. Somebody had stolen Radio One and turned it into the adventure in the bland. My body seemed to know things I didn't have any clue about, to go places I'd never even thought of. It was as if I'd been born genetically programmed to be a willing and athletic lover. Bloody hell, I was one hell of a fast learner! I liked what I learned to the extent that I was insatiable. I wanted more, much more, and I wanted to soak my body in the experience. I wanted more now!

"Come on, Sam, let's do this all day. I feel I can keep going for hours," I said.

"No!" she said.

"Why? I want it, I want you, all of you, I want to consume every bit of you," I said. I was one sexy and very randy young bastard.

"No, you must get up. Mike will be here at twelve," she said.

"Mike who?" I asked.

"Mike who you are going to play pool with later. Mike my husband. So stop messing about pretending to be seventeen and get dressed now," she said.

"You've got a fucking husband?" I said.

She just rolled her eyes and walked back into the changing room, this time to clean herself of us, and to get dressed for the town.

I knew these people, this I'd already figured. I hadn't a clue how I knew Sam who was actually Samantha. I knew Mike, I played pool with him, and he was her bloody husband!

The song "We gotta get out of this place. If it's the last thing we ever do" came into my head. I had to make an excuse. I'd just had a life changing experience and didn't think I could stand playing pool with a man whose wife had just given me all these sensuous gifts. He might see the truth in my smile.

Walking into the bathroom to go to the loo was a pivotal moment that would change the rest of my life. It's hard to describe the fear this moment instilled in my mind. What started this reaction was my reflection in the full-length mirror at the back of the dressing room. This had been unnoticed as I staggered in to take a piss with my now forgotten terrible hangover. The large mirror was a little misty from the steam of the shower. The image was indistinct, like looking at somebody through a thick fog.

What was standing before me wasn't me, it was a different me, but it wasn't another person, it was still me. Overnight I'd put on several kilos, possibly eight or ten. My hair was much blonder, longer, and I was different! I couldn't put my finger on it. The hangover was coming back with a vengeance as I struggled with this strange vision. What was so different? It was a mystery that wasn't going to be solved by standing there, gaping at a disturbing misty image.

Then I saw it. On the dressing table was a telephone, not a telephone like I'd ever seen before. Why was I focusing on the telephone? These people had money. They could afford unique things that could only be purchased in London. The phone had touched a nerve memory. It had triggered a feeling of strangeness. Something was different. Something was wrong. I was groping in the dark for an answer, any answer, or any clue as to what was causing this feeling of being disorientated with the world. On the top of the linen basket was a newspaper. It was a copy of the *Daily Mail*, on the front page a picture of the Prime Minister. I didn't recognise him. Then and only then did I see the date. It was August 23rd 1973. The *Daily Mail* had said so. It wouldn't lie, would it?

"What day is it?" I asked.

"It's Saturday," Sam shouted from the shower.

The *Daily Mail* was Thursdays. *Shit*. Today was the 25th... I went out on the 17th...

This was the point where I fainted. It might have been all the alcohol from the night before, but the night before wasn't in The Cauldron back in August 1971.

Not so bright, and in fact very, very late!

I'd walked out of The Cauldron over two years before! Two fucking years before! God this is crazy!

I've got to get out of this place, if it's the last thing I ever do. Somebody was playing an evil trick on me, though the sex was amazing!

CHAPTER 7

In the unfortunate cancerous right here right now.

Back in the here and now, I was still reeling from my first terrifying cancer dream. The following evenings when darkness started to fall and the hands of tiredness were pulling me towards sleep, I was plagued with the terror of reliving the gut-wrenching experience. After a few anxious evenings the nights turned into ones filled with peaceful sleep. I only dreamt in the mediocre normal with vague and hazy experiences, most forgotten by morning. I started to crave the total life experience the tactile dream had given me. My life was so grey in its everyday pain I had to return to the total sensations of a crystal clear reality. This was the point where I started to fear going to sleep and dreaming the mundane for the rest of my life, however long that would be.

I supposed twenty days had passed, and even the urges to have more of the intense other dimension were fading. It was like I'd almost dreamt a dream. Had I experienced it at all? This is what I started to believe until the night it happened again. I was dreaming the usual mixture of disjointed nonsense until I felt a shift, and I'd moved back into the super real. It started with a feeling of oncoming terror.

The initial reason for this dread was that beneath my feet I started to feel pain. It came from below as a sensation of burning, a hot pressure building against the underside of my soles. At this point the visual took over. I was in a black void, a complete area of empty, black, cold space. In this cold void I wasn't sure my eyes were open. I was looking but I couldn't see. The pain in my feet continued to grow and below me the merest suggestion of grey was starting to appear. From my previous experience with those flesh-eating androgynous creatures this oncoming greyness was not a good omen. The onrush carried with it anxious fear. This greyness was in the process of change becoming darker and darker with every passing second. In my gut I could feel the cancer demons approaching. I was slipping back into that world of terror.

What happened next took my breath away. I was shocked that I'd forgotten so many of the incredible sensations of living at a molecular level. My breath was coming in heavy gasps as the fear grew, and I could sense the molecules of air passing through my throat. This sensation alone was addictive. The pain in my feet had evened off to the sensation you would receive standing on a pebbly beach. I was fearful but had to look down. What lay beneath my feet was black tarmac, neatly laid black tarmac. All around my body I could feel a pressure building and coming from every direction. I couldn't understand how I could see the tarmac when I couldn't see anything else.

So there I was in this long-awaited for dimension, and I was in a black void standing on a strip of tarmac. "Was it a road?" I asked myself. In fact what was the purpose of this? It stayed in stasis like this for some while. Time didn't seem to matter. Suddenly, I could hear at almost a canine level what sounded like the onrush of stampeding horses, or the rumbling of heavy guns creating carnage on some distant battlefield. This sensation of sound grew until it became audible to the normal human ear. Around me everything was changing for the better or the worse, with the onrush of the noise bringing such fear I could feel sweat oozing from every single pore on my body. Individual beads of water pushed out by fear, driven by dread.

All around the void was in flux, becoming lighter with the increasing volume of the onrushing wall of sound. The noise wasn't loud. I don't think it was loud, but it was assaulting my senses. Given my new ability to hear at this molecular level, I couldn't discern how loud, loud could be. This sound engulfed my entire being, as was blank whiteness. I was now standing in a void of white being crushed by an oncoming barrage of sound.

Change came with breathless speed. In the white, tiny black flecks appeared. These grew and with this my apprehension that this was a swarm of cancer demons starting to grow. Everything started to fill in around me until I was surrounded by a whole universe of colour. I was falling or was I standing as the new universe introduced itself to me? Perhaps I was being introduced to the universe, or someone was asking if I could join. The price I had to pay might be too much, the inner me was going to be crushed to dust by the onrush of the super sensation.

Green, a fabulous green, had appeared all around, and was transforming itself into the most beautiful country landscape I'd ever seen. It was spoiled by man's invention, the tarmac my bare feet were standing on belonged to the platform of a very small country railway station. I was standing quite still. I hadn't tried to move. The noise I could hear was a train coming, and the feeling of dread had disappeared with the onset of all this beauty. I was now excited and full of desire to know more.

Standing on that platform I started to survey my surroundings. The place was beautiful with its hanging baskets and perfect paint on the ornate woodwork. This place possessed everything and more. A stationmaster's office announced itself in gold, gilt paint on the immaculate, clean window glass. Fire buckets full of sand lined up against the wall glistening in the sunlight. The whole thing was a complete experience as if placed there from some period movie.

The difference was I knew at some level deep inside this was not my construction. I wasn't dreaming this vision I'd been invited into it. I was a guest in a dimension I didn't yet understand. There was always the lurking suspicion in the background that things could revert back to the damp, yellow nightmare of painful death I'd visited before. This thought was fading as my eyes began to absorb this new world. Everything around me was an intense kaleidoscope of colour where I could sense the intensity of each shade with my inner feelings. An intense pleasure flooded through my being, what a delight to be allowed into this paradise.

The train was out of sight around a curve in the track that disappeared down a beautiful deep flower filled verdant valley. As the train approached I could feel a new sensation pressing against my body. The pressure grew until my outer shell gave way and a sensation flooded through my life. A wind of pleasure was in the literal sense passing through me giving an intense feeling almost like a warm wind playing in a reed bed, touching every part of my soul, my heart, my mind. The intensity of pleasure grew more and more with the onrush of the train. All my senses were on fire and the train still hadn't appeared around the long steel curve. The onrushing iron monster was several hundred yards away out of view. My senses were becoming saturated to the point where I couldn't believe there would be any more pleasure available. I was mistaken. The train came into view, and the joy was several hundred percent more than I'd ever experienced in all my life. I thought I was going to die of pleasure. Was this possibly a new torture?

Then, for some reason, I looked away from the magnetic attraction of the train and down to my feet which were bare. The rest of my body was a greater surprise because I was dressed in what looked like a tweed suit from the 1950s. Was I in the 1950s? No, I was not in England in that decade, I was sure of this. I could feel something in my pocket and with quick inspection discovered it was a mobile phone, not something from a decade long passed.

However, this was no ordinary mobile phone. It was heavier, more robust, and somehow not quite from my now, but from a different version of the modern world of now. This convinced me that I'd moved not into a dream but into an alternative universe. I don't think I was dreaming, I think I was alive and awake in a very similar but fundamentally different dimension. This fantastic place offered great beauty and had the promise of infinite sensations of new delight. The worry that came into my mind even when surrounded by all this beauty was if this place could offer infinite sensations of delight, could it slip to somewhere populated by cruel Demons willing to give an infinity of horror and pain.

The train was approaching at speed. Each passing second it consumed the track coming towards me. I could feel the vibrations of the molecules in the rails coming up through the platform into my sensitive feet. The appearance of a little round stationmaster was a shocking surprise. I thought I was alone at this quiet country station. I assumed he was the man in charge because he was wearing a uniform that would not look out of place on a Third World dictator. He took no notice of me and began to wave a flag of incredibly flamboyant colours. The dazzling cloth covered most shades of the rainbow. His exuberant waving of this fabulous flag exerted some power over the train. He was moving it backwards and forwards with a zestful vigour.

The train audibly slowing until the stationmaster had appeared, returned to full power. The locomotive was under orders from whoever this strange little man was not to stop. I was disappointed the train was going straight through, because pushing before this monster of iron and steel was a wave of pure ecstasy permeating itself through every fibre of my being. I understood at a very deep level on this particular occasion the train was not to stop. I also understood that in the future this would be a stopping point, but not today. So why was I standing there?

Obviously for some reason. My journey the other night into another dimension was to be killed with great pain and terror by the cancer demons.

Was today's experience going to attack me in a different way? Kill me with the experience of pleasure, with joy, with sheer intense delight?

The contraption, and I say that because it was no modern train, was from the age of steam, but not any age of steam we've experienced. This monster was from an arcane age of steam we never knew existed. It was sleeker, somewhat wilder and noisier than any steam train I'd ever seen. What's more, the carriages contained slightly more glass than normal rolling stock. The impression was almost of greenhouses on wheels, a moving Victorian hothouse. I don't think the train was so hugely different from anything in the earthly world of the 1950s. What made this so different was I could feel every single part of it, its weight, its movement, its heat, its fire, its approach. This mechanical marvel represented the most wonderful vehicle I've ever seen coming towards me. It was a physical delight of steel and fire invading all my senses.

I knew it wasn't going to stop. I was hoping the joy blowing through my body moving every molecule in a wonderful distracting way wasn't going to abate. These sensations illustrated that all the joy I'd ever experienced before was a mere shadow of the delights possible in this universe. For a reason I could never explain music was playing in my head. One moment a sort of Mozart concerto was playing, the very next it had changed to "Century Have You love". This song was by the Ice Crystals Type 9. The music was almost mushbie, had this universe seen the hidden nerd in me? I understood music I'd never heard before. I knew this music and it didn't exist in my dimension. I was shocked and intrigued to discover I knew more about this place than I thought.

I was on the verge of exploding with the effects of sheer joy and love as the train rumbled through the station pushing out great clouds of white vanilla flavoured steam. The windows as it passed by glistened with the flashing brilliance of the sunshine and butterfly filled light.

The next thing flowing through my head was the biggest sensation of all. There was only one person on the train. That person was the reason for the train, the reason for all this joy. It was a girl of about twenty-five years old I supposed. She was standing, calmly holding the back of a seat. She was almost a *petite* girl with short glossy hair and the most delicious and completely wondrous smile I have ever seen in my entire life. As the train passed I also saw my reflections passing by as if in a slow motion movie. Frame by frame I built up a picture of myself in the reflection. And what a reflection it was. I was quite young, athletic, handsome and, to my great surprise, me but not me!

Her stunning luminous eyes stared straight through my soul. My joy peaked in a flood of pure ecstasy. If at this point in my life, or any other life for that matter, I had died, it would've been the perfect moment. So, even if the existence of the perfect day is impossible as I once said, there are perfect moments.

The train rattled loudly in its rush through the station. As it did so the joy inside me stayed at this wonderful peak, a peak is something that by the very nature of the word cannot possibly last. True to everything I've said before, it did not. The joy slowly faded away, the winds of ecstasy were dying down inside my body, this sensation died to an ember though it did not leave me in the complete sense. I was left with a residue running through my body's memory. I didn't know this at the time, but this moment joy and love would be ingrained in my earthly soul forever.

I was desperate to know more about this girl, to see her again, to find out everything about her. Anything less would be unacceptable. Driven by molecular desire I wanted her to be near me forever.

The big problem with alternative realities you come into through sleep is to seek constant gratification you must always remain asleep. Once desire is sated you wake up, or I think that's how it works. If these wonderful places were to be in my life I would have to sleep a lot more. The greenness, the vivid brightness and clarity of the day, started to fade to grey, then to white, then to a sensation impossible to describe. It contained great calmness with joy.

I was startled when I awoke to discover I didn't live in that universe. At only the second visit to another dimension I was addicted, forgetting where I came from, once in there not realising any other world existed. I could not control my entry to this other place, so how was I to get back? Moments in the molecular dreamscape were precious and would become more so.

I woke, it was 4:30am, and within short hours I knew two things: one, somehow I'd encountered a new great love in non-reality, giving me a joy that beat so hard in my chest it gave me pain. This place, this new world, could I go there again? Could I make myself go there at will? I had no idea.

Two, was another sensation altogether. This one haunted me and over the next few days I was to learn a lot more about guilt. This feeling crawled like a vile fungus into my mind in the hours after awakening. This was an understanding I'd done something awful in my worldly life, something I'd hidden, that if discovered would plunge me into the world of depression and incarceration. If not those extremes I would be tortured by the knowledge of my hidden evils.

I lay there for the first three hours thinking about it. All the joy I had experienced with all that brilliant sensation and light. And was the me that wasn't me the person I could have been if I'd followed a different path? As the magic faded I could only focus on the growing anxiety that somewhere in my mind I harboured a great internal deception. What bad thing had I done to burden me with such depressive dark guilt? The next day this bleakness started to fade, and in the end it was no more than an ethereal sensation of mysterious guilt.

After the intensity of those joyous moments, I was wondering if this was a natural low following such a massive high. I could cope with these bad feelings if that's what it took to slake my desire to meet this wondrous girl at least once more. Sod the feelings of hidden guilt. I had to find the door to the universe I now wanted to live in regardless of any consequences!

CHAPTER 8

Summer 1971, holy shit its 1973!

My mind was a haze of confusion reeling with the revelation that I'd lost two years of my life. I was starting to think I'd suffered some strange aberration after all the alcohol consumed the night before, and once sober all the hundreds of days would come flooding back into focus returning my history. This strange situation forced me to reassess my alcohol consumption. I was drinking too much, my head told me that!

I didn't really think this amnesia was due to the excess of drink; my main concern was that I'd suffered some kind of stroke. All the while as I dressed, random thoughts poured through my alcohol soaked brain. This hangover never seemed to go away. Perhaps the pain in my head was the aftermath of some burst blood vessel, something giving way at this very moment, so at any time I might drop down dead!

We were both dressed and I was swimming in Sam's affectionate embrace. All the while she was telling me what a wonderful person I was and what a delightful lover I made. The only things on my mind were questions. Where the hell have I been the last two years? How do I know this woman? How the hell do I get out of this house and find some answers?

"Peter, I'm off now," Sam said, giving me a big wet affectionate kiss. I didn't mind at all.

"So am I," I said.

"I thought you were waiting for Mike. You two are playing pool together at one,"

My mind was racing. *Come on, come on. Make some excuse.*

"I've got to go to the farm and pick up something my sister got for me," I replied.

"You're going to the farm? You never go to the farm, ever!" she replied, looking straight into my face with the strange enquiring look. This had me worried.

"I don't go to the farm?" I enquired.

"You told me that you never go there, ever," Sam responded.

"Oh, well I've got to go today to see my sister. Can you tell Mike that I'm sorry but we'll have to make it another day?"

I was making all the usual leaving noises desperate to start my voyage of discovery. I had to suffer a few more not unwelcome embraces before I could leave. I was making my way down the drive all the while thinking of what could've happened inside my head. I heard the noise of the double front doors opening behind me. Sam's voice rang out. I couldn't quite make out what she was saying, but she was holding something up in one hand waving it at me.

"Peter, your car keys," Sam said, trying not to shout.

I was about to say "I don't drive", when it struck me quite forcefully that I didn't know anything about sex either and I'd learnt all of the techniques in minutes. I might drive. This skill may come to me in a matter of minutes from some hidden motor memories. I might be capable of many new things. After all, it had been two years or maybe more.

In the drive were two cars, a big Ford and a Ford Cortina GT XL 2 Litre, two door model. Nice car. Metallic bronze with brown leatherette covered roof and chromed wheels. The Ford Cortina couldn't possibly be mine, but then the big Ford couldn't belong to me. It wasn't my style, that much I knew, unless I got it cheap, but this wasn't the cheap car. What do you say? Saying I was a seventeen-year-old virgin seemed to work quite well, so on those lines I went for broke.

"Which car you want me to take," I asked.

"What's got into you today," was her response. No clues were given to help me identify my car. Sam didn't know that I didn't know. Sam was about to throw me the keys and I was in such a whirl I felt like slumping to the floor or throwing up, anything really to divert me from the maelstrom inside.

My problem wasn't just the identification of the car, it was the fact that I couldn't drive! I'd driven the old Land Rover on the farm, in a large field, but never ever on the road. And now I owned a 2 Litre sports model. I had to do some quick thinking on my feet, though at that time I don't think I was thinking in any rational sense at all. My body was walking around by its own volition separate from my head. A head filled with impenetrable white noise and cotton wool. *Think, come on think!*

"Oh, I think it's got something wrong with the gearbox. I'll go to the garage and get them to come and take it, see if they can fix the problem." This weak excuse was the only response I could think of.

"I am certain you had too much last night and you're still drunk by the sound of it. It's better if you walk," Sam replied, giving me the excuse not to seem as crazy as a loon. She blew me a kiss and flattened her skirt rubbing her thighs with slow stretched fingers. I could see her red painted fingernails pressing hard into the material. Just straightening her clothes, somehow I didn't think so.

From cycling around the town in my previous life I had a fair idea where I was, and where the main road with the bus stop would be located. I walked boldly through the gate and took the left turn towards Leeds Road. Exterior confidence belied internal conflict. What the eye doesn't see…

At least once I was out of sight of the house I could slow and I would have time to think. I was a suffering a solid mental block having enormous difficulty even thinking about thinking. I'd lost two years, gained a very passionate older woman as a lover, and a car I couldn't afford or drive. I had a premonition this was going to be the biggest part of what I was to discover about my life. I was very wrong! What I knew at this moment was only the very tip of a giant grubby iceberg.

What to do next? What to do next? What to do next? Stop asking yourself that question and do something! Go home. Yes that's it. Go home to the warmth of the farmhouse.

The bus stop seemed to hold some significance, quite why I had no idea. I waited, trying with desperation to think, coming up with nothing. The only thing in my head was the urge to return to the farm at least to have some good food and a rest. The bus approached, tall, red, normal. Why I thought the bus looked tall, red and normal I couldn't honestly say, but I was pleased it was. All through that journey I can say I registered nothing. All was a blur. I sat catatonic avoiding the turmoil inside my brain. Thinking nothing was the easy route.

The farmhouse looked exactly like the farmhouse. In two years nothing had changed on the facade of that 60s building. Other things were disturbing in their profound difference. Next to the farmhouse was a large new construction that could have been a barn or storage shed. To me this very large construction had appeared like a giant magic trick. The farmyard had been transformed overnight. It was as fascinating as it was frightening.

Sam had questioned me about my visit to the farm, with the suggestion that I never go there. I was more curious on several levels about this than the reception I would receive. It was obvious to me that I'd been moving about living my life in the local community for the last two years and the family would know most of my history. Once I explained I couldn't remember anything perhaps they could fill the gaps for me, or take me to the mental hospital? So as I walked up the driveway towards the farmhouse I was speculating as to what the new large shed contained: more shitty livestock or new tractors and ploughs?

When I arrived at the front of the house, all was quiet. The one thing I did notice was a new Triumph Trident motorcycle I assumed belonged to Jane, my sister. I was looking it, bending to examining the carburettors, looking at the exhausts and generally admiring this modern motorbike, a type which I'd never seen before, it was all new to me. I was standing speculating on how fast the machine could go when I got distracted.

The noise was horrendous! An enormous ear-splitting bang! "What the fucking hell," was all I could manage. The shotgun pellets gouged their way into the door of the new storage barn close above my head. I threw myself to the floor behind the motorbike. Looking up I could see my brother George at the bedroom window with a twelve-bore shotgun. George, my own level-headed brother, was shooting at me!

"What the hell are you doing, George?" I shouted.

"It's just a warning. Stay away you bastard! We told you not to come here. You're not welcome in this house," he replied with an audible hiss to the note of his voice. If he could have squirted venom I'm sure he would.

"Where's dad?" I asked.

"Dad's at St Peter's Church," George said, all the while looking at me in the strangest of ways.

"Dad never goes to church. What's he doing there?"

George stayed very quiet for quite some time. I wondered if he was going to shoot at me again. He still had the gun resting on the windowsill, and I knew it had one cartridge left in the breech if he'd loaded both barrels.

"You know why he's there," George said, breaking the silence.

"No, indulge me. Why's he gone to church?"

"You're a complete bastard," George shouted. He pulled the shotgun off the windowsill and tried to force himself to aim it at me. I ducked down behind a motorbike praying the pellets wouldn't find their way through openings in the metalwork. George fired the gun high above my head once more, the pellets biting deep and hard into the woodwork of the new doors.

"Has one of the aunties died?" I was stabbing in the dark desperately trying to find a reason why my agnostic father would visit the church.

"Dad's been there for eighteen months. He is buried there!" George gave me a pitying look as he said these words as if he was talking to a small child that didn't understand.

"Daddy's dead! Daddy's dead!" I sounded like a five-year-old child. George just nodded. The tears flowed because I understood my very straight brother was not perpetrating some sick joke. I stood out there in the farmyard wailing like a small child. I was bereft. I'd lost all those days and my father. This was becoming a terrible nightmare.

I don't know how long I was standing in the yard crying, wailing like a lost child or whatever I was doing. I felt strong arms around me. It was George, and this time he was trying to comfort me and not kill me.

"How…?" was all I could say. This was the only word that could penetrate my wretched sobbing.

"You don't know how? You know how?" George was studying me as he said these words. He could see from my reactions that I didn't have a clue I'd lost my father, or how he'd died.

"No." As I said this George took it all in, and seemed to grasp that I genuinely didn't know father was dead.

"It was that German machine the aunties didn't like. Dad was working with it and got wrapped up in the drive shaft. I was close by and managed to stop it. It didn't look much. He had a heart attack on the operating table. He was so bloody strong, so permanent. I still can't believe he's gone."

He went on to tell me the aunties later attacked the German machine with petrol and cigarette lighters, destroying it. The new barn was to store all the new modern farming equipment safely away from the aunties. Most of it was foreign made, not necessarily German, but foreign enough to have it burnt to death for not being of pure English stock. The aunties had very strange views about foreigners, even Scots, and especially people from North Wales.

I asked George where Jane was. And the new Triumph, was that hers? The reply, Jane was now working at the veterinarian hospital. And yes, the motorcycle was hers.

"She's not riding it today because she is doing a twelve-hour shift, and doesn't want to ride home tired in the dark."

I enquired after the aunties and was told by George they remained very much alive and brutally miserable down at the old cottage. With a hint of a smile he explained they spent their days smoking, bickering with each other and discussing the evils of all things not English. I think even Southern people were classed as foreigners.

I then asked George about the shotgun. All he said was it was a warning to stay away. Not to interfere any more in the house. Not to upset mother. I didn't have the slightest clue as to what evil deeds had banished me from the family farm. Even in close proximity to my old home, looking around I captured no clues, in the broad daylight hours I was in the darkest dark.

I told him about the morning. I didn't mention the details of the loss of my virginity for the second time. I wasn't telling my brother about today. What I was stressing to George was that I couldn't remember a single thing after I left The Cauldron drunk on August 17th 1971, two years ago!

George in his cynical way would probably have not believed me, but after witnessing my heartbroken reaction to the death of my father he took on board that something had happened to me, and on some level he understood I couldn't remember.

Whether George believed all I was telling him I do not know. No matter how much I thought about it nothing was coming back. Not even the death of my father. He continued to hold me and comforted me, seeming to understand something inside me was broken. He knew I was not myself. So crushed with the grief of my father's death even quarter an hour later I was still crying wretchedly with my shoulders jerking. I was George's snotty-nosed kid brother gripping him for comfort. It was obvious this wretchedness was genuine grief over my lovely, tough old father.

After a while he explained I'd never returned to the house other than sending some large greasy lout for my belongings. This was weeks after that last night around the table.

"If I don't live here then where do I live?" I asked.

"In your fancy flat," he replied.

I asked him straight out where my fancy flat was, and why I rented a fancy flat, and what did I do for money to pay for the fancy flat.

George looked at me for some while before saying, "You don't rent your flat, you own it, all paid for! If you're not lying about this amnesia, I think you're in the shit!" He said this while looking at me like a condemned man.

George then informed me I'd been "up to no good" and I knew "all the wrong uns". He also told me quite helpfully that I lived on the top floor of a very smart three-storey block on the edge of town near the posh new estate. It was a revelation to me that I lived on the same estate I'd been visiting this morning. I started to wonder how many times I'd visited Samantha's house on quiet mornings. I still couldn't understand how I would turn up at the home of my married mistress drunk and sleep on a sunlounger without her husband complaining.

I had no idea where this place was, or how to get in. George told me Jane had stayed closer to me than anybody else, and though he didn't approve of the contact she might have a key. Jane had told him she didn't, but he didn't believe her. She would have the key to her favourite brother's house.

George, whose mood I couldn't judge from our encounter, strange as it was, agreed to take me to the veterinary hospital in the Land Rover. Our journey there was almost in silence. The only thing he mentioned was my mother Iris, and the fact she was away visiting her sister for the day. George didn't want me upsetting her by turning up unexpectedly. Was he trying to say don't come back again? I think George didn't know what questions to ask or why he'd believed any of my explanation of amnesia. I think he was frightened of asking me anything and digging up my grubby recent past, distancing us again. Assuming now I was any nearer to him.

Jane was very busy with some wounded dog, and it took some time to see her. In front of George she was reluctant to admit she had a key to my flat. Luckily for me she had it in her rucksack; Jane didn't do the handbag thing. She gave it to me along with street name where the flats were situated, and told me she'd contact me later to talk to me about my amnesia. I was sitting morosely in a leatherette chair in a very smoky waiting room at the veterinarians, while Jane and George seemed to spend an age discussing something. Finally George walked by and squeezed my shoulders like a mate.

"It'll be all right. We'll sort something," George said.

"Contact me later, Pete. Then you can tell me the real truth, and what your fucking scheme is now." Jane hissed this out of earshot from George.

Before leaving I assured Jane I was genuine and not lying. I was having a big crisis, terrified about my missing years. I did tell her a little bit about this morning. My sister and I could always talk about things my brother and I could not. My father's death had faded quickly from my thoughts. Perhaps I'd already grieved too much for him. I had no way of knowing.

When I got outside again George had gone. I don't know if our reunion was too much for him, or he decided there were too many old wounds. There was a subtle sensation of change in our dynamic. If not back in the bosom of the family I was making some small headway, some move towards a normal life whatever that is.

What was normal for me in the last two years? I hadn't a clue. I decided to walk to see if I could remember anything, hoping I would pass something that jogged a memory from some dark corner. What I did remember was that walking was hard work. I must've got soft from driving the car, or my extra bulk made me heavy on my feet in my very smart shoes. I looked at all my surroundings remembering nothing.

A complete and utter void of two years stretched out behind me.

It took me the best part of two hours to walk to the flats, and in all that time the last thing I could possibly remember was walking through the battered, tired old door at The Cauldron. My best mate Bob accompanying me on a mission to lose our virginities.

I'd have to look Bob up. He would know something.

CHAPTER 9

Breaking the tedium of the now.

Back in the cancerous now, I decided my dreams were not a natural phenomenon. I was travelling somewhere, stepping over the edge into another dimension, this world but not this world. These experiences could be looked on as alternative life, the universe of joy, somewhere where love was waiting. It was at this point I decided there were two choices: the world of pain or promises of joy in another more brilliant and spectacular universe.

Sleep came, and to my great disappointment nothing happened that night or in the following three. I was sleeping not only in the night time but for many hours during the light of day. All this time nothing happened and I started to despair that I would never experience such vivid life changing moments again. The deep feelings of dread and a nagging knowledge of some twisted past deed had faded to nothing. The thing remaining constant was the sensation of deepest love. I wanted more. How long would I have to wait? Perhaps that was it, all I was ever going to get, or perhaps the next dream would drag me back into the yellow beast infested stinking cancer hell. Then it took me by surprise.

I wasn't in bed. I was watching a music programme on the television mostly with young artists, people I didn't know. Some were brilliant, and others were equally brilliant to other people's ears, but not mine. Halfway through a hypnotic set by a girl led band from the south, the music slipped into the subconscious after which it disappeared altogether.

The treatments left me chronically tired, and always on the edge of sleep. I was suffering from the cure (not the band). So the music passed from strange hypnotic instrumental melodies to the sound of hearing my train a coming!

No build up, straight in, I was there on the platform, and this time no pain from the harsh tarmac pushing up through my feet. I was wearing a very nice pair of brogues, very 1950s. Apart from that I hadn't changed. I was wearing what appeared to be the exact same suit, and I wondered if every fibre of it was new this time round, or it was the self-same suit that existed permanently in this parallel universe? If I got it dirty today would it be dirty the next time I wore it. This thought didn't last long as I was captivated by an aroma in the air. It wasn't a fragrance from one of the millions of flowers, but it was the most intoxicating smelling aftershave, impossible to buy in my world. I touched my chin caressing it, noticing it was incredibly smooth, shaved to perfection. In my other world I often went days without shaving, though I would not know this because the only reality now was this one. I looked at my reflection in the waiting room window. I was the handsome young guy waiting for one thing to make the day perfect – the beautiful girl.

Again my senses picked up the vibration of the train at a great distance, but this time it seemed to be running with the smoothness it didn't possess the first time I'd heard it. I was pondering on this visceral difference when I realised it was approaching with much less pressure in the steam, much less heat in the firebox. That was it, it was going slower. The train was winding down preparing to stop. With this possibility I felt a tingle of anticipation run through my whole body, bringing alive every nerve. I could feel my heart pumping a little faster and knew instinctively this time the train would stop. I understood it would not rush straight through the station. I would get a lot more than a glimpse of this beautiful girl. I would finally meet her face to face, and I had started to love her before we ever met.

As before the joy and the ecstasy built inside me, not to the same mind-blowing strength as before, but if I was going to meet this girl and it was as strong as before I wouldn't be able to speak or breathe. I would die of ecstasy the moment we were inches apart. The sensations felt in those next few moments were etched permanently into my brain, a curse in our world that would last all my life.

As the train slowed and the windows of the carriages flashed by I saw no girl. The train stopped in front of me. I scanned along all the carriage windows seeing nothing, I was starting to despair. Inside my entire body I had all the feelings of joy, so I knew the girl was close. My eyes darted along the brilliant reflections of all that glazing with no sighting. The disappointment was contrary to my inner sensations, but she wasn't in the carriage in front of me, or visible in any of the other carriages.

My heart was falling. No it wasn't, all my molecules were telling me she was close. The girl was pulling the window down on one of the carriage doors where she had been standing in the door space, invisible from my view but not invisible from my inner sense of her. Smiling with a radiance that took my breath away she looked at me with those amazing eyes.

At first I didn't think I would actually be able to speak. Then I thought if I do speak I will say something stupid. Finally, however, I managed a few words of greeting.

"Hello, it's wonderful to see you again," I said. Later what struck me as odd was my normal voice has a strong northern accent. My voice was beautiful, moderated and balanced, all very correct, not my voice at all.

"Hello, Paul," she said.

"My name is Peter," I said, worried she may be here to meet someone else.

"No, not here, here it's Paul. In this universe that's your name," she replied.

"I'm so sorry. I was very rude. Please allow me to introduce myself again," I said, and continued, "Hello, I'm Peter, sorry, Paul! And who do I have the pleasure of greeting?"

"Jennifer," she said. This was after a pause of a few seconds while she smiled at me, captivating me with every feature of her face. Her eyes were hypnotic… beautiful. The train let out a shocking ear-splitting sound distracting me from this vision. Something in the corner of my eye caught my attention, forcing me to drag my gaze away from Jennifer. The fat stationmaster jiggled in all his finery as he waved his gloriously coloured flag with the vigour of a nationalist fanatic. Two great jets of aromatic steam blew out from the steam boxes, and a double blow of the whistle indicated the train was about to move. Clouds of steam started to envelop me, and I was worried Jennifer would disappear from my view for eternity.

"Jennifer, will I see you again? I must," I said, into the cloud of steam enveloping her.

"Tomorrow, I'm getting off the train. Tomorrow we will speak about our lessons," she replied.

Then through the fog bank of steam she did the unexpected, blowing me a kiss, a very soft kiss. The most remarkable thing was I could feel it on my lips. It was as if she'd bent forwards giving me the very softest of kisses. I was entranced by this development so I reached forward and gently stroked her hair, touching it in my imagination, not touching the real thing because she was several feet away on the train. To my surprise she turned and smiled at me. I could send physical affection through the molecules in the air. It was a revelation like the bow wave in water. I could push the molecules ahead of me. This is how a kiss worked, I think.

To my delight she watched from the lowered window of that strange door and continued to smile at me as the train disappeared around a curve trailing its old-fashioned guards van that took her from my view, before it too was obscured behind a bank of brilliant flowers in the old railway cutting. Jennifer seemed as fascinated in me as I was with her. She wanted me for lessons or something. I wanted Jennifer in whatever form she came. I had to be with her.

I awoke into a world filled with dark thoughts, and the feeling that some time in my recent past I'd done something very evil, worried the police and the process of law would make me pay for my wrongdoings. I was burdened with a sick hollow feeling inside that would take a couple of days to fade.

Now I knew she was coming again tomorrow. So it was a good thing and a bad thing because I would see her again in that glorious parallel universe, and afterwards I would get more deep sensations of guilt. I could cope with the guilt. My life was full of horrors for me in every way, and one more horror didn't seem to add much to the burden.

At least she was coming tomorrow, but when would tomorrow be? Was Jennifer's tomorrow twenty-four hours later for her? That's if her universe had hours. If she came back one day later in the same timeline as I lived, and sleep wouldn't take me there for several days I would miss our next encounter. She may think I'd rejected her and I wouldn't be allowed back into the wondrous parallel universe. I couldn't make myself go there. This brought a growing anxiety that I would fall out of step with her by not visiting at the right time.

I knew after just two visits, a brief meeting, and one blown kiss that I felt more passionate for this spectacular girl than any physical contact experienced in my mundane life. I was addicted and craved these crystal clear experiences in the parallel universe, Jennifer's world.

Jennifer was in my head, in my life, never ever to be forgotten.

CHAPTER 10

The dark bright daze of 1973.

I got within a couple of hundred yards of the flats when the desire not to be all alone and frightened came over me. I didn't want to sit in a flat I didn't know, or search through drawers looking for clues about my own life. I wanted company, and I wanted answers, so I decided to visit my best friend Bob Wilson. He would know everything.

I wished later that I'd gone up there and looked around. The walk to Bob's was another long trek, but there was nothing better to do and I hoped the walking might clear my head. I may come across something to arouse a subconscious memory of my recent past; at this moment every detail remained a mystery. Sad to say it was to stay that way, but complications were about to set in, big style.

I arrived at Bob's sometime in the early evening. I could hear noises from the garage. Someone was in there working on something. With Bob it was always motorised. He was always trying to breathe life back into old parts often without success. On entering the dark oily space I found Bob in a pit beneath a MGB roadster sports car. He was consumed with an engineering mission hitting some component on the front suspension, whilst squirting oil onto it and working it hard. Due to his preoccupation he hadn't seen or heard me. When he did, however, it was not with all the joys of friendship.

"You can fuck off!" he said, then continued, "If you don't fucking go now, I'll hit you with this hammer and beat your brains in!"

"That's a nice way to greet your best friend," I said.

With a surprising amount of venom he answered, "You're not my friend. You know we'll never be friends again… ever!" The ferocity with which he spat the last word shocked me.

At this he turned his back on me with a studied deliberation and continued to beat the car. I was speechless, standing there for some time before I finally tried to interrupt his work with another question.

At this point Bob raised his arm and pointed up the drive. This was done with a passionate thrust of the hand and a distinct look of the crazy.

"NO!" Bob shouted.

I think I got the hint, and for now I would let it rest, but I had to talk to him at some time to find out what had happened that night after we left the pub. It was obvious, however, that everything between us had changed and I was definitely not the flavour of the month, or, for that matter, the flavour of the year. I retreated up the drive, but after thirty feet or so the desire for knowledge forced its way out of my brain and across my lips.

"I want to talk to you, Bob, I'm coming back to see you, and regardless of what you say I want to know what happened after we left The Cauldron,"

Bob looked at me for a long time before saying, "You know what happened, and I will never speak about it, ever! You can come back here as many times as you like, until I have to hit you with a hammer, but I will never tell you what you already know." Then with a deliberation that demonstrated his intent he closed the garage door. I could hear the sound of bolts being pulled, a clear message.

I would never visit or see Bob again…

He wasn't going to allow me to explain I didn't have a clue about two years ago. It was obvious my appearance had been an enormous shock for Bob. So it was back to the block of flats, I wondered what my home would look like.

I was walking through the estate, now in complete darkness, with the wild scramble of thoughts in my head no more coherent than hours before. My hangover, thankfully, had gone. I was very near Sam's house and I wondered if my car was locked. Perhaps I could sneak into the drive and have a look in the glove box. I had a vague idea somewhere in my head that I might find something significant, a clue to my recent past, it was only an idea, but compelled me to look.

Of course I didn't manage the full sneak into the drive bit, find a clue to my past life and exit without detection. I did find something, a part of my missing life, but it wasn't in the car. Any more surprises today you might ask? There were many more surprises in store today; life couldn't be that easy, could it?

Have you ever tried to walk without sound up a gravel drive in the deadly quiet of early evening? This, I assure you, is impossible! I had found the car unlocked and discovered another bunch of keys in the glove box. Some of the keys appeared to be the same as on the other bunch, others totally different. I started to wonder if I had keys for Samantha and Mike's. I could only guess, at this time, however, I didn't know anything. It would continue this way and get more interesting.

The new keys bore the legend Jaguar. When I thought about security why would you write your address on the keys? Nothing else inside that vehicle enlightened me. It was like a car in a show room, it wasn't mine. The vehicle didn't arouse any emotions, I was out of luck. I was carefully pushing the car door closed when a voice behind me spoke out!

"Pete, what are you doing?" I didn't recognise the voice, and when I turned round I was in for a surprise. Standing before me displaying a lovely pair of legs under a miniskirt, and wearing a little T-shirt top was this slim girl with long dark hair.

She obviously knew me quite well and was expecting some kind of response. Judging by how the rest of the day had gone I remained glued to the spot silently looking her up and down. I was becoming expert at the standing and looking stupid thing. She had to say something eventually. I waited to see how I should respond to this lovely looking girl.

"Are you trying to sneak away?" she asked.

"Errrrr… no," I said.

"Don't you want to see your Vic?" she asked, throwing arms open in a gesture that suggested she was my Vic.

I guessed she was called Vicky. I was a lucky man, but what was she doing in Samantha's drive? It was the eyes that gave the game away. All I could manage was a sharp intake of breath. She had stolen Samantha's eyes! Jesus Christ, she was Sam's daughter! Then I realised why I have such access to the family home, I was Vicky's bloody boyfriend! This day could only get better! What more shocking things could you find out in twenty-four hours? Sinking feelings had nothing on this. I was drowning. Would I turn into a pumpkin at midnight?

"Mum and dad are out… Fuck me hard before they get back," she purred, using what I learned later was her kitten voice.

For somebody who has just discovered the joys of sex, things were picking up in a quite unexpected way. I really needed a shower, a cold shower. I realised I was getting to be quite a randy bastard. Even after losing my virginity only this very morning, I wanted her. She looked so good. I said nothing and just played along thinking I can't ask stupid questions like, "Do I spend the night with you," or How long have we been going out?" I needed to see which way the wind blew, and today, in all things sexual, it wasn't just blowing, it was a full gale, a whirlwind of Sam and Vic! Do all these women have men's names?

To my surprise we were back in the same bed as this morning. Not Vicky's bed, but mum's bed. I didn't dare ask why we were in her mother's bed. I just rolled with it and took it in my fuddled stride. Then she told me I liked to do it in her mother's bedroom because, well… just because, that's what I'd told her. The only reason I could think of was devilment on my part, a little bit of danger, a little bit of getting it back on the old folks, a little bit of I don't know what. Something about this magnetic bedroom disturbed me.

We made love in a wild and crazy way all of which proved on a spiritual level to be a very disappointing experience. She was divine to look at, to touch, but was lacking in the pure passion of her mother. Sam had a style and her reactions to my caresses pleased me as much as they pleased her. Vicky was wild in bed; our passion was like a super physical contact sport, all commotion, no connection. Any spark beyond the purely physical act didn't exist. She was telling me how much she loved me, and I was thinking how much I'd enjoyed the bright morning making love, yes, making love to her mother.

Then it struck me like a thunderbolt! The reason we have sex in her mother's bed wasn't because of devilment, it was because it gave me a sense of lying with and pleasuring her mother. I was already imagining making love to her mother while fucking her!

Lying together in the bed we were discussing the day. Just things in general like the news, the latest fashions, music and so on. I also realised during our conversation I had very little in common with her. We were poles apart on everything, and we operated on a totally different wavelength. I might have started my relationship with her because of sexual beauty, but I definitely knew why I was with her now. I wanted her mother!

Thankfully time was passing, and soon the lovely Sam and her husband Mike would return. For some reason though Mike was much older than me we were mates. This friendship came with a price. I was shagging his wife! They would be back in a few minutes, so thankfully we had to get out of bed and drag combs through our tangled bed hair. I was a pretty jaded sod for somebody who'd been a virgin just a few short hours before.

The one thing I didn't want to look when Sam returned with Mike was shagged out. I didn't want Sam to suspect at any level that minutes before I'd been fucking her daughter. It was obvious she knew I was Vicky's lover, but I didn't want to shout the fact in her face. Today I didn't know what ground I was standing on, so I had to play it safe, though I don't think I'd been playing safe ever since I woke up bathed in hot bright sunlight.

In fact I didn't want reminding too much of the last hour. Beautiful as Vicky was I didn't want to sleep with her. It was her mother that intrigued me, she just set something off inside me, and not something you could put a finger on, a special connection. As I saw Samantha climbing out of the big Ford I knew our connection was on a different level and I also knew I was in more trouble than I imagined. How little I knew about myself and trouble? I hadn't even approached the outskirts of the City of Trouble yet!

I was uneasy meeting Mike and Samantha together, especially with Vicky clutching my arm. I knew the other me who arrived very drunk at this house last night was quite a different person to the boy who went to The Cauldron, because it was obvious this situation had been going on for some while. I'd been quite happy keeping whole thing bubbling along nicely, like some maniacal sex chef cooking the absolute perfect, if somewhat seedy, *soufflé*.

Talking of cooking, I was trying to make my escape through the back of the house by going out through the kitchen. My misfortune continued when the loving couple who'd been shopping came in through the back to access the utility room and the freezers. So there we were face-to-face, the last thing I wanted.

Sam didn't bat an eyelash. She just said hello like it was the most natural thing in the world and hadn't seen me for an age. In fact it was almost like this morning hadn't happened, until she rubbed past me to get to the refrigerator. It was just the smallest of touches on my bottom, very subtle, very quick and unseen. This morning had happened, it wasn't some strange figment in my broken head, and I wondered how many mornings a week I tested the luxury double bed?

Sam was in the process of telling Mike how brilliant I thought the new kitchen was. I was looking around the kitchen. It was very new but then the entire house looked new. She continued in this vein pointing to the new breakfast island.

"I particularly like that feature," Sam said, subtly smiling at me,

I'd spent time in the kitchen with Samantha cooking the *soufflé*. It was starting to look that I spent time with Samantha in every dammed room in the house, and God knows where else. I really did have to make my excuses, get out of there and find out who I'd become, a worrying prospect.

The phrase worrying prospect really doesn't do it justice. By this time I knew I'd got involved with "wrong uns" as my brother called them, and cultivated involvement in a sex triangle which I hoped nobody else knew about. What else?

Quick excuse time was looming up again and I might have to demonstrate my skill behind the wheel if I couldn't think of an excuse why the car hadn't been picked up. I could tell them that the garage said there was no real problem. My first problem was I didn't even know where the key fitted!

I was just starting to make all the right noises, making the excuses, "I got to go here, I've got to do this, that, the other", when I was taken by surprise.

"Do you want a drink, Peter?" Mike said. I was mid-flow when Mike winked at me.

"I know what you like," he said, with a conspiratorial wink.

I was totally baffled as to what he meant. Was he talking about drink? Does he know what I've been doing with his daughter in the last hour? I doubt it. What was it then?

Mike appeared from somewhere in the utility room with two bottles of cold Carlsberg special brew. I looked at Mike thinking of excuses.

"No thanks. Had this stinker of a bloody hangover all day," I said.

"It got you on the sun lounger last night. I thought you might be up for another session." Mike said this quite cheerfully as if I was always up for a session.

"Sorry about last night. I overdid it a little bit," I said.

"Don't you always? You're the party boy up for anything, we all know that," he said. He winked at me once more.

"Not tonight, Mike, thanks, I've got stuff to do, places to go, people to see, and am so dammed tired," I wasn't lying.

"You never stop moving about do you, but tired?" he said. Mike gave me a look. Perhaps he knew something, or from the way he was intimate with me perhaps I was involved in a sex square!

And with that spine chilling thought I didn't stop moving, made all the right excuses, or any old excuses for that matter, and escaped to the car. Vicky followed in close attendance.

"I thought were going out tonight, or was it just the sex?" Vicky enquired.

"No, no, no, not just sex. I'm damned tired and need to rest for at least one night,"

Vicky seemed disappointed and was almost sulky like a young child. She'd gone from bright and bubbly to a morose and surly five-year-old literally in a second. It was like somebody flicking a switch. Like a child being told halfway through a game, "It's time for bed".

Quite frankly I wasn't in the mood for a bipolar black-and-white girlfriend. By this time in the evening, of what had been a long day, I'd had enough of the endless shit and was quite glad to challenge myself by attempting to drive the car. I suppose it was rude. I literally slammed the door in her face without even the words, "I'm off" or "see you tomorrow".

I was in deep concentration. Operating the car was a challenge and could become a challenge that other motorists didn't need. I was taking to the highway with no idea apart from what I learnt on the farm driving the Land Rover, but it was obvious I had a licence and insurance. Or did I? I had no idea!

I started the car and selected a gear. It moved, forwards. Another gear and it moved forwards. I was trying to go backwards. Concentrating, I looked at the little logo at the bottom of the gear stick. Towards me and back, that should do it. Slowly and not too jerkily for a first timer I made my way out of the drive backwards, narrowly avoiding two parked cars on the other side of the road. Vicky looked on with a surly glare. The thunderous expression on her face suggested that she wouldn't care if I died in a terrible collision. Perhaps it's the impression I got. Somehow I think not. The other me must have looked at her in quite a different way, or handled her differently to keep her sweet while keeping her mother sweating.

As I pulled off forwards I glanced towards the house. Quite a large modern built mini mansion on the best housing estate, such a grand style without any real grand style. How did I know these people? I'll be honest, today had been tragic losing my father. Traumatic, strange, disturbing and, on a sexual level, I was like a cat with the cream.

I drove like a septuagenarian for the mile and a quarter through the estate to my apartment. To my great joy working at the car's controls was a trouble-free run with very light traffic. What amazed me was my ability to drive somewhat better than I remembered from the farm. What other tricks had I learnt, what else could I do?

In a short distance I transformed from novice driver to not bad. Arriving at my apartment I parked in one of the bays. It would be the wrong bay of course. I would learn this in a matter of seconds without any interference from the usual helpful neighbour. Walking past the other bays I noticed they had small number plates which reflected the registrations of the appropriate cars. Mine, of course, had to be moved, but I was too damned tired to be bothered.

Blue was my colour, so I wasn't surprised when I reach the door a flat 35. The experience was very strange, almost like burglary. I pushed a strange key, the fifth one I'd tried, into the lock on the blue door. As I turned it the key met no resistance. The door opened.

So this was my apartment. I didn't rent this I owned this! Going inside I found the switch and turned on the light. It was all beautifully designed with a large kitchen diner, a large lounge for an apartment and two double bedrooms one of which had an en suite bathroom. A very nice apartment, I thought. The furnishings were all the full early 70s style, everything was nearly new, nothing was cheap, and all from the top end of the market. This classy place was mine. This raised the question of how did I pay for it?

I found the bedroom and threw myself onto the bed. I would start to sort everything out in the morning, but first I had to have a good night's sleep. The light went out and in an instant so did I.

It would be ten glorious hours of sleep, and I would awaken refreshed.

Who knows, all my memories may return in the night.

CHAPTER 11

Right here right now, or at least I think it is when I concentrate.

The days of therapy were becoming shorter and shorter. The days themselves were not getting shorter, but the time I spent awake was only for eating and drinking. Apart from that I was in and out of sleep for up to eighteen hours each day. Even when awake I was crippled by an all-enveloping tiredness which demanded every action was an act of will, a monumental effort. I was so tired inside it was very difficult to even think. Each day became a blur almost beyond the point where I could remember specific incidents with any clarity.

The nights, however, when I was fortunate enough to visit the other reality, had a clarity that remained in the mind with the force of memory only experienced when you are truly moved by a great work of art, or have witnessed some major event in history. These experiences transcended the tiredness of the fatigued daytimes, and I could relive all the vivid sensations etched permanently in my otherwise addled mind.

As the weeks passed I always seem to be waiting for a doctor or a nurse. I've spent a lot of time this year sitting in corridors interminably waiting for doors to open and not, I hoped, to close forever. You always seemed to be waiting patiently for one consultant or another.

This drudgery of day-to-day exhausted existence became the dream state, the state of semi-alive. My head was losing more hair every time it touched the pillow. I wasn't waiting for the earthly dawn to come. The deep yearning inside me was for a bright dawn, not in the here and now, but in the iridescent other world that had for me replaced what people insist on calling reality.

I now can't remember how many days had passed since my last visit to the other universe. I could do nothing because I was at the other universes beck and call. Thankfully as sleep folded around me I was taken there and discovered a little more. I became more curious... more enveloped.

So it was the same thing once again. The timeless railway station appeared with the cross little stationmaster holding his fantastical flag. My clothes were from the same period, my senses alive and on fire. Once again I could feel the approaching train slowing towards the station. The stationmaster, I noticed, never seemed to wave his flag in any other manner than frantic. How the train driver (though I'd never seen one) knew what his intentions were was a mystery. Despite this vagueness of flag etiquette the train screeched and groaned to a steamy halt. A final hiss of strangely aromatic steam and all was quiet, and to my delight she was there. Then she wasn't there!

A large number of beautiful butterflies of amazing variety and colour were flying straight past my face, some even brushing my nose, others weaving between my arms and legs like a cloud of coloured light passing by. This just added to my joy. I'd been distracted by the butterflies intentionally I think. Where was Jennifer?

She stood up. She had been down behind the door bending to pick up something, and then for the first time she turned the handle, opened the door and stepped elegantly from the train. She was very light on her feet and walked straight towards me stopping only three or four feet away. She was very close. She was a vision. Jennifer was quite *petite*, not tiny, but very girlish. Not a woman or I didn't think so at the time, her age being hard to guess. It was hard to drag my eyes away from her lustrous shiny hair glistening with rainbow colours highlighted in the sunlight. Her eyes with their magnetic quality and dark beauty begged me to stare into them. And those lips, oh those lips with that most wondrous smile! I was totally captivated.

Her clothes were the most curious thing about her appearance. They appeared to be some form of school uniform in a style I'd never seen before. It was as if she was wearing a business suit that also conveyed the feeling of school uniform. In one hand she held a very large, slightly battered brown briefcase. I wanted to ask, *"What are we going to do today?"* hoping the answer would be something exciting, something like exploring more of this wondrous parallel universe, anything that would allow me to spend time with her, though I didn't know what I was expecting. Instead I dug deep into the strangest corner of my mind asking a question that even now seems a little bit odd.

"Why are you carrying a briefcase?" That's all I could come up with. Idiot!

Her reply was odder than my question. "Because I'm a schoolgirl," she said. I thought she looked a little bit too old to be a schoolgirl.

"Aren't you too old for school?" And it just came out of my mouth like an idiot stream of words. I was embarrassed by my stupid reaction. This wasn't my world, and I knew nothing of its ways.

Jennifer looked herself up and down and smiled back at me.

"I didn't mean to be insulting," I blurted out. She just laughed.

Jennifer told me she was indeed a schoolgirl, and twenty-five-years old! I exclaimed some shock at this quite extraordinary age to be at school. She told me that you stayed at school until you understood the truths you were seeking, and then you passed the knowledge on to somebody else. The people receiving your insights would attempt to pass their final insights back to you. If all the parties understood the knowledge they'd received they were no longer at school and free to move in a world of tolerance.

"You're a student as well. Those clothes are your uniform," she said.

"I'm a student?" I said, echoing her words.

"Yes, you're a student and your subject is to know yourself. My subject is to teach you. Once you know yourself and I know you understand, I do not have to continue with my studies and neither do you. Then I will be a woman. My world will change a little bit, or a lot," she said.

The next moments were a joyful surprise. She stepped forwards and placed both of her hands in mine. She then pointed her exquisite face up at mine and indicated almost by telepathy that I must kiss her. I had to bend my neck down a little to do this. The first touch of our lips could only be described one way: as soft electric. They were blissfully wonderful with a power that shocked me, delighted me and captured me. She was kissing me with an earnest soft passion for what seemed an age. At the end our lips drifted slowly apart, pulling away from each other very, very slowly.

"I'm going now. I will see you tomorrow, then I will open this case and you will see your first lesson," she said.

"Can I take a peek at it now?" I asked. I was becoming curious. I was captured.

"Paul (I couldn't get used to this name. I was expecting the stress on the P to become Peter), tomorrow is the day we start to exchange knowledge and experiences, not today," she said with a little hint in the upturned corner of her mouth of more than just a smile.

I was looking at that little hint of more than a smile when, with a sudden move, she turned and walked away, climbed onto the train, closed the door and blew me a kiss. This kiss wasn't the power of the real thing but it managed to caress my lips, a captivating experience. Jennifer indicated to the stationmaster it was time for the train to leave.

I was full of blissful joy and already looking forward to my education, whatever form that may take. It was just as the previous visits. I was full of joy which diminished only a slight amount as the train pulled away from the station, disappearing in a cloud of its own steam swirling in the light fragrant breeze. It then rumbled off around the curve and she disappeared, but not the sense of her.

Will I be taken someplace beyond this station? I didn't mind being on the station. It would, be nice in the future, to explore some of this new experience and be somewhere else in this amazing somewhere else.

I remained on the station for quite a time, not leaving the scene for several minutes. I took it all in, every single part of that beauty. I was at the centre of a little universe standing in clouds of butterflies and birds, tiny colourful birds, with their vibrating wings tickling my face as they whirled around me in a tornado of colour… I awoke to bright sunshine beaming in through the windows of my bedroom. The transition from the other dimension to the now, the so-called real world, was almost seamless as the bright sunshine appeared to coalesce out of that cloud of bright birds.

The real set in, I was nauseous. Also the other demon was visiting me. I held that dread of something wrong in the past I should pay the price for. This depressing something was hard to put a finger on, the whole sensation was never more than a tiny hint of the terrible, seeping through to break the joy in my soul. Was this dreaded guilt and feeling of malpractice some traumatic after-effect of the cancer treatments with all the poisonous chemicals perverting my brain cells?

Jennifer was going to teach me things hidden in her old briefcase. Thinking about what mysteries and profound truths might lie inside distracted me for a while. This state only lasted a few minutes before dark anxieties returned.

My friend was arriving in a short while so we could both be burdened with a visit to the hospital. I was returning once again for my dose of black fluid pumped into my veins. The chemotherapy isn't really black, it's the impression I have of it as it mingles with my blood attempting to burn the cancer away, burning my immunity away at the same time, and worst of all trying to destroy my resolve to survive. Beyond all this I had something to look forward to – school lessons!

I spent several days pondering something. Am I going to die, and if I die where will I go? Could it be to the other dimension? Was all this a preamble to dying? Was I witnessing first-hand what some people might term as Heaven?

Perhaps all this treatment was just slowing me up and deluding my already fuddled mind into believing surviving was the thing to do, but then all the chemicals could be making me suffer this illusion of going to Heaven and I would be killing myself! The decision was made. I had to get a better hold on the daytime in my physical world or I could become addicted to the other world allowing that universe to drag me down and consume me.

If I was going to stay alive to experience as much vivid beauty as possible, I couldn't allow myself to overdose on overwhelming addictive sensations. I knew that if my body died in the daytime and if the other universe wasn't Heaven, it would disappear.

I wanted to be there all the time, but I couldn't allow myself this indulgence. Perhaps my choices were some other kind of hell.

I already craved another fix only moments after deciding it was doing me harm.

CHAPTER 12

Sweet dreams in August 1973.

I awoke at eight in the morning to what I thought was an earthquake. In seconds I realised the door to my flat was being battered by a rampaging elephant. I knew something else from my immediate past was coming back looking for retribution. The pounding on my door was loud and held a persistence I knew wouldn't stop until either I answered, or the door fell off its hinges. With great reluctance and fearing the worst I got out of bed, put on a towel, and with trepidation marched to the door.

I was going to look through the spy hole to see who in God's name was out there. I'd just reached the door pushing my eye towards the spy hole when it burst inwards, wood splinters spraying across the room, some digging into my forearm thrown up across my face by survival instinct. I was flat on my back as a result of this unexpected violence, and completely naked, the towel having gone missing as a door exploded inwards. To say I felt vulnerable would be a complete understatement. I was disorientated, unaware of my past and scared witless. I'd started yesterday witless only for the witlessness to grow.

What happened next was deafening and violent. I didn't know it at the time, but the guy who stood before me was David Hartley Sparrow, known as Double-Barrelled Dave. It was unfortunate for anybody who he visited because the double barrel did not refer to his name. It was a reference to his best friend, an Italian, metal with sawn-off barrels, a short stock. Dave's permanent accomplice who fitted very nicely under his raincoat, this was Millicent his favourite shotgun.

I, in the turmoil of my new life, hadn't noticed the two other people in the room. Mike was first to perish, he was to the right of me next to the fireplace. An enormous bang, a flash of flame, and Mike was fatally wounded in the chest. He fell to the floor without a sound. There could be no saving him he was ruined, gone forever. Without even blinking an eyelid Dave swung to the left side of the fireplace shooting poor Jim straight in the face. He crashed to the floor, broken, ruined and no more. I was on the verge of screaming, or shouting something, or shitting myself. Dave was reloading, and Millicent was accepting the cartridges with a sickening hunger. My stomach gave notice forcing me to dry retch.

"Now Millicent's got those two wankers out of the way, I want a word with you," Dave said.

"Why did you shoot them?"

"I don't like Jim Clark or Mike Halewood, I'm an Ago and Surtees man myself," continued Dave.

"They were signed posters," I said, rather lamely. I should have been more worried about the fresh cartridges resting in Millicent's hungry chambers.

"You enjoyed it Millicent, didn't you?" He was talking to his bloody shotgun!

I had no idea where these posters had come from. I'd seen them briefly the night before and was quite impressed by the large framed photo prints both signed by the stars of motor racing and motorcycling. The other Peter must have been very proud of them, but right now I was registering one fact: I was sitting naked with my bollocks out on the floor in the same room as a fucking lunatic who called his sawn-off shotgun, Millicent.

"Put some clothes on you little toe rag. You're off to see Harry the Pocket," he continued.

"Who in hell is Harry the Pocket? Why would I want to see him?" I said.

"What's your game? Who the hell is Harry the Pocket? Mr Graves, and if I were you, sir! He wants to see you… Harry thinks you're trying to cross him!"

I didn't argue. I got dressed while he watched my every move. Also watching was the ever eager Millicent looking on with her two dangerous black eyes.

"I can't kill yer! Harry wants to see you first! Besides, I'd upset Vicky your lovely fiancée, or perhaps the lovely Samantha would miss your soft touch?" he said.

"My lovely… fiancee?" I was surprised. I was more than Vicky's boyfriend!

"She's going to find out about you and the old girl. Then you're really in the shit. Of course that's if you're still alive!" David was nothing but cheerful.

He hit me around the side the head, not too hard, but round the side the head with his hard brass knuckles nonetheless. It hurt and I still hadn't quite managed to get my trousers on. Overbalancing I was on my arse again. This must have been a metaphor for something.

Dave gripped my arm with a delicate touch. No he didn't! He had an iron grip on my arm and led me down the stairs, through the car park, passing my very new, very low-lying Ford Cortina GT. The car looked particularly sad. I felt sadder than the car. All four tyres had been slashed causing the car to settle on the wheel rims. It was going nowhere and inside was chaos. All the seats had been cut open with the back seat lying upside down at a peculiar angle. I was walking the slow pace of a condemned man all the while looking at the remains of my car.

"We thought you might have the hidden stuff in it so we checked it out. Harry says he don't want you running away," Double-Barrelled Dave whispered in my ear.

"I could catch a bus, or the train." My stupid response earned me more grief.

Dave slapped me around the head with his huge bearlike paw.

"The train and the bus are not quick getaways. We are watching you! Harry wants his cut, his bit of sugar icing. Worst for you is your Nazi twin has come over from the city because you owe him big time, and he thought you was a mate. Then you go shit on him." David explained these facts to me, and who the hell was my "Nazi twin"?

Waiting in the street was the large purple Ford Zephyr V6 coloured to kill, driven by the one and only Smiggy. For a brief moment I was surprised, then not surprised at all. Smiggy had always been a dodgy bastard, and now it seemed he worked for people who shared the same persuasion. The only worrying aspect was up until the point where I crossed some invisible line, these dangerous people seemed to be former colleagues, my mates until I'd done something unspeakable, which I assumed with these people, and I was correct in this assumption, concerned money. I'd somehow managed to short change them. Whoops! The gracious Mr Hartley Sparrow pushed me hard down into the back seat of the car.

"I don't wanna hear the sob stories. Save that for Harry the Pocket. Oh, and by the way, he's so annoyed he doesn't want any of your usual matey first name crap, so nothing but Mr Graves. You can call him sir if you think it will help. I'd be grovelling big style!"

I wasn't worried. No, I was terrified by everything I didn't know. I didn't have the slightest clue what these people were expecting. They could have told me I owed them £500 and I would have to believe them. I was to discover that

I'd underestimated the depth of the deep dirty water I was trying not to drown in.

I got the impression that if I failed to deliver some of the payment would be in blood. I was expected to return all the stuff, whatever that was, and avoid giving them my blood as payment. I think Millicent was looking forward to tasting my blood group. Dave impressed me with the seriousness of the situation the other me had got the new me into.

"He must be well angry with you! Harry and Baby Doll don't normally have you people to the house. Too close to home. He likes to keep business outside the family home, away from the prying eyes of the filth, so he likes all his business to be in his High Street antique emporium. He doesn't want any connection to some of the merchandise your boys sell. Good face for the general (public)." Dave said.

I couldn't work out if Mr Hartley Sparrow was a genuine Londoner or somebody who took on the affectations to sound menacing. Whichever way it was, it worked!

We arrived at this rather magnificent three-storey townhouse standing with a quiet elegance in its own grounds. Very grand indeed, all very private and the kind of place where nobody could hear you scream. I was very worried…In the drive stood a two-door Rover 3.5 L coupe, all dark blue and chrome. As I was being led past the front door towards the tradesmen's entrance, Dave, the lovely Mr Double-Barrelled, grinned at me.

"All the nights out you had in that car, all the times your Nazi mate praised you up, and now you might be going for a long ride in the boot." Dave chuckled, and I could feel Millicent pushing against my leg through the fabric of his overcoat; at least I hoped it was Millicent!

The rear entry of the house led straight to the sumptuously decorated farmhouse style kitchen solely devoted to great food and entertaining. It was all about enjoying life and all the finest things, and one of them was standing in the middle of the room. A rather striking young woman except not that young. This was Harry's wife or, to be precise, Harry's second wife, Baby Doll! This of course wasn't her real name or what we called her. At that moment, of course, I didn't have a clue. Entering behind me Smiggy assisted. "Hi, Miriam," he said.

Miriam, it seemed, wasn't as young as she appeared. She was Harry's more glamorous second wife. They'd been together for many years. Why they called her baby Doll was simple. After a few visits to Los Angeles she now appeared to be in her thirties. Somewhere hidden behind all the expensive surgery was a woman who would never be a forty again. It turned out she was keeping herself in remarkable shape in the home gym, and all this work had paid off. She had every attribute of a woman of thirty-five. Close-up you couldn't see any clue as to her real age. Being married to Harry kept her on her toes and when around the great man she had a habit of acting like a lisping teenage nymphet. Harry evidently liked this weird simpleton baby doll act.

Miriam walked over to me and grabbed me by the ear. She pulled me rather painfully to one side, telling me that she wanted a word with me. She dragged me out of the kitchen and into large half-glazed pantry type conservatory full of fridges, bottles, everything her super kitchen needed.

I was expecting the third degree, the full questioning with recriminations and accusations. I thought the dragging by the ear was just an indication of things to come. If this thing with the stuff was on her mind she never mentioned it.

We were out of sight of my guardians and any prying eyes, or so I thought. Miriam grabbed one of my hands very firmly, placing it directly onto her very well rounded, firm buttock.

"You've been a naughty boy, and I don't want them breaking you." Miriam said this in a voice that was low and earthy. This had me more than slightly worried. I knew straight away I was up to no good with the head honcho's wife. Baby Doll was my little non-teenage, teenage queen. She had a quick glance over her shoulder looking at something. I figured she was making sure the henchmen were out of sight though I'm sure they knew what was going on. Surprise was going on. She started licking my face.

"I haven't got any knickers on. You can't touch. You'd better please Harry, then I will please you some other night." Miriam told me these revelations in the moments after she finished licking. I can't imagine what the look on my face must have been like. Sexy and shocked? Appalled? Surprised I would guess!

I realise Miriam worked out when I met her husband (businessman) Harry Graves. He was sitting in an almost throne-like leather chair in a lavish fully-mirrored, fully-equipped gymnasium. It didn't take long to realise Miriam's firm bottom was manufactured in America and honed in this very room. Harry looked like a very dapper Humpty Dumpty, right down to the handmade snakeskin shoes. Somehow his skin though suntanned looked cold and oily. His eyes pale and myopic gazed at me with snake-like coldness. The oddest thought struck me: perhaps his shoes were just an extension of his body and not shoes at all. And to my surprise he confirmed what I thought about Miriam's wondrous body moments later.

"You know what my favourite thing at home is? Sitting here watching Miriam sweat, watching her pumping the iron, watching her lithe naked body trapped inside machines." He paused for a moment, staring at me. He continued,

"Of course you wouldn't know that would you? Unless you're privy to the things you shouldn't know." He said this with an air of menace, almost as if he suspected his wife of having an affair. I knew nothing, so thankfully my face stayed blank.

"This is your first time at the house, and this is my wife's gymnasium. As you can see it's filled with lots of interesting machines. These pieces of heavy equipment could be very dangerous to someone uneducated in the ways of the gymnasium… You could find yourself severely injured. There's someone here who might like to give you some "instruction". He thought you were a mate. Now he's really annoyed with you. You should hope he doesn't want to educate you!"

The shock was profound, and it came without any warning.

Out of the dark shadows in the unlit back corner of the gymnasium stepped my almost twin brother. I was totally taken aback. It was like looking into a mirror, but the image reflected was of a slightly more muscular more athletic self, the kind of image you hope for when you look in the mirror, but reality never plays ball, and leaves you with the normal disappointments associated with your sorry carcass. I knew by instinct this was my Nazi twin, whatever that meant.

"It'll be interesting when Mr John Smith spoils your deep kinship, when Mr Smith smashes your teeth in!" Harry said, continuing with, "Of course I'm all about business, and the bottom line, which for me is three grand. So if you boys make it up that'll be interesting for my pocket. Know what I mean?" No words. I didn't answer, because I was dumbstruck that this man wanted three thousand pounds!

The man himself strolled across the room into the bright light, I realise the whole coming out of the shadows thing was for dramatic effect adding a hint of mystery, and if he was trying to convey a dark menace he was succeeding.

John stepped towards me smiling in a quite non-false way, and this in itself was disconcerting. I thought he was angry with me, very angry with me, but now he approached with a jolly smile, and then I realised he might enjoy the prospect of smashing my teeth in! He was after all my Nazi twin. If we'd been twins we must have been very similar in my previous life. Was it only twenty hours ago that I came back to being good old Peter Jackson? This group of friends and associates were a grim lot making me realise that in my previous life I'd been a bit of a bastard. This thought turned out to be wide of the mark and a lot of understatement!

John leaned in close, saying, "Peter, Peter, Peter."

All this time he was kneading my shoulder very firmly with a grasp that had me almost breathless. He was one strong guy who meant business, and was far scarier than Hartley Sparrow with his fiery redhead Millicent. He leaned very close in to me as if he were a lover in the mood to kiss me gently on the ear lobe. I thought he was going to mutilate my ear with his teeth. I don't know why I had this thought. Perhaps it was something in my hidden memories. I tensed inside, I may have even moved my head back a fraction.

"Peter, they think you owe them three grand and a little bit of merchandise. This is true. Before you find their money and their merchandise what I want is my seven grand and five thousand tabs of acid. Do you understand me? Understand me? Understand me?" John whispered.

"Yes," was all I could manage. My vocal chords were almost solid with tension at the thought of this massive amount of money I'd done something with. The worst thing was no matter what torture they put me through I couldn't tell them. They could be ripping my testicles from my body with hot tongs and I'd still have no idea.

"He's good for it. He doesn't want you boys seeing his private stash. I'll go with him!" John amazed me when he said these words to Harry. What was his game with these people?

Harry was sitting deep in his throne with a furrowed brow, having all the appearance of a man in the depths of concentration considering all the options. He leaned forward and stared into my eyes before saying,

"Peter, I know where both your houses are (both!). And John has been doing business a long time, so I don't want my friend Dave to fall out with you." He looked flushed, like a man who was having problems with his blood pressure.

John intervened. "I intend to be in business for a long time. I don't want any trouble, and my ex-friend here has agreed to sort it out, but secrets are secrets. If Peter comes through we're back to being mates, back to being, as you put it, Nazi twins." His appearance was so relaxed either he was very sure of himself or a good actor.

John then grabbed me by the hand and took me over to a weight bench. At the bench he picked up a barbell with, I estimated, 60 lbs on it. Holding it out in front of him one-handed was an impressive feat in itself. He dropped it on to the leather topped bench. The barbell hit the bench with a sickening crash making an impressive dent in the leather covered surface.

"Did you see how deep that dug into the leather? Could you imagine Dave and Smiggy holding you down? I would drop it and you would see it falling straight down towards your eye sockets. Your face would be smashed. You might be dead, or blinded, or a cabbage." John loudly faux whispered these words to me and his laugh was loud given out to the whole room.

John led me by the hand out of the gymnasium away from Harry and Dave. On the way towards the kitchen we passed what appeared to be a library. It was an impressive room with thousands of books lining the wood panelled walls, all very sumptuous with its antique lamps and a huge desk. To my surprise at this desk was a large figure bent over studying books. This bulky man was sitting in a wheelchair banging away on an old-fashioned handle driven calculator. He looked up and our eyes met, it was very disconcerting. It was Lenny the Helmet! I was going to say something but Lenny, on seeing me, just shook his head sadly and made a rude gesture moving his hand up and down as if clutching a stick. John roared with laughter.

John continued holding my hand like some demented lover as we walked past the fidgety smoking Smiggy and out through the kitchen where Miriam blew me a kiss. John saw this and sniggered.

"If Harry ever found out you were fucking Baby Doll?" John said. He didn't continue, but I knew what he meant. Then he looked at me.

"Of course you're safe on that score with me," John added. At this I realised the baby doll liked both the Nazi twins. Now I wasn't quite sure if she was blowing me or my firm handed guide a kiss. I even thought we may have had a threesome. It made me shudder!

Outside, John Smith was very casual, much more pleasant and far less businesslike.

"I think you've got something figured out. You're playing those bankers aren't you?" he said to me. I had a revelation at that moment. He thought I had invented some elaborate hoax, a scheme in which the twins would come out as the top locals (businessmen). Again he pre-empted me.

"Right, Peter, where's our profit? Where are the tabs? And how does Lenny the Helmet fit in with all this?" John said. I couldn't imagine the person I'd been before today. Did I hold in the dark recesses of my mind the workings of an elaborate scheme? Questions were being asked and all were going around answerless in my head. The now very casual John was moving towards the big Rover. I had a feeling we'd shared many adventures in this car. I was wondering if I was going to sit in the passenger seat and be expected to spill the beans, or was my fate the commodious boot. I had the strangest sensation others had travelled in it, some with one-way tickets.

John stopped as we reached the car complaining about his shoe. I didn't know if this was some kind of ruse. It was not. His shoelace had come undone and he wanted to tie it. He put his foot up on the front wheel and I looked inside the car. There, in the centre console, were the keys hanging in the ignition. What was coming over me? Panic I suppose, coupled with the urge to run for it. I had to do something no matter how rash to make my escape.

The next move I was planning wouldn't be too smart, nor would it be logical. Or was it? I was in the shit, he wanted me to take him to where the stuff was stashed. I woke up yesterday morning with my mind a clean slate. Some things had come to me by instinct and not through memory. I had no way in this new old world of knowing where the stuff was. It could have even been stashed in my car, though this had been subjected to a thorough and violent search by those bastards Dave and Smiggy. They could be hanging me out to dry already in possession of the money and the drugs. They would be making off with enough money to buy a couple of houses, nice houses.

I was readying myself to give John one huge kick in the bollocks. He would fall like a wounded buffalo. He seemed able to read my thoughts, slowly looking up at me with his wry smile.

"Look, Peter, if you're playing me your fucked. We've both got secrets, and I don't want to know where you keep anything. I wouldn't let you in on all my little secrets, so I'll be about for the next day or so doing business locally," John said. He winked while looking back at Harry's house checking on the eyes watching us from the windows.

"I'll be keeping an eye on you. I'll see you at 6pm tomorrow night in that shit hole, The Cauldron. We can square up and carry on as business associates, and I hope good friends." John said this as he was taking his foot off the top of the wheel. His eyes fixed on mine.

"You don't think you could kick me in the bollocks and get away with it do you?" he said. Then he laughed once again, cheerful bastard. I was thinking he was going to take me in the car back to my place, or places.

"Be good to me Pete and run along smartish. Find me the seven grand and five thousand tabs pronto," were John's final word's as he climbed into his car to drive to God knows where. If I hadn't been sure of something before, I was certain of it now.

"Damn me, I'm a bloody drug dealer!" I said these words out loud to myself. Internally the idea sounded bad, but when spoken out loud it sounded appalling and terrible.

As I walked away in a torpor brought on by too many questions with no answers, a final question popped into my head.

"Two houses… I own two houses… Where's the other?

CHAPTER 13

Right here right now, with some serious camping in the winter of 1990.

The daytimes were sleep filled blurs, a vague broken experience full of drugs and drowsiness. I was starting to lose grip on any kind of cognitive reality, just living in a vague dreamlike state. I understood at some level I was travelling downhill on the way to death. I had to do something to drag myself back into the world of the living. My addiction to Jennifer's universe was all-consuming. I wanted to be there all the time. The more I had it, the more I wanted it!

Journeys to the other dimension of crystal clear sensation, and staggering robust physical health were dominating all my thoughts. Any hope I had of fighting in the real world was slipping away. I had to latch onto something harsh in an effort to fight back, to be aware of the world in which I lived, not some ethereal parallel universe.

What to do, how to shock myself back to reality came to me in a brutal moment looking at my reflection in the mirror.

I was shambling around the house in my pyjamas, the heavy cotton type you buy from large chain stores. These were one of the only two pairs of pyjamas I possess. Normal life is a place where I used to live, a place where I was not being looked after by various friends and nurses. In normal life I always sleep naked. Now these two pairs of heavily machine washed striped pyjamas were starting to look very disturbing as I discovered when I passed the full-length mirror in the hallway.

I was gaunt with sallow flesh, prominent cheekbones, hair just wisps clinging to my head. I was becoming a victim of the genocide of cancer. It came as quite a shock bringing back memories of two strange days spent in an emotional semi-drunk conversation with Bob Wilson's widowed mother Rachel. What I saw looking back at me was a victim from a Nazi concentration camp somewhere in eastern Poland. Why you may ask do I think of a concentration camp somewhere in eastern Poland with no specific name. The answer is quite simple. The only description I've ever had of life in a concentration camp came slowly from Rachel Wilson over the course of two long days with many cups of tea, and a little too much brandy. She could never bring herself to say the name of the camp.

The discovery that I looked like one of those newsreel films taken by the Allied forces as they moved across eastern Europe shocked me to the core forcing me into the realisation that I was slipping away from the living, so I started an exercise, a grim exercise in memory. Thinking about beautiful days full of sunshine, joy and *bon ami* was no good for me. This was a reminder of my night-time preoccupation with a parallel universe and Jennifer. Thinking of beauty was like an addict thinking of his favourite fix…

No I was going to concentrate on everything Rachel described to me after our long talk through two days and one night. This grim exercise would teach me that these survivors did so with a brutal determination to hang on to life. Others, no matter how determined they were, had perished through disease, brutality and random murder. I was not going to fall to brutality and random murder, but I was falling too easy for the soft option. I had to stand up in the daytime and fight the tough battles.

I would force myself to remember in all the details stories the widow Rachel told me just a month after the funeral of her only son Bob. It was the winter of 1990 and all the world was changing. The Berlin Wall, glasnost, and finally I could talk with someone who might know about my wilful forgetfulness.

I didn't go to the funeral because I was a long way away, unaware of Bob's tragic death during one of his very long destructive alcohol binges. It was his coping mechanisms when things were getting too much, beyond control. So it wasn't until after the funeral that Jane my sister managed to contact me.

Jane had attended the funeral. She was a friend of the family. Bob's sister Louise was a lifelong friend of Jane's. Both had been anxious young girls meeting for the first time on their first day at junior school, later, on to the same senior school. This friendship had lasted into adulthood. Louise became a doctor and my sister Jane a very successful vet, particularly with small aggressive designer dogs. She loved them all. I did not.

Jane told me that after the funeral Rachel had pulled her to one side asking if she knew of Bob's great secret. It was obvious Bob's mother thought I might have shared a confidence with my sister. They knew he had some dark secret haunting his past, but he'd never revealed it. My sister asked Rachel why they hadn't asked Bob over all the years.

"It was his father who stopped him talking because he didn't want any more suffering in his life. He told Bob he didn't want to hear of it, to be a man, and not a baby. He never told Bob about our wartime sufferings, just the edges of it. If we could live through all that there's nothing you could do in a town like this to compare with what we suffered. So I suppose Bobby sucked it back in and held it there like a toxic ball for years. He never spoke of it, just cried at night for months. I could hear him weeping through the walls and Abraham insisted he'd get over it like we all did. Did we? I don't think he ever did." Whatever it was, Rachel's explanation was no explanation at all.

This is when my sister told Rachel I'd come and see her. She was more than a little surprised I'd come to talk after what happened to me in the early 70s. I was looking for answers and didn't realise how shallow the pool was. So on a bright cold February day I arrived with enormous trepidation at Rachel's new maisonette. I was glad it wasn't in the old family home with its textures, its smells, and my happy boyhood memories of the place.

It felt very cold as I walked up the drive of the very neat maisonette. I don't know if it was cold, I think I was chilled by the thought of the ghosts we'd disturb. Rachel had seen me approaching. She had been waiting, looking out of the window, seeking answers. And by the time I climbed the few steps outside to her front door she was waiting to open it. I didn't even knock. It swung open and I was greeted by a sixty-year-old Rachel who on that day looked older.

"Hello, Paul, I'm very surprised indeed you can see me after what happened in 1973, or was it 74?" Rachel said, as a greeting.

"Hello, Mrs Wilson. Well I'm here, but I don't know exactly what you want from me. If I can help I'll do my best," I replied. It was a strange start to our day.

"Please call me Rachel you're a grown man. I think you can answer some of the things I never asked Bobby. Please come in and sit in the lounge. Would you like a drink of something?" She talked very quickly driven by nervous anxiety.

I went into the lounge and sat down on her new sofa. I didn't recognise one single piece of furniture in there. It was as if she had expunged everything from her previous life. I think she'd moved because the old house with all its memories triggered sadness. My host had gone off into the kitchen to get me a cup of coffee. "Not too much milk, a tiny bit of sugar, and yes, I would like some biscuits." I knew what she was going to ask me. I also knew I'd disappoint her.

She returned with a tray. On it were two mugs of coffee, a large barrel of biscuits, two small slim stemmed eastern European looking glasses, and a large bottle of brandy. I'd no idea the conversation was going to need so much support from alcohol. I had scant clue at that time of what was to come out from inside that truth telling brandy bottle. We sat drinking coffee for quite some time, talking of the weather, people we knew, just general chitchat. All mundane talk until after we'd finished our coffee and biscuits. This is when we got down to the nitty-gritty.

"Bobby came home so dirty and broken. What thing had happened?" Rachel asked. She talked rather strange English. She had a very good accent, but still managed at times to sound very Polish even though her accent was more or less Home Counties English. I knew all too well what she meant: the answers she was looking for. I had no answers, no truths, no anything, but how could you tell this grieving widow, who'd recently buried her only son, that I didn't know anything about the night nineteen years ago, and after all this time I'm still asking myself the same questions.

"I am not lying Mrs Wilson, sorry Rachel, but I really don't, in all honesty, have a clue what happened. I've racked my brains for nineteen years and have no answers. I visited Bob once in 1973 to ask him about that night. I told him I couldn't remember, he told me I was a liar and knew the real truth. I'm afraid Bob knew the truth. I cannot for the life of me remember anything" I was sorry these were the words I had to say to the anxious and disappointed face of a grieving mother.

She looked shocked to the core as if somebody had stolen a precious thing. In fact the news her Bobby had come home so dirty and broken was itself a revelation to me. Why was he dirty? Why was he broken? These were things I knew nothing of. I now realise the last time I saw Bob, the day he was under the car, he knew the truth about that night after we left The Cauldron. He held it inside like a slow cancer of the mind eating away at him, leading to his eventual destruction.

To my surprise and total horror Rachel was on her knees at my feet. She was clutching at my legs, looking up to me, pleading, and shouting!

"You are lying! You are lying! You know what happened that night. Please God you must know," she pleaded.

"I cannot remember anything about that night, and the only person who knew was your Bobby. I thought coming here would give me the answers. I don't know who is more disappointed, you or me," I said. It was the truth. She would not stop and was convinced I knew more. I stroked her hair, wiped tears from her cheeks, held her racking shoulders, and I cried bitter tears myself. It was a fruitless journey but what else could I tell her?

After helping her to her feet she slumped into the chair sobbing with a wretchedness that pulled at my soul. I was in two minds whether to invent a tale, make up a story to give satisfaction to her needs. In the end I made soothing noises and weathered the storm.

During the storm we opened the brandy bottle, and it started to open the bubble of truth. Rachel was starting to accept I didn't know what had happened. She did, however, explain to me how Bob had tried to tell his father, shouting and screaming. Mr Wilson had pinned him to the floor and told him to suck it in and be a man, not to be a baby, not to spoil his young promising life. At which she broke down again in tears for some minutes constantly muttering, "It killed him, I know it killed him, it killed him."

I don't know what clicked inside Rachel, but she decided to tell me something, the whole story, why Mr Wilson had told Bob to "suck it in, not to disgrace the family". It was because Mr Wilson was in fact Abraham from Kraków in Poland, and of course not born a Wilson. You would never have known this from his accent or his grammar. In this he was a pure Home Counties Englishman. He had been successful in removing any semblance of his past life from his new existence in England.

I cannot tell you his second name apart from it began with a W. Beyond that I found it unpronounceable. I never wrote it down and I don't think it matters as he wanted to be known as Mr Wilson. He succeeded in becoming Mr Wilson, English bank manager. Rachel Majka, as she was born, became Mrs Wilson, later the widow Wilson who would lose her Bobby. This loss of her son was blamed on hiding painful past truths from their siblings, so their siblings were obliged to hide their pain from them. Suck it in, let it fester, and let it rot your insides until you die!

Rachel explained how they had both been in concentration camps in Poland, not the same camp, but different ones some sixty km apart, how, after the American forces had liberated her camp, she was sent to a field hospital. This place was full of thousands struggling in a daily battle to deal with the aftermath of what had become for the Nazis the "Jewish problem". The American Jewish problem was how to feed all the thousands of arrivals, and at times how to feed their own advancing armies.

The other concern at the American field hospital was these starving people would damage themselves by eating too much of any food available, and some of the survivors died of kindness. Others could not survive any longer despite the kindness. Others like Rachel and Abraham managed to find salvation from the horrors of the previous two years, and each other, in this American medical camp.

Both were academics, Abraham an accountant, Rachel a chemist. There was a framed photograph now on display in the room. This was one of the few of her possessions to survive her own brutal regime of cleansing. A photograph taken on a beach somewhere in 1948 showed an incredibly beautiful Rachel, with a very sporty and darkly handsome Abraham. The couple that found each other at that hospital camp in the damp woodlands of Poland would not even recognise the healthy couple on the photograph taken on the beach at Broadstairs. When they first met they were grotesques who recognised qualities in each other, some survival instinct, similar wounds, something?

Rachel now well into her stride suggested there may be another bottle in the cupboard after this one was finished. She moved deeper into their stories, first Abraham's tortures, much later in fact the next day, her own. She wanted me to know the truth of their lives during that terrible time. She knew I didn't know what had tortured her Bobby, and wanted to explain why nothing could happen in a safe northern industrial town that would be half as bad as their lives in those rancid camps? And they'd survived!

"If I could tell nobody of the enormous horrors, then Bobby could hold his small story too. This is what Abraham told me." Rachel decided to tell me everything.

"I want it outside of my community into a world where people communicate with others and don't hold dark secrets festering in their hearts. A world of people knowing the truth might remember and not go down the same roads again." This statement came from Rachel, and I hope that I've remembered all the history to pass it on.

The stories she told me during our long two days of conversations formed what I was now going to use to remind myself why people wanted to go on, people in far worse situations than me, people who didn't have a choice. I didn't have a choice, but I wasn't fighting I was drifting. One way or the other, the time to make a stand was coming. Life was in the balance. I was drowsy, and of course I fell asleep.

I was transported into that wondrous dimension, so incredible. Why did I want to put a stop to all this?

This time there was no railway station… things were moving on!

CHAPTER 14

Going to a better place, away from right here right now.

The river in front of me on that hot summer's day was a slow moving sheet of dark glass reflecting the sky with its few clouds. I was shaded by the willow trees overhanging a small wooden jetty. This peaceful idyll was a hidden treasure secreted away from the busy high street by a row of Georgian buildings. One of them turned out to be a quaint pub with a beer garden. This beautiful old building had a long back garden ending at the tranquil jetty next to the river where I was fortunate enough to be sitting at peace.

I was holding a partly drunk pint of the most delicious beer I'd ever tasted in my life. It had an intoxicating aroma, beautiful taste, silky smooth, and just the alcohol level I imagined. This universe was the most delightful place. I could even feel tiny creatures walking in the grass several inches away from my hands such was the sensitive connection I had with all things in this other world. I was sitting on a step with my bare feet on a jetty overlooking a perfect summer river.

A shadow from behind alerted me to a presence. It was the shadow of a schoolgirl with a briefcase and a smile from Heaven. Jennifer had arrived. She sat next to me holding a small glass of lager which surprised me because we always build images of people in our own truth. She leaned against me in an affectionate way arousing warm sensations deep in the fibres of my being. She placed the briefcase on the jetty and released it from her grasp. She was free from this permanent attachment for the first time since I'd encountered her. For some reason I imagined she never loosened a grip on it, also I imagined she didn't drink.

When she released her grasp on the damn thing there was an air of the forthcoming. It was not dissimilar from a market trader setting out a stall of mysterious goods. I wondered what could possibly be in the damned thing.

She leaned across and kissed me softly on the cheek. Next her lips very slowly sought mine, and then I experienced the wonderful soft sensuality of her kiss. This was starting to become much more passionate than anything before, and I was drowning in sensations. There was a noise, or was it a vibration coming from some mysterious place I couldn't locate. I was scanning around to see what was causing the sound. Jennifer had stopped kissing me and was pointing along the jetty. This strange sensation of noise emanated from inside the battered briefcase.

"Paul, I think it's time for your first history lesson," Jennifer said, and smiled her brightest smile.

I didn't like my intimate moment being spoilt by a briefcase, or whatever was making the noise inside it. She leaned across, picked it up and placed it between us. I was curious about the contents of this important object. She flicked the catch and pulled it open. What I'd expected to see were books and the paraphernalia of education, but instead the case held absolutely nothing! I couldn't believe after all the build up it was empty. Something told me I should look further, so I stared into it for quite some time, discovering nothing. Full of puzzlement I looked up at Jennifer, a question on my lips.

"What am I supposed to see in there?"

"Look harder and you will see what could be the road to truth" Jennifer replied. All very mysterious I thought. So I looked again, this time much harder, and it remained a black empty space. No, something was different this time. I was making my first big discovery about this universe. I was not looking down into blackness. I was standing in a black auditorium. Whether it was circular or square I do not know, it wasn't the blackness of a pit or an unlit room painted in the blackest of paints. No it was a different black with a tantalising non-description of its limits. Oddness abounded. Dark as it was, the space held a feeling of illumination. The source of this became a shock as I looked upwards.

To my astonished surprise the sky was still above me, the same sky as by the river. I was standing in the same place though obviously much smaller, or was I the same and the area around me much larger? I don't know but I was in the briefcase. The room was probably the size of the large church and I was starting to wonder how I'd get out, or was I trapped down here? Looking up again, there above me was Jennifer smiling into the case. I was just wondering if she was several times bigger than me, or twice several times bigger than me, when a voice to my right shocked me.

"You must be Paul? You've come here to access memories." All very modern I thought. Especially as I was wearing tweed, and even with mobile phones the impression of this place was of a much older society. In terms of our universe we would be somewhere in the 1950s. Access memories were from another time, a universe apart.

What stood in front of me was a pixie. I think it was a pixie, I'm not too sure about this, never having seen a pixie in my life, but this wondrous creature in front of me was definitely a pixie. She was divine with the face of a pixie. You just know these things. She wasn't tiny which came as a definite surprise to me.

"I'm Hysandrabopel, you're access code."

"Can I just call you pixie? You don't look like an access code to me," I said.

"No, I'm not actually an access code, and I'm definitely not a pixie! I'm a real Lylybel, and I have your memories with me."

"Memories of what, and why do I need to access them?" I asked.

"In a past life you lost your mind, all very careless, I'm here to help you find it. No more questions on with the show!"

She held out one delicate little hand holding a tubular silver cup. In her other hand she held what looked like a strange silver key. She was holding this by the working end with the loop up in the air. I was quite confused by this strange arcane paraphernalia.

"Are you saying you are holding my memories, and you do not remember them yourself?" I asked.

"I wouldn't want all your horrible memories or anybody else's I educate about their history. No, I only have happy memories of my life as a Lylybel, and all the ancient marvellous traditions such as Alssnurgwodging and the like, but the like is more fun," she said with a giggle.

"Can I call you pixie?" I asked Hysandrabopel. I couldn't possibly remember her name or pronounce it as she'd done with a hiss and a rolled P. Also, though, she didn't know it. She was a pixie!

"If you're such a fool you can't pronounce things in Lylybel speak. I suppose you'll have to call me a silly name!" she said, frowning and smiling at the same time.

"Go on then, pixie, show me how it works," I said, boldness bursting forwards. At least it might get me out of this black hole though there was no fear of entrapment at the time.

What followed was not what I expected. She took the key, which wasn't a key after all, and placed it ring end first into the small silver tube she was holding. On closer inspection everything about the key, this silver vessel, was incredible in its ornate design, very arcane, and by some unknown instinct I knew it was incredibly old. It could have been as old as mankind holding all memories from day one. She removed the key from the liquid, placed it in front of her mouth, pursed her lips in the manner of a film starlet at a photo shoot, and blew very softly for about ten seconds.

Bubbles, bubbles, more bubbles were produced by this delicate breeze. They were all individual bubbles, not sticking together, just dozens of beautiful glistening colourful baubles that floated around my head like orbiting planets. None of these orbiting entities seemed to burst of their own volition. On closer inspection some of the bubbles were opaque and cloudy, others delightfully translucent, glistening, tempting the finger to probe forward, thrusting to burst.

"Pick one, pick one, pick one, go on pick one, then burst it, you'll see, you'll get the hang of this. It's the most wonderful thing, easy history, very easy history. Memories especially constructed for the wilfully forgetful."

I hadn't burst bubbles blown in this fashion since I was a child. It all seemed rather silly, and I don't know what it was going to achieve. I burst a big shiny one right in front of my face.

I was riding my bicycle on a country road in the sunshine, and it was 1968, June 16th, a Sunday. I was with a cycling group of eight people, one boy my age, all the others much older cyclists from the club. I knew what was going to follow the very next pedal stroke or the one after that. I realised in that instant the bubbles contained more than memories, they contained re-enactments. I was speaking to the boy next to me, Graham he was called. We were talking complete nonsense about girls, about what we would like to do to them, about what Cynthia so-and-so at school would allow you to touch. It was the conversation of teenage boys wanting to be far more sophisticated and worldly than they pretended to be, or in fact would ever become.

The strange thing about this past vision was if I was going to fall off in two miles I was going to fall off. It wasn't a matter of changing things, it was a matter of being there 100% with no control whatsoever, like living in a video rerun of your life. You can see all the mistakes and feel all the sensation and pain. Worst of all you can do absolutely nothing about it. You are nothing more than a passenger watching life as it was when you were full of joy riding a bike in 1968.

So I had to lay back in real time, enjoy the day, see how far it went, and the worrying thought was, *Am I back here forever? Is my fate to relive the whole of my life from this point, again?*

The ride was on a spectacular and rare beautiful English summer's day with quiet roads, no punctures, no tiredness, just a mini epic in the history of cycling. A day when perhaps some of the older men worried about work tomorrow, about their wife's health, about the finances, but a day on which young boys were racing along, wind in their hair, sun on their skin, a perfect day. I could feel… everything.

I remember the very day with great fondness. It was a day when we stopped on the riverbank, some of us swimming in a slow-moving river, others just lying in the sun taking in the rays and forgetting about the harder things in their lives. I experienced every second of it missing nothing. Another memory was that after we had dried off and eaten our sandwiches, we dozed in the sunshine. I'd been living this old memory for about an hour at least. I could feel the grass tickling my naked back as I laid there in the sun getting warm, and then I fell asleep.

I was woken from my sleep by a kiss on my lips. This kiss was much more applied than previous ones. I don't mean that in a technical sense like applying paint, I just mean at that moment it seemed to have a hidden passion I'd never noticed before. I was thinking this is strange being woken on my cycle ride by a kiss. There were no girls in the cycling club. It was one of the older men playing a terrible prank on me, an embarrassing prank that would have me blushing and squirming for hours, I remember it well.

I opened my eyes on that riverbank and looked at a vision of glossy sunlit hair, the most striking thing being the vividness of the colours highlighted by the sunshine. I drew back and there was Jennifer, smiling. I think she knew the point she'd kissed me. She laughed, and smiled simply the most captivating smile I'd ever seen. I could also hear laughter from inside the briefcase. Jennifer leaned across and closed it.

"That's how a history lessons work around here. You pick a bubble and pop it. It's then you witness your past actions," Jennifer said.

"How do I find the right bubbles to pop?" I asked.

"It's easy. You just learn to find the right one among the thousands. You'll catch on. It's quite interesting when you find how to work the system," she replied.

"Are you not going to tell me how to search or going to help in any way? No hints to direct me?" I responded.

"No, never!" Only two words, I was to find my own way. When she said never it meant never, or did it?

After a few minutes chatting I walked up a pub garden to fetch more beers for me, and the person who was starting to become too important, enticing me to stay in what was not my universe. I looked back at Jennifer as I marched towards the bar. To my delight she was looking over her shoulder away from the river, and directly at me. A beer garden table was between me and the pub, I fell over it. It really hurt. I was in agony having winded myself and coughing a terrible cough. This total realism thing had its beautiful moments and until that incident I didn't realise it had any bad moments at all.

I was convinced I'd found a place where pain would never visit, and up to that point I was correct in my assumption. It bodes ill to assume too much.

I awoke in a world where pain was every day. I was coughing, and my arm hurt where I'd dragged at the tubes held by probing needles into my battered veins. I was in strange bed in a strange room in a hospital having more therapy.

It was a nightmare and I was awake… if only I could wake up from this!

CHAPTER 15

Bloody red son of 1973.

My strange awakening in 1973 was becoming more than a nightmare scenario. I knew nothing but who would believe me? John Smith, for whatever his reason, failed to offer me a lift. He was keeping an eye on me, but not going to be my "bloody chauffeur" as I was informed. How could I find out what I'd been doing in the last two years and put it all together in time to save my sorry skin from these dangerous people?

I learnt little or next to nothing from my visit to Harry the Pocket's house. I'd learned I was a sex-crazed lunatic who was having too much of a good time with a violent gangster's wife! Sorry, he's a "businessman". What didn't I know? Too much, that's what I didn't know! Why do they call Harry, Harry the pocket? Worst of all, what in God's name had I done with the stuff, whatever it looked like? And the final question in a long list of unknowns I was asking myself was where in hell's name is my other house?

I had no choice but to visit my sister Jane once again to find out if she had any clues about this other house. Jane hadn't mentioned it when I first asked if she had keys to my place though she was incredibly busy with a rather sorry sick chinchilla. The pressure was on at the veterinarians and she may have forgotten to mention I owned another house. Unlikely I know, but then I didn't know how good or bad my relationship with Jane was. Perhaps our relationship was incredibly fragile and she was doing something to help, but as little as possible. The bunch of keys for the flat had twice the number of keys I needed, and this I surmised meant I already possessed the keys for my other place but not the location.

If you remember 1973, taxi companies were thin on the ground. Telephones were equally spread out and often vandalised. The bus service on Sunday was pathetic. I tried a telephone box it was broken, I tried another and finally got through to one of the only two taxi firms in town. All booked up, it was a Sunday! There was a scabby mini cab firm. I rang four times, no one answered.

More walking was now the necessary evil, and my beautiful shoes made my feet sore. It was something I hadn't noticed at first. My clothes were all very well made, all cut with incredible style, and all my shoes appeared to be handmade of the finest quality. I was so stunned by my out of phase appearance in 1973 that what I was wearing other than the wrong underpants seemed of little concern. Looking round my flat I'd noticed that all my shoes were high quality with only one pair differing substantially. For some reason I owned a pair of very robust industrial looking brogues. These, though high quality, looked as if they were meant for the management visiting the factory floor. Brogues with built in steel toe caps. This in itself was a worry!

The shoes fitted like a glove, but shiny leather soles were definitely not for walking in. I had precious moments of time I didn't want to waste, stupidly thin shoes, and too much walking to do. I did have a wallet, however, which contained a substantial amount of money, in fact more money than most people earned in a month.

I would stop in a shop and buy something more suitable so I could move about with a bit more speed and much less style. Of course it was Sunday in August 1973, and the shops were all shuttered and in darkness so I had to think outside the box. I walked across to the park and found a group of loutish skateboarders. I purchased some quite new and very sweat-stained American basketball boots off a big taciturn mono symbolic boy who didn't have the appearance of a businessman, but when it came to negotiation, he was good! His business style was to grunt in non-comprehension every time I made an offer. He carried on grunting until the amount of money got ridiculous. Without a word he removed his star-spangled boots and took my money, enough to buy three good pairs. A least now I could run if I had to. I had a sneaking suspicion these sweaty objects would need wings! They had a definite need for a thorough fumigation. They stank like French cheese on a hot day, but beggars can't be choosers!

"You can wear these," I said, giving the boy my handmade leather-soled loafers.

"Grandad shoes! I'll give 'em to mi old man," he mumbled. At least he could speak. I thought he might have been disabled. I suppose skateboarding in leather-soled loafers he was!

I hoped my sister would now be back at home on the farm. I prayed that I wouldn't bump into the aunties. The slow jog to the farm was three and a half miles in baseball boots and a suit. I think my body smelt worse than the pigs when I arrived.

On the way I'd stopped at another phone box and contacted the farm. I was lucky George answer the phone. "Where's Jane? I need to speak to her," I'd asked.

He didn't know but had a good idea and would try to find out for me before I got there. To avoid the watchful and often vengeful eyes of my aunties he would meet me at the gateway to the main road in half an hour.

"I phoned the vet and he suggested Jane was visiting friends at the Red Wheel cafe up on the bypass," George informed me. This greasy cafe was a usual Sunday stop for the guys after thrashing out a hundred or so miles around the valleys in the morning. Jane hadn't been out today. The veterinary emergency with the chinchilla continued, spoiling her day off.

My brother had phoned the cafe, and Jane was going to wait there for me. I would have to make my own way to the Red Wheel because George had told the aunties he was nipping out to look at some livestock for ten minutes. So George for all his farm management degree wasn't in charge of the day-to-day running of his own life. He may have controlled the farm animals but that's where any semblance of control ended, the two wily old vixens were holding him by the balls.

I knew in the eyes of the aunties George was still the wicked nine-year-old boy who liked mint imperials a little bit too much. He once felt the full wrath of Auntie Beattie after dipping into a bag of imperials without permission. The wicked old witch must have counted every single mint.

The Red Wheel cafe was another three mile hike, so as soon as I was on the main road through town I stuck my thumb out to attempt the impossible, hitching a lift. To my great surprise I could hear a car stopping before I'd even turned round, and to my even greater consternation it was a large 3.5 L Rover coupe. A grinning John Smith looked out wagging his finger in a "you're a naughty boy" gesture. He pulled the Rover into reverse and backed up about one hundred yards. I continued to stride out walking towards the Red Wheel pretending I hadn't noticed anything. John Smith idled along behind me, wanting me to suffer. On a personal level I just think he was having a laugh. It was John Smith after all. I know the town well and made for into a pedestrian alleyway. I didn't want him knowing where I was going. I'd slipped clear of the thug, or was it my one-time best friend?

The Red Wheel cafe sometimes looked a magical place with bright red and white outside lights flooding the car park. Shabby motorbikes glowed in the twilight of a day under this coloured illumination. Sometimes the whole car park glitters with chrome, and holds an oily odorous mechanical magic about it. Not today, however. It was a grey summer's day and the place look like shit. Inside on the cigarette burnt plastic floor a scarred jukebox was playing some Buddy Holly rubbish from some time in history, ancient history.

The whole cafe was ancient history. The plastic tables, the plastic chairs, the chrome-backed chairs at the bar, the Wurlitzer Jukebox, not the mighty bubble Wurlitzer, but a 1960 something crappy one built in Mexico for a price. The worst feature in that grease filled emporium of fatty foods and bad music was a constant low lying blue cloud of cigarette smoke. For somebody like me, a farm boy, this was choking on a good day. On a bad evening this cancerous fog burned your eyes making you cry. In fact the whole scene in there made me cry.

All this was interlaced with a smell of oil and fried food. I don't mean cooking oil I mean engine oil which oozed from those bloody marvels of modern transport rusting in the car park. They squirted more oil out of their old engines and fumes from the exhausts than heavy goods vehicles. Everyone seemed to have a layer of light oil on their lower legs and boots, girls included. Smoking full strength cigarettes without filters seemed to be the cool thing to do, and for some of them this would end their lives quicker than their dangerous motorbike riding.

I could see Jane near the back along with Steve, who, despite his slimness, tattoos, greasy blonde hair and general leather clad nastiness, was a very well-educated civil engineer. On weekends he became Marlon Brando's "Johnny" from the movie *The Wild One*. This was the hard image Steve put across. He was a really nice guy behind the front, but with me being younger, allergic to grease and totally uninterested in any form of transport that didn't have seats, I was a pariah. From this standpoint I painted him with the same brush as everybody else, the stereotype brush giving broad strokes. All black dogs are dangerous aren't they?

Jane nodded to me in acknowledgement of my arrival pointing to a quiet table in a smoky distant corner where nobody sat because it was next to the toilets. Without asking she stopped on the way across to order Pepsi Cola for me and another hideously frothy espresso for her. Lucky for me our table was in the corner furthest away from the not so mighty Wurlitzer. It was one noisy bastard with rattling blown speakers. We could just hear ourselves while nobody else could.

The topic of our conversation was an exploration of what Jane knew. I, of course, didn't know what to ask and she might know something important but not think it vital. You can't answer if you don't know the question. I was starting to despair at the mask of disbelief coming down over people's faces when you informed them you couldn't remember anything from more than a few hours ago.

Everything back beyond that over bright Saturday morning for two years was a blank. It sounded preposterous even to me and I was suffering this living hell. What had I done to deserve this? Perhaps I didn't want to know the answer. My preoccupation was this memory problem might be physiological and something inside my head was slowly leaking. Soon the dam would burst and I'd die in seconds with the last moments of life full of unbearable head pains. But the fact remained, no matter what the cause, I was clueless.

"So, go on, little brother, what's the problem now?" Before I could reply she continued, "Before you say anything I do know you've talked with George. He's told me everything. You'd better not tell me lies, you little shit, or Steve will come over and…" She looked me straight in the eyes. I wasn't getting a word in and she placed a hand on my lips to hold me silent and continued. "If you really can't remember you've been working for those bloody gangsters we'd better get to the bottom of what they want from you pretty smartish, or you're in shit street!" Jane was straight to the point.

The conversation continued in this direction for some time, three Pepsi Colas, three frothy coffees, and at least an hour and a half of discussion, not wasted but not very informative. Jane knew why Harry the Pocket was called Harry the Pocket. She would tell me later. My sister also knew about Sam because she'd seen me out and about in my car with her. She was curious as to what I was doing with my girlfriend's mother. I couldn't answer.

"I saw you a few weeks ago parked up at the reservoir. All the windows were misted up. You were shagging her, weren't you?" Jane stared me down waiting for the look of guilt, waiting for colour to come into my face. She was to be disappointed and at the same time not disappointed. This was some thin veil of proof to Jane that I really was telling the truth. I knew nothing about a romantic visit to a reservoir car park. I think Jane was starting to believe.

She knew about my house, centre of town, a small two up two down with little front garden and a back yard leading into an alleyway. "Not a bad little spot," she said. She also knew I'd had it modernised and it had a kitchen with a bathroom built above on the back. I was shocked to the core when she started to fully explain my dubious career. Jane knew I'd been dealing with hallucinogenic drugs and marijuana, but she didn't have a clue as to where I would hide anything, though she made an aggressive suggestion. Quite unpleasant!

She explained on the occasions we'd met up in the last two years she'd wasted her time trying to persuade me that I was being an idiot, leading a lifestyle that would lead me to prison or death at the hands of the very man I'm now trying to appease. Jane couldn't suggest what to do in my current situation. She did, however, suggest it was time I thought about getting out of the shitty business.

"Why didn't you tell me about the townhouse?"

"You only asked about the flat," Jane replied, looking at me straight in the eye.

"You were testing me? You thought I was conning you?"

"Yes!" Jane grabbed my hand bending my little finger hard back. It hurt like hell.

"What the hell!"

"Just a taste of what liars get!" Jane had made her point.

I took a sip of Jane's coffee and it was disgusting. I decided I needed to know more about one of my dangerous anniversaries.

"Tell me about Harry Graves. What's this pocket thing?"

Jane outlined Harry the Pockets secret past and what a vile dangerous unscrupulous man he was behind the facade of "businessman". She'd learned Harry's secrets from her best friend Louise Wilson, a trainee doctor, Rachel's daughter and sister of my former best friend Bob.

We lived in such a small nepotistic community where everyone thought they knew everyone else's darkest secrets. They certainly didn't know mine! Louise told my sister the shocking story after her mother Rachel suffered a hysterical rant about Harry Graves who wasn't Harry Graves at all. It all started when Louisa casually mentioned she knew Harry and his wife Miriam from the surgery where she worked during her studies.

Rachel had screamed at her, "You stupid girl! You should never help the rzezimieszek! He is evil, pure evil! He deserves to be ill and die!"

"The reservoir or whatever you said needs to be ill?" Louise was trying to lighten the mood.

"The rzezimieszek, the rzezimieszek!" Her daughter couldn't understand the Polish, so Rachel screamed it out in English. "The pickpocket, the cutthroat, that's what everybody called him in his camp. He wasn't in my camp, thank God!"

Harry the Pocket had a tattoo which consisted entirely of numbers under is left armpit. He first met Louise's parents, the future Mr and Mrs Wilson, in an American army field hospital. The man who would become Harry the Pocket was already called rzezimieszek along with accusations and rumours concerning his treachery. Harry had a Polish name, Rzezricki, which he now hoped was totally forgotten. He wouldn't want anybody remembering him from the old days. He grew into the accusative nickname the rzezimieszek during dark days when he used any means to further his ends. A name spawned in the cruel blood-soaked winter earth of a faraway Poland.

How Harry Graves came across his sombre English name no one knows. It's not even close in sentiment to his Polish name. In the current world Harry spends a lot of time talking of money in the pocket, keeping it away from the government, his percentage, and hamming it up with a continuous habit of putting his hands in the famous pockets and gesturing to all this is where his percentage should go. He continuously hams it up over his nickname probably in a subconscious effort to shift the truth of its origins. No one, absolutely no one, was allowed to even think about mentioning his nickname, it had a bleak history.

Rachel had been told by some local survivors that Harry (Rzezricki) arrived in the concentration camps late in the war. He was the son of a wealthy jeweller, and with careful spending and even more assiduous hiding he'd managed to avoid the Nazis for more than four years. However, in the autumn of 1944, the net finally closed in around Harry. Rumour was he tried to escape by implicating the innocent people in a flat below. Two of the soldiers shot a family in the kitchen, pushing the bodies from the window to fall into the street as an example to others. Harry was promised a visit to the gas chamber and did not escape.

The rumours had been rife about the Nazis hoarding gold and precious stones, so when they marched filth covered Harry directly to the showers from the train he made a final plea to a senior SS officer who beat him to the floor with his silver handled stick. Before he was unconscious Harry managed to scream out that he was the best jewellery expert in Poland. He could sort and value confiscated family heirlooms. He was very good at book work. He didn't die in the showers but awoke on a dirt covered floor in a crowded hut. He was alive! This had saved him for a few days.

To survive he made himself more valuable. Harry needed an edge to keep him alive, so he told the Nazis he was capable of finding all the hiding places in the camp, places where prisoners hid their precious belongings to barter for meagre scraps of food. He'd keep his eyes and ears open, and at the right moment would reveal where some of the more careful Jewish people kept their wealth. He also knew people hiding anything unapproved in the camps received a bullet to the back of the head, or were beaten to death in front of the others as an example.

In the final days of war, Harry used his influence and hidden wealth creamed off from his informing to hire four of the late arrivals. These Jewish men still had enough strength to fight. He promised he could keep them alive with his contacts and camp knowledge until the Americans arrived.

Tanks rumbled in the far distance, and daily retreating Germans marching past the camp in bedraggled convoys. Chaos reigned when the showers had stopped killing, the ovens had gone cold, and the guards were fleeing to avoid being slaughtered by enraged Allied soldiers.

Harry was crippled by fear after two of his "helpers" were found mutilated without throats, and the other two helpers disappeared as if they'd never existed.

Apparently a tough American sergeant was openly in tears as he described the scene after he'd opened a very thick gas tight door. He explained to the others he could hear a pathetic whimpering sound, the only noise in all that quiet horror. The hardened veteran couldn't believe somebody so brave had managed to survive all this horror. He'd plucked this man so close to death out from inside a mound of rotting corpses. The man was now being cared for and sent to the field hospital. All the others knew this man was the rzezimieszek and the truth of why he was hiding.

Many knew that he'd hidden among the rotting corpses of the very people he betrayed to prevent others hunting him down and killing him like a rabid dog.

In the American field hospital more rumours started, some of the survivors knew of Harry, and called him the rzezimieszek! Some of the stronger ones wanted to kill him, but to their annoyance the Americans cited it all as rumour and protected Harry. They moved him one hundred miles to another field hospital. This is where for a short time he made friends with Abraham and Rachel. They were soon to shun Harry because the truth was hunting him down. Others at the hospital already knew Harry only too well. A few days later they moved him again for his own safety.

The rzezimieszek reinvented himself as Harry Graves, friendly businessman and local antiques dealer, as a cloak of protection shrouding him against his purulent past.

Eventually the rumours found him in a northern town in England. Other survivors lived in this community, people with tattoos, who would like to kill him even now, their rage against him testimony enough. Harry stays very private in all things. Unguarded public appearances even seven hundred miles and twenty-eight years from his old home were a rare occasion. Rachel and Abraham arrived in that small northern town five years after Harry. They had rare glimpses and never acknowledged him.

So I knew why I couldn't call Harry "the pocket" to his face. And if I ever did I think I might end up another victim. The cold dark room with a concrete floor would probably be his basement, or someplace he rented. I wondered if I could use this information with the authorities to get out of the situation; grass up Harry to get time off. When I thought about it I was sure that other survivors would have reported him already, but what can the authorities do, all the evidence was dead.

The conversation continued with the obvious next question. If I owned a house, where was it? My sister told me the address. I knew the street, very quiet and out of the way.

"The ideal place to host wild parties, and do a bit of business with pleasure, why not?" Jane said, all the while staring hard into my eyes looking for a clue. I said nothing.

"That's how you described it to me last year!" Jane's spat the words.

She thought I was losing my mind because I'd been experimenting with the muck I sell. Now I was reaping the rewards of my decadent criminal lifestyle. She was not surprised I was suffering, nor that I had people after me. In fact she told me she was surprised I lasted this long in the business.

"All bad news, all villains your so-called circle of friends!"

The biggest surprise was who I actually worked for. I thought it was the notorious Harry, but no, I worked directly for Lenny the Helmet who I seemed to think was now doing the accounts for the businessman. John Smith worked directly for John Smith, and for neither of the other parties. It was all getting very confusing until my sister explained that I'd been taken under Lenny's wing after his accident during Christmas 1971. He could walk but he found it easier to use a wheelchair.

She'd given me the address of my house suggesting I'd be a fool to hide anything there. I couldn't even find my own house, a big pile of bricks in a street. How in God's name was I going to find anything I was hiding? Sadly, I agreed with my sister. I doubted I'd be foolish enough to hide drugs and money in my own house. I may have been rather cunning, so I had to go there and think out of the box, not looking for the obvious but the devious.

My sister had keys for both my places and even this puzzled me slightly, I don't know why she supported me. Had Jane helped me out more than I thought during the last two years, helping me hide stuff, keeping the law away from me, even earning herself a bit? I doubted the latter. However I knew she was doing things to keep me safe and I knew somewhere deep inside I didn't deserve it. Perhaps my sister was nobler with her family values than I was.

"I'll give you a lift."

"You have your bike… here?"

She smiled. "Yes, little brother."

I had a lift, I had the address and it wasn't in Shit Street.

I was!

CHAPTER 16

Trapped in paranoid daze, 1973.

I was terrified of my sister's riding at the best of times and she knew it! Jane was hammering the 750 cc Triumph Trident motorcycle along at breakneck speeds towards town. She managed to look over her shoulder a couple of times and give me her famous maniacal fast bike grin. When she wasn't doing that I was being whipped to death by long hair hanging out from the bottom of her helmet. Mind you it was a different torture from the light rain stinging my eyes. I didn't have a helmet and feared my skull would at any moment be smeared across the greasy, damp tarmac flashing by beneath my feet. I could scream and protest all I liked but she wasn't going to slow down. Was this punishment for the things she'd had to endure on my behalf during the last two years? Now was her chance to make me suffer for a while. Unless we crashed!

We arrived at my terrace house in minutes. The whole journey of terror seemed like hours of holding my breath, and wishing not to die by plunging to the tarmac from that vibrating monster. I think in retrospect she didn't want to be involved. The speed limited her involvement in my seedy affairs. We pulled up and as soon as I'd been able to get my stiff body off the pillion she revved up, shot away and didn't look back. It was as if she was helping the devil. If she didn't look at the beast it wouldn't bite her.

I squelched up the pathway, my American-style baseball boots saturated after the motorbike ride. This footwear was now as uncomfortable as the slippery handmade leather. I walked through all twelve feet of garden to approach the front door. It was locked which was a big relief. I expected it to be unlocked, broken off the hinges, or carrying some form of grim message. This could be painted graffiti, a note or a big hole blown by a shotgun, but I didn't care as long as it wasn't the last option. The door was unmarked and locked. Then I started to wonder if somebody had locked it from the inside. Until that moment it hadn't occurred to me that an adversary could be waiting in the shadows.

I entered slowly, my eyes peering ineffectively into the gloom. Inside I cannot say it was anything like I remembered because of course I can't. I was in the dark afraid to use the lights for fear of being watched. I waited for my eyes to adapt to the gloom and found myself looking in to the lounge at the same time glancing through a door leading to the back room and the kitchen beyond. It was all very tastefully decorated for a small space. I was wondering if I'd actually paid a designer do this for me. It didn't seem my style at all.

Each shadow was a muted grey, the sky outside coloured the same in a continuous light rain. In my paranoia I recalled John stepped from the shadows in the gymnasium. I could see forms and dangerous shapes in every dark shadow. Was he going to step out from the gloom now? I thought being my old friend he might have a key. This thought alone had sent shivers up my back.

I was thinking of picking up an ornamental object to use as a weapon. Nothing seemed to come to hand until I saw a pool cue. This was the pool cue used to thrash Mike on the green baize when I wasn't thrashing the lovely Sam in the marital bed, or perhaps I planted a few balls with Sam on the pool table! The cue was the two-piece type, so the obvious choice was the handle which I hefted by the thin end to make a weapon. It's effectiveness as a weapon would be very much reduced if Dave was in the room with his dark-eyed friend Millicent. I crept around my own house, scared of my own shadow, thinking every moment could be my last.

The house after careful inspection appeared to be completely empty of anything harmful. I moved back to the front door locking and bolting it. I wasn't sure it was completely empty of harmful substances, especially if the police found them. This was what I was here for, finding the stash before anybody else got their hands on it. Knowing I didn't have a lot of time I rushed at it starting with the basics. All the drawers, every little nook and cranny, all the difficult spaces in the kitchen, the pots, pans, the ice box in the refrigerator.

These are places everybody searches, and to find the stuff I would have to force myself to start thinking outside the box. Was it hidden in the house? Could it possibly be in the back garden if that's what you could call the bleak concrete enclosure at the back of the house? And so it continued for around two hours. All I had to show for my efforts was a jumbled mess. Everything strewn around looked like other people's stuff. I didn't recognise anything.

I was upstairs sitting morosely on the slashed mattress of the double bed looking out into the grey street through a small opening in the blinds. I was pondering my childhood. What went wrong to get me to this place? As far as I was concerned I had gone from awkward adolescent and arrived in this dark place in the last forty-eight hours. Gazing at nothing in particular I was consumed by fatigue brought on by my mangled thoughts.

My eye was drawn to the alleyway off to the left, attracted by a small puff of smoke. It rose up through the grey drizzle that filled the afternoon. What a joy England is in the summer. From behind the blinds (another nosy neighbour) I watched these traces of white smoke until I got a glimpse of the cigarette smoker glancing around the corner to take a swift look up and down the street. A face not unlike a small weasel, it took no effort to recognise the well-known rodent, Smiggy!

Did he expect me to leave the house with bulging pockets, filled with drugs and money? No, to my mind he was making sure I didn't run. Moments later this idea had transformed itself. I was starting to believe Double-Barrelled Dave and this little weasel had already robbed me with the knowledge that I'd be in the shit and they'd get away with quite a haul. They needed a victim to satisfy Harry's lust for revenge. Me!

At that moment I realised if they knew I was seeing my girlfriend's mother, there'd been following and closely watching me for some time. For some reason Dave assumed I was getting married or was engaged to Vicky. Perhaps I was, I didn't know! Then, of course, there was a thing with the baby doll which still had me confused. Was I sleeping with her or was she taunting John Smith because he wouldn't? I couldn't see John being worried about Harry if he wanted to share her bed. I shuddered at this remembering the thought that perhaps we'd all shared a bed.

I'd been in Smiggy's company on the last night I could remember. Did he know something about the events of that night and now used them to influence me? A nice way of saying blackmail I suppose. The last thing the weasel organised was me going off to lose my virginity with some girl at a small party. What dubious angle could he get on that?

Now I'm not a hard case by any means but you could handle Smiggy with a broken arm, so for a moment I thought about collaring the little git to make him talk. Twist his arm until he fessed up. That wouldn't work of course because it would get straight back, and I was more afraid of John Smith than anybody, or was it Harry I was more afraid of, or Hartley Sparrow? I was afraid of my own shadow and paranoia was painting a dark picture. I was in a panic and I didn't have a clue about anything. In fact I didn't have any idea if I was a hard case or not. I now carried the bulked physique of somebody who could handle themselves, but if I'd had the brute aggression it no longer existed.

Where to next? Then it struck me. Go to my flat. Perhaps it's there. No, I won't have hidden anything there for the same reasons as I wouldn't hide anything in my house, though I still wasn't certain. How crafty could I be? Then it struck me that I spent a lot of time at my girlfriend's house. This might be the best place to hide £10,000 and 6000 tabs, whatever they looked like. I was in total ignorance of what form my product came in, or what it looked like, so how was I going to find the stuff?

It was another three miles back to the edge of town where my flat was located perilously close to Sam's house. I couldn't think of that house as anything to do with Vicky, or her father Mike. Everything seemed so familiar in their home, even if only remembered by instinct. At that moment base instinct took over and I knew my main enemy wasn't Harry, but the fearsome John Smith. I had a feeling he'd be smiling as he twisted my arm until it broke, or laughing as he carried out grim tortures with pliers on parts of my body… Instincts cannot be ignored!

I slipped out of the rear door into the rain, closing it as quietly as the proverbial mouse. I was even more careful locking the door with the utmost care not to make the slightest of noises. Though why it mattered I do not know. My watcher was out front fifty yards away in a fairly busy town centre with traffic noise close by. Smiggy would need uncanny hearing ability to detect anything. I could have nailed the door shut!

Even at that distance I was equally careful with the big gate to the back. This was a hefty metal framework with tongue and groove wood screw to it, a secure gate you couldn't see through. I opened it the smallest amount and looked out into the dismal alleyway.

Millicent was looking straight back at me from very close quarters. She didn't seem to be very malevolent keeping quiet on this occasion. The owner of this very short hunting weapon was smiling. I looked the other way, into a face carrying a brighter smile – John Smith's!

David Hartley Sparrow stood his ground and lowered Millicent before slipping her inside his raincoat. He wouldn't want his favourite girl to get wet. It might spoil her looks. John Smith, however, strolled over to within a couple of feet. I was about to dive backwards through the gate and slam it, or wince in terror as he started the beatings. None of this happened because I was frozen in the very bright gaze of the magnetic John. He was smiling as he put his arm around my shoulders, all matey, pals together again.

"Not found it yet? Or are you leading us on a bit of a wild goose chase? Remind me. Didn't you know we're following you? I'm following you," John Smith whispered into my ear. He looked along the alleyway, all the while judging the distance to Dave, lowering his voice even further.

"You know I don't care a fuck about them anymore. I just want to have my end, and be friends again. You've got something planned you crafty bastard?" John was barely audible.

He used the hand on the arm draped over my shoulder to pinch my cheek very playfully. In fact so playfully it brought tears to my eyes. He was still smiling.

"Where're we going next? Do you want a lift?" he asked.

I lied and told him I was going to my flat to see if I could remember what I'd done with everything. He again leaned in close making a tut tutting sound with his tongue as if to say I was being foolish.

"You only have to remember my bit, that's all," John said. He seemed to think my denial was part of a master plan I was playing out like a method actor. Perhaps he thought I was stalling until the right time came along?

John Smith's chauffeuring service had reduced the surveillance numbers down to one. He wouldn't have Dave and Smiggy in his car. When Dave got stroppy about this I thought John was going to get out of the car and hand out a beating. He didn't seem the least bit worried about Millicent hidden beneath Dave's raincoat. John Smith owned a viciousness of spirit you could feel in a visceral sense even through his lustrous smile.

During the car journey John referred to the other two as halfwits. This was the first time I'd heard him refer to them like that. Then again I'd only met him for the first time that morning. He assured me he wasn't jealous of me and Baby Doll. He laughed like a drain after he said this. The other thing that occurred to me was perhaps Baby Doll wanted rid of Harry, sickened by his constant voyeurism, insisting she work out naked at all times so he could satisfy his own form of sexual perversion. Was she forming a partnership of some kind with the malicious John? Then again, perhaps I was being paranoid.

John dropped me off in the road outside the flats, and bade me farewell like an old friend before driving away. The sound of his car disappeared into the distance until quiet came when it was several streets away. He wasn't watching me. Was he was watching the other two pretending to be following me as his cover? More paranoia set in. John Smith's confidence was so high I started to believe he knew everything, and everybody else was living in a fog of ignorance, all the time John machinating for his own gain.

He seemed so confident about everything, including me. Had John Smith drugged me as part of some twisted scheme I'd invented, or had I drugged myself? This would explain why I couldn't remember anything. To make any sense of this I would have to write all the known facts down like they do on the blackboard in detective shows. I had the sensation of being on a very steep hill covered in ice wearing very slippery shoes and with seismic shifts the gradient was getting steeper and steeper. I couldn't turn round, I had to go on, but every moment I was more out of control.

Soon I would be in freefall plunging towards what?

CHAPTER 17

Right here right now, Holocaust versus Hysandrabopel.

They, the nurses at the hospital, were supposed to be saving my life by killing the cancer that had spread beyond the initial tumour. They fought back with the toxic nausea of chemotherapy, burning its way through my veins, destroying the cancer cells, destroying my immunity, and destroying pretty much everything, even the will to live at times. The desire to live, however, is far stronger than most of us suppose. In the bar discussion at the pub over a few drinks, people always say, "I don't know if I could go on!" Such platitudes are good for the pub, but when push comes to shove it just comes down to only two questions!

Do I want to fight on? Do I want to give up? The decision made after you've addressed those questions a lot of people believe can make a big difference to your recovery. I'm not so sure. However being positive seems to work even if you're kidding yourself.

For me, I think I turned the corner when I started to remind myself of Rachel's horrific stories, all given to me in those days after Bob's funeral. I wasn't only fighting with chemicals. I was using toxic thought against cancer's darkness, against what was trying to possess me. I was going to assist the chemotherapy and fight blackness with even blacker thoughts!

Rachel had so many dreadful stories to tell that midnight crept upon us. I had to sleep in the spare room. She had me awake at first light with a cup of tea. Half an hour later the brandy bottle was open and the stories continued until the dramatic climax.

I was listening to Rachel's harsh history for something like thirty hours. I understood any suffering I had had in this life was not suffering in the real sense. My suffering was beginning to look like a minor irritation compared to her teenage years of terror and death. In our modern society no one was going to put a bullet in the back of my head after terrifying me for several hours, or after killing all my family in front of me, or beating grandparents to death in front of their grandchildren. Political dogma was not going to degrade people with nakedness in the bleak cold, not in my part of the modern world at least.

So I focused on the horror of other people's lives, which made mine seem lightweight, and these thoughts kept me in the here and now, and not drifting off into a parallel universe I craved like a drug addict. Given the opportunity I'd overdose and I'd never come back.

I was living in a conundrum where on the one hand I was trying to avoid slipping back into incredible sensual beauty, and one short breath later was begging for it to enrapture me. Such conflict, I wanted to be in the world full of sheer joyful sensation, and at the same time I wanted to be in the world of the living, the world where I could go down the pub, come out to find it raining, this real world, wonderful despite its minor irritations.

Mr Wilson is where I'll start. He didn't know Rachel before the war and he never met Rachel in the camps. The meeting was under the eyes of an American doctor, in a field hospital, somewhere in southern Poland towards the end of the Holocaust. World War II was drawing to its final battle in Berlin, and they'd found each other.

Abraham Wysklowsi had been married for a short while. His wife had been expecting his child, and in the first hour after they'd arrived into terrible cold squalor of the camp both disappeared, snatched away by the forces of evil, never to be seen again. They'd survive so long, and this was late in the war with the Nazis in full retreat. This was the heartbreaking, bleak, cold January 1945 start to his battle for survival in that terror camp.

Abraham had survived, even against his own feelings of guilt after his wife had perished. At times his survival instinct was weak in the face of his inevitable doom. Dying a quick death could be a bonus. He was an academic and accountant. He was put to work counting gold, jewels, glasses, belongings, making accounts, grim accounts for the Third Reich who loved order, their order. He was surviving day-to-day with constant hunger. His luck was much stronger than others. They wanted him alive and working, so he was fed a little food to keep him alive at his desk. Deeply depressed, with suicide a constant in his mind, the days dragged by.

Sometimes he wanted to run from the office and be shot in the back. Other times he wanted to run to the electrified wire and find some warmth in that bleak winter as he cooked himself to death. Despite this he forced himself through the days like a man walking very slowly through a thick eternal fog. Abraham never thought about the end, but he didn't want it to end in death, and to compound his terror he could see no other outcome. There'd been a large reduction in the number of people coming to the camps because of the retreat, and soon his department would be surplus, ready to be thrown away. Abraham was a cheap tool, a disposable instrument.

One day, for some unknown reason, he became the focus of interest for SS officer Oberfuhrer Haussler. Badly injured at the Russian front he was now newly promoted to deputy commander at the camp. He was a man who took particular pleasure in any perverse act that could bring suffering and deprivation to others. Killing in all manners and forms had become an interest for Haussler, but he was growing tired of the easy slaughter. His new favourite experimental method to witness death was to subject his guinea pigs to his own perverted psychological methods.

For his amusement he set up an experiment with three of the Jewish academics, men from different countries, from different parts of the camp, men who didn't know each other. Even if they did it wouldn't have mattered. He put them in a small room. They were all issued with blunt knives, short 2 inch blades, and told to wait for something to eat. A day passed with nothing appearing. A second day passed slowly with no food, but water was given, horrible brackish water that one man feared was the experiment. This man believed it was carrying some form of the disease and refused to drink it. He was starting to suffer delirium. Sometime in the middle of the third day a sergeant unlocked the door and stepped into the centre of the room placing a tin of very poor quality meat, similar to modern dog food, in the middle of the floor. They were all told they couldn't share under any circumstance, and only one man could eat it, and only the man who took the food would leave the room.

These men were academics, not men of violence, men of reason, men who could debate world problems for hours, possibly debate for years. They had started their debate in the 1930s and carried on until the violent world they debated caught up and captured them. The state-sponsored violence was against men like them, and the thugs only believed in one credo, never regarding other beliefs or methods with anything other than scorn.

These cerebral men could not, would not, fight over food. They would share it. Haussler had a different agenda for his experiment. He enlisted the help of two more Jewish academics to take his experiment one step further. One academic was French and I do not know his name. The other guinea pig was Mr Abraham Wilson, but in those days he was just another Jew from Poland who's job was counting the profits of genocide.

They were taken to a small room running alongside the cell where the three men were sitting looking at a tin in the middle of the floor. Mr Wilson and the Frenchman could see the scene in the other room through a small grille. All the occupants were locked in the deadliest of deadlocks. All were desperate to taste the aromatic meat but could not come to an agreement on how to end the deadlock. No agreements could be made under the rules. They'd been crafted by an insane mind and the rules were final. This cruel system allowed for no agreement. It was one man and one man only to eat from the small tin of poor meat. Haussler instructed them to watch explaining the rules of the game and what had happened over the last three days, the discussion, followed by deadlock. He explained how these wretched academics would not fight to stay alive, would not fight for the chance of food.

Mr Wilson and the Frenchman had both been in custody without food for more than three days. They were so hungry their whole beings focused on one thing alone, the thing that would keep them alive and stave off the biting hunger pains. In the camp all-consuming hunger dominated every waking thought. The smell from the pitiful small tin of meat was intoxicating as it drifted into the cramped observation room. This was all part of Haussler's experiment. An SS sergeant entered the room and asked if the men would fight for the food. Two men agreed they'd come to a decision. Their decision was to be civilised and not to fight. One man, however, didn't say he wouldn't fight. He just remained silent staring at the tin, that intoxicating opened tin of food in the middle of the floor.

The Frenchman was poked violently in the ribs and pushed back hard against the wall by Haussler who asked him what he thought was going to happen if the men shared the food. He was unable to speak such was his terror cramped in the small observation room with this crazed German officer leaning on him with his stick. Haussler didn't want to touch such filth with his hands. The Frenchman was finally forced to respond, "I think they'll share the food."

This is when Haussler told them, his words emphatic, "No they won't. Only one man will eat the food. He will be the man who is prepared to leave his academic life behind, and become a killer." Two of the men, he noted, did not want to fight, but to his joy the other was focusing entirely on the pitiful tin.

Under Haussler's orders the sergeant in the room drew his pistol and shot dead both men who didn't want to fight. The bodies were not moved. Mr Wilson and the Frenchman were shepherded into the room with blows from Haussler stick. Now they knew the truth. If they did not fight they would be shot! They had witnessed the demonstration. They could not share the meat, so there would be only one survivor.

"All academics ready to discuss, but there is nothing to discuss. One of you will eat and the others will die, then I will have a candidate for my further experiments," Haussler said. All the time his perfect smile tormented them.

Seven hours later, Mr Wilson was led back to the long shed where he survived day by day. The cold tin shed was lined with bunks four high, with hundreds, possibly thousands of the diseased, the dying and the doomed. Abraham had drying blood on his hands, spatters of other people's life on his clothes and food in his stomach. He worried the others might be able to smell the meat, the taste of which was still a potent force in his mouth. If they could smell it there would be questions asked by those strong enough to be angry, but they could not overwhelmed by the all-pervading stench.

He knew in his mind only one of them would have survived. This would torture his living days for many years, never fading far into the background. At times he relived how strong he'd been in his moment of extreme violence, how his savagery had ripped the life from two other men so he could fill his stomach. As he replayed it time and again the truth of his savage actions haunting him. He'd cowered in the corner begging for mercy as the other two had fought each other to a bloody standstill. Abraham decided he wanted to live and became a savage, or was it a callous calculation, killing the weakened men?

Rachel explained during our long conversation about the few occasions Abraham Wilson had mentioned this, and how when the subject came up it lasted for days until he exhausted himself with the personal probing, and had become so tired he had no more mental weapons to whip himself with. Only then would he seem to forget this incident. However it returned from time to time to haunt him, to question his humanity. I was starting to understand Abraham. I now knew so much more about his personal fights both in the physical world of the camp, and his mental world in the aftermath.

I was still running this through my head when I started to choke, starting to run out of breath, beginning to slip under. Was I choking on my own vomit? Was this the moment when I was to be plunged into eternal dark? No, I was drinking beer! I was sitting at a table in a beautiful pub garden out in the country. I knew the inn quite well, though for the life of me I could swear I'd never been there. It was as if I'd been there many times, but each time I've forgotten the previous visit so it was familiar in every sense of the word but not remembered. Does that make sense? The beer was delicious and the company across the table was even more delicious. This time she was drinking a pint.

It was even better that she wasn't wearing her school uniform. It was a hot day allowing Jennifer to wear a sleeveless T-shirt, tiny shorts, and flip-flops. Nothing school girlish about her now. Just the two of us chatting across a warm wooden table covered in empty crisp packets and other people's empty bottles. All this was cast in cool shade and dappled sunshine. This was a perfect moment together. We were in the middle of a discussion about leisure activities and what made athletic leisure of any kind, leisure at all, and when was it not a pleasure to be doing something you liked even if it hurt a little. I think this conversation was fuelled by the fact that we were not looking at other people's empty bottles. We were a little bit drunk.

Her foot was not in one of the flip-flops and not resting on the grass. It was engaged in a game of footsie under the table rubbing my leg, and I was enjoying this with immense pleasure. It was a surprise manifestation in itself. I was beginning to believe we were getting closer, much closer than I expected, and the more physical the better was my verdict. I was starting to feel more than the joy the first molecular wind had pushed through my body on that station platform. This was something much more, not just a sensation of something joyous approaching. I was falling in love, and her open sexuality suggested she was falling in love with me. With this realisation I was revelling in profound delight.

In this glorious world of total sensuality and colour nothing could spoil this moment apart from "the briefcase", which to my horror was under the table. It was intriguing. The case was speaking to us in a manner that seemed quietly musical with a strange hidden depth of sound. Though quiet it was insistent. I had this feeling in a few moments I'd be travelling down into it again, or because I didn't know how things worked I was pondering if this time it would be different. Would the pixie whose name I still can't pronounce come out to meet me? No, of course she wouldn't, I'd be back down in the bowels of the brown leather case once again.

I wanted to carry on drinking and playing footsie. She insisted we work on my education, so initially I had to suffer the strange process in order to become fully aware, and then life with this beautiful girl would become a reality. I looked down into the briefcase, once again into the breach, dear friends. It wasn't too hard the pixie was quite beautiful and from past experiences the bubbles were sheer delights. With this in mind I stared into the blackness with almost a longing to stick my finger into more of those shiny orbs. It was so amazing to journey into your past beautiful memories.

I looked inside. I was inside, in that black space again, with just its hint of parameters. The space was almost luminescent in a blackness I now realise could be just six feet or six infinities if that's possible. My little friend walked out of the darkness towards me. She was wearing the most curious outfit I had ever seen – on a pixie that is! Worn by a fireman from the United States in 1935 it might have looked quite normal. Worn by a pixie in a dark space, the shiny boots, black trousers, red jacket festooned with brass buttons, all that criss-crossing of leather belting, and a glorious metal helmet seemed almost the most ludicrous thing I'd ever seen. She also appeared to have white leather gloves on, in which she held the now familiar implements, except this time they appeared to be larger, not by a lot, but larger.

My little fire fighter went through quite an elaborate ritual this time. Her histrionics started with her moving her arm in an enormous arc before dipping the blowing device into the liquid. I am assuming this was liquid because never once did I ever see the actual inside of the ornate vessel. For all I knew it could be as empty as the strange black space I was standing in. Nevertheless, after what seemed like an hour of elaborate posturing, adjusting stances, and getting what appeared to be the lighting that came from nowhere perfect, my pixie friend puckered her lips and blew some bubbles.

It was like the first time. I was immersed in a whirlwind of brilliantly coloured translucent globes swirling around like a solar system with hundreds of planets. This time, however, I noticed in this cloud of brilliance some of the bubbles, only a few, were very dull. These were different in form, appearing as a dull translucent grey, nowhere near as shiny as the others. Not in any way as tempting a target for the finger. However, the thought occurred to me that I should try one of the dullards today, so I did. I poked it with my finger. At first the bubble reacted with a strange indifference to my finger, a little bit like a balloon held in somebody's hands. It flexed inwards, though I experienced little resistance. It gave me the strong impression it was held stationary in space. I was pushing into it, not popping it.

"Push it harder, don't be such a wimp!" Hysandrabopel the Lylybel encouraged. I'm going to call her pixie!

A further harsh push was all that was needed.

It popped.

CHAPTER 18

Forgotten times relived, smoky amnesia daze.

The bubble had popped, and I was none the wiser. It was still very grey in the space I inhabited as if the bubble floated around in front of my eyes. Then it struck me that this greyness was biting into my body cold and wet. I was in fog on a cold night. It felt like February. I don't know why I say that, but that's what it felt like.

I was walking along a street, then I recognised where I was. I was walking towards my small block of flats built curiously in the middle of an executive housing estate. It towered over many of the houses, how did they get planning permission? The blocks modernism was a rather bland product of 1960s ugliness. I almost instantly understood what was inside the darker bubbles; the period between 1971 and 1973, the two years I'd never managed to recall.

So it could have been February 1972 or 73, if indeed it was February. Whenever it was it wasn't something I remember. It was, however, quite curious because my feet were very wet and muddy. I wasn't driving my car and I seemed to be out of breath hurrying along the pavement back to my flat, or should I call it an apartment this being an executive estate.

I was wearing a heavy dirty overcoat mud caked at the bottom. Inside there was a large object, the type of which I had no clue. Remember I was a mere observer unable to adjust the course of what was happening, so I had to be patient and discover what I was doing that night. This would be the first concrete thing I knew about myself during my lost time, other than hearsay. I had waited this long, surely I could be patient for a short while to discover something. This was no joyous return as the cycling trip had been. This return felt sleazy.

Inside the flat I removed from inside my overcoat a large bundle in a plastic bag. Placing this on the table I then proceeded to delve inside, removing wads of five and ten pound notes, to my surprise a large amount of them. For an incident I do not remember there was a lot of money around, and usually when it comes to money, in the present day at least, I remember. That night, however, remained a blank until this rewind experience. So I had to continue viewing, to reveal the truth, and this was an education, history I suppose.

I was counting the money out, all £4000 of it. In 1973 you could buy a house for less than that. There were two-bedroom bungalows going for £3650 so, as you see, it was a lot of money. I'd got it from somewhere, and I didn't think the somewhere was a bank, unless of course I'd committed a bank robbery! Besides, banks don't store money in large OXO tins! There were clues, and along with the money was a carefully made account listing all the transactions, monies paid, and goods delivered. I recognise the handwriting. It was my father's!

I stashed the money rather carelessly underneath the refrigerator in a plastic bag. This, I assumed, was because the money wouldn't be staying there for long as it was destined for greater things, bigger profits, merchandise, or something. As a spectator to my own past without a clue as to the unfolding events, I still had an idea what this money would be used for. This didn't fill me with joy because it took me back into a vile world I once occupied that crippled my life.

I sat down in front of the television kicking back large amounts of Special Brew lager. I was lounging, and obviously not fazed by the amount of money I had in the flat, or what it was for. This TV watching consisted of some awful comedy programme which I remember vaguely from that period, though never really liked. This was disturbing because the other Peter liked it! I was starting to wonder how long this would go on because I'd been watching my rerun for about an hour and a half. Nothing had happened, nothing at all. I continued to watch television right through an old version of the *Nine O'Clock News*. Some of the items I still remember from all that time ago, Mr Edward Heath, the three-day week, the power cuts, and the adjusted incomes policy. All laughable now, although I'm sure it was quite serious in 1972 or whenever it was.

I was quite drunk and not paying attention to the television. It was just a background buzz. Also in the background was another buzzing, almost frantic and continuous. This was breaking through my drunken haze, so what was it? No, I don't know what it was. I was drunk, after all, very drunk. The buzzing continued, uninterrupted for some time, possibly three minutes. There were also drums playing or so I imagined. Synchronised anger was at the door.

Through this foggy haze of alcohol I connected a few brain cells realising somebody was at my door, somebody with an urgent desire to see me, somebody who couldn't wait. Was this what the money was for? Or was it something else, something unexpected? It sounded to me like it was something to do with the large amount of money. Much to my surprise, I got up, walked to the door, and without even looking through the spy hole I turned the handle opening the door wide. It was obvious the drunken Peter thought he was about to carry out a transaction.

In front of me stood a very powerful incredibly angry man with a very red face. Worst of all he was my father!

"You thieving little bastard! Where's my money? I know you've got it! Give me it or I'll break your neck! You are no son of mine!" said my father, John Jackson, farmer.

To my surprise I replied in rather a strange way. I was very free with my version of the truth, and I couldn't believe what I was doing to my own father. You've got to remember this was a replay, a video, a DVD, the real thing happened a long time ago, I replied: "What you on about, dad?"

"I know you've stolen my nest egg, my business capital, the aunties saw you crossing the fields. So give it back, now!" he said.

"I'm not giving it back. I'm using it in business. I'll make four times the money, well, three times the money in just a couple of days. It's my stake money, gets me in the game. Then, of course, I'll pay you back straight away with big interest and you can hide it somewhere else," I said.

For long silent moments my father didn't respond looking me up and down as if I was covered in dirt, or worse still, pig shit from the farm. He was assessing me, of course, making sure I was his own flesh and blood, his son, the boy they'd loved so much, the boy who stole from his own family. A vile sibling taking money from his hard-working father, a man who'd worked hard to put this aside for his old age, and to avoid paying tax to a government who squandered it on stupid wars he disagreed with to the point of obsession. There would be no argument, because the money had to be returned.

"They kill the poor people who get in their way, make rich people richer, and politicians make their reputations by walking on the dead." He didn't like politicians much, even less the ones who interfered with agriculture.

He continued "That money was earned. That money is money this bloody government would waste on something stupid. That money is for me and your mother's old age and not for your dirty deals." My father's spat the word "deals" out.

He didn't mind selling produce on the black market, doing deals behind the taxman's back, but he was vehement in his disgust with me over selling hallucinogenic drugs to partygoers, and a bit of weed as well, actually resin, but this is just semantics and it was, whichever way you painted it, drug dealing .

"I'm not giving you the money back! This gets me in the game," I said.

Watching this I was quite amazed. I'd always been slightly afraid of my father, but now I was not only admitting I'd stolen his money, I was openly stating I was using it to buy drugs then make a huge profit, before giving him his money back with interest. It was getting me in the game? I was so blatant to my father's face, so just watching this rerun of my life gave me the shivers. How could I have been this rotten, this hard, so bloody awful?

My father was eyeing me up and down. He was wearing a very grubby stained boiler suit, filthy wellingtons, a flat cap, and some form of vest-type shirt underneath. His stance was getting more aggressive, feet apart, arms spread, leaning forwards. Suddenly he lunged and grabbed me round the waist. I responded almost immediately by attempting to get him in a headlock. This was quite a revelation because I'd never remembered I was this strong or powerful. I was a young man, a very fit young man, going through a very sad moment wrestling with my own father over a drug deal.

We were uttering guttural noises at each other, most single swear words mumbled under the breath. I've no need to tell you what they were. You can imagine four-letter stuff of the worst kind. We wrestled and swore at each other for what seemed to be a few minutes. Whether it was that long I have no idea, I was fully involved in the fight. It wasn't really a fight it was a struggle for power to see if the old Farmer John still had it, or if that young upstart son was now going to be taking over, if not on the land in a different and more criminal field. If of course, those fields of activity exist at all in small northern towns? Sadly they do.

We came into contact with the table in my dining area and the tangled family argument fell on top of it causing a loud groan to emanate from the overstressed fake wood. Both of us were thrashing around with our bodies on the table, our legs hanging out in space. I had a few items on the table, one of them a very modernist vase-type thing with artificial flowers. My father released one arm grabbing out for this object. I don't know whether he was trying to stop it falling from the table, or grabbing it to bludgeon me. It fell to the floor breaking into countless small ceramic shards. The struggle continued, my father gasping out, "Give me the money you little cunt!"

I screamed he was a silly old twat for not understanding the profit would be good and quicker than fiddling the taxman. He was roaring back that this was filthy money. His money had been gained through hard work selling produce in the farming community; pure hard work in fact, something I wasn't experienced in.

The table collapsed. There was a huge splintering of wood, chipboard-type wood with a lovely G-Plan finish. We crashed to the floor on the tabletop like hitting the bottom of an elevator shaft. We came to rest with my father almost on top of me. As we hit the floor I thought he was going to crush the life out of me. Like me he was partially winded. I think he'd injured his arm or something. I could feel his vice-like grip around my waist slackening. He released it and lay on his back gasping and clutching at his arm in pain.

"I'm not going to go on like this. I'm not fighting you for the money, but just make sure you bring me back the exact, and I mean exact, amount. No interest! Do you hear me? The exact amount! Not one penny more!" All these forceful words my father forced out while fighting for breath.

Slow and ponderous my father climbed to his feet. I remained gasping on the floor looking up at him. It was then I noticed tears running down his old face. He was crying and I was too stupid to know why. Also dripping from him was blood, quite a bit of blood. I was starting to worry, so still winded I forced myself to my feet, and gasping for breath I asked in a stupid way, "You all right, dad?"

He looked at me through his tears and just mumbled something as he was leaving the room clutching his damaged arm. I had crossed the line, gone beyond the father-son argument, into a struggle for power, supremacy, and worst of all I was doing it on the strength of a good drugs deal. He left the room crunching through the broken shards, some of which were embedded in his bloodied right arm.

Then a curious thing happened. I got a strange sensation the bubble rewind was over, but somehow not over. I was correct as the room started to go dull grey in front of me giving at first the impression I was on the point of blacking out through lack of breath. This, of course, wasn't happening. I was back out in the fog again. Then it cleared quite suddenly and it was 4:30pm or thereabouts. It was obviously the same period with the same damp, bone-chilling weather, and I was walking towards the farm gates relieved the deal had gone well and I'd made money, lots of money! I was going to pay the old man back the full amount without interest, perhaps even try to beg forgiveness.

I was thinking about begging forgiveness when a police car approached coming down the track from the farm.

Panic set in! I was wondering if my father had confessed to his tax dodging and was handing me to the police for my drug dealing, all in an effort to save me from myself. This seemed logical to me. My father would see this as a salvation, in the short-term a hard lesson, but in the long-term serving me well.

The police car was not alone. It travelled in the company of another vehicle, both moving in a slow procession, splashing and squishing through the mud on that familiar potholed driveway. As they slowly passed me I could see my sister in the rear seat of the police car, looking very tired, with an air of resignation about her. She stared at me through the misty rear window, shaking her head from left to right, like this procession was on my behalf as if I were the instigator, the reason. The ambulance passed very slowly behind the police car. There was no rush, and inside I could see two or three vague silhouettes through the opaque glass.

Once out onto the smooth open road the sirens came on with the police car escorting the ambulance at speed towards the town and I presumed the hospital.

I was thinking of setting off in pursuit when everything faded to white and green. It was now dark outside and I was inside the hospital…My sister was sitting in solitude in the corridor with no other members of the family to be seen. My mother and George were not there, not in the corridor at least, thank goodness.

"Let's go outside for a cigarette. I don't want them to see you! Come on, get a move on," Jane said. I couldn't detect any tone in her voice. It sounded so flat and detached.

I was stationary in some kind of catatonic fusion as if I were part of the hospital floor or, as people say, glued to the spot, after which Jane grabbed my arm and dragged me through a door out onto the fire escape. She seemed unable to speak so I asked, "Who's ill? Is it father with his bad arm? He's cut it and I hope it's not gone septic or something like that." My sister burst into tears. She'd already been crying for a long time, it was quite obvious. Now she just roared, gasping for breath and blubbing.

"Dad's dead, got stuck in the baling machine. George was working close by and stopped the machine before it did too much damage. We all thought dad would be okay but he had a heart attack on the operating table. He never woke up and mom had just finished making dinner." Jane broke down into wretched tears. I moved to comfort her receiving a cold response.

"Dad's dead and we have to hide out here away from mother and George. I want you to be part of the family. Do you understand? Part of the family! I'm going to straighten you out if it's the last thing I ever do because nobody else will help you!" I think she saw me as a wounded animal, somebody who needed veterinary treatment. Perhaps I was a wounded animal. I was going to respond but everything faded out so I don't know where our conversation went after that.

Once again I was outside in the biting dark cold fog. I could smell smoke and see it rising through the strange glow in the distance. This cloud of blackness seemed to be an indication, a signpost saying some strange terrible occurrence had happened here. It was like a funeral pyre with death its only reason for existence.

I was drawn towards the source of this blackness, this harbinger of evil. What greeted me was the strangest of scenes. It was a German manufactured baling machine blazing away to destruction, engulfed in flames supported by a large amount of diesel oil. Next to it, with apparent madness on their soot streaked faces were my aunties, Beatrix and Violet. Both completely blackened by smoke, wearing their aprons from the farmhouse, and what appeared to be muddy carpet slippers on their feet. They appeared riveted by the spectacle of the inferno, watching the flames engulf the machine for reasons I now fully understood. I didn't attempt to approach them. I was too ashamed.

I crept off into a cold empty farmhouse with uneaten dinners on its large Victorian table, shamefully to hide an old OXO tin under my mother's no longer marital bed.

I was stunned, not because dad was dead, I already knew that from my conversation with George in August 1973, but the fact he was distracted from his work by my involvement with the drug dealing. The fight had probably been on his mind. My father was quite a tough guy, but when it came to things in the family it was different. Mother was ill once and he fretted for weeks even after she was better. Now I could imagine him totally distracted from his work running the fight scenario through his head, what he'd done wrong, not what I'd done wrong.

He shouldn't have been working with a damaged right arm. He was probably slow moving, or using his left arm to operate things normally done instinctively with the other limb. I knew that damaged limb would slow his movement, and I was to blame for his injuries.

Whatever? Inside that bubble I felt completely responsible for the tragic death of my father.

I'd killed my own father!

CHAPTER 19

Right here right now, but enraptured or is that captured?

I was back in the black of that damned briefcase. The hand I had use the pop the bubble was on fire, and the pain was excruciating. It was as if my hand was being held in naked flame, and subjected to the biting tongues of fire. I stared at the smoking flesh turning a purulent pink colour, bubbling, and dropping off the bone. I was melting away. The hand that burst the terrible grey bubble was dissolving in a way I did not understand until the pixie gleefully explained.

"It's an acid bubble, it's an acid bubble! Yes, it's an acid bubble! All the grey ones with the real interesting stuff are!"

Then I understood the full significance of the fireman's suit. She had produced a hosepipe out of the blackness. It was an old-style hose, a canvas grey pipe with a marvellous ornate brass nozzle formed like the mouth of a large fish. Sadly for me it was only dripping a small amount of water. She was smiling at me, holding this useless fire fighting device, and not attempting to use it.

"Use the bloody hosepipe! Get on with it. Use the damn thing!" I screamed.

Pixie reached up to the helmet and removed it from her head, placing it on the floor in front of her. She then proceeded to stare at it. All this time I was suffering terrible agony, a terrifying, biting, mind-numbing cacophony of pain. I was about to scream something extremely rude at her when she held up a hand. This was a caution for me not to say anything. She was counting and looking at the helmet which I realised had an ornate clock built into the badge. So the fire crew identification badge was a timepiece. The brass numbers were counting down, 16, 15, 14, it was all happening very slowly. I couldn't take this incredible agony much longer. I had to scream out for her to use the hose.

Just as I was about to plead with her she opened up the hosepipe on to me with a terrific blast of the incredible icy water. Even though the jet was over my entire body, the water only affected the parts on fire with the acid. Everywhere else was dry. The water continued for about a minute, I suppose, before she turned it off. I looked at my hand. It was normal, not burnt, no scarring, just normal, as if all that melting burning pain had not existed at all. I still remember it with a profound agony inside my head, and if I think about it a little too much it returns.

"You have to suffer if you pop a grey bubble. If you pop nice bubbles they're not acid, but nice. All the interesting bubbles are all made of acid, interesting stuff, and you pay in proportion," pixie explained with that captivating smile on her face. Was she a sadist?

I was just about to reply to this rather sadistic, beautiful pixie, when I felt two soft, fine hands close around my eyes from behind my head. Was this some other pixie inside the briefcase, another subtle torture to remind me of a distant past, to give me my education? I was worried these hands were going to put heavy pressure on my eye sockets and gouge my eyes.

Suddenly I was in the warmth of the pub garden again, feeling joyous throughout what seemed to be every molecule of my body. Jennifer released her hands pulling me round by one shoulder. As I turned to face her I had a strange feeling something would not be quite right, that the pain and scarring inside the bag would carry over into this beautiful universe. I was wrong.

She was as perfect and as beautiful as she had always been. The scarring, that was mine alone, and for some reason I could see she understood what I'd learnt from the dull grey viscose orb. Jennifer stroking my face as if taking tears away from my eyes, though there were no tears. I was joyous to be with her. She then suggested that we go for a walk in the nearby woodland to discover a little bit more about nature.

As we walked very slowly in beautiful sun dappled daylight I talked about my experience with the pixie. She listened with patience but I understood on some level she already knew. Jennifer assured me this was the learning process. I was surprised when she confided something to me. I had been assigned as her student and against all the strict rules she was becoming too close to me. I was pondering what she meant by too close, was she starting to feel the same way about me as I felt about her? It was then I noticed she didn't have a briefcase with her.

"Where's the briefcase? You haven't got it," I said.

She just laughed in the infectious soft way I was starting to adore. She told me some character called O'Duke had the briefcase with him. I was on the very verge of asking her who O'Duke is when I heard the distinct sound of footfalls crunching through the old leaves on the forest floor. These were coming from behind us, a disturbing sensation. I was quick to turn my head, and to my great surprise saw a huge Irish wolfhound trotting along behind us in the most benign manner with a briefcase, now closed and locked in his mouth. Jennifer explained to me the Irish wolfhound, O'Duke, was a guard dog to prevent the briefcase from falling into the wrong hands – mine! What constituted the wrong hands was explained to me. I had to learn all the lessons from this mysterious past other life. People with a large amount of grey bubbles were known to steal briefcases and throw them into dark places – rivers, down wells – anywhere they couldn't be recovered from, even fires. All these actions are forbidden by the access codes, the Lylybel population.

Without any doubt, as a group of creatures the Lylybel were dead set against any tampering with history, so the wolfhound and I don't know if he was called Oh! Duke or O'Duke was sent by the glorious grand mysterious mighty Lylybel to stop me destroying the evidence of some strange past life I seemed to have lived. I explained to Jennifer that I didn't want to destroy the briefcase. If the price I had to pay to be with her was to learn the very painful truths about some distant past life, so be it. I knew instinctively I had to be with this special woman, and not destroying the case was part of the price. What could be that bad?

O'Duke stopped behind us. For some stupid reason I have no idea why I put my hand towards him, well above the briefcase handle, and attempted to stroke his head. He didn't growl, he didn't bark, he didn't move, and he let me stroke his head during which he made the strangest almost musical purring sounds. All I could think of was the sound of a big cat more than a dog. With this growing confidence I decided to see if I could touch the handle of the briefcase. Was this madness?

I could swear the dog rolled his eyes as if to say, "What an eejit"! However, he seemed to understand I didn't want to take it from him. A brief glimpse of his huge teeth, plus the immutable fact that he was enormous, with intense watchful eyes was enough to discourage anyone but the most foolhardy. He knew I wouldn't dare try. I knew I was never going to!

We continued our walk and existed as one reacting with every molecule in the woodland. In many ways it was more. The sensation of vastness running through my body gave me a perception of a great endless forest. Endless and timeless was better description of the vast arena of dappled shade filled with wonderful aromas, and populated with the most vivid strange creatures you could ever imagine, or never imagine. For my human sensibilities this was almost an overload, too much colour and movement saturating every sense in my body.

The dog slept in the long grass with his head resting on his front legs. Both were crossed over the briefcase.

I fell out of the dream and into the real world where I was sick, broken, very tired and vomiting. Despite the horrors of the real world I was entranced by the last moments in the other universe.

In these last moments I'd fallen asleep with Jennifer held tight in my arms, so tired after she'd shown me a bit more about nature.

CHAPTER 20

In a daze with my head trapped in 1973.

I was back in my 1973 post-amnesia headless chicken period. And I was going to waste more time looking around my own flat for the particularly cunning place I'd hidden £10,000 and a large amount of acid. I didn't have any idea what the acid looked like, but I knew what money looked like so that's where I focused my efforts. After I'd arrived at my flat, the first job was to firmly close the door, wedging it with a large sofa. This made it difficult to search the sofa, but I was past caring. My investigation of the sofa started with a kitchen knife, slashing it apart. Tattered material was everywhere, along with bits of foam, and when the sofa was quite dead my spirits were in a pretty similar state. There was nothing in there. That's a lie. There was one 50p piece, a 5p coin and an old biro. Perhaps I could give the 50p to John Smith as a down payment? Or poke him in the eye with the Biro?

I spent the next hour engaged in a frantic search of my flat discovering along the way all types of interesting electronic equipment, small amounts of money tucked away in drawers, nothing significant just a few pounds here and there, an amazing selection of clothes including things I would never consider wearing; but obviously did! I looked absolutely everywhere, even under the fridge, not knowing this is where I'd stashed father's nest egg. The only thing I turned up was a small bag containing about two dozen very tiny white pills. I didn't know what these were. If it was acid how could I test them? And they certainly weren't the several thousand tabs John Smith insisted I possessed. I flushed them down the toilet.

Even though it was raining outside on this August Sunday afternoon it was quite warm. I was wringing wet from head to foot with sweat. Whether this was from the effort of turning over my flat, or through pure fear I couldn't guess. I was certain my lack of "the stuff" would lead to a bludgeoning by John Smith, or the malevolent smile of the black-eyed Millicent. If I was going to visit Samantha's house, I would have to change into something fresh. After my sexual wrestling match with Vicky I discovered I had a key, one of the only positives from our post 'lovemaking' conversation. If nobody was there I could let myself in and search in peace. I was beginning to believe this was the obvious hiding place, perhaps inside the pool table where I'd played cosy games, who knows?

I was standing in the shower beneath a jet of very hot water trying to get my thoughts together and despairing because, looking around the bathroom, I realised I could have placed the money behind the tiling, or slipped it under some object that appeared to be immobile. The more I looked round the bathroom, the more I realised that if I'd hidden everything with great cunning, short of knocking the flat into a thousand pieces, I would never find it.

I wondered if Samantha knew more than I originally thought about the lost goods. But then if she didn't, going in and saying, "Hi, Sam, do you know where I have hidden all the money and the dangerous drugs?" didn't seem the best course of action.

I was slipping on some nice clothes and listening to songs I'd never heard playing on the radio. It was obvious being top of the Pops didn't rely on musical quality. It relied on something mysterious. Most I had never heard before, and some like Clive Dunn and Ray Stevens I never wanted to hear again, or perhaps hearing them again would be a good option. It would mean I would still be alive!

Why was I going round on Sunday afternoon? Of course! I was visiting the house to see if I could catch up with my fiancée, Vicky, the girl I didn't like too much. She seemed to like me, and I wondered if it was because I was giving her a low rent version of a jet set life style. Or it might have been something else, something I had been but now definitely wasn't. As I arrived I could see there were no cars in the driveway so it was obvious everybody was out on a Sunday trip – the golf club, some old aunty, who knew? I would be able to conduct a careful search at my leisure, it was important not to disturb anything that could arouse suspicion.

Using my key I let myself in, slipped off my handmade shoes to protect the light coloured carpets, I didn't want to leave wet footprints all over the house. The starting place, I decided, would be the games room with its little bar, pool table, and dartboard. The bar seemed an obvious place, and going on a hunch of reverse psychology perhaps the obvious was where I should look. I started with the fastidious search through all the nooks and crannies of the elaborate construction of bricks, wood and apparently old pieces of ceramic drainpipe, all illuminated by a smaller ersatz version of the light hanging above the pool table. Perhaps the whole setup looked better after a few drinks.

The pool table was another matter. It was a full-sized version constructed from a very heavy hardwood. It was a beautiful piece of furniture, real quality. I couldn't destroy this. The damn thing weighed an enormous amount and was extremely difficult to move. Its complexity to dismantle convinced me this wouldn't be where I'd have hidden the money.

Ten thousand pounds in five pound notes is 2000 notes, quite a large bundle. Had I split it up into smaller amounts, spreading the risk so to speak, or would it be in one big fat pile? I investigated behind the radiators which were covered in ornate grilled box-type structures, a good possibility when it came to hiding money in a hurry: I came across four copies of Playboy magazine. I searched the whole room applying a twisted logic. Where would I hide things quickly, but safe? This thought kept running through my head as I move urgently from room to room, looking into drawers, searching beneath objects, looking around in the back of wardrobes, all this time vigilant not disturbing anything, while at the same time desperately wanting to rip the whole place apart!

In Vicky's room I noticed large amount of cuddly toys, teddy bears, rabbits, strange non- world creatures, all kinds of large stuffed animals. Was I responsible for giving Vicky one of these monstrosities, and did any of them have zippers at the back like a large hot water bottle case? One by one of these creatures were carefully probed to see if deep in all that fluff there was something substantial. I was paying special attention to a rather large frog which proved to be completely vacant when I heard footfalls on the stairs. Somebody was in the house. Should I pretend to be sleeping on the bed, resting my eyes?

I'd dragged the cuddly toys down from the dresser in the order. Now I had to put them all back in seconds. It was a panicked rush. Vicky put her head round the door, eyes open wide in surprise, and taken aback by me holding two of her largest teddy bears, one under each arm. How do you explain this one? I took a dive off the high board asking, "Which one of these did I get you first?"

Vicky looked at me for some while. I thought I'd said something wrong, but after what seemed an age she responded, "Capt Snuggles." She was pointing at the chubby brown bear under my right arm, the one with the zip, the one I hadn't yet got round to giving an internal examination. So I threw him back on the bed and placed the other on the dresser. Vicky was still giving me a perplexed look.

"What's wrong with you, Peter? Yesterday afternoon you paid me no attention, and now you're positively weird," Vicky enquired.

I was very fazed not noticing Vicky was wearing the strangest white outfit including pink socks with little bobbles of fluff at the back. It was almost as if I'd never seen an outfit like this before with its white pleated skirt, and very stretchy top, revealing a slim braless torso and small firm breasts. I suppose I was staring her up and down like some kind of moron before the final click inside my brain notched it all together. She was wearing tennis gear. She played tennis. I knew I hated tennis, in fact I was very poor at all ball games apart from the ones played on flat surfaces indoors. So I wasn't going to be talking tennis with her. What did we have in common?

I didn't know what Vicky expected of me. I wondered if we had any meaningful conversations at all. For all I knew we might have a totally silent, hot sex-only relationship. I had to do something. I couldn't ask her questions like some police interrogation. I moved forwards taking her in my arms and kissed her with hot passion that was mostly fakery. She wasn't my thing. I had no mental desire for this girl, and she only inspired my base animal lust because of her lithe physical beauty. She was responding to my faked desire by pulling at my clothes, tugging her tennis outfit from her body, all the time demanding I make love to her, or something like. "Fuck me hard until I come. Go on, Peter, make me suffer!"

We made enthusiastic and at times very noisy love, she screamed, she clawed, she swore like a trooper. I cannot lie. I enjoyed most of the performance, but that's what it was from me, a performance. I experienced intense physical pleasure, and my gasps of ecstasy weren't all faked. However throughout I was thinking of someone else. Something seemed perversely criminal in the way I was thinking of Samantha and using Vicky's body to satiate my carnal lust for the very woman who'd given birth to her. Thinking of Samantha made me a better lover, so this was a strange form of proxy lovemaking and it should be illegal. Or should screwing your girlfriend's mother be illegal?

Vicky went off to take a shower. I went straight to Captain Snuggles ripping into his soft underbelly. I discovered he was very wealthy for a bear containing a sum of money that had me gasping for breath! Inside he was guarding a pair of five pound notes and nothing more unless, of course, you include a plastic bag with about 500 pills inside, all very tiny innocent white pills. I even thought about slipping one in my mouth to try it for content, not that I knew what to expect during an acid trip.

The number of pills wasn't sufficient to satisfy the demands of the businessmen, and I came to the conclusion they were probably a side issue, a little private percentage for me, not the real deal. Perhaps I ought to slip Vicky one? Oh, I already had! I don't know why I had this thought, but somehow her presence irritated me. I needed to search.

She was coming back from the shower, very naked, quite lovely, in the same sense as a nude in the National Gallery can be quite lovely. I knew I was seeing her to gain access to the house, and one of its hidden treasures. I just wanted her to go so I could continue my room to room search, possibly a fruitless task, but I couldn't rest until I'd covered every possibility, even the garage. They didn't park their cars in the garage, so it could be the usual mess of million items, providing me with a nice hiding place. The garage could be the breakthrough!

Vicky announced she was leaving. She'd been playing tennis with some friends at an undercover tennis court, one that I had a membership for. I was a member? She'd come home to get changed before meeting her parents over at her grandmother's house. I couldn't even ask where grandma lived, because for all I knew I might be the apple of the old lady's eye. God, this amnesia was awful. Rushing downstairs Vicky asked if I'd be round later. I had no idea so I vaguely said, "Yeah, I suppose."

"Don't be so bloody enthusiastic! What the hell has got in to you? You're like some kind of mental case," she said.

"I'm just not feeling my old self at the moment, must be a little bit tired. Do you mind if I rest here?" I was pointing at the bed. She tossed her shoulders back, threw me a puzzled look and went downstairs shouting back, "Suit yourself!"

I was left to search the rest of the house including sticking my head up in the loft. The roof space revealed nothing of any significance, a few reminders of Vicky's childhood, old rocking horses, toys, dolls and all manner of board games. Nothing I could give to Harry or John. Of course I did come across a large amount of money, so much money it could've solved all my problems.

The unfortunate thing was, though the money was in large denominations I don't think I could interest Harry in a hotel on Park Lane.

Only Samantha's room remained. Would I have left anything with the lovely Sam? I was starting to search the room with the same fevered correctness I'd given the rest of the property. My unreliable gut instincts were telling me what I was looking for was in this house. Now I suspecting the integral garage but had to satisfy my curiosity and finish my room to room search.

This room felt right, this place was giving me strong vibes, but of what? I'd completed a thorough search of the en suite bathroom and the lavish wardrobe system in the dressing room… nothing! It was down to the last room, the master bedroom, a place where nothing was ever hidden, or, with luck, everything.

I started searching in the top drawer of the dresser next to the bed, not the small bedside tables. This was a much larger unit standing next to the en suite doorway. It contained Samantha's underwear arranged with almost military precision drawer by drawer from top to bottom. The top contained nothing but beautifully manufactured diaphanous knickers in all their variety. In the next drawer down were more knickers, still of the same fine quality but more for everyday wear.

The two drawers below were arranged with very neat dividers, these containing bras, everything arranged in a similar system. Top for the bedroom, bottom the street. The fifth and bottom drawer of the dresser contained suspenders and boxes of stockings. I gave it a quick rummage, pulled the drawer physically out of its rails to look into the empty space below, nothing. I fed it back into the rails with trembling fingers driven by such strange desires. I closed it shutting the vision of stockings and suspenders away from my hungry eyes. Such provocative contents sent messages to my brain flashing into life desires driven by pure instinct.

I asked myself would a large bungle of money be in there, and I think the answer was no. Despite this I started the careful examination at the top drawer. I was now concentrating intently, careful not to disturb the neatly laid out lingerie. I wanted to leave no trace of my rifling through Samantha's beautiful gossamer-thin lace objects of desire. The whole drawer had an intoxicating subtle smell to it. Just the faintest hint of her perfume and I was soaking it in. My concentration drifted away from the desperate search for the hidden money. Now I was trying to recall lost memories, emotions brought alive by heady scent. Without thinking my body moved into a kneeling position in front of the draw. My whole being was soaking in the aroma. By now I was resting my face on the top layer of knickers. My mind was searching for lost ecstasy, driving me to bury my face very gently in the erotic contents.

"What the fuck do you think you're doing?" Vicky shouted. She'd returned for a forgotten handbag!

CHAPTER 21

Right here right now, sweet aromas, sometimes.

It was the perfume. A subtle aroma Samantha had caressed onto her soft skin all those years ago. For the first time in decades it was in my nostrils once again. Years disappeared as if they'd never happened. I was back with my head buried in that drawer in 1973. I opened my eyes in hope only to discover a different reality. I was lying in a very bright room, with lots of flowers, flowing curtains, and a flat-screen television. This was certainly not the 1970s. This was the cancerous now, but the perfume was in the now as well, not from the past. This beguiling aroma was here and now, and in those few moments of absolute concentration absorbing the scent I'd forgotten all the other painful constraints on my modern life.

The nurse was a very large lady in a crisp and new looking uniform, it was tight, giving the impression she'd been measured for it before she went on a diet of meat pies. This well proportioned nurse however, was the unlikely source of the wonderful aroma. I didn't want to ask her the name of the perfume, something I'd never known. I wanted it to remain a mystery, a magical essence that transported me to moments in life I'd enjoyed with a great passion. To give a product name to this magical aroma would diminish it, like knowing the answer to all the magic tricks, spoiling the show.

The aroma was pure magic. I was not adverse to a bit of scheming in order to prolong the moment. I complained about being uncomfortable in the bed, encouraging the nurse to rearrange me. I did this two or three times before this lovely woman started to get slightly irritated by my constant demands. I apologised explaining my wasted body was now so thin I found it difficult to remain comfortable. She didn't seem to mind, and proceeded with great care to try and get me just so. For a few moments I was.

I was just so, soaking in decades old sensations and memories evoked by the perfume. Why hadn't I realised back then I was so much in love with Samantha. I was too young, too wealthy, disgustingly randy and a miserable bastard. The realization I'd been in love seeped into my soul over the years and now it was all too late, but happy on this day to remember the merest hint of days long gone. I speculated if Samantha had loved me at all. I do not know. She may only have enjoyed a very interesting sex life with me, nothing more. Her husband was busy in business and too tired at night, or they'd been married for too long for the fire of passion to burn so brightly. I might have just been the latest handy new flame.

Once the large nurse had left the room, the perfume dissipated all too quickly into the very efficient ventilating system. It did not, however, dissipate from my mind. It was still very much to the forefront and it started me considering something Rachel told me. She said it took her a long time to find a perfume that didn't remind her of a concentration camp.

This may sound more than very strange, how could beautiful perfumes remind anybody of such an awful place. Perfume was a reminder of the tortures that had taken Rachel's innocence at the hands of Oberfuhrer Maximilian Haussler. As age crept into the soldier's body his uncontrollable fondness for very young girls grew with each year. With his position of supreme power allowing him to indulge in any proclivity, he investigated warped versions of physical satisfaction to satisfy his base desires.

The very slim fifteen-year-old Rachel was the special thing he was looking for. She had the appearance of a girl much younger than her years. Long-term starvation had slowed her development into full womanhood. The Oberfuhrer first laid his eyes on this young girl in the sewing shed. Rachel was repairing the awful recycled paper uniforms, often used many times over. Ten people could wear one item of clothing or twenty if careful repairs were carried out. With time the accountants could average the cost per head, and because the large turnover of people, high command could be satisfied the unit costs were low. You couldn't waste good paper clothes by burning them.

He was taken by her dark beauty thinking she was only twelve or thirteen-years-old. This excited him. Maximilian liked girls who could be "womanly". In this he meant they could be used time and time again without too much damage, because physical damage would spoil his enjoyment; his only consideration. Rachel, however, was something special, though normally Haussler felt nothing emotionally for the young women he abused. Rachel was an unexpected vision enticing Maximilian to go in a different direction for the only time in his life.

Easily bored he would use them for a few days, and when he tired of them, if they were lucky, he'd toss them back into the bowels of the camp. Sometimes if they lashed out at him he would shoot them in the face for fun more than punishment. Once he enjoyed the sensation of shooting a girl in the face as they were standing and he was taking her. Max wanted to feel the sensation of release, leaving her while she was having a death spasm. He didn't say if he'd enjoyed it, but it was an experiment.

Rachel proved to be different right from the very moment he saw her. Maximilian understood he must have her in his quarters. She would be is maid, his cook, his dresser, his personal little lady. He would find some clothes for her, pretty clothes, things that once belonged to rich families and now piled up in storage. Fine quality clothes from the best shops in pre-war Berlin, and this girl was small enough to wear the clothes of a twelve-year-old. The very thought of this made Maximilian very happy indeed. And so Rachel was fed every day, only just enough to keep away the hunger pains, not enough nourishment to bring her body into full womanhood.

Her time as his plaything started with the bath, the first hot bath Rachel had had for months, or was it years? She really couldn't remember. Then he combed her hair with great care for more than two hours. He sang soft childhood lullabies as he moved the comb with a gentle rhythm through her hair adding different products from time to time. He worked carefully smoothing the dark sooty tangle into glossy black sheen. He then insisted she always used a perfume he'd discovered while visiting Paris some years ago.

He'd bought it as a special gift for his sister Ingrid. Now in the dark days of war with Ingrid burnt to dust, a victim of Allied bombing, he lavished it all on this other young girl. Perhaps facially though, not in colouring, she reminded him too much of Ingrid. This girl was dark, as Ingrid had been fair, this girl's skin would bronze in the sun, where Ingrid's was always white. He decided it was something in the face or was it the eyes that reminded him of a childhood with his lost sister?

Decades down the road in my lovely bright room, I was getting to grips with the real world. My remembering the hideous world Rachel described was a diversion, part of my battle against cancer and my intoxication with the parallel universe. I was trying to remember the chronology of events in that camp. It annoyed me that my recollections were so jumbled, sometimes with painkillers, though I was now taking far less. It was difficult to pin down the order of events.

It was something like this. Oberfuhrer Maximilian Haussler used her with rapacious brutality as his sex toy for five months. Being his slave kept her body alive, not her soul, that part died more each day. In the sense of physical being, many of the people who had been in the sewing shed with her had now perished from disease or gas. She was feeling guilty about staying alive, because she was given small amounts of good quality food, clothing and warmth, others had nothing. Rachel was his sex slave being kept just right for a man who liked young girls, she loathes herself, but what could she do? To rage against Maximilian would be committing suicide, or fight on?

The Oberfuhrer was gluttonous in his appetites desiring many young girls, and on his more depraved days would select others bringing them to share his pleasures. This would worry Rachel, though she would never voice her thoughts to that monster. She might be replaced and sent back to the shed if she were lucky. Some of the women would be a danger, accusing her of collaboration, others would be just sad for her.

On the occasions he did bring the other girls none of them ever stayed more than one night. Two of them died in front of her, and he pointed out it would increase her diligence in pleasuring him. He told Rachel about the girl he'd shot in the face during orgasm and how he wanted to feel her spasms. This man knew no bounds, and she was trapped in his world of terror.

Eventually Maximilian never ever shared their moments together with anybody else. She was exclusively his. He was a man of heavy needs, and to this extent he used every part of Rachel's body in the search of satisfaction. Sometimes he lay there naked next to her, sweaty, drunken, snoring and so openly vulnerable. Rachel wanted to grab his ceremonial dagger, a very elaborate gold and pearl handled device, and plunge it into his heart killing the monster. She also knew for this action she would die a more terrible death than most of the terrible deaths in the camp. So Maximilian lived, and so did only a small part of Rachel.

In the final days before the Allied advance swamped the camp, bringing Rachel to the rehabilitation hospital and her first-ever meeting with Abraham, two things happened. The first was she went to sleep naked in the pungent, sweaty, post-sexual embrace of Maximilian, and woke up alone. She could hear distant guns. All the Nazis had left. Rachel was stunned. They had gone and she was still alive. Perhaps Maximilian had thought something of her, or the Allied advance had taken him by surprise giving him no time to return and kill her. Many others had taken bullets moments from freedom as the Nazis escaped. Rachel would survive!

The second was that for a few precious minutes there was a non-reality where nobody could believe they'd left. Rachel used this to scour her body of any smell of the perfume, and rubbed herself in her own filth to make herself part of the camp and not some collaborator. Again she donned a disgusting old paper uniform pulled from a corpse near the officers' block. She wouldn't stand out, and she hoped some of the more crazy ones seeking wild retribution couldn't smell her!

She'd not been guilty, but had been fed, and survived. Others had lost all their families. Blame had to go somewhere, and frustrations over the terrible inability to fight had to be taken out on something. The madness didn't find Rachel. Maximilian disappeared forever, possibly dead in the final fight for Berlin, or he'd turned into vapour and hid from his crimes in a sympathetic country. Rachel knew she would never see him again. For a long time she thought about seeing him in the street somewhere, and what would she do if she saw him again? But she never would.

I was getting very tired now and starting to slip off the edge into sleep. This wasn't an automatic entry into the parallel universe. I had to remember that only recently I wanted to be there all the time despite the feelings of terrible guilt at some unspeakable crime every time I awoke. At that time I was so addicted to the other dimension I was having difficulty focusing on the staying alive bit! I concentrated on the harshness of mankind… my world… I slipped into sleep.

This super reality didn't start off in a white void, or a black void. No, it started off with a bell ringing. A loud, ding, ding, ding, ding was ringing in my ears. I was standing by a gated level crossing with a very nice red bicycle held by the saddle with my right hand. I was waiting for the train to thunder through the crossing in a cloud of vapour. As always it was a beautiful sun dappled day, and I could already see Jennifer waiting outside the Old Vaporous Loco tavern just across the tracks. She had a bicycle with her too.

The train only took two minutes to come through and pass. It seemed like an age. I wanted to join my lovely friend. She'd already got the beer in, but then I realised I was sweating. She'd beaten me to the pub, or more to the point shot away before the gates closed. How she got served so quickly is a mystery, but then this is Jennifer's world, so she knew the train was coming. She'd probably phoned the pub to tell them she would arrive at 1.23pm, or something like that. She was laughing at me. My gaze travelled from her beautiful smile and down. I could see a little bit more of my hidden past getting ready to greet me. The briefcase was in a little basket on a rack above the back wheel. I knew it waited for me alone.

That stupid little pixie would be in there somewhere. I imagined she'd be wearing cycling gear today, or that dreaded fireman's uniform. Of course, as always, I was wrong.

Eventually the train had passed, the crossing opened, and at that moment I was free to enjoy a beer with my exquisite companion. Today she was mostly wearing Lycra, except Lycra didn't exist in the parallel in the sense we know it. This was more a silk and Merino wool affair, but the effect on me was quite profound. This is what I think caused me to spend most of the day cycling behind her, and how I got caught out at the level crossing. Too much concentration on the wrong kind of thing can be bad for your health, particularly at level crossings!

When I arrived propping my bike up against hers I asked where the large dog O'Duke was today. She informed me he was here and still guarding the bag. There was no evidence whatsoever of an Irish wolfhound no matter where I looked. I investigated everywhere, under the tables, around the pub yard, across the road in the bushes. Full investigation revealed no sign of the big Irish wolfhound. I voiced this to Jennifer who laughed her lovely tinkling laugh.

"Don't be silly. You don't have to see him all the time, but he's here," she said.

I didn't want to take the bag away from the pixies, or destroy it, but I had the urge to stand up, undo the clasp, and pull it open. Jennifer, however, had pre-empted me. She took a huge drink from her pint, and standing up grasped the bag with both hands. She then pulled it open with a flourish, and as she did this the most curious thing happened. It seemed to gain a little bit of weight and her arms sank slightly. Out of the bag came the huge head of an Irish wolfhound, it laughed at me, all teeth and grinning. Then to my surprise the big dog, and this is the truth, winked at me, then disappeared back down into the bag. As he went down into the darkness it was obvious the bag got lighter, the weight disappearing from Jennifer's arms.

She couldn't hold the whole weight of an Irish wolfhound, so I concluded the bit you could see was the only bit that weighed anything. It was still guarding the bag. This diligence would catch the unwary, those foolish enough to open it would discover the full wolfhound, and this is where I stress the word "wolf"!

"How am I going to get into the bag if the hound's in there?" I asked.

After I said this I took a big long refreshing drink of glorious beer with my head back, my eyes closed. When I opened them to put the beer glass back on the table I was standing in the blackness once again. Just to reassure myself I looked up. Above me were three things, not including the sky of course. One of them was smiling at me and he was an Irish wolfhound. The other was also smiling at me with a little bit of an ironic twist to the corner of her mouth. The sort of look that says, "We caught you there didn't we"? Finally I was still definitely in the pub yard because above both of them silhouetted against the blue sky I could see the pub sign, "The Old Vaporous Loco".

Inside, the Lylybel who I called pixie was already waiting dressed in the finest God knows what. She was dancing around making a strange little skipping arm waving dance. During this performance it looked as if the pixie weighed almost nothing. This must be impossible, I thought, as she was wearing an enormous backpack. It was a canvas device similar to a very old hiker's backpack. However, the canvas appeared to be of a very fine lightweight quality. The bag itself was colossal. It was the size of a small car hitched up high on the back of this delicate and now wondrously strong creature.

As always she pre-empted my question. I was going to ask what was in the bag. My little friend had already realised this and told me it was an antidote to the bubbles. I was just about to ask if it was full of water when she mentioned this was a different antidote, one that would work in a different way, and was sometimes a little bit more effective. This would have me back to normal with a little less suffering. I noticed she didn't say without suffering, just a little less. The pixie could be such a liar.

She produced from nowhere, or hidden back pockets in her clothes, the two familiar devices. The ornate silver cup and the blowing ring, which of course wasn't a key. Or was it the key? This time the ornate vessel in which the bubbles lived, I suppose I can use that word, was quite small, much smaller than I'd seen before, and I was wondering if the key would fit into it. Of course when I saw the key I realised it would. This too was tiny, so I was expecting a myriad of small bubbles, and that's exactly what I didn't get.

Pixie didn't take a breath. She dipped the tiny device into the silver pot, held it up in front of her face, pursed her lips, and at this point the giant haversack started to get very slightly smaller, not smaller by a large amount, but very slightly smaller. The draft, because it was nothing more coming from her lips started to produce a bubble, not a stream of bubbles, just a single tiny almost black bubble. It looked horrific, nightmarish. The bubble continued to expand as the enormous backpack became a little smaller. It was still a massive backpack, but by now the bubble was coloured light grey and enormous, the size of an elephant. It wobbled around on the end of the blowing device looking for the world like a bouncy castle version of this creature.

"Go on then! Go on then! Pop it! Pop it!" pixie demanded. She'd disappeared entirely behind the colossal bubble, and there was no sign of the vessel, or the key. Through the translucent glow of this very light grey bubble, I could see the pixie was now wearing what appeared to be an early Boy Scout uniform complete with shorts, hairy socks, brogues and an enormously stupid large brimmed Scout hat. She removed this monstrous headgear and threw it at the bubble. It bounced off the grey blob flopping to the floor. She then told me the only way I could pop this one was to run at it going full pelt. She informed me not to run at it "half arsed". Some pixie!

So, I ran at the bubble on full power. I was doing fifteen miles an hour when I hit it producing a big wet pop!

To me it sounded like I'd dived below the surface of a pool, the stunning rush of a quieter sound, full of strange ghost echoes.

Pixie heard a big pop and laughed so much she almost burst!

CHAPTER 22

Forgotten times relived, sometimes you've got to laugh!

In my hand I held a fresh packet of non-filter cigarettes, and a half bottle of whisky rested in my pocket. I was standing in a hospital corridor. I scanned this way and that looking for somebody official with who I could enquire as to the whereabouts of one Leonard Stubbington. This was his unused birth certificate name, to everyone else in the outside world this particular Leonard was known as the more immediate Lenny the Helmet, famous for his continuous carrying of a crash helmet, and that's the story he told his mother.

Lenny was on the trauma ward having had a bizarre accident a few days earlier. He'd spent the first few days in intensive care. Lenny was in luck. They weren't too bothered about head trauma or anything considered sinister by the neural consultants. The biggest worry for the doctors were blood clots coming from the many broken bones in his legs and the possibility of bone marrow leaking into his system causing heart problems. He was pretty bashed about after suffering a nasty accident riding his much loved Lambretta 225 cc SX scooter. This had not survived the brutal impact. Lenny had not been told of its sad demise. I knew the big greasy dork would be mortified at the loss of his loved one.

I didn't know the details of the accident, however, I wouldn't have to wait long to find out from the man himself. That was if I could find him in this maze of corridors, small rooms, and signposting that was useless for finding anything you were looking for, or for that matter anything you weren't! They consisted entirely of numbers and acronyms. After a quarter of an hour of looking around, I had at last located my quarry in a small side ward with three other patients, all of them young, all of them in traction, and all of them motorcyclists. Most of them would return to 2 two wheels, Lenny included.

"Hey, hi, man, cool to see you. I'm doing just great, fantastic, amazing!"

Lenny said, as high as a kite on painkillers. All this was said in a slurred and difficult to understand voice. I suggested I return tomorrow but he would have none of it and wanted to tell me all about it, how he'd come to find that sometimes fluffy clouds are solid. This had me mystified, and I asked him what he meant by solid clouds. At this Lenny laughed like a drain. "Man, the mist, it was solid, solid as a rock, and I tried to ride through it!" Lenny managed. After this he slurred out an explanation as to the circumstances of his accident. He took the long route round, and the whole tale carried on for about an hour before I could make out exactly what he was saying. It was like this:

Lenny was doing a drug deal and he dealt nearly exclusively in acid, an occupation which I apparently knew all about. Or course I only knew about this from my experiences after I woke up disorientated and clueless in August 1973. It was in the two days after awakening I discovered I was teamed up with Lenny in his business. I knew something about this partnership, not the whole story, and only little snippets I'd heard. Now I was getting the story in blur vision from the man himself on the day, though four decades too late.

It was a winter's day, typical in its greyness, with a damp low light that did nothing to relieve the dullness of the daytime. In his usual fashion Lenny had been hanging around at home (God knows where that was, or what it was like). A phone call had awakened the slumbering Lenny who was taking his afternoon nap sleeping off lunch, if that's what you'd call his daily beer with fish and chips habit. Somebody in the next town wanted some stuff, a grand's worth of stuff. This was a good call for Lenny. So, a little worse for wear, or in fact a lot worse for wear, he stumbled down the stairs to his motor scooter.

In the early days he wasn't the most careful drug dealer usually keeping most of the stash somewhere in his house. The location of Lenny's place remained a mystery to me, but I'm quite sure that a good police squad would have sniffed it out in no time. His usual *modus operandi* for the movement of acid was to use some part of his motor scooter for concealment, a fuel proof tube inside the fuel tank, or hidden in part of the frame where he'd made access during the many modifications to his beloved machine. On this day the size of the deal and the speed in which he needed to get there, along with his rather drunken state were not the best arbiters of good fortune for our jolly dealer.

Lenny concealed the acid tabs in two places. When I say concealed this was barely the case. He had far too many tabs on him, so when his normal hiding places were all full he had some tabs left over. These he stuck in the lining of his famous crash helmet. He went on to tell me he was starting to get big time paranoid about being watched, but he was drunk and the fear of being caught by a surveillance squad had diminished in inverse proportions to the alcohol consumed.

Another thing against Lenny in this endeavour was his velocity as he ripped along on one hell of a rate, speed being of the essence. It wasn't so important that he had to rush and attract attention. Rightly or wrongly, Lenny had the throttle pulled right back and at times after leaving town was touching eighty miles an hour which he informed me was flat out even from a 225. Then, he added, once clear of the town he really started to enjoy the ride, though the after effects of the booze were starting to make him sweat. Lenny was suffering a big flop sweat, wet all over.

Halfway into his forty-mile trip to the nearby city Lenny ripped through a small country crossroads, the beginning of the end? This was the moment the unfortunate circumstances of his near future began to unfold. Two bored officers in their police car had seen him travelling at great speed, well above all the local limit. To break the boredom they set off in hot pursuit. Lenny noticed the police about three miles down the road when the siren blasted from fifty feet behind his scooter. The noise grabbed his dulled attention. The only way he could shake them off was to enter the maze of little country lanes. He knew these well from the days when he used to go fishing on a regular basis with his old man. This group of lanes led to all the best fishing rivers and ponds. He knew them like the back of his hand and his fervent hope was the policemen didn't go fishing with their fathers, if they had fathers.

He went on to say that for a few miles he was thinking if he could get far enough ahead he'd ditch the stuff, or hide in a patch of woodland he knew and let them pass. They were on him and he couldn't seem to shake them off no matter what he did. Salvation came into view when he spotted a path running alongside the railway track. The path was an access route to some railway work huts, and at a glance it appeared to continue past the huts and off into the countryside. Beyond the work hut the track was a single strip of dirt, impossible for the pursuing police car. All this time the Triumph 2.5 pi squad car was on his tail. The roads were too narrow for the police to pass and stop him. They were waiting for the right moment.

The only thing he could do was make a last-minute dive onto the track. With a lot of wild leaning and a bit of luck our fugitive was on the path and away with the police car overshooting the turn. The officer in charge brought the car to a halt with a screech of tyres. Throwing the car into reverse the driver made the moves to follow him down the badly made road.

Lenny shot past the hut and sure enough the road beyond was only a single track. His luck was in the track had posts to stop wide vehicles going beyond the hut. He was away and the police wouldn't catch him. He didn't think they'd seen his number plate either. This was the old black and white type, or in his case silver aluminium with very little paint. This item was always kept in a dirty condition, so the plate was difficult to read from only ten feet away. He'd figured they wouldn't know who he was, and if by a fluke they caught him he wouldn't be carrying the stuff!

"Man, I was bricking it. I thought they got me. I thought they'd find the acid, so I got out of sight down that track and started looking for hiding places. Found a good spot under some railway signalling equipment to hide it temporary, like. The trouble was…" Lenny continued.

Yes, the trouble was Lenny hadn't got rid of all the drugs, and in his frantic efforts to lose the police tail he was sweating like a pig and strangest thing was happening. He was starting to enjoy the whole experience. "It was fantastic! Like a brilliant war movie where you know the hero will shoot all the Germans or the Jap's or whatever." He explained to me he was so excited by the chase that he decided to see if he could find a police car and spook them by doing the same trick again. By now he was really enjoying the day, he was magnificent! Not Lenny the Helmet, but now Lenny the fucking invincible!

After some effort turning the scooter around on the narrow track he headed back the other way to find the police car. After reversing back to the main road the policemen were in the process of leaving in the direction they'd come from. Lenny shot out of the track over the level crossing and off in the other direction. The two policemen in the car heard it, saw him, and decided to chase him down. This time they would catch the slippery bastard.

Lenny was more than a brilliant scooterist… he was a TT rider, a world-beating star on two wheels, uncatchable. All his fear had gone, and they were nowhere near him because it had taken them far too long to turn round on the narrow road. They were greatly disadvantaged by the big man's pure speed, agility and fearlessness. He sensed the police car would not catch him, not even get near. He was invincible. Also in his favour was the coming of evening with mist lifting up from the damp fields in strange swirling blobs that drifted across the road making visibility difficult.

He was having no problems seeing today. He had thousand mile eyes, vision of an eagle, and unstoppable pace. The mist was starting to look like objects, elephants, cows, and even small buildings, and Lenny was just drifting through them. He hit them at speed and they would fly apart in clouds of coloured light making a sound like metal tubes falling on a concrete floor. He was enjoying every minute of this. Lenny forgot about the police car in pursuit and aimed at the blobs of transforming mist. This was the ride of a lifetime, he was in the groove, and for some reason it was incredible!

The policemen realised the big oaf with the long greasy hair hanging out from under his helmet was going nowhere special, and he no longer tried to evade them. Their quarry took a left turn, and they knew the small country road was only field access with provision for a few farmhouses. The road looped back onto the country lane they were on, so they didn't follow Lenny. They continued on past the junction to where he would rejoin the road. The officers were taking a chance he'd turn left and ride straight into their roadblock. One officer would wait by the car, the other hidden in the bushes fifty yards up the road, so when their prey was stopped by the police car the other could rush up from behind to make the arrest.

Our hero of the day, the wonderful Lenny, was pulling the throttle nearly through the backstop such was his velocity. Now his skill level was beyond the impossible. He was Godlike, especially the way he and his machine cut through these strange spectres, bursting them with coloured light and sounds so high pitched they bounced inside his head. He rounded another curve and in front of him were three or four more clouds of mist. It was getting thicker, more interesting. The first cloud in his way looked like a very low-flying aircraft painted blue, a very light blue. It was travelling backwards. How he knew the direction of travel was backwards he had no idea. He cut through it like a knife through butter.

Other creatures exploded with noise and light as he drove through them. Hippos exploded, giant spiders fell apart, Lenny was in ecstasy at the power he held in the hands gripping the bars. Then there was this strange Chinese creature in the road, black and white. A very large giant panda was sitting in the road. Lenny pulled the throttle as hard as he could desperate for the sensations invading this body would bring, he ploughed through the stupid black and white creature.

Lenny hit the panda right in its stomach. It was made of metal, hard steel, it was a Triumph 2.5pi. This didn't burst apart in a bright flash of light. No, Lenny's legs burst apart with a horrible crunching sound, and it was the last thing he remembered until he found himself lying in the road. He was transfixed looking up at a blue flashing light on the roof of an ambulance. By this time he was on morphine, feeling good, and passed out again.

"I was high as a kite, man, the acid inside my helmet, I'd forgotten the acid inside my helmet, and all that sweating, it had soaked into my head. Man, I could've died from the acid alone, but, man, wow!" Lenny mumbled.

In his traction he couldn't move much, both legs stretched out in metal cages with pins through them holding bones together. He had drips, tubes and wires running in and out of him almost everywhere, but he still managed to lean over suggesting a little bit of business. Lenny was whispering to me and I knew all about it. I was his right-hand man doing a bit of running for him and doing a lot of dealing for myself. Lenny had a private contact in another city who'd send over a runner, it all worked smoothly. With John Smith's stuff we'd make a bigger margin.

Lenny carried on telling me how he was now dealing with Smiggy and they were doing all right. We were all doing all right, making deals, and polluting the stupid of other towns. Making lots of money and not caring a toss for the dope heads. At this Lenny looked at all the tubes and laughed.

"Looks like I'm one of the stupid now! Mate, can you take over for me for a while? Someone's got to keep the thing running. Anything happens to you, I'd do the same for you, man." So that's how deep I was in all this, and I suppose this was why I was given the opportunity to look into this part of my past. I find this bubble darkly funny even though it illustrates my lack of care for others and only my care for making money. Sod them, they're only acidheads was my attitude!

"Tell me the end bit again, Lenny," I said.

Lenny started to say…

Then I was on fire, the acid causing a burning sensation that consumed my entire body. Everywhere was burning, even my eyeballs. I could feel them crinkling up like big black raisins in my eye sockets. I could barely speak as the skin around my neck tightened crushing my windpipe. This was excruciating. I could even feel my genitals burning away. I managed to scream out in a blinding agony, "Stop this! For God's sake, stop this!'"

A gentle breeze, then a wind, then a gale, then the storm followed by the hurricane, or was it a tornado? The immense force would have blown me off the world if it had not been for someone holding me. My eyes were starting to clear from the burning acid, and I could see I was being held in place by the Irish wolfhound. His teeth gripped my leather belt, a very large stout belt around my waist. This belt was more like a weightlifter's belt, constructed with leather strong enough to stop me blowing away.

The wolfhound seemed to be anchored into the ground as if he was growing from it. So rock solid was the dog's stance it was miraculous.

With my clearing vision I could see the little pixie holding a tiny golden straw which was connected to the enormous rucksack by a tube no thicker than a piece of string. From the end of this tiny golden tube came this immense storm blowing away the agony of the big grey bubble. The violent wind removing the deep burning pain and the immense rucksack was getting smaller and smaller. By the time I felt no pain it was no bigger than any normal bag on a pixie's back. But what is a normal bag on a pixie's back?

I closed my eyes in relief, but could feel tugging at the large mysterious belt around my waist. When I opened my eyes I'd been transported into the open once again. I was sitting outside the pub with a drink in one hand and Jennifer pulling me playfully towards her to give me a kiss. Our lips touched with soft passion that turned into a long lingering kiss. This took away any final traces of pain, that only moments before had been so intense I wanted to die to be free of it.

Jennifer's kiss held intense desire, I wanted to be alive, and stay here with her.

"We'll cycle for the rest of the day if you like, and explore many things," she said. And we did.

CHAPTER 23

Inner daze, the pinball's rude awakening in 1973.

So there I was, only a few short hours into my awakening after two years of what? I was on my knees with my face buried in my girlfriend's mother's best Italian underwear with a very diaphanous possibility of any plausible explanation. No excuse could explain why I was softly resting my head on her mother's freshly laundered seductive lace. I was locked in a slow motion time vortex. Each second was an awful long wait for the explosion. I was using every infinite second to work on an excuse. "My cheque book, I dropped it the other day and your mother told me she'd put it somewhere safe." I tried that one.

Vicky was standing aggressively with one foot thrust forward and her hands placed on her hips. Her unflinching gaze was taunting me to say something even more ridiculous. The second silence was longer than the first. Vicky was waiting, I think, with a secret delight for me to grab a large spade to dig my own grave. She stared at me with unblinking eyes, and tapped her foot with a doom laden continuous beat like the drums of an oncoming superior army.

"Are you trying to sniff it out?" she suggested. I was about to reply when she continued, "Have you got a thing about my mother? You're always having a laugh with her. If she wasn't my mother and so bloody old I'd think you were shagging her," was her dagger-sharp comment. I don't think she knew how sharp the blade was.

I rose to my feet with the sort of hands out expression Frenchmen give you after they've run into the back of your car. The expression said "Who me?" My own body was trying to betray me. Yesterday morning's passionate sex lesson pushed its way into my head. I couldn't force it back. A blush bloomed across my face and this started an enormous one sided argument. Vicky didn't think I was having an affair with Samantha, but was jealous that I enjoyed her mother's company so much, worse still she was so terribly old and boring.

I'd had no real conversation with Vicky, none that I could remember anyway. I wasn't saying anything. Vicky was doing all the talking, or should I say shouting, building her rage until it became a rant solely about how weird I'd become since last week.

This was a bit of useful news. I was about to ask, when she lambasted me over Saturday night, not yesterday but the week before. It was evident we'd planned something special that I didn't attend. I'd postponed, going off to the nearby city for a night out with, as she described it, "that Nazi twin of yours".

"What do you mean Nazi twin?" I asked.

"You told me! Have you forgotten everything? It's something Harry the Pocket told you about Nazis in the SS," Vicky replied.

"Remind me?" I continued.

"You are really weird since last weekend. The Nazi thing is something to do with your teeth," Vicky said, with growing irritation.

"Go on Vic's. Tell me," I begged, pressing the point.

"You only call me Vic's when you're after something, and I'm telling you fuck all. You're nuts!"

"Oh, I see."

"You've gone really weird!" she said, and immediately pushed the subject to where I didn't want it to go…"What are you doing? What are you really up to? Et cetera, et cetera, et cetera," so she continued.

She shouted at me for possibly ten minutes, perhaps even longer, or the tirade was much shorter, terrible in its fury. I was concentrating on every word, trying to glean any information from her. Possible clues as to why I'm suffering amnesia, or what happened in the past to give me the amnesia. The John Smith thing was of interest. Had he poisoned me last weekend with some type of drug?

I've got to admit most things she was saying passed over my head. I was concentrating so hard on keywords that a lot of the stuff about us I ignored. The apparent lack of concern fuelled the fire of anger keeping her in an almost endless rant which finished with the words, "I really don't know why I bother with you? I loved you, you were great fun. Now you are a sad pillock. Mothers underwear drawer? You sad…bastard!"

Vicky finished with those words, I think. The truth is I can't remember, I was concentrating on the jigsaw puzzle of ideas she'd spat at me during her rampant judgements of my character. She was probably right about everything.

Vicky threw me out of the house, but she didn't take the keys off me. I wouldn't have let her. She was cold and icy as she drove me back to my flat in her rather battered 1966 Mini. At least she'd stopped screaming at me. I was wondering if I could placate her, but looking across at her rigid in the driver's seat gave me no desire to try and coerce affection from her.

I mentioned that she could ask her mother if she'd seen my cheque book somewhere, because I'd lost it. These were the only word spoken. She didn't ask me when I would be around again so perhaps she was going off me. I just wondered why I had been so attractive in the first place. Should I have asked? I knew the answer. I'd been shallow and she had a body I wanted to touch, and obviously a mother who I desired.

Back in my broken flat it looked like a bomb had exploded ripping the building apart. The signed prints of Mike and Jim remained on the floor torn apart by shotgun blasts, and the rest of the place totally wrecked by my frantic search. I had to do something. I'd either hidden all the money and drugs, or they'd been stolen from me and I was being fixed up to take the fall. In my panic I was thinking of the safe warmth in the old family home. This got me to thinking about visiting Jane and laying everything I knew out in plain terms, a third-party eye view might reveal something I'd missed.

The flat was so shattered a complete redecoration was necessary. It would have taken a week to tidy. Picking all the glass up and vacuuming from top to bottom would solve nothing. Then it struck me. I hadn't looked in the vacuum cleaner. Who would? I wasn't sure where I kept it but vaguely recalled seeing one somewhere in the kitchen during my search.

Sure enough it was in a cupboard covered in the debris from my previous frantic searching. Of course the only place you can hide anything in a vacuum cleaner is in the bag. Sure enough, in all the dusty filth of matted hair, fluff and God knows what, I found an envelope. The thick brown manila envelope contained a lot of money, a lot of money by 1973 standards. This gave me something to flash in front of the gang, some money to suggest I had more, or to run with! Not the ten thousand pounds, it was, however, one thousand pounds, wrapped with a seal announcing the bundle contained fifty £20 notes. The seal was handwritten, and not in my handwriting? So some money existed, but where was the rest?

I'd had a bit of luck, but I didn't want to carry the money and decided to push it up behind the back of the kitchen sink. In the narrow space the fat envelope would wedge nicely. Nobody would bother searching because the flat was already in tatters. I secreted the money after peeling off £40. The search continued.

I was convinced more money was concealed somewhere. Finally I gave up physically exhausted by the constant uninspired searching. I was like a blind man searching for one strand of brightly coloured hay in a barn. I was blinded by amnesia. I was leaving to see Jane but couldn't lock up, the flat was a shattered mess and with my chances of long-term survival did it matter? Habits die hard. I've always locked doors and the shattered door swinging loosely on its hinges begged to be secured. I was trying to figure out some way of securing the door when a voice from behind broke the silence.

"I wouldn't bother with that if I were you, I'll only kick in again. Might have a look round. Might even go to the toilet on your poxy sofa," Dave said. At his comment the lovely Hartley Sparrow accompanied by the weasel burst out laughing. I was immensely relieved I'd hidden the thousand pounds, or to be more precise the £960. I didn't know what these two wanted but money was certainly one of their primary desires.

It looked as though Dave didn't have Millicent with him. They were making a rare social visit, though I did notice they both sported rather sturdy boots. The shotgun was less worrying than the boots which would make less noise as they used them on me. He could only kill me the once, but beating me to death with his brutal boots would take longer. I held onto the bleak hope that the sadistic Dave would prefer to shoot me in the stomach and watch me bleed to death burning in my own stomach acids. I'm sure he would've enjoyed either method, like a stroll in the park with a tasty relish of extreme violence.

I wondered if I could walk past them, so I strode with no confidence down the hallway towards them. I expected them to bar my way. They both stood aside like gentlemen courtiers and ushered me through. I was wondering if they were going to trip me at the top of the stairs, cosh me on the back of the head, or like big children spit over the balustrade on to my hair. None of these things happened. I walked past them, down the stairs and outside. My Ford Cortina GT GLX2 litre had a big white arrow painted across the shattered windscreen. The aerosol painted arrow pointing down into the car with a word written above. All it said was "Look".

The footpath didn't pass the car. I had to walk twenty yards out of my way to look inside it. There wasn't a dead dog on the seat, nor was there a dead cat, or even in Mafia parlance a horse's head. No, one of them, I suspected Smiggy, had shit all over the front seat. It was a huge solid mass, quite the most disgusting thing I'd seen since leaving the farm. It festered there on the seat, and the most appalling thing of all: no toilet paper! My one dominating thought wasn't the defilement of my car, but the dirty little sod hadn't used toilet paper. I wouldn't ever use the car again, or shake his hand!

They were driving a green and white Vauxhall VX 490, and they didn't offer me a lift. As I walked they followed me through the estate creeping along like kerb crawlers. I think they were delighted watching me get progressively wetter in the light drizzle. I did the alleyway trick again to lose them and it was easy. They were reluctant to leave the warmth of the car.

In the next street I had a bit of luck, something that would hasten my getaway. A battered minicab with a mismatching coloured front wing was coming my way. These things are not supposed to be hailed, I stuck my thumb out in hope, and it stopped. The woman driving it I think was young, but she looked old, with a thin face, cracked lips, and thin hair.

"I'm not supposed to pick people up. Give you a lift if you tip me well, she said.

I was back in handmade shoes, and didn't desire the walk. "Yes I'll tip you generously, I need the lift."

Through my fog of disorientation I realised this was Sunday evening and I knew my sister would be avoiding the family circus around the table. I gambled that Jane would be with the other bikers. I was forced to revisit the oil and grease cafe, knowing she'd be hanging out there. The only bonus was some of the characters in there were tough, proper tough, though probably not as murderous as Dave and his metal girlfriend.

The really murderous prospect in all my troubles was the frightening John Smith who wanted his cut of the proceeds, his percentage. He was an unknown, the real danger. He could kill me somewhere quiet after taking all I had, and claim later to Harry that I'd done a runner. I didn't understand my relationship with John Smith and perhaps never will. I did feel safer in the aggressive atmosphere of the motorcyclists' café than as a passenger in John's car. Somehow I felt safer with my sister backing me. This, of course, was total illusion.

It was late into the evening as I arrived at the cafe. Only a handful of motorcycles were outside glimmering in the wetness, illuminated by the neon lights and reflected in the cafe windows. It was difficult to see individually what make the bikes were. I did see a Triumph Trident which was a new machine and quite rare. My spirits lifted, Jane was in the cafe.

As I entered the greasy place her boyfriend Steve rolled his eyes at me as if to say, "Here again, pest"! He did get up and go to the counter to get coffees for me and my sister. He then hung around the pinball machine looking hard and sexy. At least that's what Steve thought he looked! Smoking and talking bikes with the other guys while waiting for my dominant sister, she was the boss. I was going to tell her every single fact I knew in the hope she could put two and two together. The lacy contents of, and my discovery in the underwear drawer would remain forever private, Perhaps?

Jane's theory was my amnesia was drug induced. It was possible John Smith or Harry the pockets sidekicks had dosed me the other night in an effort to steal the money, leaving me to take the blame in my drugged ignorance. They would be away scot free with everything. Another disturbing scenario was suggested: did I know everybody involved? Other people unknown to me could be tracking me down at this moment for their cut. Could it get any better? Jane ran through the known facts for me one by one, even using a napkin to make notes. She started to use salt and pepper pots, and sauce bottles. It was beginning to look like a chess board, and I was beginning to look like the sacrificial first move, the pawn.

This game of chess had a bit more spice. When the winner called checkmate the loser wouldn't just have his king pushed over. (A bottle of HP sauce) No, the special loser would discover the joys and solitude of the countryside. This wasn't a traditional chess match played in Iceland by grandmasters. This match was being played out by grand bastards and the ice wasn't on the land but in their souls.

As we talked the Buck Rogers pinball machine was rattling away in the background. The ball being battered around mindlessly inside the machine, the final result it would fall down a black hole. The ball reminded me of the way I was rushing around, achieving nothing, bounced from one place to another. The ball was hard and made of steel, I wasn't.

I told Jane they were probably watching me right now, so could she give me a lift on the back of the bike. A terrifying thought! I was actually asking for this? Jane could take me to the town house, but first head in the direction of the farm to mislead my watchers into believing I was spending the night there, a place where I might be safe from their violent intrusions.

I had to revisit the town house and I might not sleep at all this night. If I'd hidden £1000 inside the vacuum cleaner I couldn't help but think there would be more hiding places. Some of my stash could be at the town house. I was haunted by the idea that my salvation in money and drugs may be only inches away. That thought drove me on.

One problem was looking for the acid. I was looking for a large amount of pills, or I assumed it would be pills. I was a virgin when it came to acid. I must've known everything about the business until I woke up a few hours ago. Now all my knowledge of the hard street-life had disappeared, and I knew nothing of the laws of survival. God I was in a mess, confused and lost. The road ahead was something I wasn't worried about in August 1973. I couldn't see past The Cauldron tomorrow.

What form was the acid I had hidden?

Acid can take many obvious and some not so obvious forms. What was I going to find at the end of all this?

CHAPTER 24

Right here right now, under the ground, in terror, in ecstasy.

I was in a far better place now, resting under the ground. No, I'm not dead! I was staying with a friend in a cave in the mountains. This is a cave with running water, electricity, and an almost constant temperature throughout the year, with little need for air conditioning in the summer, or much heating in the winter. When you say you're living in a cave people conjure up something from the movies like *The Flintstones* or *10,000 BC*. These twenty-first century caves have flat-screen televisions. This one also had the solitude and peace to focus on my great hidden battle.

I was lying in bed, my body no longer invaded by wretched tubes. My hair was growing a little bit, but only a little bit, I couldn't perceive if I was losing it quicker than I was growing it, but hope and sometimes hair springs eternal. This thought of hope springing eternal brought me back to thinking of Rachel and her beloved Abraham, who'd spent horrifying months under the special attention of the voyeuristic torturer Heinrich Haussler, mind games now his particular new favourite blood sport. Sometimes I tried to speculate as to what Heinrich was thinking, what drove him to play these twisted games?

Psychological games occupied much of Heinrich's waking thoughts, keeping him amused during a difficult period in the war. During his active service he'd been much more of a soldier than his brother Maximilian, but after suffering severe wounds to his left shoulder and face on the Russian front he now fought a different war, the economic war, killing the so-called corrupters of the Nazi system, or in his case murdering for fun and profit.

He preferred violent interrogations of captured soldiers. These Jews were easy, and since posted to this wretched camp Heinrich had become bored with easy deaths. Now he was experimenting. These tortures were much more satisfying when he practised them on academics. His ambition was to twist one so tight he'd die of a heart failure under stress. Abraham Wilson became his new object of amusement.

Heinrich's new diversion was Russian roulette. He'd found a very fine Austrian made revolver in a good suitcase. It was a beautiful smooth piece of craftsmanship with a six bullet chamber that when spun whizzed round with a beautiful crisp clicking action for several seconds. When a chamber was loaded with only one bullet, on most occasions it would stop near the bottom out of harm's way. It also had a hammer lifter fitted which prevented the hammer going all the way to the cartridge case, so if the bullet was in a position to kill the little slider on the left-hand side of the revolver would prevent any unwanted accidents. The object of his interest was unaware of the gun's special features.

On a bitter cold February day he summoned Abraham to his office wondering how far he could push this little academic accountant. When he arrived Heinrich had prepared a black bread sandwich, not a sandwich in any modern sense of the word, more just a rude piece of bread topped by a sliver of very hard cheese, a meagre offering in a normal world. This morsel of poor food looked like nectar of the gods to poor Abraham. The German officer asked him if he'd like it, and made a further offer of great interest. "You can have one of these every day."

Mr Wilson concentrated on looking at the floor too afraid to speak, never daring to catch this man in the eye, never being able to judge the situation. A defiant look may draw a laugh or a bullet in the back of the neck. Heinrich explained his little game, and his experiments didn't include a get out clause, unless death was the get out clause. Trapped, Abraham listening to this Nazi telling him he could eat this very tempting morsel every single day. The price was play Russian roulette, with Heinrich spinning the chamber, promising only to pull the trigger once each day.

He would continue to do this throughout the next month. If the accountant managed to survive, he would receive two pieces of bread on the final day, and two pulls of the trigger! Heinrich explained he had no choice. His fate had been decided and he was to visit the office every single day for a morsel of food. The price of continued life was a daily gut-wrenching nerve-shredding game of Russian roulette. It was poor hard cheese to be earned in the hardest of ways. On some of the darker days Abraham prayed with fervour for a bang he would never hear.

Those thirty long days started with a very dramatic demonstration. The pistol was pushed under Abraham's nose whilst Nazi spun the chamber. There was no time to think. He pointed it straight to Abraham's temple, and pulled the trigger… Click. He then spun it again repeating the exercise, but at the last moment pulled the gun to one side. Cordite exploded inches away from the Jew's ear with an enormous bang. He lost his balance and fell over. His head was ringing and he'd become temporarily deaf in his left ear. He could hear laughing, loud raucous laughing!

"I might not have to give much bread. I've never seen such a poor bargain," Heinrich said, laughing. He continued laughing as he pointing his leather gloved hand to the door. Abraham left the office clutching his piece of black bread with a morsel of cheese. His prize had to be forced down in the corridor before anybody outside caught sight of it. He was desperately hungry. Strange thoughts of what thirty pieces of bread would look like haunted him. More food than he could imagine after a year of near starvation…

Whilst I was lying in bed hoping I may survive, I was pondered what mind bending torture daily Russian roulette would be. Would I quickly crack and throw myself at the German in a frenzied attempt to inflict injury before he killed me? The other option was to listen to your hunger and keep walking into the office and take the food. This way you'd have a slim chance of life. Was going through the torture every morning after nightmare filled nights preferable to no existence? I think this is how Abraham saw it. Everybody was hungry, diseased, starving, and didn't have his opportunities. To call this an opportunity is insane, but the world Abraham existed in was.

The crucial point Rachel told me was that Abraham was familiar with weaponry. He knew the Austrian make and believed the gun was fixed, though he had no certain way of knowing this. He came to this conclusion because on two occasions the German pulled the trigger twice, both times aiming past his head very close to his ear. With each of these explosive demonstrations he laughed loudly afterwards, and it was obvious t he didn't expect his fine uniform to be splattered with remnants of bloody brains.

I was drifting off again down into sleep. Reliving this horror was keeping me fighting but not away from the other universe. I want to be there, I didn't want to be there, yes I did, or was it no? Of course I did. I was addicted.

I could hear a train. Not another bloody railway station I was thinking, but I sensed movement, music and the crush of a crowd. We were on what in this parallel universe was a convincing version of the Orient Express or something equally plush. Everybody on board was dressed in all their finery. I was wearing some kind of dinner jacket that was not quite the thing we have here. It was somehow slightly less formal whilst retaining an air of refined elegance.

When it all came into sharp focus, when I say focus I mean when everything in this universe joins together as one to give a complete experience, I was stunned. I could literally feel the air molecules blown out of the musical instruments because we enjoyed the full sound of a live band. You could practically taste every drink, and feel the pressure waves from the groups of people dancing. It was a glittering magical night made more so after I sensed Jennifer.

She was dressed in the style you would expect from the 1930s, a very elegant slim dress, pearls and she was perfection. We decided to dance without any preamble, and as we joined the crowd on the small dance floor she gave me a very soft kiss. Nothing too much, this wasn't the right place. To my astonishment I could move around with the fluid motion of a ballroom dancer. My partner's abilities were equally refined. Together we floated through the crowds gliding around the carriage as it rattled on through the night's cool air. The classical interior was all elegance, and everything from the lighting to its sumptuous wood crafted interior glowed, shimmering as if in a heat haze, though the temperature in the carriage was, as always as in this universe, perfect.

In this world most things were never less than astonishing and I loved being here. The feeling in the air that night was one of celebration. Something indicated it was the right time for a gala evening. The whole proceeding had a joyous feel to it. We danced, chatted with others, talked between ourselves, and drank a few delicious champagnes. It was uninterrupted pleasure carrying on like this for several hundred miles as the wheels clattered along the shiny rails taking us ever further south. In all the miles I hadn't seen any sign of a briefcase, or, for that matter, a large dog.

A large tuba roared out its bass sounds blown by a very well dressed red-faced man. We danced nearer to him now. To catch my undivided attention my magical partner tweaked the end of my nose playfully and pointed into the mouth of the tuba. I, like a fool, looked… I was deafened for a few seconds by long low roars of wind. Then it was almost silent as quickly as it had been loud. I could faintly hear the band playing on above me. Looking up out of the mouth of the tuba I saw lights in the carriage and people dancing by. Jennifer smiled down at me with that look in her eye that said, "Got you!"

For the first few seconds I feared sliding down the tube into smaller spaces until I was trapped, wedged solid, in a narrow pipe. When I'd adjusted to the darkness I was in the same space as usual, and I could see O'Duke resting in a corner watching me with luminous eyes. My little friend the Lylybel was nowhere to be seen until, of course, she caught me completely by surprise by coming from nowhere and tapping me on the shoulder. I turned almost angry at being caught out, and I was amazed to be confronted by a very elegant different Hysandrabopel. What had made this change between now and our previous meeting? Then I realised she was almost as tall as me, taller, in fact, than Jennifer.

Her attire was not as elegant as my lovely partner waiting high above in the carriage. Pixie was wearing what appeared to be a very expensive business suit including handmade shoes, and some form of college tie complete with a tie pin. She was every inch the successful businesswoman, or should that be businessman the way she was dressed. Who knows?

"Would you like to dance?" she asked.

"We have no music," I said. The pixie clicked her fingers, imperceptible at first, but then pressure waves built up pushing the air. The molecular dance that was sound slowly filled the space with exquisite harmonies, a far richer sound than produced by the band in the carriage above. That's before she turned the intrusive sound from above off. This private bag music flowed around both of us as she grabbed me in a very formal stance. At first with her attire I thought she was going to be the man, and I was going to have to dance the woman's part. Thankfully this didn't happen. We started to glide around in the darkness, the only light coming from the carriage above.

As we moved with astounding elegance in the darkness, I thought I could sense the hint of an aroma coming from the pixie. This aroma became whatever you wanted it to be as long as it was nice. You imagined chocolate, there it was for you to smell, and if this got too much, your imagination might wander towards vanilla or strawberry. This is how the system worked, or it's what I remember of how the system worked. I forced myself to try imagining something disgusting. This didn't seem to do anything. The previous fragrances continued without allowing in anything noxious. I did think of Marmite, and that worked. The pixie must've liked it!

We danced for a time so compressed or for so long I cannot remember. Pixie was now resting her head very gently against my shoulder with her eyes closed humming a little song to herself. This resting of the head didn't seem to be romantic. It was almost medical as if she were listening to my chest; which was more disconcerting than it being a romantic gesture. I knew deep down she's a slippery customer and the thought of her listening to my heart had me worried.

"What are you doing with your head on my chest? Are you listening for something?" I asked.

A reply was not forthcoming. Silence answered my question. Not loosening her tender embrace around my body she continued to hum along to some private tune, all the while with her beautiful hair resting against my chest, and her right ear pressed hard against my sternum. Whatever she was listening to I didn't like it! With quite a sudden movement she stood back, looking at me.

"I was listening to see what kind of stomach you've got. Is it a strong stomach or a feeble squishy stomach that lets you down all the time? You know, weak." After a pause she continued, "I don't want you yukking up all over my beautiful history bubble constructions because I'd like to have a nice clean experience to watch," pixie said.

We'd danced on for an age or so and there were no bubbles anywhere to be seen. I was beginning to wonder if anything was going to happen, or were we just enjoying the night dancing to a twirling fast waltz? It wasn't the true waltz rhythm we understand though the dance itself was similar and a lot more fun.

I noticed as we twirled around we were starting to make a long trail of very tiny bubbles. They came from below our feet but not exactly beneath our feet. This was more of a moving up through the floor and oozing out of the pattern of footprints we were leaving. It looked as if we were dancing across a Milky Way of stars that glistened, very small, all very bright and effervescent like champagne. These were nothing like the previous bubbles I'd become accustomed too, and to break one of these sparkling delights would be a joy. These bubbles didn't look like they were going to burn me to death.

Dancing in a sea of bubbles was the eventual outcome of our waltz. The entire floor had become covered to the depth of several inches in glistening bubbles, so bright my eyes were continuously dazzled. This brilliance, this shine, was almost unbearable. It also had another quality. It seemed to be springy underfoot like the floor had disappeared to be replaced by this soft sea of very fine bubbles. This was the moment I pushed them aside with my elegant dancing shoe. I was shocked by what was revealed. The whole floor beneath this trickery was one grey bubble, thankfully not too dark, but to be this big and grey it must've started life very black, very small, very bad, not a bubble to be messed with!

If we could stand upon it how was I going to pop it? I didn't need to ask. The music and the aromas were a fading memory. All that remained was the pixie who'd now released me from her grasp, and was fiddling around in a hidden pocket for something. What she produced was very similar to a telescopic car aerial, the extending type made of eight different sections. She proceeded without any theatre to extend this to its full length and it was almost as tall as the pixie…What she did with it next was use it like a pointer at a conference. I now understood where the business suit came in and she asked me a question,

"Would you like to see how bad you've been? And if you're as bad as some people are suggesting you are, you're in trouble in that bubble," pixie rhymed in a singsong voice.

"What…?"

"You'll see," pixie said, starting to bring the pointer up into the air and over her shoulder in a giant arc.

Hysadraboppel didn't hesitate in plunging the white board pointer into the bubble. Nothing happened for quite some time, about ten seconds, after which I could hear this very slow hissing sound like a puncture. I put my hand over the hole. I could feel no air rushing out… It was rushing in!

My hand was trapped in a violent vacuum the strength of which gave me the impression my arm would be ripped from its socket. I couldn't escape. It was pulling my fingers longer and longer, and to my horror my body was transforming into some form of flesh elastic. It hurt like crazy. This inward rush of air wasn't going to let me go. I was going to be pulled down like a piece of spaghetti sucked into a hungry Italian's mouth.

I did the only thing possible to relieve the pain. I put my hands together and dived. It was similar to plunging from a ten meter diving board, except for one thing: this was scarier by far!

CHAPTER 25

Crazy bad breath forgotten times.

Wet cigarette smoke… Lips were pressed against mine kissing me with a lot of wet tongue. I was, of course, a spectator to this, like watching a full 3D movie with sensation vision.

I had one hand on this girl's right thigh which was quite naked, no stockings. The other was up underneath the back of her jumper. I could feel the strap of her bra pressing into the palm of my hand. She wasn't objecting to my investigating touch. She was pushing against me with her whole body. This was the language of sex, and we were communicating in this idiom towards who knows. It could be the back of a car, it could be my place, or it could be anywhere. She broke away from me slowly biting my lip as she did so, giggling into my face with more unwanted aroma, this time the distinct smell of too many short drinks.

She was quite lovely. Long hair, slim, very well proportioned, and I think her young age gave her complexion a beautiful freshness despite the damage from alcohol and cigarettes. At a glance you would have guessed she was twenty. On consideration I think she was about sixteen or even fifteen. The girl looked straight past me across the pub booth, and on the other side of the table was an equally lovely girl just as fresh and just as drunk. She he was in the arms of my Nazi twin, the one and only John Smith, and in this video rerun we were both laughing together. We were big mates out on the town, and with his treacherous nature you never knew if you could trust the laughter.

The girls were giggling to each other, making signals that they wanted to go to the ladies for a chat, to talk about whatever girls talk about in the ladies. Were they going back with us? We didn't doubt it. Were they going to fuck us? We didn't doubt that either. We were the lads, out on the town, flashing the cash, and we were smooth-looking bastards at that. What more could a girl want?

The girls squeezed out of the booth past us, having to climb over our laps to get out. There was intimate touching greeted by a lot of giggling as they slipped by on hot legs towards the ladies room. We were not a lot older than the girls in years, but in terms of dispassionate taking advantage we were veterans. This is the feeling I was getting. Cynically take the pleasure, spoil, and forget.

John leaned across the table so we could talk without shouting saying, "They'll be gone ages. I got something to tell you. It's big!"

"Go on then, John. Does it have a profit?"

"Fucking lots, more than you can shake a stick at!" John replied.

So he started to tell me where he got the drugs from. This was quite worrying because he never told anybody who his exclusive connection was. Now he was telling me. Even on the rerun deep down inside my head I sensed I didn't want to be in any deeper. John Smith obviously wanted me in it up to my neck, or he was just a mate trying to cut me in on some totally class money action. I wasn't feeling cut in, more dropped in it!

"Mr Big, if you want to call him that. His real name is Raymond Nice. He runs that large scrap business in the big disused factory at the edge of the city. You know the place on the road out to the north where all the scrap cars are piled up right next the road. You can buy anything for a few bob. Well he fancies himself as a bit of an Al Capone, a big-time gangster, but he's not smart, a bit of an arsehole really. I went to see him the other week to do some business. Normally he's got this big lump of a brother with him. Now his brother Walter works in the scrap yard but he's not the enforcer. He runs a low-level protection racket with some local takeaway restaurants, the odd nightclub, nothing big time, but he fancies himself," John said.

"I digress. I was there and Raymond sends him out the room then tells me he can't trust his brother. The big dumb arse wants to see more of the action and Raymond can't trust him not to flash the cash about drawing unwanted attention." John Smith explained how Raymond Nice didn't want his brother to know who "The Man" was.

"This is where it gets really interesting. There's this guy by the name of Chas, a real ugly bruiser, who works in the yard and he's the chief enforcer. The dickhead broke his leg in an accident at the yard, and Raymond wants to go down to Bristol to see the man, get some gear. You know what I'm saying? So he invites me along because he trusts me!" At this John Smith roared with laughter until tears rolled down his face. "Trusts me! Trusts me…the wanker!"

I did not see my lovely girl again, and I wanted to. Unfortunately I missed out on the girl in this rerun, but I'm sure I enjoyed her at the time. I suffered a jump in time. One minute I'm in the pub waiting for my girls return, and the next I'm standing next to a parked car somewhere out in the wilds. It's all very dark and I can make out the shape of John's Rover 3.5 coupe. He's laughing and telling me Raymond Nice has retired from the business of drug overlord. This sudden retirement happened after a scare near Bristol when a drug deal went slightly wrong.

It turned out that the two of them travel down together, Raymond carrying five grand with him, and the caring John Smith as the minder, though John, to my knowledge, never carried firearms, so what he expected John to do if the trouble really kicked off God only knows. They'd done the deal and it had gone smoothly, a regular arrangement. The right amount of stuff for the right amount of genuine non-counterfeit money, all in five pound notes, none of them freshly printed. All that money taken for selling bits and pieces of old cars, a perfect front if you need untraceable cash, the bonus being you don't have to pay scrap value for all the cars. Some of them you can collect free whilst the owners are asleep.

This is where the drug deal went slightly wrong for Raymond Nice. The two of them stopped at a pub to have something to eat, chicken in the basket or some such delight. Now relaxed Raymond decided to have four or five Scotch whisky's, he wasn't a big drinker. John was now responsible for driving, and not too long after they'd left the odour of stale beer and chicken behind Raymond had a nasty turn.

John decided that he should sleep a little bit more soundly and pulled over into a lay-by where the snoring, overfed Raymond suddenly died. I think what he died of you could call asphyxiation, or a more accurate description would be John Smith pressing both hands across his face. The former Mr Big struggled drunkenly against a far superior force. John Smith was very strong. "It was like stamping on an earwig," he told me.

"One minute the old bastard's doing my head in with the snoring, next he's all quiet and peaceful, lovely result. I know who's "the man" so I can now take over. I'll work some story with that dumb arse brother Walt, and he'll think that he's been crossed by Harry the Pocket or that nauseating sidekick of his, Double-Barrelled Dave. So, with a bit of luck, dumb arse Walter will sort them all out for us. What a fucking result!"

John Smith opens the boot, and the dim interior light illuminates the contents. Before me lies Raymond's body, and his face is very purple especially where it's been resting on the car boot floor. I feel like vomiting. I've gone from drug dealer to accomplice in murder, and this "friend" of mine will kill me without even thinking about it if I don't help him. I was being used and tested to see what I was made of. Stupid, soft, malleable clay, that's what I was made of!

I was rigid with fear staring at the body when the location changed. We were now in another part of the country. It was still dark, and this part of the countryside seemed familiar to me in a way that as a spectator I hadn't yet grasped. Then it came to me. We were below the farm on the edge of the old copse. You can access this through a series of gates connecting the lower fields, especially if you've got keys which I obviously still possessed. How they came to be in my possession, I don't know.

The copse was a long way from the public highway and contained no fishing pond that could tempt people to visit this remote patch of woodland. It was quite unremarkable in every way, a perfect place to hide the body deep beneath leaf mulch and debris of old rotting woodland. We only had one spade between us so we took it in turns, five minutes apiece, to dig a very deep hole to keep Raymond safe from foxes and other animals. It did occur to me that the devious John might decide I was more use to him quiet than as a business associate. I carried on digging what could have become my own grave.

Well it's obvious the unfortunate Mr Nice rests alone because I'm telling you the story. There would be no story if John had murdered me, but he didn't bury me alongside Raymond for his own reasons. He needed backup with his story. Also, he couldn't cope with the sudden expansion of business, and needed an established outlet. I was by all accounts a big wheel and a pretty miserable bastard. The replay had exposed this sad fact, and as his accomplice I was deep in the spider's web!

The job in the copse was done. We were now away from the farm, and I was so tense I could have snapped like a dry twig at the least provocation. John, however, was humming to himself, contentment taking over after dumping the body. However, you couldn't imagine he'd been stressed. Killing somebody was for John like standing on an earwig. This made me shudder cold up my back.

What we were doing next made me shudder more. We were beating some guy in an alleyway with a cricket bat, at least I had a cricket bat, and John was stamping on the poor victim's testicles! I, on the other hand, was beating him around the legs hard enough I'm quite sure to break something. During all this violence John and I were discussing how much money he'd cost us. We informed him of the tactics he would use to recoup his losses, and how if he didn't return the money to us we would keep visiting until he got his life formula correctly aligned with our business plan.

We supply the stuff he sells. The merchandise goes down some more levels to the little guys who deal it out on the streets. He keeps a small margin after which he gives the money due to us. This guy was somebody we trusted. This time he'd let us down and needed a lesson. Other lowlife's need to know he's had this hard, hard lesson! He can be in the game if he pays us back, but it will never be anything but money upfront, and if he doesn't pay us back… This is the darkness I'm involved in along with my Nazi twin who I naïvely believed was the force of evil, and now I can see why we're twins.

I suffer a short series of flashbacks, all of which seem to involve doling it out to somebody who's crossed us in some way that we perceive to be bad. I suppose when you're dealing at this end of the spectrum you can't go to a lawyer and expect to take somebody through the courts. It has to be more immediate, and as I'm watching these short snapshots of my previous history I'm starting to become more and more nauseous to the point where I think I'm going to be sick in my own flashback. How did I get to be like this? What drove me to push my life down such a bleak path?

On one occasion I was sweating, and seemed to be enjoying the workout. I was wearing my steel toe capped brogues and I could feel the amount of effort I was putting into my work convincing people we weren't soft touches. The final nail in my vomit coffin was watching the pure physicality of my nauseating violence. I was getting to the point of vomiting inside my own flashback, but I was watching and not participating so if I vomited where would it land? If I threw up it wasn't going to make the past violent me vomit, so what would happen? Would I throw up all over the Pixie?

Then I was dry vomiting. It was a wretched non-stop deep gut-wrenching effort. Every time it produced a dry burning in the back of my throat, and every time I'd imagine it was the last effort, or my body could take no more. Each time this happened I was wrong. The dry burning continued in my throat, the retching so violent it seemed some inner force was attempting to pull my stomach up through my larynx. It continued for so long that my entire throat and windpipe were on fire.

The only things moist were my eyes, wet with tears produced by the strain of continuous, never-ending body-wracking convulsions. It was going to kill me if I carried on heaving my guts up like this for much longer, I would rupture something inside my body and die. Some time in this haze of bile induced agony I realised I was no longer in the flashback. I was in the realm of the pixie and this was my current fire, the result, what she'd expected. A weak stomach or no stomach at all in fact! Witnessing my hidden past was nauseating and Karmic revenge was being put upon me, I deserved it!

With a final effort I managed to open my tear-filled eyes, and with blurred vision I could see my little business woman pointing her telescopic device at me like an accusatory finger, and there was no wind or water. I was retching as if I was to die, and nothing would allow me to speak a single word to her. This, I felt sure, would be the end. This little Pixie was going to stand there pointing with the extended chrome stick and let me die.

Through my blurred eyes she looked like the Grim Reaper holding out a bony finger of death. Perhaps it was for the best. Through all this agony I remembered Jennifer waiting above in the railway carriage…Things changed.

Moments later I was standing at the bar. She was laughing at some silly thing I'd mentioned moments before. We were both drinking very cool champagne, stunningly refreshing, putting out the flaming agony in my throat. This was a blessed relief. Moments before I thought I was going to die, now I could no longer feel any terrible acid dry ripping at my solar plexus. I was no longer retching with incredible body breaking violence. Now I was standing at the bar on a train with a very beautiful woman, and the music played on, and on, and on till dawn 295 miles away. I stayed with her all night, all the way to a distant mysterious place.

CHAPTER 26

Crazy auntie in crazy daze in August 1973.

The only undamaged item in my flat came as a surprise. I had a telephone and it was in one piece. During my searching I was so intent on finding money and drugs, I hadn't noticed it. It was a slightly depressing discovery. If I hadn't noticed this searching my flat then what else was slipping through my vision filter? I might be looking straight at my stash and not seeing it.

The telephone cable hadn't even been wrenched from the wall. This was the real surprise. I'd expected Harry's henchmen to prevent me from ringing anybody. Then I started to think perhaps the phone was connected with a purpose in mind. Had they tapped in another line and were listening in from one of the other flats? I was getting too paranoid for my own good. I knew they may be devious, but not that smart. I hoped!

I didn't discover my telephone, it discovered me. Startled by the loud ringing I threw myself to the floor and rolled over into a defensive position behind the sofa. Loud noise was now associated with Hartley Sparrow and the back of the settee offered some protection from Millicent's venom. I had a feeling it might be Vicky. Only one second later I was hoping it was her mother. I was wrong on both counts.

The voice on the telephone came as a surprise. It was my mother Iris. I don't know how long it had been since we'd talked. For all I knew we may have argued bitterly only days before, or not spoken in an age. I was totally unaware of the current dynamic. We might have baked cakes last week, laughing and joking happily together. What did I know?

I didn't have time to think let alone speak. She'd already started. "Peter, come quickly to the old farm cottage. Something terrible has happened to the aunties,"

"What is it, mum? What's wrong with the aunties?" I replied, thinking not much could possibly happen to those old harridans. They were made of stainless steel after all.

"Just come to the cottage now! Right now! Don't waste any time!" were the final words before she hung up. The whole conversation had taken less than twenty seconds giving me no chance to think of anything. What did this mean? The silence ringing in my ears was deafening to the point of leaving me dazed. I think I stood still for some seconds pondering my mother's words. I snapped into action.

Once on the move I didn't waste any time and was through the door towards the street before I had time to fret about Double-Barrelled Dave waiting in hiding for me. My car was a ruin, so I started running down the road and stuck my thumb out hoping against hope for a lift. I was running on adrenaline because my mother had sounded frantic.

For once during this grey miserable Sunday the rain had stopped, and to my knowledge I wasn't being watched. My luck improved further when I saw another minicab, a rather tatty Austin 1300 in a sort of vile dark green colour with a grey front wing replacing either rust or accident damage. Minicabs are not supposed to stop when hailed by the public, you ring up the office and arrange the pickup. This guy stopped at the merest hand gesture from me. The negotiation was quite abrupt. I asked him how much money he wanted to drive me out to the farm. He said normally it was whatever, but because he'd stopped illegally it was double. I paid him anyway.

I arrived at the farm in a matter of minutes, paid the man, didn't tip him, and was greeted at the main gate by Jane who was giving me a rather strange look. You'll start to understand when I tell you what happened next. Without any further ado we rushed up the path past the new farmhouse and down onto the old lane. This led us the extra quarter a mile to the old farm cottages which originally had housed three families, and after a conversion in the early part of the century one family in cramped conditions. Now after a second restoration it was a rather cosy lair for my two widowed aunties.

Tonight it was a fortress and not the cosy quiet little cottage I'd come to know and avoid as a boy. It was like an enchanted cottage in some Grimm fairytale. You couldn't approach it without being seen, and once seen the disgruntled dragon aunties would pounce with barbed criticism. There was no escape from the tongue lashing no matter how hard you tried. Innocence was tried, it failed, and cuteness was used by my sister, which failed. When an old relation died of influenza I wondered if we could buy some for the aunties. I was only four.

About one hundred yards from the cottage Jane and I were startled by my mother jumping out of the dense shrubbery that lined the drive approaching the cottage. She was waving both arms, grabbing at us, preventing us from going any further, and she looked very scared. "We can't go any nearer! The aunties have gone insane, quite mad, and violent!" My mother said.

"What?"

"Aunt Violet is dug in with a twelve-bore shotgun. She keeps taking pot-shots at anything that moves. I keep shouting it's me, but she seems to think Beatrix is holding me hostage, using me as bait to lure her out and make the kill. I think if the three of us talk to her we could persuade Violet to surrender." I was baffled.

All three of us were hiding behind a thick rhododendron bush. This was far enough away and thick enough to stop the shotgun pellets, but also near enough to be heard. Each of us in turn tried to persuade Violet she was safe and we weren't trying to flush her out to murder her.

At first she was having none of this. Then we pointed out that Auntie Beatrix was nowhere near the cottage because everyone could hear sporadic bangs coming from down near the old copse. Violet began to believe she was no longer under threat. After four or five minutes of persuasion a white head appeared above the sofa wedged across an open front door, a floral patterned barricade and her firing position.

Auntie Violet, at my mother's request, laid her weapon on the settee, and came out of the house straight towards us. She was difficult to see in the darkness with her usual bleak, dark clothes. At that moment we didn't know the significance of the black clothes, but we were to discover for ourselves why Violet had been dug in behind the sofa. Beatrix had been blazing away with her favourite shotgun at her favourite ally in torture – her sister. It was quite inexplicable.

When Violet had settled down to a level where she was coherent, my mother ushered her off down the lane away from the gunshots towards the new farmhouse where sanctuary beckoned. My mother had retrieved the shotgun from the settee in the cottage, and I did notice she'd picked up all the spare cartridges. She wasn't going to be too cavalier with Beattie running around wild. Jane and I were left without any form of protection during our quest to discover what was eating into my large auntie. She wasn't going to be too hard to find firing both barrels in quick succession. As fast as any experienced hunter out looking for pheasant, her reloading was astonishing. The gun fired with two quick reports, only seconds passing before more shots.

We had secured flashlights from inside the cottage. The aunties always have them handy for the power cuts, though I can't remember there ever being one. They were still living in the World War II black out. We used the flashlight only when necessary for guidance. A beam of light would be an ideal target for Beatrix, but why Auntie Violet had been targeted we had no idea. Beattie was now paying attention to something else. My sister seemed to think I was responsible for this madness, and until the situation became clear I didn't understand why.

Jane had already glimpsed Beattie in action. She'd received the first emergency call from my mother, and I was only called later after this strange situation had spiralled out of control. It started when my mother received the hysterical phone call from Violet. At first she thought it was an exaggeration. After two large bangs the phone was dropped and background screaming persuaded her otherwise. She knew something strange and dangerous was happening.

As Jane and I arrived at the copse the clouds were breaking apart. It was almost a full moon, you could see quite clearly and there before us stood a sight no young man should ever be witness to. It was far worse than any werewolf movie, far worse than any other type of horror movie, and even Hollywood couldn't construct a monster so fearsome. This was my auntie out exploring free-form hunting!

She was, for all intents and purposes, trying to kill off every crow in the world. She hated crows, she had always hated crows. She found their sombre noises made in the winter depressing and loathed the amount of damage she claimed they did to the crops. I wasn't too sure they did much damage however Beatrix hated crows, black crows.

What she was doing was plain and simple. She was trying to kill them all with her shotgun. How she was attempting this was a sight for other people's sore eyes. She was dressed in wellingtons, and around her shoulder she wore an enormously proportioned canvas bag. At the beginning of this madness it had been crammed full of cartridges. The number of cartridges in her possession had diminished by a considerable amount. Judging by the rapidity of the shots she was now probably down to her last thirty. If we waited long enough she would run out of ammunition, but in the meantime the rest of her dress code begs to be explained.

Can you imagine a fully grown rhino in a wildlife documentary with all the pictures taken from behind, but in the case of this rhino it would be coloured pink, and be the fattest rhino you'd ever seen. Auntie Beattie was wearing what she was born in, but this suit of skin had grown blotchy, veined and to enormous proportions. She was shooting alfresco, naked apart from the bag and wellingtons.

Even more shocking was her language. Every single time she pulled the trigger, or thought she saw a bird, there would be swearing, always a four letter word or a derivative. So the hunting party was carried out with a soundtrack something like this: bang! "C..t". Bang! "F..kers". Bang! "C.. ts", and so on. She was a one-man, or shall I say one-woman killing machine. It was perfect synergy between cordite and Tourette's syndrome.

I told my sister to go back to the cottage and get a large blanket. I knew she would eventually stop shooting. I thought she was crazy with drink. Too much sweet sherry had finally tipped her into alcohol-induced insanity. I was slightly off the mark with that one, wrong about the drink as events would prove. My sister had returned with two large blankets. My auntie remained in the copse blazing away into the darkness with her cordite-fuelled Tourette's at full steam.

I don't know if the shotgun was scary, or all those mottled acres of nakedness. If it hadn't been so insane the whole montage would have been quite amusing. My sister, to her later shame, started a fit of giggling. I felt like roaring with laughter, prudence being the better part of valour in this particular case. My auntie may have heard us and interpreted laughter as being taunted by more f..king crows! We may have died of belly laughs.

After about ten more minutes of wild anti-crow rage Beattie finally ran out of cartridges. She continued the fight by grabbing the barrel of the gun which must've been incredibly hot. It was hefted with both hands to be used as a wooden ended club. After a few fruitless swings she slung it up into a tree in a last attempt to kill one last black crow. The swearing was unabated throughout the shooting and into the club wielding phase. Now she was unarmed and impotent. She let out one last cry finishing with, "You're all fucking cunts! I'll see you all dead you cunts!"

Beatrix slumped to the floor as if somebody had pulled the air plug out of a blow-up figure. She visibly started to sag at the end of the ammunition, and with the gun now somewhere deep in the undergrowth of the copse she was in meltdown. That's what it looked like. First she was on her knees then she flopped forward onto the wet grass and proceeded to do what appeared to be the breaststroke. She was moving in a casual breaststroke style, looking around as if enjoying a swim in some warm and pleasant ocean.

We didn't dare to approach this strange apparition. We were starting to think she was in some kind of deep trance or sleepwalking. Waking her might be fatal. After stroking casually across this imagined bay for a few minutes she tired deciding to float for a while. Rolling onto her back with arms behind her head produced the most flagrant display of huge breasts and body hair I've ever witnessed in my life. It was an overt exhibition that would last the most voyeuristic lover of the flesh many lifetimes. It was the Eldorado of skin, the Fort Knox of mottled heavy flesh.

Later in my life I was once witness to a terrible accident, unfortunate enough to be the person to cover the body of the victim. He was completely mangled, a horrible grotesque mess.. Two of us covered him up. Both of us did this by looking out of the corner of our eyes, just on the edge of peripheral vision. Similar to when you see a squashed animal on the road, you don't look directly at it but steer round it using peripheral vision. It was this method Jane and I used with Auntie Beattie. We sidled up to her both looking the other way, so on the limit of our peripheral vision she was just a pink blob, a big pink blob, but a pink blob nevertheless! We finally had the prostrate auntie wrapped in a blanket. She didn't seem to have any violence left in her until she saw my sister who was wearing her leather jacket.

"My, you're big! You must be the king of the crows. Die!" Beattie said, lunging forward towards Jane hefting one of her large, very fleshy arms. Her fist contacted Jane's jaw with an amazing accuracy for a woman who had all the appearance of total exhaustion. She connected right in the sweet spot that boxers aimed for. Jane was lying stunned and semiconscious in the wet grass. My auntie, with a gleam in her eyes, shouted, "I've killed the king, I've killed the f.. king king!" Then she appeared to pass out. The night was very quiet at last.

I tended to my sister for a couple of minutes until she started to come round, rather dazed and angry in the extreme. Whether this was because she'd been caught by the punch or with me I wasn't sure. I wrapped my sister in a blanket, telling her not to move from the spot and to remain vigilant watching the sleeping Beattie. "Don't open your blanket to reveal what you're wearing underneath. She may rear up again like a cobra." My auntie would never let sleeping dogs lie. She would use the last of her strength to make her point.

During Beattie's wild swing at my sister the blanket had fallen away from her upper body. Seeing my auntie's huge breasts swing one way and the other as she used her fists was an image I didn't want to relive ever again. The swinging breasts were more appalling than her attack on my sister. I went off towards the cottage to make some tea or soup. I would bring it out to them in one of the many thermos flasks my auntie seemed to own. When moving about on the farm these two women appeared to always be clutching a thermos ready for any cold snap or emergency, even in the height of summer, so finding one wasn't going to be difficult.

Of course I had another motive for going to the cottage alone. It was convenient to do a quick search. I had too much of an idea why my auntie was crazy. She was as high as a kite on LSD! The only way she could be high was if she'd ingested it quite recently at the cottage. Inside the cottage everything was in disarray. Both windows were blown in with the tattered curtains looking grotesque as they moved in the light breeze. The banister rail going up from the lounge had three spindles missing, and an enormous amount of damage to the rail itself. Everywhere inside the cottage was gouged and peppered by small holes. The pock marked settee was across half the doorway. It had been pulled aside so my Auntie Violet could leave the house. The back of this generously stuffed settee was in tatters from many direct hits. Luckily my Auntie Violet had the wherewithal to fire warning shots over Beattie's head to drive her back, and was smart enough to stay low behind the settee.

She had managed to drag the phone across to her command position behind the makeshift barricade. It had a cable long enough to run to the front windows and up to the bedrooms at night. The aunties liked to have the phone near them "just in case". I never knew quite what this meant, but I did now, and I had no idea their emergency would ever be like this. I imagined one of them would have a heart attack, a stroke or a nasty fall. The idea that one of them would be high on LSD was quite beyond my imagination.

When you're young you never understand the fear of decrepitude. The words, just in case, filled many scenarios, none of which included a naked female hippo with a shotgun. As a small boy suffering with aunties and their version of just in case, I always thought of illness or invading armies, even alien invasion. Tonight, I've got to admit, did have me laughing slightly too much which made me laugh even more when I thought about my aunties telling me every time I ever laughed at anything that "this is no laughing matter"!

The kitchen revealed a pile of Beattie's discarded clothes along with her favourite grotesquely frilly, flower-covered apron. The large farmhouse table was covered in baking materials. I had no idea why. My aunties relied entirely on my mother for baking skills. They had both been very capable bakers. At times when I was a small boy they produced a wondrous variety of delicious scones, sponges and pastries. However, of late my aunties relied on my mother for all their baking needs. Beattie hadn't wielded a rolling pin for a considerable time, apart of course from chasing the odd rat around. It was a farmhouse, after all, and the door was always open in the summer.

On the table was a great variety of baking goods, most of which were flour and butter, but the source of my interest were the additives. She had put out all the pots of jam, mincemeat, which isn't meat at all, a fact that always amused me as a child. Best of all she had some little bottles of essences, most of which had been high up above the electric meter in the spice cupboard for some years. To gain any access you needed a set of stepladders. I was certain Beattie hadn't risked her chubby neck on the ladders, and I had to assume Violet was co-opted to do the mountaineering.

To cut to the chase, somebody, and it may have been my mother volunteering earlier in the day, had brought down all these little bottles of essences, most of which had handwritten labels. Others had labels that were unreadable with age. One of them had a bright green label. Normally it contained some very strange peppermint flavoured essence, but time always turned this delightful flavour into a sticky solid. This little green labelled bottle stood out amongst all the rest, and on a subliminal level attracted me. I recognised it, and I knew why!

In that moment I realised LSD can be a liquid – lysergic disulphide. I was hiding it in a bottle the aunties would never see, secreted at the back of a high cupboard where in normal circumstances it would be undisturbed for a lifetime, at least a lifetime for my aunties. For some reason they'd decided to bake. The old bottles all needed tasting and relabelled. Essences that failed to meet the correct standard would be thrown away. Auntie Beattie had obviously shaken each of the small bottles against her fingertip to release the flavour and then popped it on the end tongue for the tasting. Most had not been opened. You could see that from the dust. This bottle with the bright green label was more attractive than the others. This would explain why it was one of the first to be experimented with, and this was the moment Beattie began her recreational drug experience.

It was a revelation, I knew I'd found all the LSD. This small bottle was enough, if used with a syringe to meter out the liquid it would provide hundreds of doses, if not thousands. I examined the bottles more thoroughly discovering that only eight bottles had labels low down. These all seemed to be the most attractive bottles and the least dusty. All these could be the hiding place for the LSD. I didn't want to take any chances. All the bottles were on the table, the cupboard was bare so to speak, and my cup was overflowing. Looking around I found a pillow case in the washing and placed all the bottles on the table in it, every single last one.

I could hear the sound of footfalls on the drive. I had to be quick! I dived out of the back of the cottage which wasn't as quick as I had hoped because the door was a massively bolted very thick oak, a godsend to my Auntie Violet. On opening the door the light from the kitchen revealed a ragged scarring on the outside from numerous shotgun blasts, some of which had gouged great splinters from the door, luckily for Violet none penetrating it. I had only seconds to hide the bottles outside, pushing them under some bushes and kicking some ground mulch over anything that showed white. As I took a final glance at the hiding place I turned to look at the back door. Framed in it was my sister.

"We're all going to the farmhouse. You're coming too! Regardless of what you say, we're sorting this out!" Jane said.

I wondered how long she had been standing at the doorway. Had she seen me burying the bag, or did she think I was out the back examining the door or taking a leak?

More questions, no answers.

CHAPTER 27

Crazy daze. Fighting aunties and wild mothers, August 1973.

"Your Sid was a bastard, a cheap spiv, a coward of a man!" Violet spat these words across the family kitchen. We all looked at her in astonishment. Violet was directing full venom on her sister Beatrix.

"Sailor Jack, sailor Jack won't come back. I don't think he's dead I think he's messing about with the girls somewhere. Always liked sex, used to touch me, try and seduce me. He was a fucker." Beattie remained under the influence, or so we thought!

Violet reared up and rushed across the room. She grabbed the seated Beattie by the hair. The thin woman dragged her large sister to her feet. To our horror the blanket fell away again, and we were subjected to the dreadful montage. Violet leaned in until she was less than an inch away from the wobbling Beattie's chubby veined nose. "My Jack volunteered and lost his life fighting for this country. He was a wonderful husband, a kind and generous lover to me, and ONLY me. You're jealous, you fat old cow!"

"My lovely Sidney lost his life in the war. My Sid was doing his bit. You know some people had to stay at home because some people didn't have the health!" Beattie was crying, something I'd never seen.

"Don't make me laugh. My Jack died in ice-cold oil-filled water. Your Sidney, your precious Sid, was crushed to death by a crate of contraband stockings. You know the driver panicked when the police came and the box fell on top of him. There was never anything wrong with your husband apart from greed, and his liking for fast cars and cheap girls. He never wanted to screw you, you fat old bitch!"

"Violet! Beattie! This isn't like you. Please stop it. You're sisters and you're hurting yourselves!" Iris my mother moved in separating them.

"If that fat bitch ever bad mouths my Jack again I will take the shotgun and blow her brains out!" Violet had gone from thin mouse to tigress, and I don't think she was ever going to let Beattie dominate again.

"Come on, calm down. You two (she was pointing at my sister and I) help me with the aunties. Get some cocoa on while I attempt to settle them. Beattie's had a bit of a turn (my mother looked at me with steely eyes), and Violet has been very stressed tonight. A good night's sleep and it'll all be different in the morning." My mother said this whilst pulling a grim face to my sister Jane. Would it be all right in the morning or ever again between the sisters?

The aunties were both gently wrapped in blankets and after two hours of kind words and a large amount of medicinal alcohol they were both calm enough to be helped up to the bedroom.

The aunties were now tucked up in bed, one of the double beds in a guest room. They often stayed over if it got too late and Beattie had taken a little too much medicinal whisky. Giving my auntie an alcoholic drink tonight didn't seem like a smart idea. However, normally you could never argue with Beattie, – ever. Tonight Violet had proved an exception to the rule. With most of the whiskey finished the two of them were tired. In the last hour they hadn't mentioned there violent exchange, as if the venomous words had never been spoken.

In the morning shame would prevent Beattie from ever talking about it. She would forget it, her mind was made up, and that would be it. They always slept in the same bed at the farmhouse. At the cottage they had their own rooms both with very different distinct styles, Beatrice chintz, Violet stainless steel and science fiction, but in the family home they shared a bed. Tonight Violet would be awake the whole time watching to see if her beloved sister was going to be all right. Auntie Violet was taking no chances. She was wearing a white nightgown borrowed from my mother. No crow shades!

Down in the kitchen the remains of our family were sitting round the large table, my mother, an angry-looking brother George who had returned from a neighbouring farm, my sister Jane who now sported a very bruised cheek, and myself who was not looking forward to the upcoming interrogation. Rather strangely my mother Iris set it off with something I didn't expect.

"George, haven't you got work to do? I don't want this turning into a shouting match, some stupid sibling argument. Just go and do what you have to do on the farm!" Iris said this with quiet authority, and what surprised me was George picked up a piece of cake, and he then pointed a finger at me with an almost pistol-like gesture. My brother left the kitchen without saying a word. The finger wasn't a death threat it was more an indication to behave. I think!

"So, Peter… is this nonsense about having amnesia your method of wheedling your way out of this?" Iris said. This, of course, is where I was going to take centre stage and explain everything. So without any further ado I ran most of, but not all, the story past my mother who was less than impressed.

"You're very consistent with your story, but how did you know where the drugs were? Don't lie to me. I know you hid them," Jane chipped in. She'd seen me hiding them and now my mother knew.

My mother looked at me sizing up the situation. She knew I was involved in drug dealing, and I didn't doubt we'd argued about it. However, no matter what scars she bore from past arguments I had no bitter words to remember, no recollection of cruelly spoken remarks. As far as I was concerned we had not spoken for seven hundred days.

"You little shit! You drugged up Beattie! You could have killed them both! And if you don't know anything, how do you know where the drugs were? No more bloody lies!" This came as a surprise coming from my mother. I had never, ever, heard her swear, not once in all my life apart from one time when she took a vicious kick to the thigh from a dairy bull.

I had no choice but to explain all of it to again, of course, missing out the very interesting sexual learning experience with Samantha, and the bit with Baby Doll which I still didn't understand. As I went through the story once again I was trying to clarify in my own mind what had happened. The bottles of LSD finally raised their ugly little stoppers. Questions I couldn't answer came to mind. I explained the difficult task of driving the car on the road, and how after a few minutes I gained the level of competence of an experienced driver. The skills were hidden inside but how I accessed memories was something I hadn't yet managed to get a handle on. I failed to explain my rapid learning curve in the bedroom. Some things you just can't tell your mother.

Jane believed me to a point, but my mother was less easy to convince. However, I pressed on trying to explain my instincts driving me to find the money in the dust bag of the vacuum cleaner and the strange feeling that the teddy bears contained something. I didn't put my head back in the lingerie drawer with its sensation of deep desires. That would be too much!

I told my audience I knew Beattie was high after I'd seen her in action, and even her beloved sister Violet had nearly become a dead crow nailed to a tree.

I'm not sure Beattie would have gone as far as that, or she might! Can you imagine if Beattie had managed to kill Violet and nail her to a tree? I imagine the crucified auntie story would've been the stuff of Sunday tabloid legend. I explained that I didn't know if I'd ever taken LSD. At this my mother raised a rather elegant eyebrow as if to say, *"You're quite good at this forgetting thing. Persuade me"*.

"I figured out that whatever she'd taken was in the house, so when the opportunity presented itself I searched the cottage. I saw the bottles and there was something irresistible about the one with the green label. It stood out from the crowd. That's when I realised it wasn't just bits of paper or small pills. It was really a liquid and I had all of it, several thousand pounds worth of the stuff, so where have I hidden the money and how do I get out of this situation?" My words were something like that.

Jane broke in to the conversation. "How did you get here so fast? You don't have a car, not one that works anyway. Who gave you a lift?"

"A minicab and the bastard made me pay double for thumbing him down!"

"You can't thumb a minicab, and on a Sunday night?" Jane was sharp and smart, unlike me.

"I wasn't far from the flat, you know, running along holding my thumb out. The man just came up from behind and stopped."

"You live on a quiet housing estate. I think he was following you!" Jane said. I pondered this and was certain that he wasn't. A few seconds later I was wavering. It did seem a bit odd, two mini cab rides in the same day, in the same cab.

My sister shrugged her shoulders and left the room, but not before pointing at me and menacingly adding, "Following you!"

My mother was not to be distracted by the minicab debate. She continued cross examining me. How could I possibly be the inexperienced boy who'd left the house full of innocence two years before? Hearing my story again after all these years I now understand why my mother doubted me. It was all too far-fetched and she left me in no illusion, "If this is some kind of trick I promise I will never speak to you again!"

It wasn't a trick. I was only able to pick things up when the right key hit me, and there hadn't been many of those. One day everything might come back in a flood. Something inside may push it to the front, but for now it was like dancing with shadows.

Jane returned to the kitchen, I thought she'd been upstairs dressing her wounds. My sister was being more proactive and she'd gone down the farm track to the gate to see if I was being watched. Both of us were surprised when she announced that the minicab was parked in a field entrance about two hundred yards down the main road. She could see the glint of the windscreen in the moonlight.

She'd followed the hedgerow until a full view of the car was possible without letting the driver ironically see he was being watched by what he was watching. The minicab driver wasn't having too much luck. He was watching me, but of course in the days before mobile phones he had no way of telling whoever put him up to it where I was. The only way he could do this was leave the scene of his surveillance, a risky move.

My mother rose from the table, walked over to the electric kettle, filled it and turned it on. She fixed me with a steely gaze and spoke. "You two have a cup of tea. I've got a little errand to run." With this she went to the cupboard in the corner and pulled out a very nice double-barrelled lady's shotgun. She used this to shoot rats in the farmyard. We both rose to stop her, she held out a calming hand,

"I'm tougher than you think and I've got some rat hunting to do. Don't follow me!" She donned her wax jacket, placed a large number of cartridges in a pocket, and marched out of the kitchen. My sister and I just stared at each other dumbstruck.

What happened next was described to us by my mother on her return minutes later. It went something like this. "I found the little rat in the field entrance and shot him!" We were speechless for several seconds, stunned that my mother would go out with vengeance in her heart and murder somebody in cold blood with very little evidence of any crime.

"He's not dead, but I think he wet his pants." Then she laughed. My sister told me later this was the first time she laughed since my father died. Jane went on to say that was the moment my mother seemed to become herself again. It was a strange way of finding yourself, by making some weasel minicab driver piss his pants.

My mother explained everything. She'd seen him sitting there with a window open smoking probably his sixtieth cigarette of the day whilst he stared up the road in a casual manner, but it was obvious he was keeping the farm entrance under surveillance. Despite our recent history she was enraged that somebody was watching me. She'd already lost her husband, her older son George was so wrapped up in the farm that nowadays they never seemed to communicate. This left Iris stranded in a house full of women. She was determined they were not going to take me away from her, no matter how dark my past. She was starting to believe my story, but then mothers always do believe their sons are angels, true story or not. "He's a good lad", how many times have you heard that from the gangster's mother?

Iris was a good shot, having years of practice as a girl brought up in a family of doctors on an old farm run by her grandfather, and of late shooting rats by the dozen in the farmyard. The first shot glanced across the windscreen of the car shattering it into the lap of the driver who immediately spat is cigarette out which burnt its way through his trouser leg to his testicles in a matter of seconds. He was too scared to look for it, or to jump from the car. The second shot my mother put through the back side window making him feel that the next one would be for him. The panic set in. He was being burnt alive by a cigarette he didn't have time to look for, and he didn't need to find as his fear did the job. He pissed his pants.

He was frantically trying to find the keys he'd placed on the floor of the minicab. Probably he'd left the vehicle on occasion to mope about in the lane trying to catch glimpses of the farmhouse through the trees along the drive… My mother quickly reloaded and fired two more shots at the car. The first was aimed squarely at the door panel, the second scraped across the rear window blowing that into fragments as well. She reloaded the gun yet again. These cartridges did not contain particularly large pellets. A shot to the face would be very serious, but a hit to the body at that range might bring some blood up through the clothes, or at least a lot of high-quality bruising.

She fired two more shots at the car, both into the rear door. The driver was cowering on the floor by now, so she poked the shotgun into his ear. What he hadn't realised was my mother was very careful not to murder him. She hadn't reloaded the gun. Having a hot barrel thrust into your ear can be quite persuasive. She asked him who'd sent him to watch me, and he didn't hesitate in replying that somebody called Dave had sent him. He owed him a favour, a big favour, and was desperate the gunmen didn't find out he'd spilled the beans. This driver was clearly in trouble. The poor man was now clearly terrified of both Dave and my incredible mother.

The minicab driver was in a miserable state, though he was a particularly miserable creature to start with having a very dilapidated body for a man of his age including a lack of teeth. He only had three all stained brown with nicotine, and his breath wasn't going to win him any favours either. His misery was growing by the minute: he was stuck between a rock and a very determined woman from the farm. My mother informed him I'd left by another entrance at least half an hour ago. I could be anywhere. His cab was a mess, his trousers soiled, his luck gone, and now he had to tell the lovely Hartley Sparrow he'd lost me. She finished the one-way conversation, "If any of your friends come up here I will not hesitate to shoot. There's nothing here for your kind but lead! Take this message to anybody who's interested!"

I was going to enjoy a good night's sleep in my old bed, tucked up warm with cocoa, all supplied by my ferocious mother, a woman who'd rediscovered herself on that damp moonlit night. She was still full of fury at my father's untimely death, but had stepped out from under a blanket of grief. I know she didn't blame me for his death, because she was unaware of our fight and would never learn of it. My tough mother had defended her cubs like a wounded lioness. All I hoped was the cab driver shit himself as well. I know I would have!

The next morning was a big surprise for me as 6am was something I haven't seen in a long time. I was on a farm after all. Jane missed work phoning in to say she had a headache which in some ways wasn't far from the truth; she had a shiner from the massive ham-fist of a blow delivered by Beatrix. The aunties were left in peace, and this was not just so they could rest. This move was considered prudent so that we could search their cottage, their intimate items, without their knowledge. My mother insisted we never ever tell the aunties the real reason for the madness. We should suggest perhaps one of the bottles had got some form of botulism or some other such food poisoning that my auntie had a bad reaction to. Perhaps she was lucky to be alive. Violet was.

This was a good explanation because it gave us a good reason for the missing bottles. Iris wanted to get rid of them permanently at first. Then she realised they might be a bargaining chip if I were to avoid some evil fate. Whether they were going to kill me or not, I didn't know, neither did my family. We didn't want to take any risks so the six little bottles were moved back down to the farmhouse and stashed carefully away in my mother's hidden private safe, not the farm safe.

I took one bottle with me, the little bottle with the green label to demonstrate if the need arose that I was in possession of the stuff, and the rest of it was safely stashed away. This seemed to be a very thin insurance policy, a sort of whole life with no profits policy. They could torture me to reveal the location of the stash in my mother's safe, and I could think of two or three people who would enjoy the job.

We conducted a thorough search during which I spent ages staring at different objects, looking trancelike at different pieces of furniture, various cubbyholes, and anything to ignite the fire of memory. In two hours there'd been no inspirations. It was now 8:30am on Monday morning with my evening trip to The Cauldron approaching too quickly, and not a penny found. The only money available was the £1000 I found in the vacuum cleaner, but I suspected it was part of my profits, not part of the missing £10,000! How was I to know?

Where to next? I needed inspiration if I were to survive.

CHAPTER 28

Right here right now, with a bit of sartorial camping.

I was resting outside in the cool morning sunshine. In some small corner of my body somewhere not detectable by medical tests, I was starting to feel slightly better. Not a great leap forward in bursting physical health, more of a subtle change. The number of pills I was taking every day had gone down to about fourteen which is quite a low number when you're suffering from this illness. To me I was taking far too many of these damned drugs, and a future without the constant tyranny of medication will be just fine by me. When I think about it, having a future even with some pills is also fine by me.

Doing anything physical for more than half an hour was almost impossible leaving me wrung out like an old dish rag. One day I walked a dog very slowly for about six hundred yards. On the return I had to go to bed and rest for several hours. Inside me the feeling of total fatigue nagged at my psyche. I was like a torch fitted with very old batteries functioning in a limited way, throwing out a dim light of little use. I functioned in a way that was alive, not really living.

Other people had suffered far more than I ever would. I continued fighting my inner diseases with other people's terrible experiences.

Rachel focused on Abraham's relationship with Heinrich Haussler, the SS officer who picked him out for special attention. Whether the attention was special is debatable. The German officer was bored, often seeking out little games to play. He may have had a dozen different people he played mind games with. Sometimes, if deep boredom set in, he would turn his little games violent in a fatal way. This was his way of passing some time. He would have preferred to have been killing real soldiers, not eliminating a bunch of bankers and tailors.

Heinrich's other victims did not matter to Abraham. The only thing on his mind was staying alive until freedom came. The Russian roulette was now over which meant the meagre supply of hard bread and cheese was no longer available. Two weeks had passed since the last terrifying click of the revolver including moments later when the German opened the chamber of the gun and placed five more bullets in it. After doing this he spun the chamber around and pointed the gun at Abraham's head and laughed to himself. "I haven't finished with you yet. I'll think of something else. Go!" Haussler said, with his usual smile.

Rachel told me she thought this long-term stress, coupled with the appalling concentration camp diet, was what led to Abraham's heart attack some thirty years later. I wasn't sure about this as Abraham Wilson, by the time of his death, had grown to a considerable size, making up for all the years of desperate hunger through the 1940s. As a few family dinners round the table at their house had revealed to me, Abraham possessed a voracious appetite. This and the fact that Rachel swears he was killed by a Mercedes, a German car doesn't really add up. However, this is Rachel's story.

In her story he was killed by a Mercedes car. In fact he was more likely to have been killed by the *patisserie* he was heading for across the busy high street to purchase God knows how many cakes. The car didn't manage to hit Mr Wilson. The driver applied his brakes producing a massive screech of tyres as a large man in a suit stepped out into the road. The driver's hand was pressed hard on the chrome horn rim in the centre of the steering wheel producing a very loud Teutonic bellow. This made Abraham jump forward with surprise, and even break into a lumbering run for a few strides. When he reached the sidewalk surprised and breathless his heart was pumping on adrenaline, its cholesterol filled arteries fighting to supply the muscle. It was all too much for a man who'd overindulged for thirty years. He dropped dead right there on the pavement in the doorway of the *patisserie*, a massive coronary taking his life in seconds. After surviving all those years on a knife edge it came to this, death by cake knife.

Rachel likes to believe that without the shock her beloved husband would have gone on for decades. He may have lasted another month or had a mild heart attack alerting the doctors to his problems. This could have led to surgery or a bypass operation, but it would not have been as straightforward as today with the technology used in 1985. However, it might have given him a chance. That is, of course, if he'd had a mild heart attack and was somewhere near help. Abraham suffered a huge coronary outside the very food emporium that had helped to clog his overburdened arteries.

Back at the camp Abraham had lived through the last four or five days of the thirty day Russian roulette thinking that Heinrich would let him believe he would live, only to shoot him on the last day. No matter what he ate it never stayed inside him, the constant stress and the diseases of the camp making his bowels weak. Heinrich hadn't killed him on the last day, but it was a two-pronged sword. It gave hope, but he knew the officer would think of something else. Rachel told me about the last great torture.

The cold in the winter was horrible with a poor diet and the inadequate clothes letting in the terrible biting, icy wind. The summer coming was even worse. It spelt the beginning of disease breeding with a voracious appetite for human flesh. There were the flies, millions upon millions of flies. In all the rest of his life Abraham couldn't bear a single fly in the house. His paranoia about these creatures was profound. In the accounting shed the heat was starting to build, sweat was dripping from his forehead, and the sergeant in charge didn't like marks on the paper. Even if everything else was covered with a layer of filth, the accounting paperwork of the Third Reich had to be perfect.

It was in this environment along with a few other accountants and former bankers that Heinrich delivered his final psychological test. The German decided to create a fiction that somehow a devious Abraham was now helping him. Others could believe this because even with the starvation he had a metabolism that hung on to some of his fat. He wasn't very large, but compared to the others he was positively glowing with health even if this included a grey skin parlour. Occasionally one of the others zealously pointed out he looked remarkably healthy, almost suggesting he had secret supplies because he was passing information.

Rachel told me he remembered the day with a vivid frightening recollection. He was sitting at his desk when Heinrich entered the room and strolled over in a casual friendly manner, then insisted Abraham were to go immediately to his office. All this was spoken loudly as if to tell the others how special this man was. He had no choice but to do as ordered, and discover his final torture.

Heinrich suggested many things he could do to him; have him throw children's bodies into the ovens, or he could chat to people as they arrived assuring them the showers were really good, and they had nothing to fear. Abraham either snapped inside or found great courage when he told Heinrich to kill him because he wasn't going to do that to his own people. He'd already killed to stay alive, but something inside him said he wasn't going to betray anybody else.

"You are very brave Jew, and very lucky. I don't want to kill you yet. I want your own people to kill you, and if they don't before the end of this war, I will!" the Nazi officer confided to him. To Abraham's great surprise the officer told him the Russians were getting close. It had been a rumour in the camp for a few weeks, and nobody believed it. Everyone thought the promise of liberation so close was a cruel joke. He confided he wouldn't be there when the Russians or the Americans arrived in their push towards Berlin.

What he did tell Abraham, however, was if his own people hadn't killed him by then, just before he left, he would put several bullets in his stomach. He would die an agonising death. There was no escape from his death camp. In the meantime he would be his friend, his closest buddy, somebody who was always there for a laugh and a joke.

Two days later in the accounting shed it was midday and hot. There were so many gold teeth, dozens of spectacles, various bits of jewellery, anything that could be exchanged for money or goods to power the Reich's defiance of the Allied advance. There was always somebody willing to sell them armaments through the back door if the price was right, and the gold collected was of good quality.

He didn't realise Heinrich was standing behind him watching over his shoulder. Then the arm was around him, Heinrich loudly proclaimed his clothes to be disgusting and he would fix him up with something better within the day. After all, he was a very special man. The others in the shed watched intently without apparently moving their eyes away from their work. They watched in the way of the camp, in a way you'd never notice. Not for one second would they dare to fix the German in the eye. For that single moment of contact they could be beaten to death on the spot, or just kicked around for half an hour, then shot or left with injuries so bad they would die the same night. All of them secretly witnessed this exchange and were shocked.

Abraham prayed new clothes wouldn't arrive. Unfortunately he was taken away at seven in the evening by a young officer and instructed to pick out of the pile of clothes something not too good, but a lot better than what he was wearing. These should be clean and of good quality, clothes that would be his death sentence. Others looked on in disbelief as Abraham returned to the squalid dormitories dressed in quality clothing. All they had were meagre rags made of dirty paper.

"Why has he got those clothes? What has he done to deserve them? Is he a quisling, the big informer?" This was on all their lips. Very few would believe this was a form of torture. How can you be tortured when you're given good clothes, and look at him, he's not even thin. This was only the first day of suspicion.

He explained to anybody who would listen that the German was picking him out for some terrible psychological torture, wanting his own people to kill him. Some who knew Abraham and had been privy to his previous trials knew Heinrich was singling out this particular man for his twisted pleasure. Many others, however, didn't know Abraham and they thought him a traitor.

For Abraham things began to cool. After a week without a single visit from Heinrich he was starting to feel the German had forgotten him. Perhaps he was tied up in some war business now the Russians or was it the Americans were approaching. In the last two days in the still of the night everyone could hear rumbles like distant thunder. This would be the guns of the Allied armies coming towards them with rescue possibly only days away. The big question was would he survive those final days?

Nine days after the clothes incident Abraham was starting to look very similar to everybody else. The clothes were of good quality but the camp quickly degraded them into no more than expensive rags, so he began to relax a little looking more like the others. This is when Heinrich appear again. He marched into the shed accompanied by four other soldiers all with submachine guns. This looked like the end.

Lighting a cigarette he very carefully held it between his fingers before drawing on it with a joyous indulgence, and to Abraham's terror Heinrich sauntered over. He wasn't looking up at the German officer. Concentration on the work in hand seemed to be the only way he could react. He was quite shocked to feel a friendly arm around his shoulder. Heinrich whispered in his ear. "They think I'm having a joke with you. They think you are giving me information. I'm going to make them think you're helping me, a German. Now laugh or die," Heinrich said. Abraham laughed. It was very hollow.

Heinrich continued to have his arm around Abraham's shoulder. His cheek was almost touching the Jew's cheek. One of them smelt of expensive Paris aftershave and the other smelt disgusting. This didn't seem to put the officer off. He continued to stage mumble into Abraham's ear, then, much to his surprise, he reeled back in a roar of laughter saying to a startled audience, "That's really funny. I didn't know you Jews could be so amusing."

Heinrich pointed to a man in the far corner whose name was Benjamin. Heinrich ordered the guards to take him outside and shoot him immediately. The orders were carried out with the old accountant screaming all the way through the door and out into the yard beyond. He put up a good fight. He was kicking, gouging and clawing at anything he could, fearing not death but going out without a struggle. Seconds later there was a roar of machine gun fire, then silence.

"Good man. Thank you for the information," Heinrich said, still smiling. He then left the accounting shed to a silence that terrified Abraham. Benjamin had been one of those who understood.

The SS sergeant who had been overlooking the accountants was also summoned out of the room leaving only the prisoners. Abraham was berated by many for being an informer, a filthy quisling who was on the take. A few of the others defended Abraham knowing the Nazi's game. The sergeant was watching everything through a spy hole and he could see who was defending Abraham against the hostile reaction of several inmates. These men would be eliminated next leaving this particular Jewish man an isolated island almost certain to die at the hands of his own people.

No matter what he said he was the one in good clothes, the man who had blatantly condemned another. Some of the other accountants continued defending him. This wouldn't last, because two days later Heinrich appeared again producing much the same stage act as before, this time picking another of Abraham's allies. He wasn't shot outside the shed like the other man. No, he disappeared, until one of the others reported seeing him lying dead next to the electric fence. He'd been badly tortured to the point where he might have thrown himself on the fence to finish it. His other supporters melted away frightened of being eliminated, and now no one would protest his innocence!

Two days later he remained alive, and there were no visits from the officer to the accounting shed. There could be no possible relaxation because he knew if the Jews didn't kill him, Heinrich would! On the third day Heinrich came to him with the same act as before this time whispering the good news and of course the bad news. "The armies are only two days away at the most. I'm going to leave this dreadful camp very soon. Tomorrow, if you're still alive, I will kill you myself. I'm not going to waste ammunition. I'm going to beat you to death, very, very slowly!" He whispered all these words into Abraham's ear. After this he pointed at another unfortunate, even slapping Abraham on the shoulder saying loudly, "Good, very good!"

The last of his allies had disappeared. Abraham defended himself with an intense vigour against all accusations, pointing out the facts. "This is exactly what the Nazi bastard wants, my own people killing each other. It saves them the trouble of putting us into the gas showers then wasting fuel on the ovens."

The next morning the Allied armies were tantalisingly close, everyone had a glimmer of hope. The prisoners could hear the guns a short distance away. The fact Abraham could hear gun's was to him a miracle. He was still alive, not murdered in the night by his own people, now he dreaded a visit in the next few minutes. The Nazi butcher Heinrich would beat him to death so close to liberation, so close to a new life, so close, so desperately close!

Some of the senior Germans started to disappear. Abraham went into hiding under the latrines in the filthiest place on earth with a stench so appalling he emptied everything in his stomach within minutes. He was lying in excrement, along with several others all there for their own reasons, for thirty-one hours, until he heard cries of happiness from some and cries from others. Through a very small crack in the woodwork at the bottom of the latrine house he could see a pair of brown boots with green trousers above them. The Americans not the Russians had arrived. This was a better form of liberation, everybody knew that, and he was alive, thank the gods he was alive. He had to slap his own face to confirm he lived. Every part of his body was numb from the hours in that filth.

A few of the camp guards were in captivity. Most of this ragtag beaten army were lower ranked men who had been ordered to stay and fight to the last man. This enabled the senior officers who would be brought to trial for committing genocide the opportunity to escape. Heinrich had forgotten all about his little games.

At this point, hiding in filth so appalling he made a vow to himself. With the excrement only inches away from his face and his whole body smeared in the vile beyond vile he swore if he ever saw Heinrich Haussler again, regardless of a prison sentence or the death penalty, he would kill him with his bare hands. He was sure that with good nutrition and renewed strength he could physically kill the war-wounded Nazi with his bare hands.

This thought made him glow with joy. It would be tremendous as he crushed life from him. He could almost feel his hands around Heinrich's throat, and no more twisted words could come from his lying tongue. If he ever saw Heinrich nothing would stop him destroying this harbinger of evil.

He realised it was this thought of revenge that had kept him alive through those thirty-one soul sapping hours.

And I thought I was having a bad time when I suffered some urinal incontinence!

CHAPTER 29

Right here right now, chicken soup with a bad taste.

On reduced medication I had started to indulge in a little alcohol. We are only talking a couple of small glasses of red, or a couple of small cans of beer and no more. I was still ingesting a lot of medication by normal standards. However, compared to where I'd been I was barely in the league of pill taking at all. With all the sitting around I was starting to find it difficult to sleep, a big change from some weeks earlier when I was sleeping eighteen hours a day.

The beers help me to fall asleep. After that it's up to the other dimension to suck me in. I believe with all honesty, even now, that these experiences were not coming from inside my head. They were sliding in from another dimension. It was the profound reality of the experience, everything down to the tiniest detail, windblown insects crawling on your skin, the wind ruffling your hair, dust puffing up around your toes if you walked barefoot on the dry soil. Everything was there in those dreams, and unlike the normal world your capacity in this dimension was to understand all the sensations at once. There was no need to cherry pick the moments. It was all there in one glorious bright instant. No wonder I wanted to go to sleep so much, balancing this against the fact that I now want to be awake and alive full-time.

I'd floated off this particular evening thinking of an incident concerning Mr Wilson. Every time he saw blond-haired blue-eyed muscular men of a certain age, he scrutinised every single detail convinced that one day he would come across Heinrich Haussler. The chances of this happening were incredibly slim, almost impossible. It was an uncontrollable urge inside him to stare and assess anybody who could have possibly been Heinrich. On occasions he would strike up conversations with them, sometimes quite surprised to discover they were Scottish or, on one occasion, Swedish. This was a constant gut reaction seeing the Nazi in every blond-haired man on the street. I had started to see

Jennifer in the crowds, though on second inspection none of them looked remotely like her. She did only exist in that other dimension.

I was living in a conundrum, wanting to be in one place and wanting to be somewhere else. It was not an every night occurrence, however, joy of joys, tonight was one of those journeys of brilliance, tempered with trepidation over what the Lylybel would bring me. It wasn't always a joy to see this pixie, who assured me quite sternly that she wasn't one. Though she introduced me to my past memories and exacting the painful price, she was nevertheless captivating in her chameleon beauty, seemingly changing with the passing of the days, always recognisable but never quite the same. She was certainly the same person all the time. I think the mischief in her eyes changed with different stories. Her manner would reflect something she didn't know about but could sense coming.

Most of these dreams seem to entail some form of railway travel. It was never a great surprise to arrive in the other universe and to be standing on the station, or leaning on a level crossing gate, or even sitting in the sunshine outside a railway themed pub. On this occasion, however, I was wearing tweedy hiking gear from a bygone age. The day was not cold though you couldn't describe it as hot either, and the wind was blowing quite strongly, as always carrying the scents of a million flowers. In front of me on the bench was the inevitable pint of perfect real ale. I've never been a real ale drinker before. Now I was becoming quite an aficionado of the dark liquid. I burst out laughing as the pub sign bore the legend "The Steam Dragon". The sign itself was a curious mixture of a steam train at full speed with its belching stack producing a very exotic twirling mist that formed the shape of a dragon engulfing the rear of the train transforming it into this mythical creature. The painting was the most perfect pub sign I'd ever had the pleasure of sitting underneath.

Jennifer looked ridiculous with the sturdy boots, woolly socks, enormous Boy Scout-style shorts, and what could only be described in today's language as a hacking jacket. The image she presented was straight out of some 1930s mystery novel. The only saving grace was that her hair was free to the wind reflecting all its subtle chestnut hews in the sunshine. I knew hidden in her modest backpack, a canvas affair, would be lodged some hideous hat I would laugh at. She, of course, would defend it as perfect for the day. Perfect if you wanted a laugh!

We had a typical pub lunch, the usual affair of bread and cheese, all topped off with an enormous amount of pickle thankfully washed down by another pint of particularly glorious real ale. We hung about outside the pub for a good half hour before marching off towards the moorland fell which was hidden by the bulk of the hostelry. As we rounded the back of the public house I was amazed to see such a daunting rock face with steep crags looming up in the middle of what was essentially rolling countryside. The sky all around was a brilliant azure blue, but the crag itself was topped with swirling clouds forming a constant moving picture of shapes as shadows danced around the pinnacles of rock.

It was the first time in this dimension I'd seen anything you could call threatening. The whole of this wonderful world was perfect. Now before me stood this grit stone monolith with its crown of swirling cloud and mist. The profound contrast with the rest of the country side made it look ominous. I think in our world it would've just looked like another hill. Here it gave the impression it existed solely for the purpose of fell walking in a different weather to the normal perfection. There was no fear in me as we started out. The only thing scaring me was I knew Jennifer would put on some hideous hat!

The giant Irish wolfhound appeared out of the mist and fine rain to our right as we were three quarters of the way up the mountain, beyond the trees, walking across open moorland. It was carrying the briefcase in its teeth without any strain at all. This case must be weightless until it's needed, then assumes the proportions of weight and size necessary for the task in hand. The dog was wearing the strangest of hats that I feared would be presented to Jennifer. However, as it got closer the hat turned out to be the pixie dressed in what could only be described as a pantomime frog suit. All the while as they approached she was eating soup from a bowl using her webbed hand as a spoon. I was wondering if her fingers were burning. You could clearly see the steam rising from the little earthenware bowl. More disturbing than the soup eating was the constant supply of bread. All seemed to be plucked from inside the dogs left ear. A source that was strange and disgusting. The bread, however, looked white, fluffy and dry.

As the dog marched towards us with this strange creature perched on its head I was laughing with tears rolling down my face, or was it rain. I couldn't help myself. The appearance of the pixie was ridiculous. They stopped in front of us. I was concentrating hard on the bread eating exercise, looking deep into the dog's dark ear cavity every time the pixie fumbled to find some more bread. It was so dark I couldn't see anything until the bread was outside in the light.

It appeared too materialised in her hand as it came out of the shadow. This magical appearance had me captivated, concentrating every time she put her hand into O Duke's huge ear cavity. I was watching the darkness; a sudden difference in the atmosphere told me I was standing in the darkness. At least in there it was dry! I was disconcerted with the thought of standing inside the waxy darkness of the great dog's ear. It was dark, there was nothing I could do and I couldn't detect any wax.

I didn't dare move because the pixie was quite devious. I could have been standing on top of a very thin wall, so I concentrated on my balance in this total blackness. I had to check several times to see if my eyes were open. Even if they were there was nothing to see. A flood of grey light came in from above. The briefcase was being opened and looming above me were the huge faces of Jennifer and the Irish wolfhound. The pixie was nowhere to be seen until she sprang down from high on the dog's head and plunged into the case feet first much the same as a giant frog, because now she was as big as me. Had I shrunk? I'm not sure, or had she grown? She landed with perfect accuracy directly on top of my head.

This had me lying stunned on the floor tangled up with a frog pixie. To my amazement the Lylybel still held the bowl of soup, but this time when she put her hand in and pulled it out again something was different. She formed a small O with her webbed thumb and forefinger. Her whole face appeared out of the frog's mouth, the enormously proportioned eyes were made of glass, all the time she had been looking out of the frog's nostrils!

I didn't get a choice in which bubble to pop. It would be just one made from the grey coloured soup, looking a little bit like chicken soup, or even worse chicken and mushroom soup. This is my least favourite in any world, and I was surprised such a culinary horror existed in this dimension. The bubble produced from the soup had all the flavour of something I wasn't going to like. This greasy grey bubble rolled slowly into the air. It floated as if suspended on grease or oil. This was the impression as it came clear from her hand. It burst almost like pus from a septic wound on the end of my nose. I was off into a past life none interactive video ride.

The 1973 me was walking towards an attractive and almost new small bungalow surrounded by well maintained shrubbery. The bungalow had a small ramp up to the front door. This was telling me something. However, I wasn't seeing any significance until I produced a key, opened the door and marched in as if I owned the place. I didn't own the place.

I was there to do business with the owner, Lenny the Helmet. This was the explanation for the wheelchair ramp. Lenny could walk, however being on his feet for more than a few minutes gave him a lot of pain in the knees and hips. He could jump out of the chair and lumber to the door if the house was on fire. Lenny preferred to sit in the chair most of the time. His house was adapted for this, though he could get in the bath, stand at the sink and other such things. He was a large man, and the chair gave him an even larger presence.

I was about to speak when Lenny gave me a look, as if to say, "Be quiet". This startled me until the shadow behind my left shoulder moved. It was sunny outside. In the bungalow sombre shades prevailed with the curtains constantly closed to the prying eyes of the curious walking their dogs in the street. With business to be done you had to be careful. The shadow turned out to be my first meeting with the lovely Dave Hartley Sparrow and his friend Millicent. The very fact his gun had a name and he constantly referred to what it was saying gave this particular gunman a very nasty edge over anyone else who was an insane killer.

Thankfully the gun was held loosely down at his side. He wasn't pointing it at anybody, though in the twilight I did see Lenny's coffee table was now firewood and it hadn't been stamped on. Killed with both barrels, not a fate even a coffee table deserves, particularly when as I found out later Lenny was lifting a cup of tea from it at the time. Perhaps that was the reason. Lenny was using it for tea! He'd been unaware of Dave's approach. His stealthy entrance had been made through the kitchen door always left open for Lenny's Yorkshire terrier Mimzie, a dog with a bitches name. Lenny had a way of calling things what he felt appropriate. He wasn't about to call Dave anything other than Sir!

"Are you the guy who moves the stuff around for Lenny?" Dave said, addressing me, all the while strolling towards me until we were nose to nose. My space was being invaded, he knew it, and he knew I didn't like it. He had me figured as a soft touch in an instant. Dave knew I didn't carry any weapon. Lenny told him I carried nothing after he suggested he might have to shoot me as I came in. I was told this later though I wasn't convinced he'd use his gun in the middle of the day on a quiet housing estate. However, he'd shot a coffee table, twice!

I was considering if I should tell him I was indeed the man who moved the stuff around for Lenny. We worked more as a team nowadays with Lenny doing all the admin and handling the supply chain. I shifted it out to the dealers, never selling to anybody I didn't know or on the streets, always careful, always watching. I was putting it out there while taking as little risk as possible. I didn't get a chance to speak. The previous question was rhetorical. He knew who I was all along. Lenny had told him I was coming at 3pm and was always on time.

"You're working for Harry now," Dave continued.

"Who's Harry?" I said. Dave looked across at Lenny and indicated with a wave of the shot gun he should speak.

Lenny filled me in on the details of our little team's demise. We were still going to be a team, but now playing for a different leader, and for a much smaller percentage. Dave had pointed out to Lenny that with the financial clout Harry could bring to the LSD game we would make as much money as before, if not more, that was a certainty. I realised we were no longer in control, and if this Harry person wanted some deal to take place in a high risk area, from the look of Dave Hartley Sparrow it would be impossible to refuse. It turned out Harry did like to have full control, and watch everything!

There was the sound of a car horn outside the bungalow. This was from a large black Rover saloon driven by Smiggy who now worked in a pawn shop owned by Harry the Pocket. And it was this slimy little piece of work that persuaded his boss of the large profits to be made in drugs, far more than fencing stolen property, or taking illegal bets on horse races, or even lending money at high rates of interest. All these other activities required more risk for much less gain than the large profits available in the early 70s from LSD. Weed could be shifted as well with very little risk and good profits. Other people could deal heroin or cocaine, LSD was something that could be produced in a laboratory at low cost. No need to smuggle it in from another country. Smiggy's sales pitch had delighted Harry, and the cherry on the cake was how little security our nascent drug business possessed.

"You can meet Harry right now. He has a little weekend cottage near the river. Somewhere quiet for him and the family. You'll enjoy it. I hope you enjoy it. So lovely and quiet there, you get my drift?" Dave grinned all the time he said this.

Dave raised Millicent pointing her in my direction suggesting I was going to be one hell of a good worker for Mr Pocket, "and never to call him Harry the Pocket to his face. Everybody calls him that, but never, never to his face!"

Lenny climbed out of the chair, picked up a pair of walking sticks and waddled off with his strange gait to the car. As we arrived at the car Smiggy was grinning at us and laughing. I spat directly in the little weasel bastard's face as I climbed into the car. I knew he'd suggested this move of direction in Harry's business.

The weasel wiped his face with a handkerchief. "You'll get yours one day. You more than deserve it and I'll give it to you!" Smiggy informed me.

I didn't know why I deserved it, and I wasn't going to ask him. Nobody in the front seats spoke a word during the car journey. Lenny was sitting in the back with me, and this car had child protection locks on the back doors, something new in those days. We might have been trapped but Lenny was not afraid to explain the situation, though he whispered. You could see Dave almost craning his neck to hear, never suggesting that we either speak up or shut up!

I was getting to know the situation. Dave understood it already and Lenny understood also. From boardroom to shop floor in one scary afternoon!

CHAPTER 30

A forgotten family get-together in Toad's house.

A little place in the country David had called it. As we crunched into the grand pebbled driveway through the magnificent Gothic entrance gates it was obvious this was not your ordinary little place in the country. This was all an illusion of grandeur. It transpired that the main house had been saved from dereliction by a property company who very profitably turned it into eight luxury homes. Harry's little place was the hunting lodge belonging to this once grand estate. Constructed in rugged stone next to a river that ran through the extensive grounds, it had been built for the pleasures of hunting and fishing. Just beyond the lodge there was a small weir allowing water to fill the estates ornamental lake. This meant the cosy three-bedroom lodge was effectively isolated on an isthmus. There was only one approach along the strip of land dividing the river from the lake. Anybody approaching invited or not, was in clear sight.

As we drove along the isthmus to the turnaround outside the lodge, I noticed it had a small jetty into the river. Tied to this jetty was a rubber boat with a large engine. Was this was a getaway vehicle if any visitors arrived without a formal invitation?

A woman was standing watching the river and smoking. Even at a distance I could see she was very attractive wearing tight jeans and a big fluffy sweater. Her attraction was very physical suggesting a latent sexuality in the way she moved. It was almost catlike and very athletic. Both Lenny and I were watching avidly when Dave leaned over from the front and said, "Anybody sniffs around Miriam they'll get big trouble. She's Harry's baby doll and don't you two ever forget it!" Dave was quite forceful, poking Lenny's stomach with Millicent he added, "I've heard why they call you the Helmet, so keep it in your pants!" Dave moved Millicent down and rested her in Lenny's crotch.

We pulled to a stop outside the lodge and as the car's engine fell silent the front door opened. Lenny was peering into the gloom and gasped. "Fucking hell, he's in on it!" then said no more. .

The figure in the doorway on that late spring day in 1972 was me! On closer inspection it wasn't my twin. It could, however, be my very slightly older brother who was hewn out of much tougher material than I was made of. There was something disturbing about this man. His movements were very catlike, similar to a panther, always ready for any action, ready to pounce upon anybody moving into its territory. I could see why a woman like the one on the jetty would be with him even though it was obvious she was at least a decade older than my rugged double. I was wrong about the woman on the jetty, and wrong about John Smith who I thought was Harry. He was sitting in a fine colonial wicker chair on the back terrace.

Dave opened the rear doors from the outside and we clambered from our prison. I even thought about sprinting for the river and diving in. Then, of course, they had the power boat. They could chop me up with the propeller, or just come alongside to hold me down with a boat hook. Lenny and I marched into the house like a pair of lambs to the slaughter. We had no option but to join this man's game. The only thing we could do was negotiate the money side of it. We were, after all, going to be doing the same job, now watched over by very unpleasant henchmen.

We were led through to the back terrace overlooking the river and greeted by an older round-faced man lounging back in his colonial chair with his feet resting on a similar designed footrest, all the while he puffed away on a large Havana cigar. Being there next to the river I had a sudden vision of a childhood book my mother used to read to me some evenings. This character was toad. I was wrong about that as well, he was a rat!

We were pushed in front of him like naughty schoolchildren in front of a headmaster, and were expected to stand silently until summoned to speak. Our future employer couldn't see us and apparently was looking straight through us down towards the jetty admiring his property. Eventually Harry decided we'd been hanging around for long enough. The cigar was dispensed with, flicked from his fingers directly into the river, only half smoked, a dreadful end for such a fine cigar. This was his money no object, I am the man manoeuvre, impressing us with his little place in the country, and his command over his thugs. Lenny and I had moved up a notch in the business, descending further into the sewer as we did so. I admit we were not good boys, but this was a different league. This involved shotguns and nutcases willing to use them.

"Hello, boys, I'm moving into your territory. You will be working for me from now on. This isn't a negotiation. I'm telling you directly that I will expand your operation, and you're going to run it for me. You'll do all right." This was Harry's opening gambit. He laid it all out for us in one statement.

"I built this up. It took me years and what's he got to do with it?" Lenny said, with astounding bravery. He was pointing towards my double who grinned back totally nonplussed by this accusation.

"Lenny, Lenny, Lenny, old mate. They followed you to my old place in the city and made a proposition to me. They wanted to take over this town, not my pitch, your pitch! Harry told me about the increased flow, and I won't be paying a percentage like you, so it's all business for me."

"Go on Lenny introduce me to your friend then." My double said this, and he was looking at me with a strange interest. I stared back in disbelief at my double.

He stepped towards me smiling, holding out a hand to shake. "I'm John Smith, and I'm quite fascinated by you. We could become friends, very interesting with the girls as well… oh, sorry about the business thing, but you'll do all right, better than before, and with protection." This is how Mr Smith introduced himself to me. Confident of course!

As he talked to me he glanced towards Dave Hartley Sparrow. A grin was crossing his face as if Dave with his shotgun was a joke, like a child trying to stop a drunken father beating its mother. It was obvious John wasn't the least bit put out by the takeover bid. He would make more money, lots more money, and if they leaned on him too much he would see to it they stopped pressuring him. They knew it and he knew they knew it. He was one scary bastard!

Harry then became the chameleon, mine host, holding out both his hands towards a table in the sumptuous room behind the open French windows. The table was set with a full spread of food and drink ready for a little business party. First of all Harry introduced us to his wife Miriam, known to Harry as Skippy and to everybody as Baby Doll, again Miriam to her face. I thought she was with John Smith and somehow I could see them together. It was the catlike movements, a shared physicality. I couldn't see her with Harry the rat toad.

We might as well enjoy the business party because the negotiation was more on the lines of half the previous profit margin, but shift three times the stuff.

We would make more and expose ourselves to more risk from the police. This is where, yet again, I was wrong!

To my surprise Smiggy appeared holding a very expensive reflex camera ready to take some family shots of a happy gathering down by the river. We were all going to march onto the jetty and pose, but first he must take a few profiles shots of me and Lenny. They knew what we looked like so why did they want the pictures? It made no sense. Until of course Harry informed us the drug squad had a large interest in our business.

"No, no, no, no, it's not like that, boys. It's so they know who not to arrest. I want my business to run smoothly, and my friends on the force, who shall remain nameless, want no one spoiling the profit margin or the construction of their luxury villas near Torremolinos." Harry reassured us the photographs would keep us safe, not to the contrary. If trouble did occur the individual and group photos were evidence that we'd consorted, the bastard.

We all sat at our assigned places around the table. The open French windows offered a very intimate view of the tranquil river flowing outside, but inside I was far from tranquil. I could not argue with this situation. I was in a dirty game and sometimes you have to bend with the wind. What surprised me was the places had been set with nametags written in beautiful handwriting on bows around the napkins. Baby Doll knew the names of the guests and had planned the seating in advance. There was a confidence about the whole setup that was as disturbing as it was professional.

John Smith turned out to be the most amusing of dinner guests, telling stories, cracking jokes, and even breaking into a short romantic song in the style of Engelbert Humperdinck for the benefit of Miriam who appreciated the attention. She seemed fascinated by Mr Smith. Then again perhaps she was just being a good hostess. Harry didn't seem bothered he was more preoccupied with how the business worked, questioning Lenny at length about the most reliable dealers on the street, and how the money flowed. He knew already where the drugs came from, and they came from one John Smith. However, who supplied my smiling double remained a mystery to everyone. This is the point where the story gets a little hazy.

The strange thing about John Smith was, if he wasn't your enemy he became a very amusing man, and at this time I wasn't his enemy. He was very curious about our almost twin appearance even going to the extent of questioning me about my background, this proved fruitless search. Thank God!

He was seated next to me, and John laughing told me during a rowdy period towards the end of the meal that Harry had tried to move in on him, but he'd persuaded the small-time businessman otherwise. Evidently Dave Hartley Sparrow had followed Lenny to the city and his meeting with John Smith one month earlier. Then they moved in on John Smith sending a thug who did a bit of part-time knife work for Harry. This particular hard case was known as Pana Pucci. The small-time thug had travelled over to the city to persuade Mr Smith to reveal his contact, allowing his boss to work directly with the main man, maximising the profit margin. Pana Pucci was a brooding dark menace of a character, very good with blades, persuasive in the extreme, he went in hard. He disappeared!

The unfortunate Mr Pucci turned up a week later, unwashed and covered in his own filth. He'd been locked up somewhere very dark and cold by John Smith. He was a changed man, never the same again. He'd moved in on Smith with his usual heavyweight knife to the throat routine. In seconds the tables turned and the knifeman was beaten unconscious. After which he took a terrible battering all over his body with his hands coming in for special attention. There was no more menace left in this hapless blade-wielding thug.

He'd been locked up in a large metal tool chest for six days with only water being supplied through a pipe similar to a feeder for a hamster. It transpired that when John Smith dragged Pana Pucci out into the light of day he lectured him on the negative merits of wrongdoing, or attempting revenge. The knifeman only ever returned to the town once telling Harry of the frightful power of John Smith. He fled the town that night and no one had heard of him since. Or had John Smith followed him and once the message had been passed to Harry, assisted in his permanent disappearance?

Harry had only one good quality henchmen, the redoubtable David Hartley Sparrow. However, if he shot John Smith the whole thing would fall to pieces, so for the moment Harry had to be pragmatic, approaching John Smith with an attractive deal. John Smith was still the big wheel in the city, so Harry had to content himself with three local towns. It amounted to a business as big as John Smith's, though dealing direct John had a bigger margin. Harry, of course, wanted more. He wasn't going to get it, not yet, at least. It wasn't a bad move for a man who was a petty criminal on many levels, nothing big in any one area of crime, money coming in from a series of small, nasty scams. He did all right on this, but now he was determined to do even better.

Harry leaned forward and asked a question that became something else. "Are you two boys related? You look almost like twins."

"No, Harry we're not related. We've been through all that," John shouted back.

"You both got the same perfect smile!" At that moment the nickname came. I shouted back that I doubted it because mine was perfect with no fillings. This is when John surprised me. He opened his mouth and was very proud to show me he had no fillings either. This was the point in the evening where Harry told us about the Nazis. How in the early days of the Waffen SS you had to have perfect teeth to represent the master race. Later this practice, through necessity, fell by the wayside. Our nickname given to us that drunken evening by Harry was "Nazi twins". It stuck, and for good reason.

I wasn't really involved in the negotiations between Lenny and Harry, just questioned over my precautions when trading with the street dealers, and what was my security with the money. He even suggested it might be safer using Dave to help me collect. I pointed out it was a trust thing I was operating, and having a twitchy shotgun-holding moron on board would really sour the game. I didn't call him a twitchy shotgun-wielding moron that night! Harry agreed that I should carry on as before, though I would have to work harder with the increased workload. This wasn't exactly true. I was just going to sell more produce to the same number of dealers. Harry seemed to think everybody wanted to do LSD, and if we pushed it hard enough everybody including housewives and grannies would be taking it. They, of course, had Valium.

As the business lunch was drawing to a close I noticed Harry was now chatting animatedly to Dave, whilst he puffed nauseatingly in that smaller space on a giant cigar. Was this ego boosting? I was involved in my conversations with John Smith. To my surprise Lenny and Baby Doll were getting on like a house on fire. How this greasy-haired lumbering lout entranced her I do not know, but that's what appeared to be happening, the unexpected. This is probably why Harry didn't take a blind bit of notice. If Baby Doll had laughed at everything John Smith said perhaps Harry would have become wild with jealousy.

John Smith suggested we go to a nightclub together to see what effect we had on the girls. I had no objections, because this move would get me away from the hunting lodge and back out into the real world where I would feel safer away from shot gun wielding, deal making, crazy bastards. Of course I was out on the town with the craziest one of all. It was only our first encounter but I already knew that. He was, however, amazingly good fun to be with. He was a very good actor but I do not think he was acting with me. I may be wrong but I actually felt he was becoming my friend. I'm quite sure it's foolish thought.

We were living it up in a nightclub when a very attractive girl came over to me. She was probably too young to be in there legally, and not the type of girl I tend to go for when left to my own devices. However, this girl seemed to think I was wonderful and flattery can get you anywhere. I was becoming interested so I asked the blandest of nightclub questions. It had to be shouted. "What's your name?"

"Vicky, my name is Vicky." I already knew who she was when my stupid past manifestation met her, and I could do nothing because I was the spectator. She was following me on behalf of Dave Hartley Sparrow, her brutal, much older boyfriend who didn't mind what she did to help him out. He had lots of young girlfriends, and I suppose she thought he was exclusive to her. There was to be no sex that night. We danced it away. Things changed when we returned to her house in the early hours of next morning. It was the moment I met Samantha.

She came to the door as we walked up the drive to the impressive new house, and stepped out in a housecoat to castigate her daughter for being very late or very early back. Then our eyes met. It was like instant electric, a magic conjuring up a different future. I couldn't break away from the magnetism her eyes held me with.

I was looking into her eyes as they transformed by getting larger and larger until they were massive reptilian eyes made of glass. This was one of the most confusing moments of my entire life. One moment I'm looking into the eyes of someone who was invading my soul, the next I'm looking at giant glass eyes. I'd gone into a trance inside a dream I suppose. Now it was a shock to be back in the room, or, to be more precise, back in the bag.

I wasn't in that bag. The eyes in front of me were transforming into beautiful brown eyes. These belong to Jennifer who was now wearing her hideous hat, a brutally enormous tweed cowboy hat festooned in its leather band with pheasant feathers, a sort of Miss Marple meets John Wayne look. Then, of course, my body started to burn with the acid from the grim soup bubble. My whole body was on fire though it wasn't too awful, and now I understood why we were on this dark wet mountain. The rain was coming down with an almost biblical force, washing away the burning sensation, finally leaving me cleansed of pain. Jennifer's hat was more painful than the bubble!

"Let's press on now. There's a lovely bed and breakfast on the other side of this hill. We can take breakfast together there!" Jennifer said this with her lovely smile beaming out from under the preposterous tweed hat.

Breakfast seemed like a wonderful idea. Whether we would manage to sleep much before our breakfast was a matter for debate.

CHAPTER 31

The lead door closes, sometimes it opens.

Welcome to the radio club! This club has nothing to do with amateur radio electronics. The nature of this club is based on waiting and support. Members can sit for twenty-six minutes one day, five the next, and sometimes an hour. You become expert at watching doors. Every time one opens and a nurse appears you expect your name to be called. So rarely is it called that when they finally shout your name it comes as a shock.

Everybody has a cycle of treatment and mine was five days a week for eight weeks. You're not allowed to join the club unless you've got tattoos. These come free with the assessment and are permanent markings to align you perfectly for the Chernobyl effect, a reminder that lasts a lifetime. At first you're the new boy starting out with a batch of five other people, half a dozen at the time, week in week out. I couldn't believe I'd got cancer, and the others couldn't believe they had it either. Some had lived in denial for so long letting the disease run its cellular mutation that the therapy might be more psychological than meaningful.

It's a siege mentality where you all become a group of smelly friends in adversity. Everyone in that waiting room smelled like sickly burnt peaches. I thought it was a combination of heavy perfume and fear, until the day my car's air conditioning packed in, and I discovered it wasn't just them, it was me! We were all being systematically cooked alive. Some of your group have shorter cooking schedules than you, others more. In the final two weeks everybody goes into countdown mode, then its kisses and cuddles, and congratulations all round. Some people have burnt faces, others blistered skin, I suffered from chronic mind numbing tiredness.

You are sealed in the room alone behind a fourteen inch thick lead door. Just you and the machine set on automatic, forty-four seconds in four bursts of eleven seconds. It feels like nothing but it is this great illusion. It's cooking you alive. If some poor unfortunate child is in for therapy it takes an age because they need anaesthetising. This morning we were all in for a long wait, a little blonde girl was brought in, no hair, five-years-old with her favourite teddy bear. Snowballs deserted her during the treatment. She never knew because her mother insisted Snowballs had stood guard, watching her as she slept. The nurses watch on flickering blue grey monitors. Perhaps they're not in colour because the blue grey makes it somehow old, less immediate, less the real now.

After a few weeks we all know each other stories, so everybody had a book of some description, real paper or electronic. On this day I'd forgotten my glasses so I closed my eyes and started to think of the darker days in which I thought I'd sleep forever wanting to stay in the alternative universe. I wanted to be with Jennifer, and was desperate to discover all my dark forgotten past. Curiously the more I knew of my bleak past the less guilt I suffered on returning from the other universe.

I was thinking of the tortured lives that made my troubles seem like walking in a sunny valley. During the extra long wait that morning I didn't go back to the concentration camp but to Willesden in North London. I was at a branch of a well-known bank with a new deputy manager, a man with the ambition to push hard in the hope of gaining good position and a comfortable life.

Mr Wilson was now deputy branch manager. It wasn't a large branch, not the one located in the centre of the high street. He was only three streets and two promotions away from the level where he could be running the main branch. This particular morning Mr Wilson was behind the counter, not a usual position for a man of his standing. He was teaching some new recruits the finer points of careful paper handling, making sure all the receipts were correct, every bit of paper was organised and nothing in all the mass of paperwork was misplaced. Everything had to be accounted for and not a single item lost. Abraham Wilson knew all about record keeping and the harsh penalties you could pay for being tardy.

Abraham was mentoring two new recruits who had done everything in theory and now were working the counter for the first time. They were seated in adjacent windows, and Abraham floated between them making sure everything was in order. He dealt with the odd unusual request, all the time subconsciously surveying people coming and going, watching the world he loved, the world of commerce and numbers. Then he saw a blond man, thickly-set, of the right age. He told himself to calm down, just another on blond apparition.

It had been years and there he was, this former Nazi officer standing before him. Heinrich Haussler, but it wasn't. It was just a man who looked remotely like Heinrich, and on closer inspection nothing alike. Abraham Wilson returned to his new recruits, the cold raising of the hackles on his spine slowly subsiding, perspiration driven by adrenaline breaking out on his forehead. He could feel the dampness in his armpits under his jacket. He had to stop imagining every blond thick-set man was Heinrich. Every week he was haunted at least ten times phantom sightings.

He looked up again to survey his kingdom. The old manager would be retiring soon and he'd had a whisper that the branch would be his. A London branch at that! There was another blond man in the bank two counters along changing some traveller's cheques, and in front of him another blond man. This time he wasn't going to be fazed. He'd had his one shock for the day, and decided only seconds before he was going to stop looking. He couldn't go through this reaction every time he saw blond-haired men.

"Can I cash zis cheque please?" the man asked.

It was his accent, watered down by time living in England. A wash of adrenaline rushed through Abraham's body. The young assistant serving this blond man was pushed harshly to one side, he was over forceful and she let out an audible groan. .

"I'm the deputy manager. What do you want, sir?" Abraham asked, fighting to keep his voice level under control.

"I have zis check I would like to cash. I am a customer at the other branch. Unfortunately it is full today and I cannot wait," the man replied.

Abraham decided to confront this man, and pushed the girl back in front of the cashier's window. Pointing at the customer he instructed, "You deal with this one. I've got something to do." He left the bemused girl at the counter. She was flustered and inexperienced in processing traveller's cheques.

Miss Smurthwaite was the girl's name. She took a deep breath and started dealing with the very distinguished-looking customer, all the while wondering what was wrong with the usually quiet Mr Wilson. The young bank clerk was only in the preamble when something extraordinary happened.

A chair, a large heavy chair that was testimony to the bank's wealth and power struck the blond customer a shuddering blow to the right shoulder. As the blond man started to collapse another large man in a suit plunged on top of him. Miss Smurthwaite stood up and was appalled to see Mr Wilson the deputy manager grabbing frantically for the customers throat. The young assistant pressed the panic button. That's all she could think of after seeing the look in Abraham Wilson's eyes. He was deranged.

The moment he spoke Abraham knew this was Heinrich Haussler. There was no mistaking the Bavarian accent, and of course he looked exactly like Heinrich because he was. For a moment Abraham thought about following him home. Then he thought how stupid this would be, he could find the address in the records. In a matter of seconds he'd run through every scenario, his mind a whirlwind of wild emotions. Rage guided his actions. He'd vowed to kill him, to choke the miserable life from him, or to beat him to death even if it meant his own demise. His wife and child at home were forgotten in his bloodlust to kill the beast.

The man was so strong. He'd gone down hard after the blow from the chair and was already fighting back. Abraham's s left hand was an open claw as he lunged towards Heinrich's throat. There would be no mercy today. He would crush his windpipe. The strength in the deputy manager was of a well-fed man with no fear. No guards were going to rush in to save Heinrich now. He would perish like a dog on the parquet floor of the bank. He was taking no chances. Holding the German down with his knees was a bit of luck. He'd fallen across the German's chest landing heavily on his biceps with both knees pinning Heinrich to the floor.

Abraham tightened his grip from the left hand crushing the throat. The final weapon was his right fist that he plunged hard time and time again into the left side of this evil monster's head. Already he had blood on his knuckles, bloody vengeance. Only seconds would pass before he would be arrested. It was enough to send Heinrich to hell. His head was swimming in a sea of boiling rage. If his wife had been there in front of him with their child she couldn't have persuaded him to stop.

Their eyes were locked on each other, the German struggling to gain some ground, Abraham staring into those eyes waiting for them to slip to the dullness of death. It was the deputy bank manager's vision that started to blur. Something was wrong and he couldn't in his driven rage understand what was happening. His vision was greying and blurred. He was losing sight of the German. Was he having a stroke because of the physical effort of killing this man with his bare hands?

The third blow with the heavy wooden chair dislodged Mr Wilson sending him to the floor unconscious. Miss Smurthwaite's policeman father had versed his tiny daughter in the art of self-defence and now apparently the art of self-confidence. She'd stepped up when all the others in the bank had stood by watching the attempted murder of an innocent Swiss businessman. Seeing no weapon other than the small wastepaper bin, an umbrella and the big chair, she picked the object that would give her inertia to replace strength, and three blows were enough to dislodge the attacker.

Abraham awoke in hospital with a policeman at the end of the bed. The Swiss man had gone off to a private clinic, and fortunately his injuries were only superficial, he was released home that evening.

On waking Abraham Wilson recalled the horrible face of Heinrich Haussler lying below him on the parquet floor. He shuddered with a terrible realisation. The man had looked like Heinrich, but he knew in his heart that it wasn't. He knew he'd made the most massive mistake of his entire life!

The man he'd been so desperate to kill had an incapacitated arm from the Russian front, and a huge Y-shaped scar on his cheek, testimony to the power of Russian artillery. Another inch and the shrapnel would have taken his eye or killed him.

He couldn't believe he'd attacked a man who looked quite like his nemesis. He doubted he would have a job to return to. All his ambitions would be crushed forever. The bank wouldn't want him back in the branch and everyone in Willesden knew about the incident. He knew the Swiss man would bring the force of law against the bank looking for compensation.

Abraham Wilson experienced two of the luckiest moments in his life. The first was Claus Steiner from Switzerland wasn't going to press charges or sue for compensation. The bank had agreed, however, to allow him a top rate of interest on all his accounts for the next year, and he wasn't poor. The area manager supposed Claus Steiner didn't want the police involved because of the amount of money he had banked in what was an austerity ridden UK.

The second bit of luck was the area manager's son had been shot down and held prisoner for five years. Since then he'd been dark and taciturn, prone to fantasy, driven sometimes to wild rages. The area manager was sympathetic and knew Abraham Wilson had endured terrible suffering and lived through years of deprivation. He understood Abraham was scarred for life. For this one reason alone he was going to give Abraham Wilson one chance, one very last chance. He would be demoted to head of counters, after which he would be moved to a bank well out of the way, and fortuitously a new branch was opening in a small northern industrial town.

The area manager arranged a few meetings with his son's psychiatrist. These meetings were difficult and Abraham attempted to respond, but kept many things inside. The psychiatrist seemed satisfied he would never attack anybody again. He never did.

Three weeks later the refugee family were on the move once more, a damaged father, his secretive wife, and their happy young child Louise. They arrived on a dull grey day in a small Northern industrial town, a town where nothing terrible ever happens.

The strain of these events profoundly affected Rachel. The family had to get someone in to help out. A local woman was recommended. She was very good with children. Everybody said so. Somebody had to look after the child because Rachel, worn out with stress was incapable of doing anything. She had to go away for a few days to rest. Her much older sister had been studying languages in London at the outbreak of war, and never returned to Poland to be captured. Rachel Wilson was now so thankful her older sister Mila was there to comfort her trauma. The incident with the German hadn't changed her view of Abraham. It had changed everything!

She'd been looking after Louise the day it happened, washing nappies or something when the phone had started ringing. The call changed her life forever. Abraham had attacked a man at the bank.

Two days later when her beloved Abraham returned home he'd been very reluctant to talk. This ridiculous incident had ruined them and he wanted to it block from his mind. Everything he'd set out to do had been destroyed in that one moment. He didn't know at the time the Swiss man wouldn't sue for compensation and he didn't know the area manager understood his trauma. Even so close to the end of the war people liked to forget about suffering and get on with enjoying life. He'd been fortunate but didn't know it yet.

Rachel pressed him long into the night before he finally told her about his obsession with this officer. He had never spoken of this in the years they'd been together. He admitted his obsession required every blond man he saw to be inspected.

"How could I have been so stupid? All the millions of people in the world, he's not going to turn up in my bank!" He cried as he said these words. Rachel pressed him for more information.

Everybody has secrets, some darker than others. Abraham knew most young girls were systematically sexually abused in the camps, and he knew his new wife had been violated by German soldiers. She'd talked only once about it, telling him that it wasn't much because she was so skinny and filthy. Contact was also forbidden. Germans couldn't fraternise with the filthy Jews. Abraham pushed it from his mind. He loved his wife with all his heart. She could do nothing other than survive in those camps, and he thanked God every day for Rachel. With the move to England the past was never forgotten, but never mentioned.

Rachel knew the Swiss man was a Bavarian German living in London under false papers. Working as an art dealer, living the happy afterlife, his stolen gold safely locked away in some vault. Maximilian had possessed a collection of photographs displayed in ornate silver frames stolen from a dead Berlin family. Alone for many hours Rachel had often inspected them with a hidden jealousy, seeing happy times next to the lake, the sailing, the picnics and the skiing. She fantasised of a life without war, a life with food and a life of freedom. She knew that Maximilian had a twin brother, Heinrich. Something Abraham never knew.

Rachel had expunged her past the moment she met her lovely husband, and became a fresh teenage girl once again. With the war starting before she was a teenager she'd never been a fresh teenage girl, and now she had the chance. She'd never been a childlike sex slave. Rachel never told him about her level of physical experience. She'd learnt to love in a creative way at the hands of her husband. Maximilian had been very creative from day one, now Rachel decided she would be creative. She decided to go down into a depression. She needed a break with her sister Mila, something to cheer her, and let her relax.

Rachel knew Maximilian wouldn't recognise the shapely dark and beautiful woman she now was, not the skinny child woman that had been his pleasure toy, his little rag doll clutching his massive arms. Rachel shuddered at the memory of his power and her feeble protests the first time he took her, a long night, a night of blood and pain.

She was confident of standing directly in front of him and not being recognised. Rachel wore a disguise. She bought a pair of very weak glasses from a second-hand shop. Dying her hair a lighter chestnut colour and wearing it long around the face all added to the mystery. Abraham would not have recognised her if he'd passed her in the street. Her husband might have recognised her lovely legs, but she didn't know if Abraham looked at things like that. He looked at her legs in their bedroom. Always a good man he never seemed to look at anyone else's. She had the best leg's, he'd told her so, not ever saying that even about film stars.

Cafe Roma was a coffee shop down the street from Abraham's old bank. This was one of the new ones with noisy Italian espresso machines. It was all the rage. Rachel was sick of the taste of the froth, the milk, the whole Italian experience. She'd been in the cafe for more than three days, buying one cup every hour or so, reading a book or pretending to read a book. All the time she watched the street, watched the bank. She'd been in London for more than a week. Mila knew her purpose and argued at length about her unhealthy obsession.

"You weren't there! You don't know! Support me." This was Rachel's argument. Her sister tired of the arguments and reluctantly vowed support for her younger sister. Her older sister was at a loss as to what she was going to do. Report him to the police, or face him to discover that she was wrong, deluded and confused into thinking he was Maximilian.

After several long days Rachel was losing faith in her commitment, and this man may turn out to be genuine, not the man she sought with such desperation. This Swiss man might be an honest Swiss businessman. She had to see him… she had to!

Rachel was freezing cold. She couldn't remember if the weather was cold or something was running through her soul making her cold. She had changed tactics moving down the street to another location. This meant she had to be outside hour after hour, with nowhere to sit down, no rest for her tired feet. The change of location came about when she realised the more affluent regions of London were located in the other direction, and sitting in that steamy coffee shop the passing crowd were going to a lower level of life. She needed to be located for people going up to the city.

The Swiss gentleman didn't use that branch. He'd only come in on that fateful day because the other one was full. Poor Rachel could have stood in that street for a thousand years and never seen him. She returned to the tube station each day more and more dejected, broken on the wheel of misfortune. She was in the last gasp of any hope. She had to go home tomorrow. She had to go back to the north, and she had no chance of ever finding this man. All those days looking, all those millions of faces and not one of them remotely like

Maximilian Haussler. It was all over and her feet didn't want to move, reluctant in their every stride, with the tube station creeping towards her. Once she went down into that tunnel, and jumped onto a claustrophobic train she was lost. This was the last trip back to Mila's before returning home.

Two stations had passed. Each time the train juddered to a halt, small parts of her spirit died, and as the yards of tunnel became miles the more wretched she felt. Each passing station diminished her. The train had been stood for some time with Rachel staring without seeing the passing crowds. She'd seen so many passing crowds, now they now all looked like a blurred colour. If it wasn't for Louise and her lovely Abraham she could quite easily climb from the train and throw herself to burn on the electric rails. To find this man and learn she'd been wrong would've been enough, but not everything. To learn that she'd been correct would release her from the dark past. He would be brought to justice for his crimes.

He was on the escalator, she could see him. Was this him?

As the door started to close she made for it through the packed carriage. Rachel stamped on a man's foot and pushed another man reading a newspaper hard in the face throwing him backwards. To make the door she pushed a woman with a child off the train. Rachel steadied the woman and child on the platform making excuses, glad in her heart they hadn't fallen. She wasted no time, her kind words lasted short seconds before she threw herself into the crowd towards the escalator.

Luck was finally with her. All she had to do was catch him before he disappeared. On the escalator Rachel pounded up the left-hand side, the people on the right stationery. The people on the left were rushing home, and some not fast enough for Rachel. These unfortunate people were pushed to the right as Rachel ploughed on upwards, all the time she was looking ahead, all the time the blond head was nowhere in sight. Head down, glancing up occasionally, she ploughed on upwards, certain he'd unknowingly escaped her, this was a last chance and she'd missed it. She would run on regardless until fatigue stopped her.

Another stupid person stood in her way and she grabbed this teenage commuter and thrust her to the right pushing one of the slow commuters forwards almost making him fall. The commuter cried, "Hoy!" As he stumbled forwards clawing at the man in front to gain some balance. Fortune shone for Rachel. The man didn't fall. He'd grabbed out at a coat in front of him and clutching at it managed to stay upright. Rachel herself was losing balance and she also clawed at another commuter to keep balance. She couldn't go on like this. She'd been pushing too hard. She wasn't going to find him with this crazy chase.

"Can I help you, young lady?" the man said. Rachel was almost on her knees in front of him. The only thing stopping her from damaging the new stockings on the metal plating of the escalator was this man's jacket she clutched with fierce grip. She was out of breath and out of luck. She had come to a shuddering halt behind a crowd of people.

"Sorry, sorry, I'm in a rush," Rachel said. She looked up into eyes that had stared down on her naked body many times.

Three seconds passed, a long three seconds, followed by a fourth then a fifth. Rachel's heart was beating so hard she thought her chest would explode.

"Are you all right? You looked shaken." Maximilian enquired.

"Yes I'm good, very good," Rachel said, knowing he didn't see his toy, his young girl. He saw a beautiful, mature woman.

Making quick apologies she broke eye contact and pushed on ahead into the street forcing herself into a small crowd in a newsagent's doorway. She watched him cross the road towards some very smart apartments, a place where rich people could live a contented quiet life. She followed at a distance. All the time she couldn't keep a smile off her face. The muscles in her face were locked in place by what she felt inside. Was the rigid smile one of joy or insanity?

Mr Jackson, Mr Jackson, Mr Jackson were ready for you! Oh yes, I was dark daydreaming. I was in the bright light of a lead lined day at the radio club.

My tattoos were ready for the laser beams.

CHAPTER 32

We're all going to the zoo tomorrow, the zoo tomorrow, to the zoo tomorrow.

Perhaps it was thinking of Rachel waiting for hour after hour in an aromatic coffee bar, or I was starting to feel well at some background level. In hindsight I think it was peculiar to that day alone, but I decided I could manage some breakfast, a big breakfast. Full English that's what I wanted. A proper honest to God big breakfast, and it came courtesy of Bert and Edith. They owned little enclave of Englishness in a big Spanish city and provided in all its greasy glory, the gastronomic delight, full English for the lowly sum of 4.99 euros. This was a bargain not to be missed, a mistake, I should have! Due to my illness I hadn't eaten anything other than porridge for months. A big breakfast would be a wondrous culinary moment to linger in the memory. It did.

Bert and Edith produced a magnificent breakfast which I wolfed down along with extra fried bread. The whole thing reminded me of fatter times. I tipped them, it was that good, and I left the small cafe bar with a jaunty step. I think the trouble kicked in halfway back to my weekday therapy flat when my weakened stomach revolted. I was lucky to make it home without disgracing myself in the street. "Never again, never again," I uttered this in between diarrhoea and vomiting. By the time I was empty, one hour or more had passed, and I was so exhausted I could hardly think. It was 11.15am and definitely time for bed. I could've been a small child.

Sleep came as my head touched the pillow, then a train passed, and a few moments later a train passed. This was followed by sheep, a donkey, and a cow. Though in retrospect I think it was a bull, and the final apparition, a large green crocodile. Then it all started again, first with the train. I could feel the electric motor driving the spectacle, not inside the train, the one driving the merry-go round. I could smell ozone, electrical discharge. Trains were featuring, and all my senses were on fire. I knew in that instant the dimension I was living in. This was the real world.

The merry-go-round was at the edge of a village green for the entertainment of local children. The green a perfect swathe of grass was bordered with picture postcard cottages, a church, and a pub nestled in the shadows beneath some large ash trees. This was a perfect village green. The centre of the green was given over to playing a gentleman's game, cricket, in all its leather on willow glory. In the middle of cricket pitch the wicket was perfect. Even the stumps were set, but no match was in play.

The only person out there other than a bemused me was a little umpire crouching at silly mid-on. He was wearing two or three hats, four jumpers and a large white coat. All the while this strange little man was scanning the pitch as if the game was in progress. I was standing a yard inside the boundary with the roundabout rumbling behind me like a large oversized music box. The umpire's chubby face with eyes hidden behind sunglasses looked at me square on. He was pointing past me towards the roundabout. So fierce a command I turned to see something unexpected. I was expecting to see the woman who was becoming the love of my life.

The roundabout continued to turn and standing on the back of a donkey was the little umpire unchanged from one second before clad in far too many clothes. I spun round to stare at the spot where he'd stood only moments ago. It was empty. Returning my gaze to the roundabout I half expected the umpire to now be missing. He continued to circulate remaining steady on the back of a moving donkey. The animal had real movement and I started to notice that most of the animals on the roundabout were moving, not in the sense of going round and round, they were live animals! I am certain they weren't alive when I first looked, but they were now.

My concentration had gone. I no longer watched the umpire. My eyes had been dragged away by the fascination of watching the parade of animals passing my eyes. The roundabout came to a shuddering halt, the animals did not. They climbed down off the circular platform and walked towards me, led by the donkey carrying the little fat umpire. The little man bounced like a ball of jelly on the donkey's back, his clothes started to fall from his body, shedding spare hats and spare jumpers. The sunglasses had fallen from his face. They bounced on the donkey's shoulder and fell to the floor to be crushed under hoof. If he continued like this there would be nothing left of him. He would be rattled to pieces or be naked. As the strange procession got very close the little man was wearing a gossamer ballet dress, and the smile of a pixie. I might have known.

"No Jennifer?" I asked.

"She's outside the bag in the pavilion watching, a spectator," the Lylybel said.

I scanned the ground and there she was, sitting just to the left of the screen wearing a ridiculously large, white trilby, and very enormous dark sunglasses. She gave me her biggest smile and an enthusiastic wave.

"I'm in the bag?" I asked.

"Yes and Jennifer is a spectator."

"A spectator to what?" I asked.

"It certainly isn't cricket! It's not cricket when you call me a pixie, and that's not cricket either!" the Lylybel said. She was pointing first off to the left then off to the right. I thought she was indicating a boundary. Six runs! "What's not?" I enquired.

"This isn't normal even here. It's… especially for you!" She laughed and laughed and laughed.

Each laugh came with its own pulse of molecular happiness, and between I could feel another pressure building. This sensation contained a much more solid presence, a feeling of latent power. Then I realised it was an onrush, a bow wave of aggression.

I didn't have time to think about what wasn't cricket. This game was run faster than a crocodile, or was it the bull? Both these roundabout animals were now very much alive and attempted to charge me down coming at me from different directions, so I did the only thing possible. I ran and ran and ran! In the original dark universe of the cancer Demons, driven by adrenaline I could run faster than humanly possible. In this universe I'd never had the adrenaline until this moment.

I was running at great speed towards Jennifer hoping to hide behind the screen, or leap over the small picket fence and make for the top of the small stand. I didn't have a clue as to what I was doing other than running. Don't think for one minute I was leading the animals towards Jennifer. She was beckoning me to run in her direction. I was running hard towards her offered sanctuary. As I approached she started to point to her left and down behind the screen. I thought there must be a players' tunnel or something hidden behind it.

The cricket screen was innocent blank white boarding. What it was concealing was something else. It was the briefcase, open, ready and waiting for me.

"Jump in feet first, feet first!" Jennifer cried.

I obeyed the instruction and was waist deep when I stopped dead, the open mouth of the briefcase too small to take my upper body. I could hear the approaching animals, the thunder of the bull's hooves, and a slippery rush through the grass of the crocodile's deadly body. They were almost on me.

"Don't worry they won't pass the boundary. Unlike some people they know when to stop," Jennifer said. She then kissed me passionately on the lips. It was full of every sensation the sensual body could understand. I was enraptured. Putting both hands on my head she pushed down very hard and I began plunging downwards gaining speed every inch of the way.

"Land feet first and you won't come to any harm, not until you break the bubble!" Jennifer's voice faded to an echo as I plunged hundreds of feet into the bag.

Below me was a sea, black and illuminated by moonlight. It was glistening and rolling with a long lazy swell. All the time I was falling towards it, I struggled to keep my balance and remain feet first, waving first my arms then my legs to keep some precarious equilibrium. There was no wind rushing past me, only the vision of the sea coming up towards me. It looked like a sea of pain that would shatter my body as I hit it. This strange, glistening, rolling blackness never got any closer. I wasn't falling. I was suspended above it, not miles above it as I thought, but to my amazement only one inch, one tiny, insignificant inch.

I stretched my toe downwards pointing my foot, stretching to touch the surface. The very moment I touched it I could smell urine, strong pungent urine. The stench was so strong my eyes were watering. I had to clench them shut until the acid had been washed from them by my own tears. Would I dare to open them? I knew I was no longer on the cricket pitch. I smelt bad things the other me had experienced and chosen to forget.

This was a sea of blackness and I was inside it. The smell was more than urine. It was pungent, so disturbing I could taste it. If I opened my eyes I was going to be a spectator to something I didn't want to experience. I wasn't in control, the other me was. Another forgotten horror was about to bite me more viciously than any crocodile, and hit my emotions harder than a charging bull. Then, I realised, I was the foolish donkey!

"No, No, no, Please no!" I was saying. It was more of a pathetic keening sound than real speech. As a spectator I could hear it, as the protagonist I don't even think I knew I was speaking. I opened my eyes to discover I was hiding in a disgusting alleyway in the centre of town. Bright lights filled the night in the main street only feet away. Everything was shining brightly on the 2am night-time bustle of early Saturday morning. Happy voices sounded, some shouts, even the odd argument. Some couples passed silent in embrace, no other person was cowered in filth crying into the back of their own rough, dry throat.

As I moved I could smell my dirt stained clothes, and a pervading smell of urine. Had I pissed my pants or was I dragging the stench of the alleyway with me. People in the street stared at me as I hustled along. I didn't know if it was my terrible street manners barging my way through the thinning crowds, or how I looked.

Somewhere behind this vile stench I could smell the great smell of Brut for men aftershave. The smell forced open a door in my mind. This was the night in August 1971 after we'd left The Cauldron. The fragrance had awakened me to this one fact: this was later the same night. I'd managed to live for forty years with no memory of these tormented times, buffered by my psychosis of wilful amnesia, successfully protected me from myself. If I was honest did I want these memories back? I had no choice here in my new dimension but to sit on the shoulders of a fool and watch the horror show.

Where was I going, and what was I looking for? My other self was running and pushing his way through some of the knots of stragglers. My head was moving left and right watching every single road junction, and every street corner became a threat. This paranoia continued and all the passing alleyways were dark dungeons where evil creatures could be hiding. I was moving with a purpose I didn't understand. Sound was supplied, however internal emotions seemed to be hit and miss during my playbacks. Sometimes I could feel all the angst, all the joy, and all the anger. Other times it was vague, and tonight it was particularly thin. Perhaps on some level I was still blocking it out. I knew what was happening and what was said, but not why.

I was pressed hard against a wall in another filthy alleyway, and I was concentrating on the bright yellow sodium lit street only a few feet away. Moments later a small panda car passed. I'd forgotten how funny they were. A blue and white minivan with a single rotating blue beacon in the middle of the roof, small, twee, vulnerable and ridiculous by today's standards. This comic apparition heightened my fear to a point where hyperventilation was now the normal state of breathing.

I was hiding from the police for some reason, it was obvious. Perhaps the filthy clothes were a product of some escape, climbing over fences, dashing through industrial properties. Whatever it was, the police figured large in my flashback. I was very careful looking out into the night-time street. I was very wary I might be trapped by a couple of regular bobbys on foot patrol, or another panda car close on the heels of the first. I hustled back out into the streets now becoming quiet as late stragglers disappeared into their homes. I was in another alleyway pressed hard against a cracked rusty downpipe that poured cold grey water down my arm. I didn't move. I was keeping myself tight in the shadows.

Now I was watching a nightclub across the Street .This venue was for members only allowing the proprietor to keep it open until 4am if he had enough customers. Sometimes in the summer this place would be closed up by midnight. Sometimes in the winter near daylight would greet the revellers. Tonight it was open and I was waiting. It was at that moment I realised what the other me was waiting for.

Across the street there were several motorbikes and scooters parked front wheels to the kerb. They were segregated into two distinct groups. No mixing between the hard grease of the motorbike and the soft-handed users of the scooter. I was segregated from humanity because I'd broken the rules and wasn't part of any group you'd want to be a member of. I was the leper hiding in dark shadows, keeping the segregation complete, not soiling humanity. I waited overburdened by some horror to seek the help of Lenny the Helmet.

Rain, why was it always raining as you waited? God only knows what time it was when Lenny appeared, staggering, full of drink. He'd started the night in The Cauldron with several pints. Now he was full to the point of falling over. Lenny made straight for his scooter, drunk beyond thinking of the police with their now dreaded breathalyser bag. Green crystals, no licence! Then again, who knew if Lenny even possessed a licence, or the will to take the test? I was out of the alleyway so quickly I thought I was going to leave myself behind. No such luck. I was glued to the other me, the Peter I don't want to remember. At least the emotion was dulled, almost non-existent.

"Lenny! Lenny!" I shouted.

This didn't seem to register with the big fella. He was working away at the kick-start as I prodded him in the shoulder from behind. His fist hit me squarely on the jaw sending me sprawling to the wet street, adding to my misery.

"What the fuck… Peter? You scared the shit outta me! What d'ye want?" Lenny's words were so mangled it was difficult to understand anything. The sentiment was obvious.

"That bastard Bob has done something terrible. I was there when he did it!" I said, and I wondered if the filthy other me was going to get to the nitty-gritty and explain what had happened. I waited.

"And?" Lenny slurred.

"I want to forget. I need something to make me forget," I replied. As this was going on I was starting to wish I could hit myself hard to force myself to tell the truth about earlier that night. It continued in language veiled in the obscure. At some point Lenny suggested I climb on the scooter. I'm still alive years later without dreadful scarring. I could safely assume drunk as Lenny was, he wasn't going to crash that night. This was already ancient history.

"I'll fix you up with something. You won't know if it's Christmas or the summer holidays!" Lenny said.

I was hesitant to climb onto this scooter. However, the other Peter was only too willing to climb aboard, and I didn't have the option to say no! I'd always imagined Lenny was very small time, and possibly he could get me some drugs, cannabis, weed and nothing more. That night I was to discover how Lenny made his money. The journey could have been terrifying with an inebriated Lenny on wet roads. It was nothing of the kind. The speed was moderate and the scooter was rock steady. He possessed an enormous capacity for alcohol.

We arrived in minutes at a small terraced house in a quiet street near the centre of town. This could only be described as tatty. The downstairs windows were covered over with metal sheets. The front door looked industrial and the upstairs windows were covered in wire mesh. Two or three bore the scars of diligent stone throwing or airgun use by local youths.

"Welcome to my house of fun," Lenny said, as he staggered up the short path to the front door. The little garden to the right was chest high with weeds, but more than weeds appeared to grow in the small patch of oily dirt. Other things pushed their way up through the soil and to my amazement they were remains of old motor scooters and motorbikes. It was as if Lenny had half buried them in the garden before the weeds grew, most were so embedded in the ground I think he'd inherited them with the house.

Off the scooter Lenny staggered so much I didn't think he'd make the door. It was remarkable he'd ridden the motor scooter arrow straight, stopping at every light, and never veering off of line. Lenny reached the door and had it open in seconds, then staggered back out towards the street!

"What you doing Lenny?"

"Riding the scooter in. Not leaving her outside for all the local wankers!"

Moments later the scooter roared past me over the step and into the hallway. There was an inch to spare either side of the handlebars and Lenny was inch perfect. The scooter was leaning against the wall and the fabulous Mr Helmet fell to the floor in a heap, dragging himself towards the open front door. Moments later we were behind a locked metal door, the hall illuminated by sickly light from a fifteen watt bulb. With no wallpaper or carpet this place was more than depressing. A pit!

Lenny told me to stay still and wait. He reappeared only seconds later holding out his hand. What he held out to me was probably in his possession all along. This could be a trick to fool people into believing he never carry anything. If he didn't carry the drugs they must've been on a tabletop in the next room, it was that quick.

"I'll give you these four. A gift for a mate," Lenny said, offering me four small white pills. To my surprise the other me, the desperate me, didn't hesitate and threw all four into my mouth.

"Jesus Christ! Spit them out or make yourself sick. The toilet's down the passage," Lenny said, in a voice even and sober. Jesus, this man had some capacity.

The other me took no notice swallowing all four pills in one gulp.

"I need something strong, I need something that will make me sleep," I heard myself say.

"It's LSD you daft twat, really good stuff. I don't know what four tabs are going to do to you!" Lenny said, as the other me slumped down onto the settee in the small lounge. This settee had seen better days. The person sitting on it had seen better days.

I was thinking I'd gone to sleep, but deep down I could hear a keening sound, Silent crying, bubbling painfully below.

Then I was on my feet, then I was on my knees, then I was on my stomach. I was slithering along like a snake attempting to get out of the front door, a seven-foot-high front door. I struggled to get under the top of the frame that was crushing me down trying to keep me in the house. I struggled myself free out into the fresh air, and the open countryside beckoned.

I had no helmet, I had no care, I was kissing the sky, I was touching everything in existence, colours that sang, and doorways that shrank. I mounted Lenny's motorbike. It started first turn of the key, not even a kick required. I rolled the machine off the stand powering it into the night, the road a glistening ribbon of blackness passing beneath my wheels as Lenny's street rushed away behind me.

Lenny looked out into the street, looked out into the silence. He hadn't seen the motorbike go. The apparition he witnessed was me sitting on a derelict weed entangled motorbike growing out of the garden. I was holding the bars with a firm grip, rolling and leaning as I went through the corners, wiping hair from my eyes as it whipped my face. I was doing 50 miles an hour, no 500 miles an hour, no 5000 miles an hour through a night where the road was long dark and fast. I was screaming out the engine noise at the top of my voice. How I didn't do permanent damage to my vocal chords I'll never know!

"Stupid bastard!" Lenny mumbled, as he moved outside to drag me indoors for my safety and his. Mostly his!

I pitied myself sitting on a derelict broken motorbike growing out of a front garden as the drug fuelled Peter became gripped by a terror at the approach of a monster. The past me was racing along dark roads and now out from pitiless oily blackness came a giant spectre with huge grabbing claws. Something horrible and alien happening, something the insane me couldn't explain!

"Noooooooooooooooooooooooooooooooooooooooo! I screamed.

The wild motorbike ride was over, but not the crazy journey.

CHAPTER 33

Driving the carriage too hard, and crashing.

To travel hopefully is better than to arrive. This is often said, but to travel with hope you have to know the direction. I was travelling with no signposts, with no map down the road I didn't know, full of dangers I couldn't perceive. What to do next was always my big question. Time was sprinting by. I had the drugs, but after talking with the family I'd gained a new sensibility. I didn't want to pass them over to the businessmen. This was a sensibility that could change with pragmatism if my bones were at serious risk.

Where to next? I would go to Samantha's and if everyone was out I'd search the garage. Was she privy to some of my darkest secrets? We shared many things, some already dark secrets. Perhaps Sam was in deeper than I realised. Then again, I knew her in one way and I didn't know her at all. I would have to be careful what questions I asked. This was Monday, and I didn't even know if Samantha worked. I didn't know anything about her. Time was flying by, it was almost midday, and in only six or seven hours I would be trapped in The Cauldron with the lunatics. I was desperate even with the backup of my mother and sister. I was starting to think about running away rather than wasting my time looking for what I was starting to believe I'd never find. The problem with running; I'd put my family in grave danger at the hands of the lunatics.

My sister would drop me off after another ride of terror on the back of her Trident. It was as if King Neptune himself was torturing me. "White-knuckle ride," is how people describe rides. I can tell you my knuckles were so white they were almost luminous in the dark. We arrived in minutes, and anybody following me would have been hopelessly distanced in seconds. This was my sister's excuse for having the throttle open. If you could achieve 120% throttle, then my sister had it on! She was the caring one who looked after animals, but human beings?

I was stepping from the motorbike as the seat rushed from under my leg, Jane disappearing into the distance, again with unnecessary haste. Her need to hold the throttle open had not diminished. She was still giving it 120%, and that's how I was going to search. If the booty was there I was going to find it!

No cars in the drive, including Vicky's, I was thankful. Mike must be at work and Sam would be out somewhere. I let myself in with my key thankful the house wasn't equipped with one of the new alarms systems everyone's installing. More affluence meant more burglars, more alarms. My calculation was poor.

The alarm went off, a loud bell on the outside, a siren on the inside. Surprise made me go rigid. There it was on the wall next to the front door. It had been there all the time and I'd not seen it. The alarm box with its legend, "After 30 seconds the police will be called automatically".

Minutes passed and the alarm was screaming into my head. With these minutes I was lucky because panic had trapped me in a time warp and only six second's had passed. The entrance to the house seemed so full of noise it penetrated my nervous system. I would have to run. First I stared at the box looking for something, and I spotted a small keyhole. I had keys for everything, my flat, main door, front door, some other key for something, and more keys that didn't belong to anything. Did I have the hidden safe in the house? I started this question in the middle of my search for the alarm box key! How could I be so distracted at a time like this? The police arriving would bring up no end of unanswerable questions.

It would be on the same key fob, you fool. I couldn't find it! With what I'd found in my flat I had twenty keys and not one of them was remotely like the barrel key for the alarm box. I was going to have to run. Time was moving on, another ten seconds wasted in fruitless search. In the time it takes to hyperventilate once or twice, if I didn't find the key I would have to go. Five, four, three, two, silence!

The alarm had gone silent with a second to go, was this some kind of trick? James Bond movies always have bombs that stop with a second to go, and didn't they start up again when nobody expects it? Then it struck me the police were on their way. I had no alternative but to run.

"Have you forgotten everything?" Samantha said, from the top of the stairs, naked apart from high heels, red high heels, Monday shoes.

"What?" One adrenaline driven part of me was getting ready to run, and another part of me looked upstairs. That part too was driven by a different adrenaline and hormones.

"The key, you remember we lost one, so at the moment it's under the phone table," Sam said.

I shrugged my shoulders in an expression of, "Oops I forgot". She'd turned it off upstairs with a hidden remote switch that doubled as a panic button. I didn't know I had a Monday morning appointment, and I was late, not by much, but late.

"What part of 11am is midday?" Samantha said. She was smiling down at me, and didn't look too worried about my tardiness. She looked amazing to me. I was thinking she'd spent the extra time making herself look special. Bright cherry lipstick smile and red high heels, it's the little things that count. Perfect nails, hands and feet, the perfume, the exact amount of tousled hair to look sexy without looking unkempt. Then of course the jewellery and the one piece she wasn't wearing. This was the only finger on her hands free from expensive baubles.

"I want you to be the teenage boy again today. I liked it, a lot!" all said in a soft voice. It turned out I wasn't going to disappoint!

"No problem, no problem at all," I said. I had, after all, lost my virginity only forty-eight hours before! I was a seventeen-year-old boy lost in a maelstrom of unknown intrigues. Perhaps being with her now wasn't just sex. Sam's age gave me a strange twisted version of mother like comfort. In my state of amnesia I didn't know what my relationship with Samantha was, totally sexual or more?

"You didn't tell me you loved me on Saturday morning," Samantha said. I was halfway up the stairs, and more than halfway to knowing the truth of our relationship. During the sexual teaching on Saturday morning she repeatedly said she loved me. I thought she was talking about the physical. I now knew our relationship was stronger and stranger. How I'd coped with the thought of Mike coming home drunk from the golf club wanting his conjugal rights, and Samantha had coped with me in her daughter's bed, I had no idea! How I'd managed to work my way into half the situations I now lived through I had no idea. Was I crazy?

I vowed to myself that I would make furious love to Samantha until she was exhausted, giving me chance to see the inside of the garage, it could be empty for all I knew. Of course nothing goes to plan, does it?

I drifted into the afternoon wrapped in warmth and pleasure. Time floated by, minutes passing in luxurious passion filled seconds. I let myself go, immersed myself in the pleasures and comforts of the flesh. Sometimes we were in an Olympic wrestling arena with a frantic haste, an athletic concert of movement. Other times we lay almost within stillness, the comfort so loud in its silence, to be broken once again by frantic hard muscle and flesh, against soft feminine form. All this seeped into my memories of love and desire. Lying wrapped in each other's embrace in the bright early afternoon sunshine, remains a singular moment, so ingrained in memory it has become the mark by which all such moments are measured.

We had returned once more to the Olympic arena. The urge to satisfy our carnal lusts drove us towards the wild, coupled in a frantic tangle looking for a moment of wonder when we could be at the pinnacle of satisfaction together. I think I was pulling at her hair, clawing at her buttocks, her hands tearing at the back of my thighs, and I was driving us on at full charge down that lustful highway, high in my seat being the carriage driver, pushing her on in front of me, looking for the moment when climax would stop this onward rush, and once again we'd embrace as exhausted lovers.

"You fucking disgust me, you filthy cow!" The words were shattering. This was a large brick breaking the symmetry of a perfect picture, smashing the moment. Breaking the sensual comfort we'd created on that bright afternoon. These words moved the story of my stupid life further down its crazy road.

"How can you fuck an old woman?" Vicky said, home early after suffering stomach cramps at college. She'd returned to rest quietly, discovering a house full of musk and copulation.

With the first words I had thrown myself off the side of the bed, pulling myself clear of Samantha with a violence that made her cry out . I left her face down on the ravaged bed, alone under the scornful eye of her daughter, a stupid knee-jerk reaction to a vulnerable moment of sexual nakedness. The moment my body hit the carpet I felt like a coward, a deserter. The floor was a sanctuary away from accusing eyes. I was beginning to look under the bed for more cover, so small in a situation where I should have been so much more.

Samantha rolled herself over moving towards Vicky, she swung her bare feet to the floor, not rolling off my side into the pit of cowardice. No, she moved to expose her full naked womanhood to her daughter. This was a form of physical defiance, a way of not losing her place, showing her daughter she was desirable, and physical love wasn't just for the young. She rose naked standing inches away from her daughter. In all this time Vicky's vitriolic barrage of words never stopped.

Most of the words referred crudely to parts of the body. The remainder denigrated her mother Samantha to the status of trash…The whole tirade was focused on her old body, how she looked naked, not how she'd acted. Vicky didn't seem concerned who she'd been sleeping with, or the fact she was married to her father, Mike. Everything in that household circled around the planet Vicky, and this girl was mortified because a young man could find –her mother – more attractive than the centre of her universe. Herself!

They were standing only inches apart, her mother shorter by not wearing heels. Vicky raged on taking everything in at a glance, accusing her Samantha of having bad hair, saggy skin, mottled flesh and too little of anything attractive. By now I was less than a man and stood watching from the other side of the bed. In essence the classic fool, I was re-enacting a farce, holding one of the crushed pillows across my manhood, hiding it from both women who'd been so close they could taste it. What was I doing? I didn't leave the room in shame, I didn't retreat into the bathroom to get dressed and worst of all I didn't defend Samantha against her horrible child.

How this woman could love a man so weak was a mystery, but then I didn't know what we'd been together. I didn't know the man I was a week ago, and I was a frozen spectator. What happened next should have pushed me into action if only to save the relationship between mother and daughter. I watched on from the edge of the arena, a voyeur of the terrible, somebody who should live in shame for this lack of spine.

A harsh blow with a clenched fist woke me from my trance. I think I could have been accused of catatonic voyeurism if that's possible.

The power of the punch was startling, connecting hard on the edge of the jawbone, a full haymaker of a knockout blow. I didn't sway under the impact of the blow. Nothing in my body juddered after the contact, though the blow hit me very hard. It had shocked my senses, because the clenched fist had been delivered with firm purpose on Vicky's jawbone. She was semi-conscious on the floor, now silent and pathetic. She looked like a collapsed pile of clothes, her face hidden under a tangle of hair. The shocking silence in the room was counter posed by the shouting inside my head, voicing a hundred different instructions. None of these I obeyed. Useless is a term used for many things and can encompass many forms. At that moment I was the genuine definition of useless, fully awake, and asleep on my feet.

Mother and daughter were together now, Samantha cradling her daughter's head, stroking tangled hair from her eyes, looking with desperation to see if she'd done permanent damage, ruined her perfect, not so perfect little girl. I watched as if it were a television programme, some dark comedy or a tragic tale of a broken home. I think I'd managed to achieve the broken home. I hoped there was comedic interlude coming up to soften the blow.

Vicky was alive. She hadn't swallowed her tongue, nor had she suffered a broken jaw or lost teeth. With agonising slowness life was coming back. She was crying and mumbling words of love to her mother. Samantha was just pouring out the word, "Sorry", over and over again.

"Peter! Peter!" Samantha was shouting at me.

"What?" I managed to say, breaking myself from this sad useless catatonic voyeurism.

"Go now. Please leave, Peter, get your things and fuck off!" Samantha voiced this sentiment with aggression.

The look on her face said it all. I had done nothing to intervene. I hadn't defended my lover with declarations of love and support. I hadn't poured oil on raging waters. All I managed to do was stand there like a dick holding a pillow across my genitals. I should have been hiding my face in shame for my lack of action. Running would have been better than standing there. At least it would have provided a diversion, something to break the women's toe to toe confrontation. Nothing looks more stupid than a naked man running downstairs with an armful of clothes.

My grasp on the situation was weak, and I moved from catatonic to stupid. I retreated into the bathroom to get dressed, to cover what both had seen. I could have collected my clothes and walked downstairs, even got dressed outside. No, I took three minutes to get dressed in the privacy of the bathroom. When I emerged into the bedroom still heavy with the scent of physical passion Samantha was wearing her dressing gown.

Vicky was sitting on the edge of the bed next to her mother. She leaned on her soft shoulder, all the while being stroked, loved and told she was special. I emerged into this world and the next words spoken didn't come from Samantha.

"I don't know who you are! Last week you were a man, now you're just…" Vicky said. Her voice was quiet, but the look in her eyes was very loud. She continued, this time with more force, "just a stupid bastard. I was only with you because of Dave. He wanted to know what you were doing. You were a good laugh and I began to love you. Now you are just some stupid boy!"

I might have known she was seeing Dave in my previous life, and I might not have cared, staying with her to be near Samantha. She was correct in her assumption, I was a boy. Vicky wouldn't understand it was only forty-eight hours since I was a seventeen-year-old virgin. A boy was leaving the house and I knew that Samantha could see it. I wasn't ashamed of being caught in wild passion and I wasn't bothered Vicky loathed me. The realisation I loved Samantha made me sad, I could have done more, I didn't, and in that moment returned to being a seventeen-year-old virgin.

I was not the person my lover thought, I was who I was. Each step on the stairs was taking me down physically and mentally. I was moving into a very dark unknown. Even if the money was hidden here I would never have the opportunity to find it. I placed my keys on the telephone table below the alarm box. I knew I wouldn't return for Monday morning coffee, Tuesday morning tea, Wednesday morning scones, or any other morning. I could have been wallowing in infinite sadness over my stupidity, but today I didn't have time to wallow.

"Goodbye!" Samantha said, looking down from the top of the stairs, a tiredness creasing her face.

The pebbles crunching under my feet on the long walk to the front gate seemed to be shouting four letter words at me in cold repetition, crunch, crunch, cunt, cunt, and on. That quiet afternoon filled only by the mocking sound of age-old rock beneath my feet, the crunching sounding out a broken retreat from some kind of manhood. Would I ever find the guts to turn and fight my way back?

I'd only walked a few yards with each mocking step driving me back towards childhood. A few yards later each step was bringing me back to a very adult and harshly real world.

John Smith was waiting in his car. He leaned out of the window with a radiant smile across his face, and he waved a joyful greeting, happy to see his friend again?

"Let's talk!" John Smith said.

CHAPTER 34

Johnny and his friends, August 1973.

Feet of lead, my legs didn't want to move. How do you describe my short walk over to John Smith's car? Reluctant, very reluctant! I don't know to this day how he knew where I was. That was the kind of guy you were dealing with. He was so smart it was scary, holding a magic power when it came to pre-empting actions. The other thing about this immaculate thug was he always gave the impression of being cheerful. Smiling, his bright boyish smile in every situation. This was far more sinister than any hard man's face twisted and distorted by anger.

"All going to plan then? You haven't been searching, you've been shagging." He roared with laughter as he said this. He thought I had some master plan leading us both towards creating a power vacuum which we would fill, with profit.

In a couple of hours or so we were all going to be in The Cauldron, and I had this heavy dread my next journey in John Smith's car would be in the boot. I didn't know what to say to him. Telling the truth was the foolish idea beginning to hold credence in my muddled head. The truth, if he believed me, might give him the full picture, but his reaction could be anything including my death sentence? Silence filled the car with an uneasy friction, or it did from where I was sitting. John put his arm around my shoulder like a loving older brother, squeezing me a little bit too much, a little bit too matey.

"I bet it was fun in there, what with the girl coming at the same time as you." He was still laughing.

Between his belly laughs he continued, "I need your help and you have no choice. I've got a little present in the boot." The laughter had stopped his tone flat and filled with stone cold menace.

"A… what?" I asked. I shouldn't have.

"It's all right. He's still alive!" John said. His tone brightened by the thought of the fun to come.

"He's still alive! The present is a person?" I said, and I could hear the trembling tone to my voice. I hoped John couldn't. This oscillation may have only been inside my head, but I doubt it.

"It's not a present for you, Pete. This is much more fun. It's for Harry the Pocket," He started the car, driving off through the housing estate, and to my surprise turning out towards open countryside, a move that had me instantly concerned. Had he been twisting the truth, winding me in to his web. I was convinced he'd been talking rhetorically and I was going to be the present in the boot.

Our journey was down familiar roads, the same twisty country roads I'd enjoyed so much as a boy, free and out on my bike. I knew the area well and only minutes into our journey I realised John hadn't lied in some of what he'd told me. We were on the way to Harry's little place in the country, his water bounded hunting lodge. No matter how I thought about this, the sensation was one of being delivered like a parcel. Brought back into the fold, a deluded relation with Alzheimer's who's forgotten where the family jewels were hidden.

John chatted about girls, his plans to have a week's holiday and learn sub-aqua. He fancied diving in an exotic location because it reminded him of James Bond. With John this gave me an image of *Thunderball*, and all those men underwater killing each other with spear guns. This might be the piece of equipment he desired more than the air tanks and exotic locations. I could see him using a spear gun with a cord attached to attract people's attention and pull them into his circle of confidence.

The whirlwind of scared, crazy thoughts rushing around in my head drowned out most of what my Nazi twin was saying. I don't even know if I was thinking. The noise in my head was everything from the last two days shouting at me giving me every clue at once, and the only answer white noise. My eyes were fixed on the road. Somewhere on another level I was imagining cycling on a quiet Sunday morning on these very peaceful roads. I was thousands of miles and hundreds of days away from the now. I'd been cycling last Sunday. Of course that was now two years ago, though not as I remember it. I decided this void inside my head couldn't be the result of a stroke or small brain haemorrhage. I was functioning okay, if that's what I was doing.

We swung in through the big gates onto the crunchy gravel drive towards the big manor house. John settled back in the seat of his Rover looking smug.

"I own four of those flats and rent them out. All under different names of course, the same as you with your bank accounts all opened with different passport identities. One day I'm going to own them all, then this will be my drive. Harry gave me the idea. Investment in the future, that's what he called it. This is what we're doing right now," John said, all the while leaning back into the thick leather seats enjoying the drive along his road.

We pulled to a halt in front of the not so modest hunting lodge, and my companion wasted no time in leaving the car. The ignition was off, but with the keys were hanging in it. The temptation to slide across the seat, start the car and make my escape to God knows where was almost magnetic. The pull towards the driver's seat was almost irresistible. Then the thought of somebody or a body in the boot gave me the idea this was John Smith's intention. He wanted me to take the car and the blame. The running option disappeared, so I climbed out and walked towards the front door, joining my companion as he tapped very politely on the woodwork.

"Rang the bell, didn't seem to work," John said.

Knocking on the door was having a similar effect until John suggested we walk round the back. He tried the bell again. I was sure I could hear it inside. With the noise in my head I could have heard laughter on the moon. We walked around to the back of the lodge and were both surprised at finding a small fishermen on the jetty.

"Hello, where can I find Harry Graves?" John asked.

The fishermen had all the kit, green clothes, silly hat with flies stuck into the rim, and an assortment of nets and rods. He turned unsurprised by the request. This was Smiggy on his day off, or guarding the place with a diligence. He was taking full advantage of Harry's fishing rights. The boss never went near the water, couldn't stand the stuff, owned a boat, and owned a house surrounded by water, all of this was a statement. Harry himself liked whiskey, never went near the wet stuff.

"Wadda yous two want?" Smiggy enquired in his usual happy way.

"We've got some stuff for Harry. My friend here has found the goods. Come and look!" John said, with a definite upbeat sound. I was starting to wonder what he did have stashed away in his black Rover. Smiggy walked into the lodge through the open French windows. We followed. All the while he was muttering about having his day off interrupted, about can't a bloke have a bit of peace and quiet for once. I had a feeling he was here without permission and should have been following me. Now the boot was on the other foot and we were pursuing him.

John didn't waste any time. He felled Smiggy with one forceful blow to the side of the head. The active cold brutality took me by surprise. John Smith had knocked his victim cold with the brutal full power swing of the cosh, all delivered without a moment's thought. He may have even killed him. I was dumbstruck and worse, I had become part of this aberration. I didn't want to be part of anything to do with this man. With John Smith once you were involved, you're always involved. The other option was permanent retirement.

John Smith smiled at me swinging the weapon he'd used on Smiggy. It was a very well-constructed small cosh. This was a ten inch long double thickness leather strap with a small lead ball sewn between the leather at one end, and the wide strap spread the load giving a knockout blow without too many fractures.

"Wait here. If he comes round kick him!" John commanded. He left the room in the direction of the front door. I looked at the victim who was twitching, small spasms moving through is almost inert body. I had the impression he wasn't going to wake up. This would be the truth because Smiggy, the little weasel, wasn't going to steal any more eggs from other people's baskets.

John Smith returned wearing the most curious garb. He had his smart suit on with the trousers rolled up to the knees, and above everything was the same as before. It was the lower bare legs grabbing my attention. He was wearing a pair of huge steel toe capped boots, much too large for John's feet. They must have been size fourteen or more.

John walked over and looked down at Smiggy. He enquired if he'd said anything. The answer was obvious. He was unconscious three minutes ago and he was unconscious now. This was about to change. John kicked him hard with the boot in the same spot on the head he'd put the cosh in. John stamped with tremendous force on Smiggy's sinewy neck, then he drove his right foot down for a second time, it was nauseating.

The crack from the breaking vertebrae was audible with a crunching sound like crushing large popcorn. This sickening sound had me retching. The wave of revulsion was forcing anything in my stomach up. John smiled at me, and followed this up by putting the boot in again, this time stamping hard on Smiggy's ribs. The crunching sound echoed around the room. I had my hand over my mouth fighting to keep my stomach.

"Go and spew in the river you soft git, and don't come back smelling like it," John said. He wasn't examining the body. He didn't have to. As calm as someone out for an afternoon stroll John left the house and returned to the car wearing the murder weapons.

"Like I said, just like crushing an earwig!" John shouted these words as he retreated, laughing.

I thought about diving in the river and making a swim for it. I looked in hope at the boat, but it had a lock and chain fastening it to the mooring point. The questions in my head all concerned John Smith who I assumed could swim far faster than me and for much longer. If he didn't bother to pursue me I knew in my heart he would track me down. I wiped my mouth with some of the foul tasting river water. It tasted appropriate for what I'd just witnessed. After my moments of hesitation I returned to the lodge and found an outside gardening tap to wash my face. I wasn't going to walk through the French windows past the broken and death soiled body of Smiggy. He'd been a little weasel but surely he didn't deserve this. I walked round the outside and out onto the drive.

"Come on, Pete, I've got to show you my present," John said.

He was leaning against the boot of his car, one leg crossed over the other in a casual stance. The boots he'd worn for the murder were now placed beside him. His trousers were rolled down and he was wearing a pair of beautiful black leather loafers. I was standing a few feet away, something inside holding me back. I didn't want to be too close to my monstrous twin. John was smiling at me with amusement flickering across his lips. Casually he turned away and pulled the release for the car boot. Slowly and with a dramatic hand gesture he pulled it upwards. It was similar to a stage magician revealing his assistant moved by magic from one box to another. I expected him to say "Da… Da."

Inside the boot was a huge blob of a man, very powerfully muscled and very fat with it. He had large feet clad only in socks. John Smith had used this man's boots to stamp on poor Smiggy's neck. The boots had left a vivid, easily identifiable bruising on the victim's neck. The problem for the victim in the car was he didn't know he'd just murdered somebody, and who would believe him. He was an aggressive angry man looking for the killer of his brother. This was Walter Nice whose brother Raymond disappeared a few days before. Despite cries of innocence from Mr Smith, this man knew who the killer was.

"Walter didn't get on with big brother Raymond because he used him purely for muscle, never letting him in on the deal. Walt thought he deserved more. You know, thought he was underused. He's a dumb arse. So I turn up and get in on the deal, and he gets really angry, 'not even family, I get no respect' is what he shouted at me!" John laughed, "Didn't get respect from me either."

The man in the boot remained unconscious. He had a huge bruise across the side of his head. John Smith leaned into the boot and prodded the man hard in the stomach. Other than the wobbling of fat nothing happened. My evil twin carefully fitted the boots back onto the huge feet taking great care in tying them just so. It was as if he was putting booties on a baby such was the care he took.

"The big lug hasn't got to know he's had his boots off. If something goes wrong with the plan I don't want him to know about this until the police arrive. Anonymous tip off, you know the kind of thing!" John said.

I was about to ask him "How?" but I didn't have to. He explained he'd been expecting Walter Nice ever since the other night. He was ready, and the big idiot thought John would be easy meat. He was very wrong! John explained how Walter had cornered him as he was coming back to his car. The big man was convinced he could use brute force to grab and then bludgeon the truth out of John before he killed him. He wouldn't get his brother back but he'd give out retribution to this smiling little prick.

"That's what he said to me. 'Stop smiling you little prick. I'm going to wipe that grin off your pretty face forever,'" John told me. He continued, "I twatted the pillock about a second later. Then he was asleep. Fat git took a lot of moving." John slammed the boot of the car hard down, locking it for good measure. He climbed into the driver's seat giving me a nod to join him. I was moving around like a zombie following instructions and unable to think for myself. I was fighting an internal battle and the only question was do I run? Or do I run faster? The only problem was I seemed incapable of getting my legs to move, because I was totally unaware as to where they should take me. Did a hiding place exist where John couldn't find me?

John was lying back luxuriating in the leather seats as the car cruised slowly across his gravel drive leaving the big country mansion. I was watching him, and he was playing the country squire, the landowner who'd purchased everything through the miseries of others. John would justify his source of income as nothing more than nature's justice, the strong against the weak.

As we passed close to the farmhouse John was waxing lyrically about all the improvements he'd make to the estate when he owned everything. He may even purchase the hunting lodge to complete his kingdom. I heard some of his plans, but for the most part his words were ignored as I watched the countryside rolling past with dim interest. Everything crushed into in these frantic hours had been a surprise from the unexpected sexual initiation to my mother being a tigress with teeth. What could I possibly find out now that would change anything? In a couple of hours I was supposed to be in the pub to sort everything out. I lacked the slightest clue as to what I was sorting out. I had the drugs, they were my insurance. The money would never be found, that's if it was ever all in my possession!

John pulled the car over to the kerb, stopping in the middle of town only a few streets away from Harry's house, and not very far from my own little town house. Was I supposed to get out of the car now? John Smith got out and walked across the street to the phone box. He'd left the keys in the ignition. As if I was going to steal a car with an unconscious murder suspect in the boot? He was wearing the murder weapons and this was several years before DNA.

My brutal companion returned smiling, I assumed because his phone call had been a success. He gave me no clue as to who he'd been talking to. It may have had nothing to do with the situation at the moment, but more business to keep the wheels of the John Smith moneymaking empire in motion.

"Peter your still here? You've got to be ready for our big night of fun in The Cauldron. Go on! Get out! Go and get yourself ready. It was your plan in the first place to find the source and make a killing. As you know I made a killing, and in a short while possibly another," John said.

"My plan, some of it must be yours," I said.

"Fucking too right! I just hardened it up a bit," John said. He was still smiling as he drove away leaving me standing by the side of the road with only one thought in my head. My plan! Yes, he'd hardened it up a bit! I assumed I'd planned a coup, and John had decided to eliminate all the opposition!

But this terrible slaughter was mostly my plan!

CHAPTER 35

Right here right now, rocking the boat.

The radio club had captured every minute of every day. I had no time; this was my life. Every day key noted by waiting to be let into the secret lair of the radio club, and fried behind lead doors. This is not a complete lie. My days were passing by in a blur of chronic tiredness.

The first few weeks had been a joke for me. I had no skin burns, I had resistant skin, or would that be thick skin? I wasn't suffering from diarrhoea. Perhaps in this instance I was lucky. Radioactive rays were pointing very close to my stomach. I didn't suffer anything until five weeks in. This is when I noticed the days getting shorter, because I was asleep for much longer.

Every waking hour was geared to one purpose: drive to the hospital to be irradiated then return to my flat. Other than this I did nothing but dark daydream to keep in touch with a real world at some level. The rest of the time I was eating, moving very slowly or sleeping. To my regret the number of other dimensional experiences did not increase with my amount of sleep. Most of my sleep was filled with repetitious irritating nonsense, forgotten the instant I awoke. Nothing brilliant with crystal bright light and vivid all-encompassing sensation! So perhaps I was fighting back. Or did I need to?

Another poor child was anaesthetised and alone behind the foot thick door. I had a long wait for the Chernobyl effect. This gave me a lot of time for reflection, and as usual I returned to those brandy filled days listening to Rachel as she freed herself by voicing all her past horrors.

Discovering Maximilian Haussler had survived the war and now prospered dealing art in London, had tortured Rachel. She was obsessed by a desire for revenge. At night she would lie in bed safe in Abraham's arms with her baby girl in a cot at the end of the room. She couldn't bear the thought of being apart after all the separations in her life. Yet she'd left the baby for two weeks to search out the man her husband had described, the man who'd nearly cost him his dignity and his job. Her initial obsession had been finding him to prove it couldn't be Maximilian Haussler, she prayed he was dead, burnt in the war. He was alive and she was obsessed with bringing him to justice. Many times at night she thought about telling Abraham her story, but it would destroy him knowing the whole sordid truth. He didn't know she'd been used daily as a prepubescent sex toy by only one sadistic man.

Rachel explained that as the months passed the feeling she must seek revenge never lessened. In fact it grew to a point where several times she picked the phone up and dialled 999. Seconds later before any answer was given to her plight, she would slam the phone down. How could she prove this Swiss businessman was anything other than what he claimed? He would have all the papers and all the proofs he needed to make her the mad woman. The police had too many crimes and too little resource to follow up the crazed ravings of a Polish Jewish woman.

She then told me of a day she found the answer. Rachel had been shopping in the market and was strolling down a very narrow street which was lined on each side with a variety of interesting shops. Some of these were selling musical instruments, others clothing and shoes, for which after the camp she had developed a secret addiction. Her wardrobe hid too many pairs of shoes bought because they were pretty. Abraham wouldn't have understood especially all that expense just for shoes.

The street was so varied and Rachel was enjoying her time looking in the shop windows. One particular shop caught her attention. It was an antique shop and they needed a nice clock to go on top of the fireplace, nothing from the 30s but something similar to a Victorian carriage clock. This is what she'd got in mind. The proprietor showed her two good quality clocks. Rachel enquired if he had more. While the shopkeeper moved off into the back to delve into his stock she spent her time looking into various display cases. This is when she found the answer.

It came in the form of a 1938 Nazi ceremonial dagger. This particular dagger was the SS model, and this made it irresistible. Barley sugar twist ivory handle with gold braid in the bottom of the twists, a T-bar made in the shape of very fine eagles' feathers followed by the thing that grabbed Rachel's attention. This ceremonial dagger had a stainless steel blade, diamond in section and ten inches long. It came in a lovely gold dimple worked scabbard with two hanging rings and small scar where the Nazi insignia had been prised off at some time.

None of the details interested Rachel. The justice of having this ten inch ceremonial blade driving into Maximilian's heart while blood rushed out along the blade was enough. She could watch his life forces spurt out. Thinking of this Rachel didn't care if the blood squirted all over her body, her face and her arms. Thinking of the hot sticky metallic life force oozing from this abomination made her catch her breath. The thought of it excited her in a way that also appalled. She needed the knife, this knife, not any other knife. This ceremonial representation of Nazi power was going to destroy the man who'd taken her, penetrated in every way. Now he would be penetrated in a final ugly end to his degenerate murder laden life.

Rachel didn't buy a carriage clock. She made more of her accent pretending it was from further south, somewhere in Germany. She purchased the SS ceremonial dagger for the purpose of her own little ritual of ceremonial slaughter. The shopkeeper wrapped it with great care for her because he knew he was selling it to somebody who'd supported the party. He didn't like Spics and Jews. He'd spent the war hoping a man with real charisma would conquer this wishy-washy nation, and he would've become an avid supporter of his strong pure views. He'd sold the dagger for cost, plus a little bit. A true old-time party member would understand. He winked at Rachel as she left the shop.

The dagger was hidden away in the house, and with the weapon to kill Maximilian the urge to carry out the final act subsided. A few weeks passed in which desire for revenge had disappeared, or perhaps she'd understood the gravity of buying the knife. She could go to the gallows for what she planned. With a good judge she might serve fifteen years in prison, and Rachel wouldn't survive in any prison after her hell in the camp. The dagger would remain hidden until the day when she threw it away, unused. Rachel would never get the opportunity to stab Maximilian in the heart.

The dagger was easy to forget until a neighbour put a sign up in his front garden. "House for sale". Abraham had noticed it, mentioning it casually as he came in for dinner. He was very pleased with himself, things were going well at the bank, and an official whisper of his promotion to deputy manager had been passed to him. Abraham was delighted that he'd climbed back to a good position in such a short time. It wasn't London, and it was a provincial branch, but nevertheless. With her head full of panic Rachel wasn't listening to a husband, and every word he spoke was a background jumble.

"House for sale" had terrified her. Now there was no time to waste. In a handful of seconds it had all rushed back in. If Maximilian moved in London' it would be almost impossible to find him, and if he moved to another country her chance of revenge would be lost forever. Rachel could feel one of her depressions coming on, a time when she needed to be with her sister Mila in London.

Only a couple of weeks rest and time away from her demanding child would brighten her mood. Another thing was praying on Rachel's mind. She hadn't had her period for two months and was starting to feel nauseous in the mornings. She had great joy at the thought of a new child coming into the world, and now great panic to get the job done before Maximilian moved or she got wrapped up in family matters for the rest of her life. If she was going to kill him it would have to be in the next three weeks!

I was imagining Rachel on a train going down to London clutching her small cardboard suitcase. Abraham had begged her many times to buy a new one, but this was the case she'd brought from the American army hospital camp in Poland. The case became the only thing left from those dark days. She decided that after Maximilian was dead a complete purge of the past would take place. The little battered case would go, and she would buy a shiny brown leather case to represent the bright new future.

Then I was looking at the brown leather case and all my other reality had vanished. You've got to understand in the alternative universe I have no past in this world. I was no longer remembering Rachel's small cardboard suitcase. In this world it had never existed. The brown leather case was placed very carefully under the legs of the table. I looked up expecting to see a train, or a pub, or a village green with a game of cricket. What I didn't expect was a connection between two of them. It started with a cool breeze followed by a sensation of every molecule in my body flowing across a sea of moving oil. I opened my eyes and I was on a ferryboat, a large ferryboat. I could feel every movement inside the engine and fish swimming at great depths below the keel. I needed something to concentrate my attention away from the millions of sensations. Full focus came into my world.

She wore no make-up. Jennifer never had to. She was looking out across the sea watching brilliant white almost iridescent silver cliffs passing by several miles to the south. I know it was the south. This is how sensations work in an all-encompassing super reality. I watched her looking across to the land. I could feel the wind blowing through her hair and the essence from her body passing by me on those vapours. Salt was everywhere in a fine mist in the air. I didn't want to distract her. I was looking at something far more beautiful than any painting. The *Mona Lisa* was a dull daub executed by a poor artist. What I was seeing not only delighted my senses. It poured through my heart.

"This is the train ferry, owned by the railway company, linking the two countries. We're going to Paris for dinner!" Jennifer said, turning to me as she did so. As if she'd known I'd been watching the whole time. Then again, I might have been with her all day. This is something I don't know. Perhaps I am always in this dimension and only join myself from brief snippets of my better life. I don't think this is true. It's just I like to imagine I'm never without her.

"The train ferry? Do you mean the actual train is on the boat?" A stupid thing to ask, I could sense cooling water, dying steam.

"Of course, silly. How else are we going to get to Paris? We don't have to move our luggage. It stays on the train," Jennifer replied.

"You brought the bag," I said, looking down at it, discovering it was now open-mouthed.

"Yes, this is an educational school trip."

"After my last visit at the cricket match I didn't burn, and I didn't see you!"

"I think the education burnt you enough, but I was surprised when you didn't return. The Lylybel wasn't!" Jennifer said. She was looking downwards and my eyes followed hers.

I looked into the bag and I could see the ferryboat from the air, on the very sea we were travelling on, so fine in detail I could make out myself looking down into the bag. I wondered if this went on for infinity, down the scale of dimension and up the scale also. I was concentrating on these thoughts when I started to fall. I was plunging from a thousand feet in the air down towards another deck where I was sitting opposite Jennifer. I was in danger of crashing down on top of myself. Then I noticed…

The other me had also disappeared. I landed very gently opposite the smaller Jennifer. At this point the only thought in my head was if a version of me from above had landed opposite my Jennifer. The girl opposite me was the same girl, the same size. There was one difference. She was wearing a very wry smile and pointing up at the bridge of the ship.

The captain wore Mediterranean whites, a spectacular uniform with gold braid encrusted epaulets. This captain's hair cascaded over her shoulders in wondrous glistening curls. Yes, the captain was my favourite pixie.

"Welcome to the SS *Nimrod*, the ship that hunts. You'll notice we are running purely on memory. No coal or oil involved here!" pixie stated. Then she added, "You still think I'm a pixie. One day I'll put you right. Now look up at the funnel."

And there it was, SS *Nimrod* steaming along in all her glory with millions of bubbles pouring out of the funnel. They were all being blown away to leeward with no chance of me popping one, as if this trifle would stop the pixie's plans. The funnel started to produce a giant grey bubble that grew in size moment by moment until it was as large as a house. It detached itself and flopped onto the surface of the sea. All the other bubbles were landing softly on the surface of the sea, and none ever broke. I had a temptation to dive in and find the brightest bubble I could, prodding it to release a happy glorious memory.

No such luck. The pixie ordered the crew onto the deck. They were all dressed as doctors wearing white coats with the obligatory stethoscope around their necks. She snapped out an order in a high pitched voice, all in a language I didn't understand. The doctors moved in around me, all eight of them. I was lifted bodily from the deck, and without ceremony thrown off the leeward side of the ferry. I was joining the big grey bubble floating in the sea.

"Just what the doctor ordered. A nice swim, it will do you good!" The pixie shouted through a megaphone, followed by a long giggly laugh.

I remained still treading water. The wind was blowing all the other bubbles across the top of the waves. The grey bubble was moving contrary to nature advancing towards me giving me little choice. This great grey blob rolled over the top of me pushing me down under the water. The only thing I could do was claw at it. I was drowning. So this was how it was going to be. I would die under this bubble of grey memory, or burst my way into the fat horror.

I was thrashing at the bubble, fighting to hold my breath, when two strong arms pulled me up out of the cold water.

"I thought you'd gone forever. You've been out of it for two days like a bloody zombie!" Lenny said to me.

I was in the stained bath at Lenny's place. He'd been plunging me into cold water to see if he could break me out of my catatonic state. I was wet through and fully dressed in the same dirt stained clothes I'd arrived in.

"You've got to stop doing this. Throw those clothes away. Stop doing the acid!" Lenny said.

The memory of me in the bath knew what Lenny was talking about. I was starting to get the idea I'd been at Lenny's for more than two days.

"I'm trying to forget what Bob did. I take the acid to go somewhere else. I don't know why I keep putting these clothes on," the other me told Lenny.

At this Lenny punched me hard in the face, stunning me with a blow to the jaw. After the blow he started to rip every shred of clothing from my body, and pushed everything into a large carrier bag until I was naked. Not even the shoes were spared. All my fine bird pulling clothes from the old days disappeared. Lenny fumbled in his pocket and produced a small glass bottle, and from it he took a very tiny pill.

He grabbed my face in a vicious handhold, his fingers bruising my cheeks. Forcing my mouth open he pushed this small white pill between my teeth and then put his hand across my mouth until I swallowed.

"You either forget whatever it is, or go and sort it out with Bob! If you don't straighten up you can fuck off out of my house!" Lenny shouted as he marched to the door with a bag of soiled clothes I'd never see again.

It was one of those drifting memories. The next thing I was in the same bath naked and wet with warm water, half drunk on champagne. Sharing the now very clean bath with me was a pretty girl. We were both drunk and having a whale of a time. Lenny staggered past the door with a very dark-haired naked girl clutching his not inconsiderable hairy girth. He disappeared into another room with a look over a shoulder and a big wink of the eye.

"Things are looking up, and by the look of it everything's looking up!" Lenny said, laughing as he left the room.

The next thing I'm laid back on Lenny's sofa watching snow come down outside. Months had passed since the August day when I set off to lose my virginity. Things were very different in the house. The room was decorated and furnished with good taste. The dirt covered broken old furniture had disappeared. Lenny was bent over a small desk in the corner, a very nice bureau, possibly an antique. After a few minutes in which I was content to watch the snow, Lenny stood up from the desk in his usual lumbering manner and came over to me. The wad of notes must have contained £500 in a variety of denominations. You could put a deposit on a nice house for less.

"Here's your share this week. We're doing really well. Are you going to buy the place in town or that poncey flat?" Lenny asked.

I watched as the other me put the wad of money with a confidence I've never possessed into his top pocket, then the other me announced his intentions.

"I'm buying both. The poncey flat for me and the place in town as a base when I'm pissed or I find a pretty girl," I said. I was laughing all the while and smug with my success.

Lenny threw me a can of beer, one of those new ring pull ones. I pulled the tab and the bloody beer squirted in my face and all over my new clothes. It was burning my skin and I was nauseous with the movement. Everything was wrong. Seawater surrounded me on all sides, and because I was alone in the open ocean the only shadow in burning sunlight was cast by my solitary figure. All around me this water burnt into my skin like a million fire ants trying to devour my body. I was screaming loud and long but nobody could hear me. I wasn't drowning, I was burning to death.

Such pain, such a time trapped inside it without release. One minute or was it five minutes? I had no idea. People quote things from the movies, "like a sea of pain", and I was immersed in it. So intense was the burning that I believed it had reached my bones. I was trying to drown myself without success. This time I couldn't scream at the pixie to put me out. My lungs were burning on the inside full of corrosive liquid. This time I was going to die, going to crumble away to nothing in a sea of acid.

My mouth was full of liquid. I was going to drown and not suffer this agony for much longer. There was no saltiness to this water, it tasted like real ale. My eyes were closed tight in an effort to prevent the acid water dissolving them. Hops and barley persuaded me to open them.

Across the table Jennifer was putting her glass down and smiling at me. I was dry.

"I've never seen anybody underwater for eight minutes. Pretty impressive," she said, then asked me an important question. "Where would you like to eat in Paris?"

CHAPTER 36

Right here right now, would anybody like London gin?

Things were looking up. That's if you consider chronic fatigue and urinal incontinence are improvements over before. The other option: you don't have treatment and your disease metastasises into bone cancer or other secondary cancers. So, all in all, things were looking up. The treatment was over, but I had to wait for three months until next blood tests which could reveal if it had all been for nothing.

I'd fought my way through the last week, every day a struggle, with one goal in mind. To finish the treatment and say goodbye to all my friends in the radio club. With that goal taken away from my sight line, fatigue from radiation sickness grabbed me with both hands throwing me down a hole into what I knew wasn't depression.

Totally fatigued? The doctor usually assumes you're depressed. This is the most depressing thing about doctors. I wasn't depressed I was tired from radiation sickness. Once again I'd retreated into the cool dark of the cave house. Being half alive with drowsiness wasn't helping fight my desire for absorption in alternative universe. The last few times when returning from the sensual universe my emotional response had changed.

The last couple of journeys into paradise I'd woken with emotions more muted in their angst. As I learn more about my dark period (my wilful insomnia) I suffer far less from the feelings of a dark hidden guilt. I suppose with some of the truth now in my consciousness I no longer have secrets prisoner in a tortured corner of my psyche. The new emotion I experience is regret, a large regret that I live in this hard and dull world. Though I've fought against it, I remain addicted to Jennifer and all the sensations of the alternative reality. I am determined to break this habit, but conversely I hope to visit the other reality periodically for the rest of my life. I need this to survive.

Courage is a strange word. People keep telling me how brave I am, how courageous I've been against the cancer. In truth at first I was terrified, then I came to except my illness, after which what do you do? Curl up in a ball and die? The alternative is to fight.

Rachel's courage came from a cold corner of hatred. She had to kill Maximilian Hauser by thrusting a Nazi ceremonial dagger through his evil heart. This vile beast of a man had kept her alive by using her as a sex slave. He'd made her his toy, gave her food, kept her away from disease and the gas chambers. Rachel knew she may not exist if it hadn't been for his sexual cruelty. Then she thought about the poor other girls who he shot in the face, one whilst in the act of so-called lovemaking! She had survived because her young body had looked like a prepubescent woman, and he had some unaccountable fixation with her.

She was staying with Mila once more. Five days had passed in which she sat in the window seat and watched the traffic go by. Sometimes she would read an Agatha Christie murder novel; this wasn't to give her ideas for the execution. Was it only to pass the time? She knew standing face-to-face with Maximilian was the way she wanted to kill him. At the moment he realized the beautiful shapely woman in front of him was his little Rachel she would drive the dagger through his heart and look into his eyes. Once he'd looked into Rachel's eyes as he shot another girl in the face. Smiling, always smiling.

On the sixth day after several intense personal arguments, Rachel decided she would execute him that evening. Months earlier she'd stalked him all the way to his exclusive apartment where she waited and watched until a light came on in a fourth floor room. She hung around watching the window, and finally was rewarded by a sighting of Maximilian as he strolled past the window his head buried in a large book.

Later that same day as darkness took the light, Rachel walked round the back of the building to discover that the staff, one porter and a caretaker, propped the fire door open so they could slip out for a fag. Even in the early 1950s in this class of establishment only the clients could smoke in the hallways. The staff members were always polite and never smoked; not in front of the gentlefolk. This would be her point of entry, and if it was closed she would have to think of something else.

To prepare herself she dressed in the oldest clothes she could find. They would be incinerated in the heating boiler down in the basement of her sister's block of flats. It was so premeditated. She carried a roll up plastic mackintosh, not to put on before the murder. She had brought this to cover the bloodstains because she wanted time after the murder to feel the life force outside his body, proof in the stains on her clothes that this death blood was real and not some illusion. She arrived at 6:30pm. It was dark and the light was on. He was at home. At that moment a new panic emerged, Rachel never imagined he might live with someone, and at the eleventh hour this disturbing idea came to her. What if he had a wife and children? Could she slaughter the pig in front of people who almost certainly wouldn't know his crimes? The rear fire door was propped open, only an inch, but it was open.

Rachel was very careful not to make a sound as she pulled at it. She could not stop herself and impulse had her stepping inside all too quick to look casual. If somebody watching had seen her, suspicious would be the only word to describe the way she was acting. It wasn't dark enough, it wasn't late enough and she wasn't sure if she was courageous enough. She could hear the sound of a radio playing in a small room by the front entrance. This would be the doorman's cubicle where he rested when he didn't have duties to perform. He was listening to some music on the BBC, humming along with the string section.

The service stairs didn't leave the front entrance hall. Her luck was in because they went up towards the rear of the building only a few feet from the back fire door. Fate seemed to want this thing to happen, giving her a good hand to play.

The building was a very fine example of art deco architecture. The entrance hall was glass fronted with a full sweep of curved glass broken up into dozens of small panes by a curved steel frame. This was repeated all the way up the main stairwells for five floors. Maximilian lived in the second apartment to the right on the fourth floor. Coming from the back of the building she would only be visible through the front glazing for a few moments. The gods were with her that night because the light bulb on the fourth floor stairwell was broken. Her visit to Maximilian's would be unseen. The door she must knock on would be the second along the corridor. Would she hold her nerve and knock?

She was going to talk her way into his apartment if she could find the courage. On the way across London she'd bought a clipboard and would pretend to be from the water board, surveying who had lead pipes that needed removing. Copper was now the thing and the lead dangerous to your health. She laughed at herself. This was her plan and it didn't inspire her. With her nerves in tatters she reached his door. It was a massive oak structure with a huge brass knob in the middle. The door also featured a spy hole but not the modern tiny glass monocular. This was a four-inch square eye level hatch. You could see out and, but with the massive door as protection, nobody could get in.

Rachel could hear music playing inside the apartment. This was no old-fashioned record player. He owned a radiogram that played those new long-playing records. She could tell by the quality of the sound. Wagner, he was playing Wagner, and singing along with it. This gave her confidence because Maximilian's singing was as atrocious as it was loud. With her ear pressed to the door the full power of his terrible singing could be heard. This convinced Rachel he lived alone. No wife or child could stand such an awful sound. His singing made her want to kill him all the more, plus she hated Wagner.

A minute passed, followed by another agonisingly slow minute, after which another minute passed. Her arm was frozen by her side. The music played on and the arm disobeyed any order inside her head to make a move. It was frozen solid, incapable of knocking on the door, incapable of acting out this slaughter. The record finished and all was silent for about a minute until Beethoven burst onto the scene. The intro to the fifth sounded like somebody knocking on the door. For reasons she couldn't understand, her arm decided to move in synchronicity along with Beethoven's music.

Da da da, daaa. Knock, knock, knock, knock! Her eyes opened wide in surprise. What the hell was she doing? She was a pregnant Jewish woman attempting to kill her Nazi persecutor in the hallway of a nice London apartment block. She'd never get away with it. He'd realise who she was and murder her along with her unborn child, my future friend Bob.

"Alright, alright, I'm coming, no need to make too much of a fuss!" Maximilian shouted above the music. From the sound of his voice he was only feet from the door, and she was only moments from attempted murder. No, not attempted murder, but rightful execution. She could hear him fumbling, but not with the door lock. No, he was fumbling with the little door, the spy hole. The plan melted away in less than a second, and in less than another second she turned and ran, making the corner onto the landing before the spy hole opened. She told me she could hear him bellowing through the hole, something about the bloody doorman being a lazy idiot! The sound of his angry voice made her shiver in terror, she was fifteen again and naked at his behest.

Rachel didn't slow until the ground floor where the radio played on and possibly the doorman slept on, though Rachel would never know this. She started the six-mile walk back to her sister's by throwing the Nazi dagger and the clipboard into a dustbin in a nearby alleyway. Crying a deep mournful sob with every step away from Maximilian's apartment she was as low as possible, and every step back towards her sister took her away from the stainless steel blade. She was halfway back walking in the rain, the water on her face hiding sorrowful tears.

This was the moment fate told Rachel it wanted her to take his life. Outside a public house, a poor excuse for a pub, the low end of the low end, a couple were arguing.

"Always think you're right, don't you? You're a stupid bitch!" the red-faced skinny man was shouting.

"You don't tell me what to do you drunken slob!" a little sparrow of a woman in poor clothes was screaming back at him.

He hit her as hard as he could in the face, his fist catching her between the nose and her top teeth. Blood spurted everywhere as she fell to the floor.

"That's what a real man can do. Don't you know you women are nothing? Stupid cow!" He turned without looking at her and walked back into the pub for some more drink. She was nothing!

Other people rushed out of the pub to help the woman crumpled in a miserable heap on the floor. Rachel could see the thuggery in this man's brutal attack, and this brought back memories of brutal buggery by Maximilian. If only one man in the world wasn't going to get away with his crimes it was that German, that Nazi officer. The thin man came bursting out from the pub doors. A heavy set grey old man had him by the throat, and he was beating him without mercy, all the while whispering to the skinny man, "If you wanna fight, fight a man!" Rachel was frozen to the spot watching this tableau unfold. A big crowd was forming and she could hear a police whistle. This wasn't a time to get involved with something like this.

Panic had set in. She had lost the SS ceremonial dagger. It was in some dustbin. She knew exactly where it was, in an alleyway one street after the apartments, three miles away, and no telling who could have looked in the bins since she threw it there. She started to run, and this wasn't difficult because she wore flat shoes put on for balance if she got into a fight with Maximilian. By the time she arrived at the dustbins she couldn't tell if she was soaked in sweat or rain. She had to get the dagger back. She had to use it on him tonight!

Rachel started to search in the over laden dustbin. The clipboard could be seen clearly lying on the top of the rotting garbage. The dagger was nowhere.

Old vegetables and God knows what else filled those bins. She didn't care about the squalor. Rachel dug furiously into the stinking rubbish, it had to be found. The dagger which carried brutal significance in her plan had slipped down the side of the rubbish to the bottom of the bin where it was half buried in a stinking jelly of rotten goo. She didn't care. It was a glorious moment. The weapon had returned to her hands. There wasn't a thought for the stench of rotting food on her clothes. Her hands were black with this sticky filth, but she didn't care. Nothing so trivial was going to move her from her purpose. She was blinded by the desire to kill, blinded by the desire to penetrate his body.

It was a lot quieter now. I was nodding off.

I suppose transport of information could be looked on as lines or conduits. This is what I was starting to think on reflection about my parallel universe. I slipped off into a dream remembering nothing of Rachel joyously standing in the rain in rapture at finding her ceremonial dagger. I was now in the best of all worlds, waiting for the train, or the bus, or the ferryboat.

I had a feeling of *déjà vu* because we were sitting across another table from each other. This time no breeze played in Jennifer's hair. The boat was fully glazed, and the interior was *haute cuisine*, beautiful white tablecloths covered in an array of crystal brilliance. There was a glass for absolutely everything in the world you could possibly think of, and in this universe, some you couldn't. We were enjoying a very fine steak, and I don't think the flame had kissed it for more than three seconds. It was melt in the mouth delicious, and in this world delicious meant out of this world. The boat moved along with a smooth elegance. A string quartet played light lyrical music in the bows of the restaurant, and our conversation was intimate and fascinating. The whole day passed slowly in an array of light, sounds, smells and stunning sensation.

No briefcase was visible, no pixie anywhere to be seen, nothing to spoil this perfect day. We were finishing the gourmet experience with a gin and tonic, a beautiful effervescent green gin from France. This was the perfect *coup de grace* to the whole afternoon. I placed my empty glass on the table looking at the melting ice in the bottom, when Jennifer pointed something out to me. In the bottom of my glass among the ice I spotted the dead fly.

"Hoy, you up there. Yes, you. It's me, Hysandrabopel. You know your pixie." She was wearing what appeared to be black sub-aqua gear.

"Have you been there all day, watching?" I enquired.

"No, I have been with the dog in the invisible briefcase. They're both under the table!" pixie said. And so they were.

I shouldn't have concentrated. I was squinting down into the glass to get a better look at the tiny pixie with her ridiculous rubber suit on, the flippers far too big for such a small girl. She was, yet again, a frog. I suppose it was appropriate in Paris, if it was Paris? I concentrated too much and the next thing I knew I was swimming among the icebergs and the cold was extreme.

"Paul, take the bubble quick before you freeze to death!" Jennifer said, with great affection for my well-being in her voice.

Pixie walked over splashing through waist-deep icy water. Most of the gin had gone and all that remained was the residue of melting ice. She was as large as me which always came as a surprise. Grinning like a loon she handed me her spear gun.

"You'll need this to burst the bubble!"

I was about to ask what bubble when she put her snorkel down into the icy water and sucked. She then, with an almost violent deliberation pointed it at me and blew as hard as she could. Out of the snorkel came a bubble that was as black as coal and the size of a golf ball. The damn thing shot towards my face at one hundred miles an hour. I had no chance of aiming a spear gun, the only thing I did was swing and pull on the trigger. The spear gun was no ordinary weapon. It had a mind of its own sending the tethered spear on a direct course into the black orb. The spear struck the orb digging deep into its tough flesh. So there I was holding a spear gun with a fierce grip, waist-deep in icy water with what felt like a twenty ton weight pulling on me.

The tether on the spear gun wasn't strong enough to reel in the tiny orb, but it was strong enough too real me into the tiny orb. I tried desperately to release the contraption from my grip, but my hands were frozen hard to the handle with ice. The only way to release the gun was to rip the skin off my hands. I was willing to go to this length, however, time had run out and the cord was rushing in. There was nothing I could do but follow my harsh fate hard into that black orb.

CHAPTER 37

Clothes, different envelope, same old bad news, August daze 1973.

They, whoever they are, say that clothes maketh the man. My clothes were making me sick. No longer the gauche teenager, I appeared to have gained impeccable style in the last two years. My suits were not cheap or nasty like those worn by plain-clothes police officers. Mine were Reed and Taylor cloth, precision cut by a local master tailor, and impeccably finished with the finest silk linings. All the accessories, shirts, shoes, and the dozens of ties were of equal quality. All these fine clothes shouted money in a small town. What they also shouted was criminal! I made money not through hard work, but by working a hard product into other people's lives.

Smiggy had been broken like a plastic doll by the psychopathic John Smith. I probably knew he was a psycho before. This time it only took me only forty-eight hours to rediscover the lunatic inside him. There were no laws, because John was a warrior in a different world, living in an older time without governments or constraints. A world in which he could shape his own form, become as terrible as he desired. In a different era he could've forged a kingdom through terror and guile. I was in league with this lunatic, and I'd even suggested the basic bones of a scheme he now carried out. I knew I hadn't suggested the gory mayhem, but realised John Smith liked permanent solutions, no comebacks, no surprises in the middle of the night. With adversaries dead he was at peace, and so were they.

The quality clothes I wore reminded me of everything I'd become. I was the dismal coward who stood by and watched a murder. I didn't like Smiggy, but I didn't dislike him enough to lash out and kill him. John Smith, saw him in a different light. He was a little snitch, and John didn't like being watched. His solution was to murder. What I feared most of all was I would become a victim in John's constant quest for credo, another victim to put others in fear.

He wanted to run the show, having everybody in awe of him. A cold void lived inside this lunatic and you had to be in awe because being involved with him was more dangerous than juggling nitro glycerine. It wasn't a matter of will it explode killing you, that was given, and the only question was, when?

The summit meeting in the pub was closing in on me. I saw no reason why I should go. Of course, if I wanted to live in this town there was no way I couldn't go. I couldn't run, John Smith wouldn't allow it. He'd seek me out half a world away, and kill me as a demonstration of his powers to others. Returning to my wrecked flat would be a wasted walk. Normal teenage street clothes weren't part of my lavish wardrobe. Also I imagine by now most of my clothes had been ruined by the terrible duo who'd been watching me. They would've taken delight in slashing my handmade suits, and urinated in my shoes. This is the kind of thing they thought was funny. There was nothing much in my other place. I now realised it was used after a good night out, somewhere to rest my head or spend the night not resting with some girl. I didn't know if Samantha had ever visited, though I doubted it. My clothing was impeccable, and the whole ensemble reeked of a person I didn't want to know – me.

In 1973 the new late shopping was coming in. Some of the outlets in the new shopping centre stayed open until 7pm, and the town was taking advantage of this new business opportunity despite the three-day week and the frequent power cuts. (My aunties were right!) I decided that if clothes made the man I would form myself in a new image. I desperately wanted to rid myself of the past two years, expunge the unremembered. The irony was not lost on me. I would be buying my new clothes with money from the same miserable trade. The new look would be no different from the suit I wore unless the clothes purchased today became a first step on a long road to reform. This was the moment I took the first faltering step on my journey to the present day. And I started this journey wearing the latest in sports shoes – trainers!

I spotted them in the middle of the window on a plinth. The shoes were of blue suede in three colours, not in vivid contrasts, but more subtle shade differences. The sole was made up of three layers of blue rubber, also subtle in its contrasting stripes. This *soufflé* of sporting delight was topped off by the outer sole formed to look like miniature motocross tyres with a small block knobbly pattern. The price was quite extraordinary for shoes, and they were only shoes. I would pay far more for my smart black shoes, but these were only sports shoes and the price was vicious.

I tried them on. They only had three sizes, nine, nine and a half, and ten. One pair fitted perfectly. They were the most comfortable things I'd ever worn, light and springy. Somewhere deep inside a voice was shouting, "Buy them!" So I did. I dumped my beautiful shoes in the wastepaper bin, and from the corner of my eye I noticed they were retrieved by the assistant before I'd even left the shop. I saw him slipping them under the counter in the reflection from the plate glass window. If he knew where those shoes had taken me he'd have left them in the bin.

I hadn't owned a pair of Levis for over forty-eight hours, or two years in real time. I wanted to get back into something casual, to slip back to being a teenager rather than a gangster, a drug dealing lowlife, an idiot who suggested business plans to a psychopath. The 70s were an era of terrible fashion and innovation, this depending on your view. Stonewashed jeans, this was the first day I'd ever seen these. Again the pricing was vicious, and they had a pair that fitted. I stayed in the shop until I purchased everything right down to the underwear. I placed everything apart from two items in the carrier bag in the changing room, leaving it all sitting under the bench.

I didn't feel anything like the seventeen-year-old me, and with my much heavier frame I didn't look much like that teenager either. I was nearly twenty and feeling so much older. The fitting had gone well. Now I wore a white T-shirt, dark blue V-neck sweatshirt, and with a defiance to my past two years no need for a coat. The young shop assistant couldn't believe his luck when I told him the suit was in the changing room. I hope he didn't want the underclothes!

My associates loved coats, big coats, overcoats in the summertime, somewhere to hide your angry girlfriend, Millicent. I'd strolled about with my heavy overcoat draped across my shoulders. Who the hell did I think I was, Al Capone? It was as if a burden had been lifted from my shoulders, the simple act of relieving myself of the weight of those clothes gave me the slight feeling of hope. I stopped at a phone box and contacted my sister at work. We talked for a few minutes. I explained the deep worries I held about tonight's meeting and I told her I believed John Smith was insane. She told me she had no doubt at all about that. I asked her at the end of the conversation if she had any ideas. My sister didn't raise my spirits with any suggestions to give hope, and nothing was forthcoming apart from some vague promise to think about it.

It was almost confrontation time. I walked in the direction of The Cauldron. The trainers were a revelation. Each step was a new freedom allowing me to bounce along at a pace. I was in no hurry to get to the pub, but the shoes were in a great hurry to show me how good they were. Then I came across the Old King. I decided that I needed some Dutch courage. I was going to invest in a pint of beer, and then changed my mind opting for a large brandy, after which I had a pint of beer. You never knew who was drinking in some of these lowlife establishments, and this place had no quality. No lounge bar, no restaurant, and the eating area always between your thumb and fingers. Only a bar, but this in a way was a lie. This drinking establishment had two bars, the better equipped with dart boards and a pool table, the other bar for the serious sport of drinking yourself senseless.

I was at the bar in the quiet end, the bar that didn't have any "sports" equipment. It was too early in the day for people to be drinking themselves senseless apart from two semi-conscious figures slumped at a table in the corner arguing about boxing, "Ali, he is the man, Ali."

"No, Frazier, yeah Frazier." This was followed by a long silence until another name was thrown into the hat, and again Muhammad Ali appeared from nowhere. He was magic!

"Greatest. Yeah, greatest." They may have been more coherent. I was in deep conversation with myself. It was a shouting match between several idiots, none of whom knew the answer to anything. They all shouted at once. Run, run for your life, fight, fight for your life, negotiate, and negotiate for your life. All bollocks! I was like a sapling in the wind waiting for the storm. I ordered another brandy. As I sipped it inspiration came! I had an inkling of an idea that might work.

Other people had other ideas. Some lowlife looking through from the other bar had seen me. The word was out and he could make a quick five pounds. The Cauldron beckoned me and I was in no hurry to get to the happy hour reunion. Rushing would only make me hot and I'd had a premonition of the heat inside The Cauldron. Leaving the Old King by the side entrance, I'd taken only a few steps towards the side gates of the pub when a friendly voice beckoned me over.

"Hello. Millicent wants to ask you a few questions… Now!" Dave Hartley Sparrow said. Millicent was shy this evening, hiding under the ubiquitous overcoat. He was wearing his usual light beige coat with a double-breasted front and dark contrasting collar. Two deathly black eyes peeked out from behind the unbuttoned front. Millicent was being very persuasive. With a drink inside me for courage I managed to be very scared. Without the drink I might've had a heart attack on the spot, but then the quick coronary infarction might be better than slowly bleeding to death with half my face blown away.

"Harry's dead! I wanna know before I kill you right here, right now, If you helped?" Dave was spitting in my face as he said this. More worrying was I could feel both barrels hard against the bottom of my pelvis. He had the gun pressed hard into my penis, and I could hardly speak. Pain was one thing, but my vocal chords were crippled by fear.

"Kill Harry? Nobody's killed Harry! Have they?" I think these words came from my mouth in a squeak. It felt like it.

"Harry's dead! Blown away by some big fat guy. He's dead too. Only thing is Harry doesn't use a gun. He uses me!" Dave said, no truer word ever spoken.

Inspiration can change the world, inspiration can change how you feel about yourself, inspiration can come at the moment when you most need it, and my inspiration was a small square of paper in my pocket. It may save my life. No, I wasn't going to offer him money.

"I saw John earlier. He said he was going to Harry's. I went shopping. I have receipts!" Pathetic I know, but at that moment I was grasping for the lightest straw imaginable. He pressed the gun even harder in the top of my testicles. I reached into my pocket in a slow deliberate movement, his eyes never leaving mine. One of them may have followed my hand for a fraction of a moment. He was not going to be diverted from his purpose, and was concentrating fully. My hand touched the flimsy piece of paper from the boutique. Very slowly and with great care I drew it from my pocket. It was so slow that for a second I thought he might shoot me in frustration.

"Look, I was shopping an hour ago, I was shopping an hour and a half ago for shoes, and I have another receipt. John dropped me off in town. You've got to believe me." I sounded like I was begging for my life, a pathetic beggar of a man. This was true. Dave snatched the receipts from my hand and drew back a few feet so I couldn't rush at him. Then, to my surprise, he squinted at the receipts. The man had poor eyesight. I thought he was a marksman, and now the shotgun made sense. Panic was setting in. What if he couldn't read the times printed with weak ink on cheap paper.

An age passed before he was satisfied. He then did the most extraordinary thing. He gave me the receipts back. This was the moment I think I decided that I might live. He had decided something. The smile of a happy man crossed

Hartley Sparrow's face, after which it grew to a positive beam. He had a knack of thinking outside the box, and outside of his box usually contained some form of retribution.

"Don't try and run. I know where you live, or I know where your family lives. Pretty girl that sister of yours. Jane, that's what she is called, isn't she? Fuck her. Yes fuck her hard and kill her. That could be fun!" Sparrow said these words with all the menace of a Hollywood gangster, except this was very real. I didn't want my family involved in this stupid mess. Without any options The Cauldron beckoned me, and my new idea grew, after which it seemed ridiculous.

"So I'll see you in The Cauldron will I? Peter your pathetic!"

"Yes." I don't know which one I was saying yes too.

"You've got no money! I'm going to watch John Smith rip your legs off. When you're dead, or nearly dead, I'm going to kill him! I followed the blonde twat a couple of weeks ago to Raymond's place. When he's gone me and Smiggy, with Lenny's help, will take over!" Dave said this as he turned dramatically away. His overcoat hanging over his shoulders almost slipped off, but the bastard managed to carry it off. He didn't seem particularly worried over Harry's death.

I wasn't going to mention Raymond Nice was dead. I walked the walk of a dead man. I was on death row walking towards the chair, or being English would that be the gallows pole?

More bloody questions? "You've got no money." How did he know? Double-Barrelled Dave and John Smith had both been in the alleyway behind my town house. Was it just a game and they worked together? Did Dave know that Raymond nice was dead, and I would never know if he was working with John because I would be dead before they celebrated their new partnership? Was it my idea to form a new syndicate, and were they keeping me in the dark until they sent me towards the light. As the distance to The Cauldron grew smaller and smaller chronic paranoia was growing and growing.

There was no Rover 3.5 coupe in the car park waiting. There would definitely be no visit from Harry the Pocket, and there would be no visit from the blubbery Walter Nice. It was obvious Dave knew nothing about his missing sidekick. I wasn't going to pass the information on, not with a shotgun pressed into my testicles, or anywhere else for that matter.

With a heavy heart and light legs from the new trainers I pushed my way through the big wooden doors and entered the bar in The Cauldron. What met me inside was so appalling I could have turned and ran. I was faced with a horrible nightmare, a spectre attacking me on every side, but I had to stay in this place and there would be no escape.

Appalling noise filled every part of the pub. "Knock three times on the ceiling if you want me, twice on the pipe, if the answer is no". Dawn was belting from the jukebox, loud at the request of the big crowd. They were enjoying beers and music before the sound was lowered for their quiz night. This was a Monday night for God's sake, a Monday that may be the last day of my life, and I knew that the music selection playing me out would be tragic. The Cauldron was full to the brim with mushbies, nerds without computers or girlfriends. There were some mushbiettes waiting for the quiz, I think they were girls. I've never seen so many badly-dressed people with so much acne in one place. I needed a drink, and my stupid idea returned.

This is where a little local knowledge comes in, and the desire for the biggest diversion on the planet. If I'm very lucky I may yet live. Many times before now, before I changed into a cool gangster, we'd often drink late, very late in Billy's pub. One night unbeknown to a very drunken Billy we watched him boost his profits. He liked to slip a percentage of water and a couple of bottles of brandy into his beer. This sound's extravagant until you realise the basement of his pub was equipped with twelve hundred pint tanks of real ale, and six hundred pint tanks of lager. Punters couldn't tell his beer was lower gravity, and the sting from the couple of bottles of brandy put a nice edge on it. People often commented on how good the beer in The Cauldron was.

Understaffed was the way he liked to play. His wife helped, also his daughter, and on special occasions he would get a couple attractive female students to help out for cash. Tonight he was doing it on the cheap because the mushbies drank at a steady pace all evening and over time consumed a considerable amount of beer. All he had to do was be patient and put up with the shite on the jukebox. He loaded this machine with special attention to his captive audience. He prided himself in being the only pub in town with a box loaded with "classics".

I had a stupid plan, it wasn't a great plan, and the only thing great about it was its stupidity. The beer cellar was entered from behind the bar. This cellar had more than one entrance. A fire door closed off the end of the corridor after the toilets. On summer nights he opened it to let in the breeze creating a draft to push the heavy fog of cigarette smoke around the pub; the air never seemed to clear. Inside the enclosed back yard were set of steel double doors in the ground. These were used when the tanker arrived from the brewery to pump the beer in. The tanker would reverse through the rear gates then deploy a hose to fill the tanks much in the same way as a petrol tanker at a garage. The beer tasted a little better than petrol, and tonight would be a good night, a very good night!

Two years ago the steel plates had a dodgy bolt. Bob and I had speculated if we could open it and borrow a few bottles of beer, we never did. Relying entirely on landlord Billy's tightness with money I figured that nothing would have been changed. Fingers crossed I grabbed the edge of the metal doors. The bolt only engaged a fraction because it was misaligned with the other plate. I took a hard pull at the plate…Nothing! Again I tugged, this time harder, all the while trying to keep the sound down…Nothing! Balls to it I thought! Just give it everything. What have I got to lose? I was starting to think the tight old git had actually put his hand in his pocket and money into the structure of the pub. I tugged and the damn door popped open almost smashing me in the face. The tight old git had kept the money in his pocket.

Part one of my dastardly master plan was now complete. I was standing silently in the yard listening to see if the grinding wrench of metal had disturbed anybody. Inside the pub during these moments I could hear the mushbies enjoying a very loud chorus of "Bridget the Midget" by Ray Stevens. Was I sick with fright, sick with effort of lifting the doors or nauseated by the sound of the not so mighty Wurlitzer?

Part two of my dastardly plan was about to be put into place. It would be interesting if it worked. It might save me and it could change everything.

CHAPTER 38

Beauty and the beasts.

Inside the sinister black orb the tranquil quietness shocked me. It was cool, it was dark and I was walking with Bob. This must have been the first thing I'd forgotten. I could remember everything up to the moment we pushed out into the night. Going through the grubby side door into a dark future was my last old memory. I was intrigued to know more.

It must have been the drink, because in a situation like this I should have been very nervous. My friend and companion on our journey to manhood, gabbled away like a man possessed. "Blow job… hope I don't come too quick… I hope Smiggy as it all arranged… should I have a wank now?" And so it went on, I was walking in my own soft bubble of quiet.

I was very drunk, but not pissed enough to stop me getting hard, I hoped! Relaxing and being cool was my thing, whereas my friend was driving himself towards a hyper frenzy. At that moment if he'd seen a woman naked I think he would've exploded. He raved and I drifted along the grey brick road towards the mythical world of manhood. My focus was on staying calm, but Bob infiltrating my mind, like a swarm of bees buzzing around inside my head. He must've been very drunk or very scared.

I was back in the viewing seat, sitting on my shoulders watching the rerun, knowing what was going on inside my head down to a certain level, but not into the deep subconscious. I was holding a bottle of wine, a nice low vintage red. By low vintage I mean low price. We were big spenders! This bottle was our sole contribution to the little party. Smiggy had made it very clear, he expected us to sort things out with him later, especially if we lost it! If this girl didn't fancy our little party we wouldn't even give her the bottle. We'd drink off our sorrow at remaining virgins on the walk home, and talk up our chances of losing it tomorrow night.

The Victorian streets got narrower, the buildings taller and closer together. These streets were no longer elegant, now the crumbling tenements of bedsit land. This was a place inhabited by small flats, people on low rent, low rent people high. This was the less elegant end of town. As far as the police were concerned, this area was the town sewer. We were stepping into the shit in the hope that just some of the depravity would rub off on us. We inhabited the world of the fortunate. At the end of the night we could leave, others were trapped here.

We possessed a ticket to the game. Smiggy had given us an old betting slip from the shop next to The Cauldron. Scrawled on it in barely legible handwriting was the girls address. We didn't know if there was going to be one or two of them, our friend in the pub suggested she often had friends staying, dossing down as he put it. Some of these friends might want to join in. We were too naive to understand their motives.

Bob was still going at eight hundred miles an hour. "What if they're scamming us… what if the address is wrong… what if he's bullshitting?" And so it went on. I watched myself inside the acid bubble. I was drifting on a wind of fate towards a different future. They say you make your own future and you probably do. Tonight a certain black fate dragged us down dark streets that for me would become too black to remember. All the streets were named after local Victorian dignitaries, all now forgotten. We were having difficulty finding the road in the poorly lit maze of housing.

We were looking for 2B, Worthington Road. Whoever Worthington was he'd been celebrated with grand houses for a handful of select families, now home to hundreds. There was very little movement and not many parked cars. Nobody seemed to walk the streets. Everybody was either out, or out of it, on whatever rocked their boat.

Clinging in fear to the shadows across the road an old man was taking a slow walk with his small dog. We spotted him and I bounded across to ask him directions. Imagine it from his point of view. A big young man is running across the road towards him, with another man raving on the other side of the street. The poor old man was frozen in terror expecting to be struck down and robbed of his 44p. He waited to be beaten to a pulp for less than the price of a couple of pints of beer…All I could see were the whites of his eyes, and his yellowy-white teeth visible in his forced smile. In my state this man's terror did not register.

"Worthington Road, do you know where Worthington Road is, please?" I asked.

He understood I meant no harm and the rigid fear left his body. It looked like I'd pulled the plug out of a blow – up toy. His little sausage dog was involved in a passionate affair with the base of the tree and didn't seem to care what his master suffered.

"Down to the end, turn left, two streets along on your right. That should do it," the old man said, and moved off into the shadows tugging young Nigel (the dog) away from the delicious scent he'd found. Nigel was unhappy, the old man happy he wasn't facing a trip to hospital, or worse.

Part of my tranquil state disappeared when I knew where I was heading. The tension in my stomach grew because I might actually have sex. Was I also nervous because I knew the manner in which I was going to do it? I was going to lose my virginity to a girl who was prostituting herself for reasons I didn't understand, or didn't want to. I stupidly thought a couple of paid for fucks would give me the confidence to chat up all the girls who wouldn't give me sex now. I was seventeen and crammed full of raging hormones, like Bob, but slightly less raving.

A few minutes later we found the house, on the corner, the first house in the street. The address was 2B, which brought me straight back to school Shakespeare. To be or not to be that was my question, a man or not a man, tonight would tell. For some reason we walked up to the front door, six steps above the street. There was no flat 2B, only numbers one to six. Bob used his Dunhill cigarette lighter, a thing he carried even though he smoked about three cigarettes a week. The flickering flame confirmed what we could see under the dim doorway lighting. There was no flat 2B, yet this was definitely number two Worthington Road.

"The bastard! The lying little bastard!" Bob said. He was angry at being misled. I thought I could hear relief behind his cursing. I was convinced Smiggy had been truthful.

Walking down the steps I glanced down to my right and could see a faint yellow light through some gruesomely designed orange curtains, all very 1970s. It came to me flat 2B was the basement, the bottom of the house, the old servant's quarters. The place where people who served had been housed. Those above God had smiled on, and those below for reasons never explained in church had to live in servitude. Nothing much had changed apart from servitude now occupied the entire house. This was still the bottom, the basement, the lowest point.

The door looked as if it had been dragged from The Cauldron. The same worn and peeled look of the door leading out of the pub, and now we were faced with the same door leading us somewhere else. The cool tranquil walk, the interlude between, need never have existed. The door leading from one squalid establishment to the other may well have been the same. I suppose we were looking for a certain kind of squalor, but what greeted us shocked me. Not the old me, but me!

Hesitation was the key. I looked at Bob, and Bob looked back at me. Neither of us knocked. My friend was giving me the go on you go on, look with his eyes. I didn't want the other me to knock, and I did want the other me to run. Hormones were beating on every door, screaming to be freed. I raised my arm and knocked firmly on the door, too firmly I think. The sound echoed around the lower yard. It sounded like a police raid, too much pressure on the door, too much tension in the arm.

Nothing happened. A minute and a half and still nothing had happened. By this time I was convinced the girl was out, and the lights had been left on by accident or for security. I knocked again confident it wouldn't be answered. I'd only touched the door once when it moved away from my hand and there before me was a vision. It didn't shock the teenage me, but I, aware of all the passing years was shaken to the very core! The girl was the most beautiful pixie of the creature I'd ever seen, *petite* and beautiful with tumbling hair. She was the Lylybel, Hysandrabopel, the pixie.

"Come in! Don't stand there like dicks. Get in here," the girl said. She had a nice way with words.

"What you two saddos brought me? Go on, show us!" The girl continued.

I nervously proffered forward the bottle of cheap wine. She made a snorting noise down her nose and then laughed. Not happy laughter, but the laugh of somebody in trouble. It had a tone of the maniacal, the desperate.

"You wankers can make yourselves a cup of tea. I'm going out to the phone box. Don't touch my stuff!" We'd changed places and now we inhabited the basement while she was out on the dark streets. We were left to look around. What there was to look at was not much, but one thing had surprised me, it wasn't squalid. The smell was the first thing to hit my senses as we entered. The place had a slight musty odour combined with the smell of fried food, and a cloying dampness that stuck in your throat. If you took the sensation of smell out of the equation the place was very neat if poorly furnished.

An old single speaker record player was in the alcove where the fireplace used to be. A few LPs were scattered on the floor in front of it. The settee was hidden below hideous loose covers made from the same material as the orange curtains. The bedroom had to be looked at. We couldn't resist this investigation, and were more than surprised with its neatness. There was no wardrobe and a piece of rope strung across the alcoves either side of the blocked off old chimney breast. She owned few clothes, but her scant possessions were very neat. The room was dominated by a large king-sized bed, out of keeping with the rest of that mean basement. This bed had a quality about it, and looking at this lavish piece of furniture had an effect. My stomach turned. I was looking at the place where acts of love, if that's what you could call them, took place. A few minutes from now I could be lying there naked. I've never been naked in front of any woman other than my mother.

At first glance I didn't notice the strangeness of the bedroom. It contained no windows, only a very high slotted skylight partially obscured by a large poster of Paul Newman. The only light was as artificial as calling this a place where you'd sleep. We wanted expunge the image of the threatening bed, so Bob and I headed for the kitchen to make our cup of tea. He'd gone quiet and I felt sober, though I knew I wasn't.

The more time we spent in the kitchen listening to nothing the more nervous we became. Clutching our cups of tea we sat on the sofa then turned on the record player. The record was a surprise. She seemed to have a lot of Simon and Garfunkel and late Beatles records, however this was "Metamorphosis" by Iron Butterfly, a strange choice. Minutes passed and we started to feel like spare ends. The tea was finished and drink-fuelled lust had turned into sober fear.

This *petite* beautiful girl was going to give us sex for payment. We weren't losing our virginities somewhere in the woods, fumbling and awkward with a long-time girlfriend. We weren't fumbling in the dark bedroom at a party, fuelled on cheap cider with the girl who'd let everybody do it. No, we were paying a prostitute to have sex. She may have been very young, but the connotation was of some old girl on the game, a woman too old to show too much leg, and using too much make-up. This was how I saw a prostitute, not wondrous and beautiful in her delicate form as this young girl was.

An old girl showing two young boys the way seemed more acceptable. This thing tonight almost seemed like the rape of a desperate child. Even to my naive seventeen-year-old self it all seemed very wrong, and I think Bob who was now silent had gone beyond that point. He stood up and suggested we leave. I agreed. We were halfway across the kitchen when she opened the door.

"All arranged. You two want it together or separate? Smiggy tells me you're both virgins!" Then she laughed. She walked straight past us into the bedroom, her mood higher, and she now had a bright confidence about her.

"Toss for it if you can't make your minds up, but come on, let's get started I want to go somewhere later!" Pixie was nothing but direct.

She was wearing a small man's white cotton shirt and tight jeans with some kind of tiny army boots. Our fantastic duo stood looking at each other, both wanting to be first, neither brave enough to run or say this wasn't what we wanted. We had to decide. Moments later she appeared at the door still wearing the man's shirt now open to the waist where it revealed the slight mound of each breast, but not enough to reveal her nipples. We were not concentrating on the breasts because other than the shirt she was completely naked. We could see her beautiful slim legs topped out by her womanhood.

She was standing in front of us on display without embarrassment. This emboldened one of us. Bob moved forwards and she held out her hand smiling. She dragged him into the bedroom, all the while he was fumbling in his pocket looking for his supply of condoms. I wondered if he could last long enough to put one on. I, despite myself, had a very solid erection and I didn't want to let Bob have something over me.

Bob was going to lose his virginity before me. His birthday was six weeks earlier than mine, so I was still ahead of him. What I needed now was to make sure I didn't come before I did the real thing, so I headed into the small bathroom behind the kitchen. Masturbation was the key, and with the image of pubic hair in my mind thirty seconds would do the trick. As a teenager ten minutes would recharge the batteries. I just hoped at the second attempt the bulb wouldn't go off like a camera flash.

"Pete, Pete, it's your turn," said Bob. I'd only been 20 seconds and was pushing my way out of the bathroom. Bob had lasted less than a minute. He was grinning like a fool.

"She sucked it like a lollipop. She fucking sucked it then swallowed!" Bob said.

"That's it? No proper sex?" I asked.

"No. She's knocking the edge off. Says she wants a little bit of fun out of it. Wants to see us virgins suffer a little bit. She says if she's doing this she's going have a bit of fun with it," Bob said.

The 1971 version of me looked very nervous. He may not be able to get it up, and my friend had actually had a blow job. Now watching the rerun inside the bubble I could see this girl had the devilment of the little pixie in her. I feared for the other me back in the past.

I took brave strides into the bedroom closing the door behind me, thanking God it was lit only by a table lamp. Under bright lights I think I would have been too embarrassed to perform. Sweat was breaking out on my forehead because it was very warm in the bedroom, much warmer than I remember from our earlier inspection. With the door closed it was positively hot. She was very relaxed sipping on a glass of something that had appeared from I don't know where. It looked like a dark spirit, rum or brandy.

"Anne, you can call me Anne, and please don't call me Jesus when you come. Your friend did!" She laughed at this. The shirt had remained on and was now open enough to reveal her dark nipples, and her womanhood was on full display, her legs very relaxed. She swung round dropping her feet onto the small fluffy rug next to the bed. A little bit of luxury. She beckoned me towards her. I obeyed. Then without hesitation she started with slow deliberation undoing my belt with one hand, and rubbing my testicles through my trousers with the other. She pulled my shirt out of my trousers, and was kissing my stomach flattened hard by too much work on the farm.

"Nice. I might enjoy this!" Anne said, continuing to work on my already stiffening penis now exposed to the soft light of the room. A woman, a girl, was actually touching me, kissing my stomach, and not laughing. I wasn't in a hurry to get on with it. I wanted this experience to last more than a few minutes. It wasn't because we were paying for it. This girl was beautiful.

"Can you take your shirt off? I want to see all of you," I asked.

Anne looked up at me from down by my waist, hesitating for a few moments before firmly saying, "NO!" Taking her shirt off would have revealed the true nature of her need, her desperation, and expose the real reason why she was giving the best of her young body away. I was too naive to realise her arms were already bearing the scars from the needles. I was too naive to realise a lot of the time she wouldn't be giving sexual pleasure to virginal teenagers. A lot of the men who visited would be much older, much more violent, some demanding everything in the pervert's dictionary of horrors.

Tonight was an easy fix for this desperate girl. Two nervous young men who appreciated this girl's ethereal and soon to pass beauty.

To me as a spectator to my own loss of virginity she looked very relaxed, and time was passing slowly for us both. It looked to me as an observer as if Anne had decided to pretend I was the boy next door who she might fall in love with, a small escape from her sordid world. Her slow caressing moved into kissing me on the lips with a passion I hadn't expected. For reasons known only to her, this girl had decided to treat me like her lover.

"Get the fuck on with it. I want a fucking go. I am paying for this!" It was Bob from outside the room banging on the door. He had a nastier edge to his voice than I'd ever heard. He'd been drinking the cheap wine topping up his inebriation. Now he was raving again banging on the door with an insistence that couldn't be ignored. All the while I wanted to relax and enjoy what would be remembered for a lifetime. This girl was a prostitute, desperate to fill her veins, but this night she was a girlfriend, this night my angel saving me from the devil of virginity.

"Shut up, Bob, shut up! I'll be ready when I'm ready. Until then shut up!" I shouted over my shoulder in a loud whisper. I was desperate not to break the mood.

There was a splintering of wood around the lock as the door burst open. Bob stood there in a drunken rage. He was drunk out of his mind. I am sure he'd finished the whole bottle of wine.

He was pulling at his trousers, opening the front, fumbling with his penis.

"Get off her. It's my go!" he raved.

"Make me!" I said.

He walked towards me wild-eyed.

CHAPTER 39

Right here right now, champagne nights and wellingtons.

I was bracing myself ready for Bob's attack and pushed Anne back down onto the bed behind me to keep her safe. Whatever path life had pushed her down she didn't deserve this. My adversary lunged towards me and I experienced the unexpected force of a rope around my waist pulling me backwards with huge force. I was at a loss as to understand how this tiny girl on the bed behind me could've put a rope around me, and where did she get the strength from?

The pull increased and I shot down a black tunnel backwards, a tableau of the three of us in the room shrinking to a small dot of light before disappearing. There was an audible pop and a huge splash as I came out of the bubble. To my horror I was attached to the back of the riverboat being towed along at four knots in the grey water. This strange coloured murky water was thick and oily like acid. I did not think my sins warranted it, but this acid scoured at my entire body, even my eyes.

The towing continued for hours it seemed, and I was in an age of agony, dissolving until I could feel the bones of my body held together by sinew alone. Imagine some sadist with a passion for putting cigarettes out. This is practised on your eyeball. The nerve endings never die and the pain is continuous in its bleak agony. Imagine this a thousand times over with your entire body slowly melting without nerve death. In this world you would be unconscious or in cardiac arrest, but you're not!

The rope was towing me towards the exposed propellers, thrashing white water. This was the end. After all this agony I was going to be cut to pieces. The foaming water behind the riverboat salved my pain, slowly washing away the oily acid. Each beat of the propellers threw cool refreshing water over me. As I got nearer vortexes from the propellers started to draw me in for decapitation. I closed my eyes when the blades were so near I could reach out and touch them. Suddenly I'm pulled upwards at speed my toes missing the rotating blades by an inch, and thrown unceremoniously like a landed tuna onto the observation deck. I'm cold and shivering.

The sensation of cold rushes up from my feet, through my knees and from my hands up through my arms. Everything is centred inside my mouth which is freezing. All the wetness of the River has gone from my clothes. With my mouth numb with cold I look across and with clearing vision I see Jennifer smiling back at me.

"Why are you sucking on the ice cube from your gin glass?" Jennifer said.

I spat it into my hand and threw it back into the gin goblet. The ice cube swirled around the glass slowly spiralling to the centre. The Pixie had to jump twice to avoid the cube before it came to a halt. The Lylybel leaned against it and crossed her flippers. She smiled at me and laughed, raising her middle finger at me in defiance. The whole sensation of punishment had finished, and making the pixie jump had given me a little bit of comeback, for once. I was ready to resume my life in this otherwise unspoiled paradise. Once all the truths are known this world will carry no pain, only sublime pleasure.

In the background I can hear the pixie frog woman laughing like a drain at the torments she made me suffer.

"Would you like a gin and tonic? I think I fancy another," Jennifer asked.

"Go on have another. Please do it will be delicious!" the malicious frog shouted up from the glass. She was ready for me still wearing her sub-aqua gear. I declined.

I was beginning to understand Bob had been the instigator of something I knew would be terrible. The pain I'd suffered was sufficient for a lifetime. Did I really want to suffer more pain to find out what' we'd done? The strange thing was I didn't question where this other life had been lived. Somehow, in this universe, it seemed the punishment was for another life, an old life lived before in a distant place, and I suppose in a way it was!

The three days in Paris were wonderful long relaxing days of sightseeing. Boat trips along the Seine, laughter on the steps of the Louvre, and walks around the beautiful gardens at Versailles. This is how all our days passed, all the time seeing everything through new eyes was a revelation. The *Mona Lisa* was made up of a quarter of a million brushstrokes. I could feel Leonardo de Vinci's deep passion in every single crafted stroke of this centuries old painting. Some of the other pictures in the gallery were equally amazing. The madness of some of the great artists made me shiver with cold, my stomach a sea of nerves driven by crazed thoughts. I could not look or go near van Gogh or Edvard Munch.

The days passed in wonder, we were arm in arm, hand in hand, together most of the time. Three days in the alternative universe, and I'd never lived anywhere else. On the third night, the night before we were to catch the train back to another England, I fell asleep in her arms content in knowing I'd found the love of my life. Bright light greeted me as I woke in the morning. The bed was empty next to me, and my senses had gone numb. I was bitterly disappointed I wanted to live in enchantment forever. There were no feelings of lingering guilt, because now I was learning all the dark secrets.

For reasons I never understood when I awoke to an empty bed my thoughts immediately returned to Rachel. I began to recall the closing hours of our two-day conversation and the moment she revealed too much leg for her age. I've always had a vivid mental image of the moment Rachel described her revenge on the man who'd tormented and tortured her young life.

Rachel, that vision of Rachel, clawing at her dress, was heavy in my mind.

She'd been telling me about recovering the knife from the dustbin, and she told me something that had shocked her. Digging in the trash aroused deep memories of the desperation of the concentration camp. She'd pulled a filth covered hand from the dustbin. On her wrist was a smear of aromatic grease from a discarded fish and chip wrapping. Rachel shocked herself by licking it. She was also tempted into licking the sticky goo from her fingers. At the last minute she stopped herself by wiping her encrusted hands on her old dress. It had been a close call.

Jumping up from the sofa Rachel placed herself in front of the fireplace and she revealed most of her legs to me. The action was totally unintentional, a manifestation of the torment inside. She wasn't looking at me. Her eyes were closed. Both hands were down by her side and she was pulling at the material of her dress as she recalled her story. Throughout she was kneading the material in her hands. The subconscious gathering of the material filling her hands to stop her fingernails cutting her palms, such was her tension. I was slightly embarrassed and at the same time fascinated, she still had great legs. I felt guilty looking and dragged my eyes away to stare into her intense face. Her eyes remained closed throughout, but fascinating expressions passed across her tired but still beautiful face as she told me what happened next.

She returned to the back door of Maximilian's exclusive block of apartments. The caretaker was snoring in his chair, while the loud radio was spreading the news, something about the Princess Elizabeth becoming Queen. On any normal day Rachel would have listened. All she could hear was her own heartbeat. She tried to move with the silence she'd learnt when trying not to disturb Maximilian in his concentration camp "love nest". Now she was using the same techniques not to get away from Maximilian but to meet him face-to-face.

Like a statue Rachel had been on the landing outside the door for several minutes. She had no way of knowing if it had been two or twenty. Inside her head was a violent dialogue. If she knocked on the door would she run, if she didn't knock on the door would she regret it for the rest of her life. If she managed to infiltrate his apartment to plunge the knife hard into Maximilian's heart would she then be caught and hung for murder?

One deep breath and Rachel knocked on the door with confidence. She was ready with the dagger hidden behind the clipboard. She would be a woman with a questionnaire from the water board, something about a better service with more pressure to the apartments on the upper floors. This was all she could think of. In the event it didn't happen like that because she never got the chance to get inside his apartment. Rachel never stood on the same piece of carpet face-to-face with this monster, and she didn't get the opportunity to stab Maximilian in the heart. No blood would squirt onto her clothes so she could hide the stains under the plastic coat. She would not feel the heat from his body soaking into the material of her dress. None of these things would happen.

The little spy hole door opened, and Maximilian's very pale blue-grey eye looked out of the hatch.

"Can I help you?" Maximilian enquired.

"Yes, you can. I am from the water board. May I come in for a few minutes?" Rachel asked.

"At this time of night? It's very late!" Maximilian said. He was suspicious and Rachel knew this. How could she persuade her way into this man's home?

"We are all part-timers, people with families, and we do this in the evenings," Rachel said, pleased with the explanation. What came next was the moment she'd dreaded.

"I know you! I know you! You're that little Jewish bitch!" Maximilian said, his voice rising as he did so. Little Jewish bitch, the little Jewish bitch that he'd taken in every way possible way, and now she couldn't get to him, her chance gone forever. He would call the police, or would he?

Maximilian's eye filled the small hatch. It grew wide with a building incredulous rage against this little Jewish bitch soiling his threshold, threatening his anonymity.

She was found out. He would never let her in, and she must return to the north the next day. It was a hopeless situation made worse by this man's rising anger. Soon people would be alerted and she would be found out. Intent to murder was an offence. Maximilian was explaining what he and his associates would like to do with a Jewish bitch like her.

The knife was brought from behind the clipboard in one swift movement and pushed with every muscle fibre of her body towards the open spy hole. All the hatred in her body was driving the blade forwards. This was a long diamond sectioned blade made of stainless steel by the Third Reich. It was going home.

Imagine piercing a kiwi fruit. A little bit of resistance and then a soft giving into the body of the fruit. This was how Rachel described the sensation. It nearly didn't get there at all catching the edge of the hatchway in her wild thrust. Another quarter of an inch and it would have stuck in the door. Luck was on her side and the blade glanced inwards towards Maximilian's wide open pale blue eye. The piercing sensation was experienced for a tiny fraction of a second. This moment Rachel would expand into a lifelong memory. The knife passed through the eye in less than the blink of an eye. The mad charge of steel through tissue continued. The blade was being muscled deep into Maximilian's brain. There was a big shock up her arm as the sharp point came to a halt against the inside of the back of his skull.

Whatever she'd pierced inside his evil mind had made him go rigid like a heavy plank of wood. He didn't utter a word, there was no cry. The man didn't crumble to the floor. This tableau continued for several seconds with Rachel holding the knife handle a couple of inches away from the spy hole. Fear was building inside her that this man was invincible. Rachel was about to pull the knife from his rigid face when he started to fall backwards. The knife with her fingerprints was almost pulled from her grasp as he toppled backwards like a falling tree. The crossbar of the knife made in the fashion of eagle's wings stopped it continuing into the room along with Maximilian. These fine outstretched wings caught against the edges of the spy hole pulling it clear as the former Nazi fell backwards.

Rachel retched, not at what she done but the noise the knife made coming out of this man's head. It was like pulling a wellington boot out of mud. There was sucking noise, a terrible wet sucking noise as the blade exited the brain cavity and finally his eyeball. There was a thud to the floor like a falling sack of coal as Maximilian Haussler became no more. Rachel continued to clutch the knife without removing the blade from inside the apartment. She pressed her face to the hole and looked in to see, with deep satisfaction, Maximilian, the man who had tortured her, the man who had ironically kept her alive, now twitching in death spasm.

Rachel could feel urine running down her legs. It wasn't released with fear just a total relaxation of her incredible body tension. So complete was her story she told me every small detail, and her eyes never opened. She was recalling each precious moment. The urine hot on her legs woke her from her trance-like state as she watched this monster on his way to hell. Rachel slipped the knife inside her coat along with the clipboard. The caretaker was snoring in the chair when she came down into the hallway, and he was louder than the radio. It had amazed her that she noticed this in her desperate bid to flee without detection.

She slipped out of the apartment and down the road back towards her sister, back towards a normal life. This was the moment when she thought she'd closed a chapter on the past, but it keeps bubbling back to the surface. Rachel would walk across the river on her way home. The River Thames with its dirty grey water would become the hiding place for the murder weapon. No one would ever find it, and if they did would it matter?

All the time she recalled her moment of revenge her eyes remained closed. Now, at the finish, she had them wide. The smile on her face was one of genuine joy, and the look in her eyes was not of madness, not of anything strange. Her eyes sparkled like a woman seeing her new child for the first time. She had shared her joy with me. This was Rachel releasing her secret to the world. This woman was one victim who sought out revenge and succeeded.

The moment passed and she looked slightly embarrassed, realising her dress was more than halfway up her thighs. She smoothed it back down to just below the knees, and came to sit next to me.

"Another brandy Peter? Any more questions?" Rachel asked. I was dumbfounded at the time, but now I wish I'd asked her more.

I did follow this up some years later when with time I started to disbelieve the story. Perhaps it had been Rachel's fantasy because she'd never seen Maximilian again. I knew the night because of Princess Elizabeth becoming queen. I found it in several papers. A Swiss businessman had been brutally murdered in his flat. It came out later that the murder weapon was believed to have been a German SS ceremonial dagger. This had been discovered during the autopsy from the shape of the wound, a fact later included in the coroner's report. The chief suspects were escaped Germans on the run from the authorities. It was believed that this man was possibly German, part of a network helping former SS get to South America or to assume new European identities. The press suggested some suspicion against stronger factions of the Jewish community in London. The case was never solved, but nobody cared in those days about the death of a Nazi sympathiser. He hadn't cared, and now they didn't!

That was the end of my conversations with Rachel. It was a bit of a showstopper. What more could you say?

We talked on for some time about everything we'd discussed, reliving particularly poignant moments. Later we recalled happy memories of me playing with Bob as a child. More memories were relived of happier days when we all went to the seaside in the family car. All these things were covered and we knew the conversation was over.

I was putting on my coat ready to leave, ready to walk out into the cold damp afternoon, a whole day and a night after arriving. Rachel kissed me on both cheeks, and as I stepped back she was smiling. Rachel moved her right arm holding it out as if thrusting with a dagger. We were on the doorstep and it looked to the world as if this woman were giving me a Nazi salute, a strange irony. As I turned at the gate to make my final farewells Rachel pulled her arm back and down by her side. I was shocked!

As she did this she sucked in through her teeth making a squelching noise like pulling a rubber boot out of soft mud. Then she laughed, smiled at me and waved farewell. Her eyes were as bright as diamonds and her smile was electrifying. She had told the world of her victory.

The sucking sound was in my head for the remainder that day. All through my journey back to where I lived I could hear that suction. I laughed too!

CHAPTER 40

Very much in among a daze, in The Cauldron, August 1973.

These new trainers were supposed to make you light on your feet. Mine were heavy with foreboding. The last sixty hours had been a whirlpool of half thoughts, broken ideas, and I was being sucked down into the maelstrom of the unknown. Now I faced the final black hole at the bottom of that rotating tunnel. With all my senses stunned during my new awakening, I was incapable of understanding what I'd done in my life to get me into this terrible position.

As I re-entered the pub from the rear yard the horribleness of my position became clear. Mushbies were enjoying more of Dawn, not knocking three times, but now with Tony Orlando tying yellow ribbons. I didn't know anything about the current pop charts but didn't believe everything could be this turgid. I strolled over to the not so mighty Wurlitzer. The first five listed records included some people called Peters and Lee, The Sweet and the Simon Park Orchestra. I noticed that Gary Glitter featured several times. I put my money on David Bowie and "Life on Mars". This was how I felt, like I was living on a different planet.

"Nuvva pint, Pete?" Billy the landlord asked me.

"No, Billy, I fancy one of those new bottles of Heineken you've got in the fridge," I replied, and was duly served by Billy who'd broken off serving some mushbies to get my drink. The embryonic nerd's were getting into the evening and starting to swill down the pints now with a little added something to liven up the proceedings. I was hoping for a big enough diversion to allow me some breathing space. I'd put a small amount of the liquid LSD into the tanks of beer and lager, not too much at first, and then on second thoughts a little bit more. With the vast quantity of beer I didn't know if my mass medication would work in the slightest, or I might have overdone it! The tainted crazy beer had not yet arrived at the pumps, and my tainted murderous friends, if that's what you could call them, hadn't arrived either.

The mushbies were now singing along in chorus to something called "Part of the Union" by The Strawbs. I'm not sure if any of them worked or had anything to do with a union. Most of them were unemployable until the onset of the computer when, like butterflies, they spread their wings and became nerds.

"Why has your face turned blue? And why has your face gone yellow?" I could hear this from over in the corner. The beer couldn't have been at full strength, but already a big man with wild hair was delicately touching the faces of the people opposite, incredulous because the colour didn't come off on his fingers. He couldn't believe they'd suddenly changed colour. He thought they were taking the piss by putting make-up on. He started to rub with a rough vigour at the face of the maroon one, who happened to be a girl, a mushbiette.

"Don't touch me with your tentacle. I didn't know they allowed octopi in the pub!" she screamed in his face. "Life on Mars" started to play on the jukebox, and against my better judgement I laughed to myself. This wasn't funny but I was hysterical with fear. Unable to run for fear of reprisal against my sister Jane, I was trapped into this meeting.

I was by this time well down my fourth drink, my senses softened by the alcohol. Fighting against my urge to laugh was difficult. I couldn't stop myself when one of the pool players climbed onto the table. He was a big man wearing a Liverpool team shirt. This was ripped without ceremony from his torso by his own massive hands in order to display a huge tattoo that shouted Liverpool down the length of his chest. My hysteria increased when I discovered the tattoo didn't end in the letter L. This statement about his favourite team ended in the letter O by design. The L was for the bedroom and made his team triumphant by desire.

"Gary! What the hell is Liverpoo?" one of his friends was shouting.

"I'll show you wankers!" the big man said, at which he started to pull his trousers down and all became clear as he starting to exercise himself to produce the letter L.

The landlord Billy didn't know which way to look. In the last quarter of an hour the whole pub had turned into a madhouse. Billy himself was starting to see everybody in a glowing light with all his favourite customers looking like angels. Billy ignored the mayhem and made his way along to where I was sitting.

The bar curved around into the corner producing a little alcove. I was sitting at the end of the bar watching the staff work. The staff, if that's what you could call them, consisted of just two people, Billy, and Mabel who offered lots of forty plus cleavage with endless innuendo. He insisted I was an angel and deserved one of his best foaming pints. I took it with many thanks and as soon as his eyes left me I pushed it along the bar into the corner well out of my way. My drink was bottled lager, straight unadulterated bottled lager. One beer that didn't reach places other beers do.

"Saving this pint for me, arsehole?" Dave Hartley Sparrow enquired. He leaned heavily against my back, whispering the words into my ear. He was so close to my neck I could feel the moisture on his breath. There was sinister intimacy in the way he was leaning against me. His lips so close he was almost kissing my ear like an ardent lover. His arm pushed against my back with a harsh pressure. I had a feeling he was going to crush me, consume me on that spot, and make me disappear. He reached around me and stretched to lift the pint from the bar. Dave downed half of it in a single refreshing drink. My internalised laughter increased.

Liverpool man had been dragged down off the pool table and was lying on his back between the table and the domino players. He clutched the black ball in one hand and was intent despite his drunkenness on spelling the last letter of his favourite football team.

"Nobody is having the black ball until you've seen Liverpool in all its glory!" he was shouting for everyone to hear. Many of the mushbies had gone over to study the phenomenon. One of the mushbiettes had changed her spectacles in order to see more. The whole pub was stamping its feet along with Suzi Quatro Canning the Can, urging our drunken hero to fulfilment.

"What the hell is going on in here?" Double-Barrelled Dave asked. I shrugged my shoulders in the worldwide gesture of I have no idea. Dave downed the remaining dregs of his pint and shouted down the bar for Mabel to get him another. She was serving nobody because the whole rugby scrum of a pub was down at the pool table end, the octopus and the coloured people included.

Dave placed his elbow on the bar and propped his head against one hand. His malevolent smile was only inches from my face. He said nothing, he didn't move, we were locked eight inches apart in a game of who will speak first. He was trying to panic me into a confession or something. Then I realised he wanted me to take him on, he wanted me to make the first move. I did. I reached for my lager and took another small drink. This gave me an opportunity to look away from his continuous unblinking stare. He broke off this intimidation as his second beer arrived on the bar. Dave didn't move away physically, but gazed towards the beer. His zone was firmly overlapping my space.

Dave's arm was slowly reaching out for the second pint, but it never got there. John Smith pounded his fist hard down into the spread right hand of Dave Hartley Sparrow. I could swear to this day that I heard an audible crunch as he did so.

"I could have you any time, and I'm having your pint… now!" John Smith said. His smile was radiant, happy to have inflicted pain.

Double-Barrelled Dave muttered something heavy under his breath. I thought I heard the words "kill" and "tonight". He moved away to the other end of the bar near mushbie corner. The Liverpool display had come to a sticky end and the mushbies were returning to their enclave, stopping at the jukebox to load it up with even more nonsense. "Paper Roses" by Marie Osmond had started to play. If I hadn't been so distracted I think I would've cried tears of despair, except inside I already was.

John Smith finished his pint of John Smith's in seconds, and was in the process of ordering another from Mabel. She thought he was the best thing since sliced bread, and always served him before anyone else regardless. No words passed between us, but he had replaced Dave Hartley Sparrow. John wasn't invading my space. He was standing three feet away looking in amusement at this crazy pub on a Monday night. Before ever a word was spoken between us he drank half of his next pint. I'd seen the effects on the mushbies after just one pint!

"Lenny's got what he wants from life. He's got all the local business and Baby Doll," John said.

"You mean?" I said.

"Yes. She was teasing you in the kitchen to wind up Lenny. The soft git could see into the utility room from the library." John said.

"So she didn't want to shag me?"

"No, not any more, she tired of us," John said. Tired of us! I was horrified, but in no place to be worried. Baby doll was working on Lenny, something I would have known about under normal circumstances.

"How did Lenny manage that?" I asked. I was pretending I didn't know Harry the Pocket was dead.

"Harry the Pocket's dead, killed by that big fat arsehole Walt Nice. Harry went down fighting, and he managed to shoot Walt before he died. Tidy," John said. His usual pearly grin was much wider than normal. I had nothing to say, I really didn't know what to say other than make allusions to us working together.

"So, where do I fit in to the team?" I asked. I think my voice had gone up to a higher pitch. It was hard to tell with all the mayhem inside the pub. John never had the opportunity to answer as a lanky greasy mushbie began stroking his hair.

"It's so golden. Is it real gold? It must be real gold," the mushbie said, entranced by the beauty. He caressed the locks as if they were the most precious thing in the world until John knocked him cold with a single blow. The greasy youth slumped to the floor. In the growing madness nobody noticed. John, however, glanced across the bar and seeing Hartley Sparrow he went rigid, he almost looked afraid. My Nazi twin screamed out something about Dave's red eyes destroying his brain, he raged for a few seconds about the injustice of such an arsehole possessing so powerful a weapon. John wasted no time, he attacked, weaved at great speed through the throng at the bar, pushing no one as he passed through with the magical grace of a hunting cougar.

My best hope now was that they would kill each other, or Dave would manage to maim John to the extent he needed my help. I didn't expect Dave to survive. In the Monday night lunacy nobody would have witnessed anything that could have stood in court. I left my position at the end of the bar and walked towards the rear courtyard. My welfare depended on the outcome of the battle. What I hadn't calculated on was the effect of the LSD.

John had hunted down Hartley Sparrow as he was going I suspected to where he'd secreted the not so lovely Millicent. Dave only made it halfway across the yard before a brutal blow from John's cosh brought him down. I didn't witness the first blow. What I saw was John with the cosh high above his head ready to swing down for the second killer blow. This second blow would be well aimed to shatter Hartley Sparrow's skull.

It didn't come. John Smith was standing almost like the *Statue of Liberty*, the cosh held high and symbolic of his violence. His other hand was rooting around in his pocket for something. Then he pulled it out of his left-hand pocket to fumble fruitlessly in his right-hand pocket. He was looking for something. A knife? A gun? I had no idea.

What happened next shocked me. John took a huge swing down with his cosh making contact with Hartley Sparrow's right arm. The harsh cracking sound as his radius and ulna shattered under the weight of the hard driven weapon is a horror that sticks in my mind. I was looking out from the shadows inside the doorway. John raised his cosh once more and I wondered if this would be a killer blow to the head, or the other arm. It was neither.

John Smith slowly brought his arm down and touched Dave on the cheek with his cosh. Was Dave aware of it? I'm not too sure he registered it in his semi-conscious state.

"You're not going to burn me with those red eyes! I'm going to put them out!" John said very slowly.

I heard it with shocking clarity. Was I going to run out there and prevent John from cutting Dave's eyes out? This was more awful than his brutal slaying of Smiggy. He was looking for a knife to cut out those burning red eyes. The cosh had disappeared inside his beautifully tailored jacket. He was fumbling with his trousers again and at that point I made my decision. I was going to intervene and stop this abomination from carrying out his brutal butchery upon Dave Hartley Sparrow's eyes.

My Nazi twin attempted to put out Dave's eyes, but he didn't have a knife and had no intention of using one. Before I could move John Smith had got his weapon out and was using it. I laughed out loud without thinking, and the man putting out the eyes looked over his shoulder and laughed along with me. He was pissing in Dave Hartley Sparrow's face, his LSD driven hallucination was being quenched by water. I thought he was fumbling for a knife, but he'd been fumbling with his zipper. He seemed to possess an enormous bladder because he pissed on a semi-conscious Hartley Sparrow's face for what seemed an age.

Before he'd finished I slipped back into the mayhem of the pub. The whole place had now moved into the bizarre. There was an elderly couple possibly in their fifties wearing very little and sitting cross legged on a table, they were gently stroking each other's faces. Stranger and more disturbing was one of the mushbiettes seemed to be experimenting with lovemaking in a corner, a horrible mixture of spots, greasy hair, groping and sweaty expectation with another mushbie.

All the worshippers of the arcane in that band of mushbies were in deep discussion about fire eating. Without asking they'd gone behind the bar and collected all the spirits they thought could be used to blow fire from their mouths. The discussion had become more like a science debate with a dozen ashtrays already in play as test tubes to examine the burning properties of the different liquors. The madness in that corner was compounded by one guy claiming he could see ancient figures dancing in the flames. Others then joined in a discussion about pagan religions and the influence of fire on worship.

Elsewhere in the pub people were fighting, others were arguing about the colour of the sky when viewed through the huge hole in the roof. No such thing existed. Billy the landlord was lying on his back on the bar smoking a cigar demanding Mabel install snooker lights above the entrance to the toilets. Billy suggested you needed the bright light to guide your balls into the corner pocket.

I returned to my seat at the end of the bar which was now occupied by a young girl in glasses who announced she was an eagle in her eerie. I pushed her out of the nest and took my seat. I was waiting for the return of John Smith and had no idea what would happen next. I started to wonder if he'd gouged Hartley Sparrow's eyes out after deciding that pissing was not doing the job. It had been several minutes and I helped myself to a stiff brandy from the optic behind the bar. The brandy hit me with its warm intoxication, and like a sailor on rum I was ready for the fight, or I thought I was.

John Smith appeared at the end of the bar and walked very slowly towards me. He stopped twenty feet away looking at me through the mayhem. He seemed to be puzzled by my appearance and I looked back shrugging my shoulders with the question of "what"? He then raised his voice into a loud shouting chant,

"Red eyes, red eyes, red eyes, everybody's got red eyes! You're their leader, you must die!" As he shouted he moved towards me. The hunting cougar had returned for its prey.

Before John was upon me I managed to grab my bar stool to use as a weapon. It might've been the LSD slowing him down, but I managed to swing the stool holding its legs and made hard contact against his shoulder. I was aiming for his head but this blow managed to knock him down to the floor. I didn't have time to put the trainer in or hit him again. John was off the floor in a second and looked at me filled with a black anger. I swung the stool again in the confined space and managed to catch him a glancing blow across the cheek which sent him spinning away. He didn't make the floor. He clutched at clothing in the crowd stopping himself halfway down.

I was on the move towards the door figuring I could run faster than a drugged John Smith. I was driven by the adrenaline of terror, but he was driven by the LSD madness and the thrill of the chase. Driven by fear I moved quickly, pushing my way through the crazy throng inside the pub. The main entrance was blocked by a rugby scrum playing a game of God knows what with a pool ball. The idiots were blocking the doorway, but I'd made them idiots so I suppose I deserved it. I made for the side door, the very door Bob and I had walked through two years ago.

An enormous flash of heat burst up in front of me as I approached the rabid mushbies. Whatever liquid they were playing with had caught fire and taken hold of the heavy curtains covering the window behind them. The reactions varied from fascination to wild panic. In only a handful of seconds there was an inferno up the back wall. A crowd of retreating mushbies dived into the passageway leading to the side door, my exit was blocked. I swung round and dived below the clutching arms of John Smith as he lunged to grab me. He ploughed on into the crowd of mushbies. In frustration he lashed out at three or four of them, giving me time to go for the fire door. My escape had me passing very close to the inferno and into the corridor towards the back door. Cool salvation and freedom awaited me in the yard if I could move quickly enough.

I headed down the corridor past the toilets towards the back yard. I would have to climb over the gate to gain my freedom, but I was fired up with so much adrenaline this would be no obstacle at all. It would put space between me and John Smith. Not enough space it seemed. The corridor was long and I was halfway down it. My pursuer was close behind me, but at the other end of the corridor, waiting, bloodied and vengeful was Dave Hartley Sparrow.

Conscious, with his useless right arm dangling by his side he waited. His shoulders were saturated as if he'd been walking in the rain. I think I could smell him on the breeze being sucked towards me by the rising heat in the pub. Millicent was not her usual steady self, his left arm never used to wield the shotgun. It didn't matter. His intentions were clear. He raised it and fired. The unfamiliar left-handed stance saved my life.

I could feel the draught as the lead shot passed me by. There was a sharp sting to the very top point of my left shoulder as just one single lead shot dug into my body. I dived to the right to avoid the second barrel and smashed my way into the toilets.

Outside I could hear the second barrel go. Millicent had shot my pursuer and now I had to get outside to escape before he could reload. I would have to climb over John Smith's shattered body. This didn't worry me. I opened the door and dived out into the corridor to discover to my horror John Smith alive and well. He was giving a beating to the shotgun wielding Dave who with bad eyes, and using the wrong arm, had missed once again. Two or three sharp blows had the gunman unconscious or even in a coma. Each blow was delivered with such force I thought his head would snap off. In those moments you could see he would never be the same man again.

John Smith turned to look at me, and with slow deliberation brushed his suit down making himself look presentable. He had a small trickle of blood running from his left cheek, the result of my second blow with the stool. He was dabbing this very calmly with an immaculate white linen handkerchief. He looked at me and shook his head as if he was a disappointed father. Then he made a cutthroat gesture with his right hand and pointed at me. He made no sound and mouthed the words…

"You're next!"

CHAPTER 41

Right here right now, the fires of passion.

Back in the modern day world of instant communication and instant gratification my post-cancer treatment was going slowly. Urinal incontinence had backed off to become the embarrassment of small leaks. The tiredness was very slow to leave my body. Little by little, day by day, tiny parts of my strength and functions of the body returned. To do this I was getting a little help from my friends. This is something I mentioned much earlier.

To help stop urinal incontinence I used pelvic floor stimulation, an electric device to contract the muscles. I won't say where it fits. To recover my sexual ability I used an erectile dysfunction device. This exercises the tissue and reminds the body of what it can do; it works for some people. Finally I used a power breathing apparatus to help strengthen my lungs weakened by chemotherapy.

All done in an effort to regain full pre-cancer function, but to me I seemed like the biggest pervert on the planet. To save time I was doing all three exercises at once, pelvic floor, penis excitement and heavy breathing exercises. I was like a sex crazed one-man band, every orifice in action, but I must add that I can now run upstairs without collapsing at the top through lack of breath, or pissing my pants. Finally, when I'm up there, I can make it into the bedroom with more than half a smile on my face!

It will be a long and sometimes frustrating road, but it is my great fortune to have survived to walk that road.

Over a month had passed since my trip to Paris in the other universe. I knew that each trip revealed more, and during the last the pain was almost unbearable. If I think about it now it makes me shudder and come out in a cold sweat.

Despite this I was desperately missing my lovely Jennifer. She had become the love of my life. I was tormented because she only existed in another dimension and I only visited when summoned. I was convinced I'd never go there again, and everything was over. I wanted to know the truth about the poor heroin addicted Anne and what happened that night. What I didn't want to experience was the suffering to pay for the knowledge. Night times didn't bring any return to a train station or a level crossing gate. No public houses with incredible real ale appeared. The mundane and the ordinary were my nightly staple.

I fell asleep in the middle of the day reading a novel while relaxing in the dappled shade. The beer was slipping down and the pages were turning so slow as to not make sense. I was slipping out of the zone and some lines were being covered five times and still not understood.

A hand shook me awake. I could feel the heartbeat of the person shaking me, and I knew in an instant it was my Jennifer. We were sitting in the pub garden by the river. In the far distance I could hear and feel the vibration of the train passing through a cutting. Never a moment passed in this paradise without travel along the iron road of truth, all those rigid rails are as unmoving as past history. Not the mutated truths received through opinion and education, but your real history, the truth you know to be true, not the lies you sometimes use to deceive yourself. The whole experience was how it should be. She was radiant and the mood was high. She talked about us being together forever. One day I would live in this place all the time. We would get old together, though it would take far longer than in my dull normal world.

Our conversation sparkled for an age until I could see something strange in the distance. The glassy surface of the river was being broken by the approach of a craft. At first I thought it was a long distance away. It was much nearer than I imagined. What I was looking at was a large dog paddling along in the river, and on its back stood a very familiar pixie complete with sub-aqua gear. I knew where I was going. What I couldn't figure out was how. Then I could see a small chord wrapped around the dog's waist. O'Duke was using the briefcase as a buoyancy aid strapped to one side of his large body. It was back to the old dark space routine inside the briefcase. All I had to do was sit and wait for the little armada to arrive at the dock.

I lifted the pint to my lips and took a large delicious mouthful of this wondrous real ale. My foolish move was to close my eyes in ecstasy at the taste. When I opened them I was sitting in the dark. I was sitting inside the briefcase which was leaking river water more and more by the second. The pixie was standing on the bridge of the good ship O'Duke looking down into the briefcase.

"Do you want me to throw you a line and get you out of there?" pixie said, saluting as she did so.

"Yes, pixie, throw me a line." I said this with a resignation. I knew what was coming.

A line coming down towards me was unexpected in itself. This little tyrant was actually throwing me a line. On the end was a Turk's head knot, not unusual in itself, except as it plunged down towards me the knot appeared to be wrapped around a shiny black ball. This object was as big as a cricket ball with a surface as shiny as a diamond and as black as the darkest night. I dived out of the way not wanting to be involved with the evil blackness coming towards me.

"Don't call me pixie, my name is Hysandrbopel and I'm a Lylybel. Get that through your thick head!" These angry words from her lips were muted by this hard black ball seeking me out for a pummelling. At the last second I closed my eyes fearing a shattering impact. Surprised at feeling nothing from the impact I opened my eyes to discover the blackness wasn't solid. I was travelling at speed down an ever widening tunnel. At the end of the tunnel I could already see a wild-eyed Bob waiting for me, one hand forming a fist the other thrust down his trousers.

It had been several weeks since I'd been to the other universe. It was as if a moment hadn't passed since Bob told me he was going to take what he wanted. Without any hesitation he charged directly at me in a drunken madness, his eyes frightful and deranged. His inebriation made him duck and weave like a prize fighter. It wasn't intentional. He was intent on moving in on me, getting me out of the way and then taking what he thought he was entitled to. It wasn't hard to hit him. I took a swing and connected with his jaw just in front of the ear sending him crashing into the corner of the room.

Bob was lying in an untidy heap on the carpet, he breathed heavily without moving his limbs. He appeared to be unconscious, or the drink had finally got the better of him.

"Thank God for that. I thought the mad bastard was going to beat you and rape me. Now who's going to pay for the door?" Anne said to me.

We both stared at the unconscious Bob apparently snoring on the floor.

"I'll get the door fixed, don't worry!" I said.

I smiled at her and indicated that I was enjoying the moment before we were interrupted. Without hesitation Anne slipped back into her girlfriend fantasy, and within seconds she was pulling me back into her arms, working away on my lower body. Bob was out of the picture. Thinking back to her actions, I'm quite sure Anne was out of the picture also. I was well on my way to being very drunk and my judgement was not the best in the world. With hormones rushing forwards, and a very beautiful girl by my side, my mind was a complete void, only filled with lust, and the desire to finally be inside a woman.

A couple of minutes had passed and our rising desires had become a restless passion. Bob remained still and quiet in the corner. He started to make very loud snoring noises. I snorted to myself in derision at his stupidity and he heard me. He wasn't asleep, but growling like a wild animal. I was too involved in the hot pleasures and moving towards my sexual emancipation to notice my derision had garnered a response. Moments later he was on his feet. This time he went for a weapon and it was deadly weapon as it turned out. He didn't manage to kill me with it.

"What the fuck?" was all I managed to say. He was lunging towards me holding a big metal box above his head. It looked like a metal storage trunk, and the way he handled it seemed dangerous. He hurled it straight at me with all the fury of his strength. It never contacted, passing wide of the target, me. The metal box caught on the light fitting and crashed to the bed hitting Anne's head with a glancing blow. The poor girl didn't suffer a bad injury. There would be bruising but she was only stunned. The box hit the bed's headboard and rolled onto its side. My mouth opened in horror on seeing what Bob had thrown in his drunken rage.

Before I could even shout out a single word the small paraffin heater had spilt a gallon of pungent fuel onto the bedclothes, and within a second of stunned inaction half the bed was engulfed in a wall of hot flame. This was the half of the bed nearest to the headboard. This was the half of the bed in which a near naked beautiful seventeen-year-old drug addict was burning to death. The flames in their first seconds were hot beyond the point of approach. This heater, the source of the cloying throat catching dampness in the basement flat was now warming the whole place to a skin mutilating furnace.

Bob looked at me, his face gone from rage in one instant to a wide-eyed terror. Anne was writhing on the bed in a sea of human shaped flame, and her skin was visibly shrinking by the second. This accompanied by a smell of burning hair as her lustrous mane frizzled and died in the flames. I was in a terrible panic because I had to do something. He didn't help the girl he'd set on fire. He ran past me and out of the bedroom door, and out onto the street and away into the dark night as fast as his drunken legs could carry his miserable body. The coward had no guts to confront what he'd done. This man was not a man, and the possibility was, neither was I.

The sheets on the bed were now engulfed in flames. I tried to drag the curtains down but they were pitifully small for the task. I rushed into the bathroom and pushed a bath towel under the tap which took several long seconds to saturate. In my panic this seemed to take an age. By the time I got back into the bedroom the girl had stopped writhing and screaming in agony. The room itself was now three quarters full of acrid black smoke from the foam in the mattress. I wasn't burnt by the fire, but I could hardly breathe even with my head down at floor level. I knew if I managed to quench the flames the girl would never survive. The black cloying fumes were burning my eyes and the horrible black heat in room drove me back. In the end, in my panic, I ran!

I never called the police. Bob never called the police. The man who was supplying her drugs, the man who was also her cousin, never called the police. This man would die two years later kicked to death under the boot of John Smith. The little weasel Smiggy had set us up with his drug addicted cousin, a girl he'd got addicted whilst trying to sell heroin to her group of friends. That very night she'd phoned him and asked what the payment would be. He'd arranged for her to have a little advance before we got our wallets out. The money would go to Smiggy and not help the girl. Perhaps what goes around does come around; karma bites!

I ended the night hiding in a piss and shit smelling alleyway. I was seeking Lenny looking for a way out from this nightmare. Where mad Bob ran to I do not know. When I tried to converse with him in the garage the final time I saw him he wouldn't admit the truth. He'd used outrage to make me feel I'd done something wrong. I'd been part of it, but not the instigator! I'd been there and seen what he'd done. I didn't help either. I couldn't with all the heat and fumes, but to my shame I ran! I didn't go to the police, an action I lived to regret.

This was my first double memory. I'd already lived that moment of filth covered terror in the alleyway. Now I was suffering it again. I stepped forward to leave the alleyway careful nobody should see me. I was moving exactly as before. This was history all over again. This time I trod on some greasy paper or a loose can in the rubbish and fell backwards, hard backwards.

I landed with a very soft thud on the lawn next to Jennifer. It was as if I'd dived down onto the grass to be next to her. I winded myself on landing, but only a little, nothing too serious. Jennifer handed me a fresh pint and a lovely beef with horseradish sandwich. Over by the boat pontoon the pixie was now dressed in her beautiful gossamer outfit. The briefcase had disappeared along with it the dog. That was until the dog padded past me and down to the dock where he dived into the water. The pixie climbed onto his head.

"Goodbye and… good luck?" O'Duke and Hysandrabopel said in unison. The dog could speak!

I looked over to Jennifer, and she pulled me into her arms and gave me an embrace as if to say it was all over. I'd suffered my education and now I knew the truth. I suffered no acid in the final moments of discovery because this time I'd done no wrong other than being foolish and seventeen driven by wild hormones.

"No more briefcase. Do you want to live with me for the rest of your life?" Jennifer asked.

"Yes, I love you. I want to be with you always," I said, and pulled her once more into my arms.

In the next three glorious months I discovered so much about this other universe. My senses were almost overpowered. However, I learnt to control sensual input until it was needed. The first few days were hard work; overdosing on pleasure can be very tiring. Within a month I'd mastered the control, within two months my life was complete. Jennifer was pregnant with our first child, and it was going to be a glorious life. The third month cemented the solidity of our relationship. We were inseparable and as one. Nothing could ever come between us in this almost perfect universe. As with everything new you always find out there are hidden issues, and sometimes dark secrets. Compared to life on Earth these were trivial, centuries ahead of our evolution now.

I woke up one morning to find Jennifer not lying next to me because I was sitting outside on a bench half drunk with my finger holding the page of a novel. The book was, *Das Boot*. It relives the traumas of wartime life in a submarine fighting a gruelling battle for survival deep under the ocean. The realisation that I was back in my post-cancer recuperation world sickened me. If I was in the submarine I would've opened the hatch and let the water flood in to take my life. I got up from my bench and drank four more beers before dragging myself off to bed. Once there I blindly watched the television and drank four more beers to quench my tears of misery, after which I slipped into a drunken coma. Next morning I awoke, not in our bed next to Jennifer. I was, as always, alone.

My head was an appalling mess of battered nerve endings, my dried out brain was desperate for any liquid to take the hangover away. The question, "Would I ever go back to that incredible universe?" was the only thing on my mind. Life here was so grey and dull it sapped all my sense of being. I was grey living in grey.

I now knew how all my troubles had started, and that I was driven insane by the sights and smells of that night. I escaped into Lenny's drug soaked LSD world where fact and fiction became so blurred I transmuted everything that happened into a cloud of broken memories; during that period anything happening day or night could've been just a bad dream. I stayed so long trying to forget I was sucked into a life far worse than the crime that had started it. I was down a dark road to easy money and wild times. So, after my insane period at Lenny's, I had two years of twisted big-money living full of brutality and horrors, many more I'm sure than I've been shown.

My understanding is I became so twisted in this evil web that my mind looked back to better times. Inside my tortured thoughts I wanted to be back in an age of innocence. Finally, with all this horror growing to the point where John Smith's lust to kill was all pervading, something inside me snapped. I took myself back to my last night in a life of sanity, back into The Cauldron. This brought sixty hours of confusion before the showdown with my criminal associates – I cannot say friends. This final confrontation in The Cauldron would consume more than my body!

Despite Jennifer knowing the truth about my past she'd assured me she loved me like no other. Nothing would ever break the bond of joy between us. I had to get back to and live in the other universe. I had it figured like this. I lived with Jennifer for three months in only an hour of sleep, so a week of sleep here would give me more than fifty years, possibly a lifetime. If in that sleep I was locked in my apartment without a drip feed to keep me alive, I would probably die at the end of the week. I would synchronise my death in this unlovely world with my other passing after a lifetime in paradise. I wouldn't mind this, so I longed for a week of sleeping my joyous way to a glorious end in a beautiful place. People restricted to living in this world will never ever remotely understand where I've been.

I phoned around and told everybody I was going on holiday for two weeks. I closed the shutters and locked the place down. I felt foolish and restless. What if I wasted a fortnight in my flat and didn't return to the alternative universe?

I fell asleep in the middle of my hangover day, and slipped back into my universe of perfection. I would, in the end, live in a world where you could have a perfect day.

CHAPTER 42

The Cauldron boils over. It's the end for you and me. August 1973.

My sixty hours of life as a particularly confused young man were about to end. The last grains of sand were running out, and I had no way of stopping the flow. My adversary was in no hurry, finishing his tidying up without approaching. He wasn't going to become dishevelled again tonight, not at my expense at least.

I was wearing fast shoes on slow feet and it was about time I got into gear and made a move. Pivoting, I launched myself back towards the pub, only to discover a wall of heat and flame. I could hear laughter moving closer in the corridor behind me. There were no weapons to grab in the corridor, no fire extinguishers, no spare brooms, or anything that would fall to hand in a Hollywood action movie. I was completely defenceless against a cosh wielding John Smith.

My only course of action was escape through the toilets. These were equipped with barred windows though not of very high quality. I thought I could prise them off. First of all I had to keep John out of the way until the fire took hold in the corridor. The intense heat would break his vigil. Then he would be waiting outside the windows! It was all very hopeless. I had no choice so I dived into the toilets, jamming the door with my foot, leaning hard against it with my shoulder. I was my own barricade against the firestorm approaching.

A minute passed. I remained tense against the door knowing he would sense me weakening. Time in a situation like this releases the tension, your strength ebbs away. I was determined to keep my weight on the door, to keep him outside until it got too hot in the corridor. I wondered if I could hack up through the roof of the toilets into the bedrooms above. It was all a fantasy. I had no tools to get through the substantial building's fabric.

An enormous blow to the door stunned me awake from this fantasy. Also my shoulder hurt like hell. John Smith hadn't rushed at the door with a shoulder. He'd brought the full weight of his cosh hard into the woodwork were he thought I'd be standing. Such was the vigour of John Smith's violent single blow the low quality paper cored door had shattered. The contact point on the inside panel of the door was my shoulder. I thought it was broken for the first few seconds. Higher up and he might have managed to hit me in the head. My pressure on the door was beginning to ease. Another blow delivered at full force next to the door handle saw the door begin to disintegrate.

"Pete! I only want a few quiet words," John said. He was using his best friendly voice with an inability to hide the honeyed malevolence in every word. I could hear behind his soft-toned voice the same inflection he'd used when he described how he'd suffocated Raymond Nice. The same voice he used moments before he killed Smiggy, worst of all I've heard hints of that voice somewhere else before, but I couldn't place it. Perhaps I'd used a similar tone in my forgotten life.

I wasn't considering letting him in. I was frantically searching the room for a weapon. I didn't have any time left. A huge force pushed the door. It could have been a bear on the other side using all its cold power. It was off its hinges before I had time to think. He kept coming, pushing me backwards at speed while I was trapped behind the door. I nearly went down because I was unable to move my feet backwards. He just pushed me across the urine slick tiled floor. This movement only lasted a second until I was sandwiched between two doors, the one off its hinges driving me backwards and the other to a toilet cubicle. The cubicle door opened outwards and remained solid against my back. It wasn't locked, it wasn't occupied, which I suppose was lucky in the event.

I was winded. There wasn't a single breath left in me. Gasping like a goldfish thrown from a broken bowl I slumped to the wet floor. My new clothes soaked up whatever it was making it so wet. Under normal circumstances this would have disgusted me. Out of breath and out of luck on this strange Monday night I didn't care a toss. He smiled down at me, all the while tidying his suit. I'd managed to ruffle his princely feathers a little. The feeling that this would be the full extent of the damage he suffered sickened me.

Fighting for breath I was in no state to react when he dragged me along the floor using my hair. We came to a stop by the trough of the communal floor level urinal. The drain was half blocked with cigarette papers and those smelly little blocks of lavender that's supposed to take the smell away. What they'd succeeded in doing was to make the trough two inches deep in a thick pungent yellow liquid. In one swift movement he pulled me into the gutter, my head bashing hard against the porcelain splash back of the urinal. The throbbing inside my head was ignored because he pushed on my neck with one foot forcing the side of my face and half my mouth down into the piss.

"Now, Peter, tell me where all the stuff is. If you're good I might only cripple you, then again?" John said. Credit to the man. He was wearing his very best Nazi twin perfect smile. I was trying to breathe through my nose. I couldn't speak. I didn't want to drink any of that disgusting liquid. He kept the pressure on my neck until I gasped. Urine flooded into my mouth making me splutter. I was fighting for breath drowning in second-hand real ale. He eased his foot to let me breathe. I was coughing like a seventy-a-day smoker first thing in the morning, my lungs rebelling against the pungent liquid.

The respite was only a few seconds before he pushed down hard again. I was drowning this time, going down for good. My head was twisted round as he pushed his foot forwards towards the back of the urinal. This time both my mouth and nose were under what you could loosely describe as water.

"If you know where our stuff is… bang on the floor twice. If you don't… don't bother," John said.

I banged on the floor twice. The pressure on my neck eased, but John didn't help drag me out of the trough. If I'd not had the strength to push myself out of that hellish place he would have taken the pleasure of watching me drown in piss rather than have LSD and money.

"I got all the acid, and I got £1000 at least!" I spluttered, my voice pitching up. I could hear it and so could he.

"Not interested. You got yourself out of the piss and into the shit. Now I'm going to look in your eyes as I kill you." John said this and his smile never moved. The man was some kind of LSD driven homicidal robot, insane with the joy of his own power. He raised his arm high, the cosh at least eight feet above my head. He was going to bring it down in one terrible crashing blow to shatter my skull. I didn't know how long the pain would last as my head exploded beneath the impact. I could already see it breaking with the classic vision of a watermelon dropped from a roof. He brought the cosh down hard and I waited for the end. I waited for the last sands of my time to run out.

There was a huge shattering of porcelain as he took an enormous chunk out of one of the two heavy washbasins. The cosh went up again, and this time the target had changed. The second of the two washbasins exploded into a myriad of shards. These scattered across the wet floor in that dismal lavatory.

"Brutal isn't it?" John was demonstrating his power over everything. There was a moment when I wondered if I could inflict any damage on this psychopath, and the moment didn't pass. I summoned all my strength and made one last desperate effort. Before he could raise his cosh again to bring it down on his third target which I was certain was my head, I was up on my feet.

"Throw that fucking thing away and fight like a man!" I screamed. I sounded stupid to myself, as if I could believe for one second that he had some twisted honour. I knew there was nothing other than brutal thug in his soul.

"Okay! I'll kill you with my bare hands!" John said. The bright smile had turned into a grotesque sneer. To my surprise he threw the cosh over the toilet door into the cubicle. I couldn't make a dash for it because the door opened outwards. I hunkered and made myself ready, getting my balance just so, ready for the fight. John prepared himself by straightening the sleeves of his suit and adjusting his tie. He was looking down at his shoes in disapproval. In my low stance I swept my hand through the trough of urine throwing it directly into his eyes.

"You little cunt. You're dead!" John said. He continued to be concerned about his appearance not about a man-to-man fight to the death. This nonchalance was coldly disturbing because I wanted him angry and not cold with his calculation. I had time to scoop another handful this time containing several cigarette butts that were floating at one end. Some of these stuck to his face. His smile had slipped, and he charged at me like a wild bull. I'd achieved my aim of getting him angry, taking away the cold and calculating. Now he was going to rip me apart in three seconds rather than enjoy a leisurely two minutes for his own pleasure.

I was waiting for the impact which came with an enormous bang as John passed by inches away and continued straight through the cubicle door next to me. It shattered on impact sending John sprawling onto the lavatory. The porcelain which was full to the brim blocked with shit and toilet paper shattered. He was swimming in filth. Even in a situation like this I had a moment for just a fraction of a second to enjoy it, even though I couldn't understand it.

The understanding came seconds later as Millicent entered the room wielded left-handed by Double-Barrelled Dave who'd suffered from bad eyesight before he'd been pissed on by John. He took one look at me before he fired. The pellets ripped past me and into the cubicle. John Smith was a hard man to kill. Without a second of hesitation he was on his feet and had pushed the remains of the door back to fill the space. The first shot that belched from Millicent's dark eyes had ricocheting off the tiled wall digging at least a dozen lead pellets into John Smith's left bicep.

The second barrel was aimed at the shattered bottom corner of the door. This barrel took its toll on John Smith's right leg. This wasn't a direct hit and some of the pellets were wide of their target. Others dug into the door but he'd sustained enough hits to make him cry out with pain. This didn't stop him. He staggered bloodied from the cubicle straight towards the indestructible Dave Hartley Sparrow. This time the blows came from his fist, delivered with a vicious brutality to the side of Hartley Sparrow's head. The already badly damaged gunman buckled under the first blow falling to the floor unconscious. My Nazi twin decided to kick him in the ribs as hard as he could just a couple of times. This delighted me because John, in his haze of pain, got it wrong. He used his football leg, his wounded right leg.

Doubled up in pain John slumped to the floor and I saw my opportunity lying in the excrement in the corner of the broken cubicle. The deadly cosh was clearly visible and waiting for my grasp. Only a handful of seconds later I was wielding it down towards my adversaries head. Contact was never made as John Smith saw me from the corner of his eye, pivoted, and pummelled me with a huge haymaker straight to the testicles. I folded up like a deckchair in a gale and went down.

The room was a shattered wet mess. One man was lying unconscious on his way towards death. The other was rubbing his right thigh and holding his left arm, injured far worse than it first appeared, but not enough to stop him killing me or getting away. Not enough injuries to cause permanent damage, only enough to slow him on this one occasion. Right now was my only chance.

I was in a sea of pain, and my one-time friend, if that's what he ever was, climbed with great effort to his feet, every movement slow and deliberate. I was fighting my way upwards, breathless with the pain in my groin. In my hand I had a weapon. I didn't have the cosh. This had flown from my grasp during the blow to my testicles. I wouldn't be able to move quickly enough to retrieve it from the far corner, but I'd found something else. We staggered together like old prize fighters at the end of sixteen hard fought rounds. John, with only his right hand usable, took a swing. With the weight going onto his leg the agony was too much, and the limb gave just enough for his fist to whistle under my chin.

I swung with my weapon and missed his body. I missed his head. It was like a bloody comedy, a very bloody comedy. I feared stopping, so I pirouetted on the wet floor like a ballet dancer and made contact on the second pass. My weapon was a large triangular-shaped piece of shattered porcelain. To my horror, when it made contact the shard produced a strange, meaty squelch as it pierced John Smith's jugular vein. Blood shot across the room, staining the mirrors, the walls and running dark across the floor. To my surprise I noticed it turned orange as it ran into the yellow of the urinal.

He didn't move. His blue eyes concentrated on my blue eyes. John Smith, with blood squirting across the room, was refusing to die. Standing quite still he wasn't moving a muscle, so I remained tense and ready for anything. In a final effort he did something that remains strange years later. He broke out into a big happy smile.

"Thank you," he whispered. To this day I don't know what he meant. Was he being sarcastic because I soiled his expensive suit, or was it for taking away his misery in life, for proving somebody could get one over on him, or for being at one time his best and only friend. I don't know of any other friend he had. Nobody would go to his funeral.

He crumpled downwards like somebody had pulled the skewer from inside a kebab. One minute he was erect and smiling, the next a loose pile of dead meat.

The blood was spreading out across the floor all around him. He was now lying in a warm red lake covering most of the slick floor. It was more than horrible. It was ghastly in the extreme. Then I noticed the roof in the toilets was starting to bubble. It was blistering, making the yellow paint on the ceiling go darker and blow into bubbles. The fire started by the warring mushbies was taking the whole pub down.

The Cauldron was not boiling above the fire, but being consumed in the devilish inferno. The fire had spread quickly into the roof space and tongues of flame were probing for new fuel. The pub always smelt of old oil from the heating system mixed with the smell of stale beer, and this had proved even more helpful to the rampant fire. Once the flames reached the boiler room at the back of the bar the place went up like a tinderbox. The years of leaking oil leached into the floor exploded instantly into a fireball, shattering windows and sucking in more oxygen to fan the inferno.

Sirens could be heard in the distance. I had to act with speed. I'd killed the man, and he'd been a man without scruples who would have killed me. That, however, doesn't stand up in court without evidence. We were Nazi twins with our perfect white teeth and no dental records. I swapped his wristwatch for my own Omega. This was inscribed with my name. I don't know if I bought it or if it was a present. The watch might be returning to its original owner. I didn't know if it was a gift from the late John Smith. It certainly wasn't from my parents. I thought the fire might not consume everything, so I emptied my wallet of some money and put it in his jacket pocket. I took his wallet and at the last minute noticed his monogrammed cufflinks.

As I was pulling these from his shirt sleeves I noticed he was wearing a monogrammed gold ring. Was this man branded everywhere? The gold may have melted if the fire was hot enough, but I was taking no chances. It was very tight on his finger and I was running out of time. I hacked off his finger with a sharp-edged piece of the broken porcelain. I worked away for long seconds cracking the bone and cutting through flesh. During this time parts the ceiling started to fall into the room. Dave Hartley Sparrow was not dead. A loud groaning was coming from his mouth, and he was staring from one eye.

It took me a long grizzly minute to remove the gold ring. I placed the finger where it belonged next to his hand to give the impression falling debris had severed it. Pungent fumes were now filling the room coming down black and acrid from above. I grabbed Dave Hartley Sparrow by the feet, and holding him like a wheelbarrow dragged him along the corridor towards the back door. No human voices could be heard coming from the pub, only the sound of the Osmonds singing "Let Me In", and the roaring of the inferno in the bar.

As I pulled him towards the fresh air the black fumes became lower and lower. The ceiling at the pub end of the corridor started to collapse. A huge piece of furniture came crashing through into the corridor only inches away from Dave's head. It was a large Chatwood office safe. This coming from upstairs and not behind the bar must have contained all of Billy's fiddle money. There was a hysterical laugh coming from me at the thought of being crushed to death by the profit from all that water. Water was what we needed right now, and lots of it!

I pulled Dave into the middle of the back yard well away from the pub. I didn't know what to do with him. He was conscious but not in any state to move. I went over to open the large back gate. It was locked with a padlock and two chains with more locks. If the pub collapsed it would fill that back yard with burning rubble. I didn't like Dave Hartley Sparrow but I couldn't leave him lying in the middle of that yard. I was pondering if I could put him in the farthest corner and cover him with something. It would be impossible to lift him over the eight foot high gate with steel spikes on the top.

"Look out, Peter, for God's sake look out!" a voice shouted in the dark.

Numbed by the fumes from the fire, and the fierce battle I had just survived, this was an illusion, a hallucination coming from outside The Cauldron. This voice had come out of the cool beyond the inferno. Two seconds of numbness passed by. I could not imagine what I was hearing. A woman's voice shouting for somebody called Peter to "look out".

"For God's sake, Peter, look behind you!" the female voice shouted.

I turned to see Hartley Sparrow still lying on his back. His fierce grip would never leave his beloved Millicent behind in the flames. He was pointing her at me, unwavering in his aim. It was sawn-off shotgun with a wide spread. He couldn't miss in that small yard. Both barrels were fired at once. The noise was terrible and the pain must have been only for a second before death.

Over the top of the gate, to my surprise, I could see my mother's pale, frightened face. I didn't know it at the time but she was standing on the bonnet of the Land Rover. I could see two smoking barrels above the gate next to her horror stricken face. She hadn't waited to see if Millicent was going to fire, she'd come to help after Jane's frantic requests to save me. They had arrived during the evacuation to be informed by a local policeman who was the first man on the scene that everybody was out of the pub, and remarkably nobody was trapped in the inferno. My sister knew I was somewhere inside and insisted to my mother the showdown would be at the back out of sight in the pub's yard. They were in the process of looking over the locked gates when I dragged the semi-conscious Double-Barrelled Dave out into that small enclosed area. My luck, for once in my life, was in.

I think he was dying, but he wanted to take me with him. I don't know to this day if his beloved shotgun was loaded. It may have contained the empty cases from the two shots fired at John Smith. With his one good arm I don't see how he could have reloaded it, though he'd managed it before. I never went over to look, and I never ever told my mother that I thought it wasn't loaded.

She'd brought along something heavier than her four ten used for rats and minicab drivers. With her that night she carried one of my father's double-barrelled shotguns. This was hefty twelve-bore with the equally hefty cartridges.

"Stand clear. We're going to ram the gate and knock it down." My mother shouted this and then disappeared.

A few seconds later there was a loud splintering of wood as large back gates broke free from their hinges and crashed inwards almost filling the yard. I had to stand well back in the corner behind the mutilated Dave until the gates had fallen. They only just missed me and fell hard on top of the gunman's corpse. I staggered out of that terrible sixty hours towards the Land Rover and was pulled safely into the back by the loving hands of my lioness mother.

My sister accelerated away into the night, back to the farm where I would be hidden. We nearly didn't make it as my sister had to swerve up onto the pavement to avoid a police car and the following fire engine. It was a close shave! As we raced back to the farm they didn't know they were carrying a man who would die, and later were both delighted to find out that as a dead man I would have to start a new honest life.

John Smith's immolated body was examined, and from the evidence it was decided that Peter Robert Jackson had been the fires only victim.

My family were not delighted to discover they would have to attend my funeral and grieve. They were supported by my aunties who were never told the truth. Gossip was Beattie's middle name though she always claimed it was passing on news and information. George was horrified to discover the truth. He was amazed by my mother, proud of my sister, and tolerant of me. We still speak today but only of the present.

After the pub had collapsed it filled the yard with the tons of hot rubble. Days later the mutilated body of Dave Hartley Sparrow was dug out of the pile of bricks and burnt wood. It was a grisly surprise for the JCB driver. He'd chopped the corpse's head off with the digger bucket. Some people have no luck even when they're dead! Police managed to identify him, and with the wounds to both victims it was decided they had died at each other's hand in a local drugs war that claimed three other victims of known gangs that same day.

It had all happened during the last and most legendary crazy Monday quiz night in the heat of The Cauldron.

CHAPTER 43

Right here right now, crime and punishment.

You never think the police are going to visit. I wasn't aware policemen existed in the other universe. The four policemen were all dressed in white uniforms bedecked with gold braid. They carried nothing offensive with them apart from their very large ornate hats. I answered the door to our little house tucked away in the most idyllic side street in the universe. Another three months had passed and I was now working, tinkering with old vintage cars. In this place you could pursue any career you desired. I don't know how the pay scales worked or how the greater economy functioned, but everything ran like clockwork. A perfect universe to live, and with my only love four months pregnant I was in rapture.

"Mr Paul Redondo, would you mind taking a stroll down to the courts tomorrow? A Lylybel has accused you." The officer was nothing but polite. I could even sense the calmness of his heartbeat. He was not here to push me to the floor and force handcuffs around my wrists. This was a volunteer police force, people doing it to be helpful. The uniform made it a pleasant task by looking so smart in the sunlight. He didn't even suggest a time in which to appear. "Take a stroll down tomorrow."

Jennifer was standing behind me and I could feel her heartbeat speed up. I could also feel the heartbeat inside her respond to the tension.

"Paul, I think I've broken the rules! You're in trouble because I've not completed my education," Jennifer said. We were face-to-face, and her lovely eyes had lost their brilliance, that unforgettable glint. She emanated an aura of sadness.

"What do you mean, 'broken the rules'?" I asked.

"I don't know, Paul, I just think I have." She took my hand, pulling me back through the house towards the sunshine in the back garden. It was obvious she didn't want to think about anything that could spoil this. I could feel her dread and nervousness passing right through me. Outside of my own education this was the first time in this universe I'd felt anything sinister creeping in to the bright beauty.

She held me very tightly all through the following night. The next day I dressed as normal in my tweed suit. Putting on a smarter tie was my only concession to the court appearance. Jennifer came with me, never leaving my side, never letting go of my hand. The courthouse from the outside looked like a Victorian junior school. We entered into a large hall through colourfully glazed double swing doors. The stained glass panels illuminated the hall with a thousand brilliant colours. I was shocked to see the inside. Unlike the outside it was elaborate in the extreme. Every surface was covered in gold leaf or some rich colour. The fabrics covering the chairs were so vivid they were hard to look at. Topping this all on a high podium was a large gold and purple throne. At once I assumed this is where the judge or the adjudicator would be positioned for the hearing.

The room was empty, echoing with our movements. Fine dust hung in the air illuminated by the shafts of sunlight through the high stained- glass windows at the far end of the room. Nobody else was there, so this must be the wrong day. Some kind of sick joke was being played on us, but the only problem was that in this perfect universe nobody played sick jokes. I could sense footsteps coming towards me from under the ground. Whoever was coming was walking along a subterranean corridor, walking at speed, with very light footsteps.

A hatchway in the floor next to the throne was thrust open. Out of it, in all his fine judicial clothes, stepped the judge. Similar to a knight of the realm in all this finery, this man was all velvet and ermine, with a more than generous powdered wig topping his head. From where we were sitting he appeared to be very tall and slim, almost gaunt for his height. He slipped the wig off letting his mass of flowing locks tumble out. I was shocked to see the judge and our accuser was one and the same, Hysandrabopel of the Lylybel, the creature I had teased with the name pixie.

"All rise, and face the search for truth and justice," pixie said, banging her gavel with sharp insistence against the side of the throne as she spoke.

We rose together holding hands. Through her hand I could feel Jennifer thinking, *No... Not now!*

"Would the accused please remain standing for the charges to be made?" pixie said. The voice was full of the echoes of officialdom. There was no fun in this pixie today. No frog uniforms, no little fireman, all business. Jennifer didn't move, and neither did I. Were we both accused of crimes against whatever the state consisted of in this place? Jennifer pulled my hand to capture my attention, then to my astonishment pushed me down into my seat. She was the accused, the committer of a crime.

"Jennifer Alicia... you have failed to finish your education. You have failed to educate Paul Redondo about all his failings in life. And worst of all, you subverted the purpose of bringing him to this universe," pixie said. This little speech was delivered with a grave voice.

Jennifer started to cry and I could smell the salt in the tears. I could gauge how much water was in each one. I could feel the misery oozing out of her tear ducts with every drop that ran across her cheeks. I moved to stand up and say something. Jennifer pushed me down making it quite clear in action and sentiment alone that I was not to stand.

"I fell in love with him! Is that a crime?" Jennifer said.

"You will both be punished. He will have to go, and hell won't be good enough!" the pixie said. Then she indicated that we should sit and listen to what she was going to say. We were not to interrupt, and at the end of it her judgement would be final, and without appeal. No jury of our peers, no defence lawyers, only the ringmaster of all my memories, the access memory bringing a verdict. She outlined very clearly what was supposed to happen.

"I knew all the things you'd done wrong before you got here. It was decided we would send you to the darkness. The slimy fools in that grisly place couldn't kill you. I couldn't believe you could survive so much pain. Afterwards it was decided that you would fall in love with this place, and if not this place with the woman who was so perfect for you she would be irresistible. With this you would stay in this universe forever. Time, sustenance and cancer treatments in the other world would cease. One day this universe would fade away because in the other world you would be dead. We were going to keep you trapped here until you died for your crimes." I didn't mind this. Three thousand days here were only one day in my dull universe. Being here was the best punishment in the world!

Pixie continued. "The educational package with all the acid bubbles torturing you, I put together, having a little bit of fun at your expense. Then to my annoyance, you started to get better. You kept leaving, and using this place for holidays. Jennifer wasn't a very good junior adjudicator. The stupid girl fell in love with you and that was a bonus for me because I could sense you were deeply in love with her. Like a big stupid fish on the hook. The problem I now have is she's carrying the child of someone who shouldn't exist in this universe. This is very serious. The Grand Council don't like it one bit."

I moved to stand and say something. Jennifer held me down, and I could feel her saying "NO" to me, or was it to what she knew was coming?

Pixie had paused because she could sense I was going to stand. In her gravest voice she continued. "You may think this trial is some kind of game, and Jennifer is pretending to love you. Feel her heartbeat through your hand, feel the sensations you share together in your mind, remember all that has gone before. Yes, she's in love with you, and her punishment is that if she wants to stay with you she will lose the child. You've murdered one child already, so do you want to murder another?"

She looked at me then as if waiting for an answer. I hesitated for less than a fraction of a second.

"No, I'll do anything to protect my child," I said. Jennifer next to me let out a sob. She knew the sentence.

The pixie explained that Jennifer would never be allowed to educate again. She would be the only sad person in this beautiful universe. Her only joy the child, who would live and become a new part of the parallel world. The child would be special, a child in a hundred billion, half of this world and half from somewhere alien and grey. My fate would be simple. They couldn't kill me with sensation and they couldn't burn me to death with the truth. They would separate me from my greatest love, and in my world I would suffer nothing but deep depressing sorrow.

"You can't do this! I wasn't that bad! Bob was the one who was crazed. I tried to help the girl!" I pleaded. It was to no avail, the pixie was having none of it.

"Jennifer Alicia didn't finish her education because she didn't finish yours! Now I will!" The pixie said. The note was doom laden as she said it, and before the words stopped echoing around the enormous room I could hear a rumbling sound coming from four different directions. It sounded at first like a train coming, then wooden wheels on floorboards, and after a few moments I recognised the sound of that iron road of truth coming towards me.

In seconds I was standing in a box formed by four perfect, unblemished mirrors. I could see hundreds of myself. I was everywhere in my tweed suit and smart tie. Jennifer appeared in one of the mirrors standing next to me. She clutched me very tightly not wanting to let me go, and in failing to release her grip started to melt like a hot candle, and in a final moment when the heat got too much her whole body collapsed in on itself.

In another mirror Jennifer was standing alone with tears rolling down her face. They may have been tears of joy because she was holding a young child with blonde hair and, in this universe, perfect teeth. I don't think they were tears of joy. The sadness coming from her eyes told another story. The child in her arms gave great consolation, but the truth remained she'd lost her greatest love. I knew instinctively a new great love would form between a mother and a child who would remain forever fatherless.

The mirrors had told me two truths but nothing about myself. Then Bob appeared in one of the mirrors, after which he started to come into view at random in a hundred mirrors, in a thousand mirrors, and finally I was feeling suffocated by him; he was all around me in every mirror. There was nothing in the mirrors but a million pictures of Bob Wilson. I didn't get it at all because I didn't understand what the mirrors were trying to say. Then I could see Bob putting on sunglasses. These glasses were aviator style with mirrored chromed lenses. He stared at me from every mirror, and an infinite sea of reflections looked in on me. His head was getting larger and larger until the lens of one eye filled all four mirrors, his face dominating an infinite amount of space in that mirrored universe.

Then I could see truth reflected in his sunglasses. The crazy drunk, the rapist driven by testosterone, the man insanely raving, and the man who'd drank a bottle of cheap wine topping up too much beer was ME!

I was the one who got jealous when the girl decided she wanted some love for a short while to fill her empty cold life. The horror of this struck me. In my rage I'd hefted the fire at Bob not the other way around. The man who isn't called Peter Robert Jackson threw a paraffin stove at his best friend Bob in a drunken testosterone-fuelled rage. The outcome was a young heroin addicted prostitute burning to death on a bed far to lavish for her meagre basement flat. The other thing that came from the mirrors was a cold rank cowardice when I ran. I was more afraid of being in trouble than trying to help.

The cowardice was hidden in a sea of LSD, and finally the memory of that night was just another bad trip. By this time I was deep in the clutches of Lenny and too afraid to admit to myself what I'd done. This is the moment I started to enjoy the fruits of my drug dealing, this was the point where I started down the road of debauchery finally slipping into the clutches of Harry the Pocket and John Smith. From lifting that paraffin fire above my head to wielding a shovel to bury Raymond Nice on a Thursday night just thirty-six hours before I woke up with amnesia was one small step for a disgusting rank coward.

This amnesia was retrogressive. From the moment I threw that fire and started to run, things in my life went from bad to worse. Or terrible to appalling! I suppose after I'd buried the suffocated Raymond Nice in the small wood on the old farm I could stand myself no longer. John Smith was carrying out a master plan I'd outlined in the pub, suggested as a joke whilst a little bit drunk. This psychopath was carrying it out to the letter. He was going to get rid of all the opposition and I was going to help him. I'd never discussed how I was going to help him, so I suppose he thought my amnesia was an act, some part of the twisted plan. Finally crazed on LSD John Smith thought I was going to eliminate him and take the prize, everything!

All this information was flooding into my head from my sad reflection in those chromed glasses. I wanted him to go away, and I wanted me to go away!

The amnesia wasn't an act. My mind had rejected all the horrors I perpetrated after that drunken night in The Cauldron. The last innocent memory I possessed was when we marched out to become men. So this was the moment I'd returned to. My mind desperately wanted to stand in the moment before we became something entirely different from the men we hoped we would be. Bob may have become a man, but he was hidebound by his incredibly tough father's insistence on silence. I think holding in the horror I put him through killed him in the end. I buried it for forty years until cancer was killing me. At this point I was allowed into a parallel universe to let it all out, and pay for it!

At this moment I'm being suffocated by mirrors of intense power. I can feel Bob breathing, so tactile the sensations. I can see the spectrum of light in the reflections. I am still in a parallel universe without leaving. If I'm imagining this why is it so beautiful? Is all this some other force bringing me to justice? And I do know that this universe is not coming from inside me. I can sense every molecule of movement in this glorious place, and I know I cannot generate so much inside this average head.

With surprising suddenness the mirrors rolled back away from me, going further and further away until they disappeared into the fabric of the courthouse. I'm left looking at Jennifer who is crying bitter tears.

"The sentence is final and without appeal! Jennifer, you will be alone with only the love of your child! You can go with him but your child will die, the same as the young girl" The pixie said this in a grave tone. Jennifer had no choice, and I experienced the solitude coming from her. It was a cold space.

"The sentence is final and without appeal! Paul Redondo, known in your world as Peter Robert Jackson, you shall return to your world. You shall never return here. The misery you suffer for your sins is up to you! I hope you enjoy it!" After this statement the pixie known Hysandrabopel the Lylybel burst out into a hail of hysterical laughter. Tears were rolling down her cheeks and as they fell to the floor turned into bright bubbles that floated high into the shafts of sunlight, glinting like diamonds. She was free from my sinful past. This pixie was no longer a conduit for my wrongdoings.

Jennifer walked over to me and took me in her arms for the final time. The kiss that followed for a few seconds held more passion and love than all the kisses I've experienced in my entire life. She broke away and smiled at me. I was about to say something when I woke up, crying hard hysterical tears.

I knew without doubt the fabulous universe had gone forever. Never again would I experience life so vital and raw. All the beauty of molecular sensation and movement was gone. The blueness in my soul turned to grey, and then to the deepest black. It was the longest three days of my entire life. Every moment was like waiting on death row for an execution. One every day!

Nothing brightened my dark soul. I had survived the mental and physical rigours of cancer with its terrible treatments. I was getting healthier every day. In a few days I would start work again after nearly a year, a year of teetering on the edge, and sometimes looking over it and seeing darkness, and at other times light so brilliant it changed your soul.

I walked out onto my terrace holding a very large brandy in my hand because my course of action was to get blind drunk hoping to fall into an alcoholic coma. This course seemed like the only answer to my bleakness. It was a cold winter's day outside, and on the distant hills I could see fresh snow had fallen. Higher up in the sierras it would be powder. The skiing would be fantastic. A day to change my state of misery, so tomorrow could become my perfect day.

Positive action and positive thought followed. I tossed the contents of my glass from the terrace and went inside to plan. I looked at the snow forecast on the computer, making a decision. I couldn't keep my life on this black level any longer. Things were going to change.

I couldn't stay off the drink altogether. As I watched a Tarantino war movie I downed three or four cans of lager and pondered the coming tomorrow.

I was going to make sure that this one fabulous day was going to happen. I was positive this would be a life changing perfect day. I was becoming very optimistic for the outcome.

Me being optimistic? I think so!

CHAPTER 44

Right here absolutely right now, around and around and around we go.

More stuff to add to the voice recorder.

The digital recording device ran out of words. The story was told. I travelled 300 km out of my way, zigzagging across the country, using the motorway system as a reading room. The more precise explanation would be a listening room. I got close to home before I realised how long this story was going to be. I didn't want to sit in the quiet of my apartment. I wanted the world to pass by in the physical sense as the timelines in the story passed into my consciousness. What seemed like hours later than intended I was filling up at a petrol station. During this stop I studied the readout and discovered I had several chapters more to listen to. I headed off in the other direction at the next interchange. I wanted to experience everything this man who'd thrown himself to his death had experienced.

The truth is I did experience everything this man had lived through. If you haven't already guessed, this was my story. We are one and the same. My alter ego had thrown himself off the parapet and into the deep void to be shattered on the rocks below. The intention was to have a perfect day, unspoilt by the knowledge of a bleak tomorrow… I'd planned to have my perfect day with an optimistic ending. No pessimism at the thought of tomorrow bringing back the horrors of my past grievous mistakes and the all-pervading misery of a lost love.

I'd survived the cancer and lost the will to live because my mind or some other outside force had insisted I face my turgid forgotten years. I was sickened by what I learnt, but in all seriousness I could learn to forget again. I'd done so once so why not again?

What had broken me was Jennifer. The reality we shared together was far more than the sum of any number of normal lifetimes, so intense were the sensations in the parallel universe. I do not believe for a single moment it came from inside my head. This place is parallel to us and they somehow dragged me there to show me the truth.

After the early morning discounting my day was full of hope. The snow was perfect, and a bonus was I got to ski with good company for more than the two hours as I mentioned at the beginning of this strange confession. What a day. I started with the intention of throwing myself to my death, to make it a perfect end to a very imperfect life. I met the London boys, after which I met one of their sisters who was on the long weekend skiing trip with them. She must have seen it in my eyes because she didn't hear it in my voice. I couldn't speak. Alice wasn't similar to Jennifer at all! Alice didn't remind me of Jennifer… Alice was Jennifer, every single perfect part of her!

I encountered Alice as a real person in a very real world. She was tangible, alive and there with me. Alice was Jennifer in the absolute sense. It wasn't just in the physical; she was in every sense the same person. It was a miracle beyond miracles. We understood some incredible fusion was happening between us the moment we met in the sandwich cabin. The boys stayed on for a few beers, and we skied on for two more hours. It was the strangest thing. We didn't have to speak, we'd known each other all our lives, and knew in a single moment we would be together for the rest of them. She was divorced with two children, now teenagers. I had lived alone for some years by choice. It was instant and magical between us, and so incredibly close to the sensation of oneness I felt with Jennifer in the strange alternative universe, that it made no difference.

They were leaving late that night to catch an early flight back to the UK. She would return to Spain or I would go to England within the week. I'd used my smart phone to find a number of vacancies open in my field. The job I had here no longer seemed important. I didn't have the job in England at that moment, and I didn't care. I would find one because I'd found something far more important.

We had to be together, and it wasn't just me thinking this. Alice admitted she felt an instant bond with me but had been tentative at first to suggest some connection. When I replied that I felt the same we just moved into a strange knowledgeable contentment. We parted with just one kiss between us. It held everything, that final beautiful kiss in the courtroom with Jennifer had held. In that lingering moment in the cold sierra air it seemed this was the end of a kiss that had begun in a courtroom in another reality. In a handful of days I'd gone from bliss to bleak to black, and now I'd returned to incredible bliss in a real tangible world.

I was amused to sit there on that terrace looking at the girls, thinking to myself that I'd got the best girl in the world coming into my life. I was amused to imagine myself ending my pitiful existence by plunging off that parapet, exaggerating my movements whilst hanging on the ornamental lamp post, and playing to the crowd to give them maximum horror. If I'd killed myself that afternoon the probable course of action was to drink the most expensive champagne on the wine list, or the finest brandy. Once in a state of numbness I would have run at the parapet and dived over like an Olympic swimmer starting a race. No showboating for the crowd. Now I amuse myself by laughing at what would have been if not for Alice.

You may be asking why Alice isn't with me now. This is quite simple because she is the organiser of a significant birthday celebration for one of the other ski trip guests. Being with her had distracted her from party organising. We knew our love would remain with us for the rest of our lives, so with that lingering beautiful kiss I bade farewell until we are together to enjoy thousands of days more.

Now the story is over and I'm only a few kilometres from home. It was a little bit shorter than I imagined, or I stuck in too much of a diversion by going halfway to Madrid and back… Suddenly I have to brake!

The road in front of me is blocked, and there's lots of flashing lights. Hazard lights on the back of cars blink orange, dazzling my eyes, and all the traffic has come to a halt blocking the two-lane motorway. Up ahead it looks like a nasty accident, and being the middle of the night I pull up to a halt only fifteen cars back from the carnage. Time passes slowly as I wait for things to be cleared. Like everybody else I'm curious to see if there's anybody injured. An ambulance coming from the other direction stopped on the hard shoulder of the other carriageway. It was not called to the scene, but was there only by circumstance as it was returning to a hospital somewhere.

The police arrived on the scene coming down the centre of the two lanes of stopped traffic. Their headlights illuminate the mangled car. Under the bright lights I can see that a large saloon has run into the back outside corner of a small low loader; a lorry used to bring single cars in for repair. The car has a quarter of its roof cut off where the back of the lorry punched its way into the passenger compartment. It looked like the car had hit the lorry first, and I think the damage wouldn't have been too bad until the lorry hit the barriers coming to a dead halt, after which the mass of the car pushed its way onto the cutting blade that was the loading bed of the lorry.

The car in front of me was empty when I arrived, a large Mercedes-Benz, with its engine running, the keys in the ignition and no driver. There was a man leaning in through the front window on the passenger side of the mangled car. He was dressed like me in lightweight skiing clothes. It turned out he was a doctor coming back from a late dinner at the ski resort. He'd come across the accident and rushed in to help the injured. The ambulance man could be seen picked out in the bright lights of the police cars. He was carrying a large medical bag equipped for emergencies, but he seemed to be hesitant in his movement.

The ambulance man left the scene carrying the bag with him. I thank God that the injuries were not sufficient to use his medical expertise. The doctor remained leaning into the car as if he was comforting somebody. Whoever it was sitting in the car was probably a little bit fazed by the shock of the accident, not requiring medical attention for physical wounds. The ambulance man returned carrying something else. A large white sheet was illuminated as he opened it. With the contrasting black shadows from the lights all around, the inside of the car could not be seen clearly. I'm glad I never saw it.

The doctor and the ambulance man draped the sheet over something in the front passenger seat, and moved away a short distance in deep discussion. Now I could see a white lump in the front of the car, and it was obvious that whoever was beneath it was no more. Within seconds I could see black shadows forming, coming through the white. Whoever was in the front had been brutally injured. The accident had been quick and bloody. I thought about my own death that afternoon and how lucky I was that my life had changed for the better. Then I thought about how these people in the car who were going back from somewhere, or off to visit someone had experienced violent change in a matter of seconds. Now they would face misery and a funeral. Recriminations and guilt would probably follow, after which tears for Christmas and at birthdays. The police were doing their best to move the car to open the outside lane so everybody could move on. We'd all seen too much.

Every time they attempted to move the car there was an outburst of rage. I couldn't hear what was being said but it was loud and angry. Then the biggest shock of all that cold night; the man who wouldn't let them move the car wore only his underpants! I wondered if he was drunk coming back from one hell of a party. Had he caused the accident driving drunk in his underclothes with bare feet?

No, that wasn't it.

Then I saw the other two and my heart went cold. One was another man in his underpants standing in the cold, helping the police calm down the angry man. The other was a woman in her forties, a woman who kept herself in good shape. I could see this because she only wore small panties. She wore no bra and her breasts were exposed to the cold night air. Such was her state of distress that under the bright lights she showed no sign of noticing she was nearly naked. I couldn't imagine why they were dressed like that. In one cruel instant the truth struck me as cold as a sledgehammer made of ice.

They were naked because their clothes were all covered in their friend's blood and brains, or was it the wife of the screaming man? It could have been a sister. I didn't know and I didn't want to know. They had thrown their blood and brains soaked clothes over the buckled barrier into the darkness expunging that part of their horror. I was saved and they were lost and I couldn't imagine what it must be like to have a loved one's shattered skull sprayed all over you!

The big man was really going crazy every time they tried to move the car. You could see the police trying to explain, and I could hear the shouts of anger coming from him.

"Don't you touch her, you bastards!" he said. I was shocked he was speaking English with a London accent.

I went cold right through to my soul as I noticed he was Tony, one of the London boys. The other man in his underclothes was Michael, his friend. The woman I knew to be called Jacqueline. She was Alice's best friend. They'd all been travelling together on the short ski break. They were all returning to England on an early flight the next morning.

I closed my eyes and prayed that when I opened them it wasn't the same grisly picture. I open my eyes and everything is more horrible than I thought. The woman in the car is a love I will never have. Alice is decapitated and spoiled. The vision I met only hours ago who saved my life is dead!

She was going to change everything in my world, and now, like Jennifer, she'd gone forever in a more horrible way than I could ever imagine. People dressed only in their underwear on a freezing night screaming and angry only feet from her body. It was the thought of their discarded clothes soaked in Alice's brains that turned my stomach. I walked over to the barrier and vomited until I had nothing left inside me.

I had nothing left inside me before I vomited.

The road wasn't cleared for another twenty minutes, so I sat in the car thinking and not thinking, a constant loop of horror going round in my head. I'd killed enough people in my life. Did I make their car thirty seconds slower in leaving? I was talking to Alice on the phone as she was walking to the car. She told me it was very slippery and she couldn't concentrate on both things. She stopped and we made plans for several minutes. These minutes would have changed the history, so I'd managed to kill Alice before we'd even begun.

I couldn't look at them as I passed. I could hear their frantic voices, and involuntary nerves made me glance for a fraction of a second towards the gathering. Jacqueline was now wrapped in a white blanket, little spots of black coming through showing on the surface. I don't know if she had small cuts or it was blood from Alice's body. Inside I was reflecting on everything that had gone before. As I passed by my senses were invaded. I could smell ruptured diesel lines, puddles of fuel evaporating on the road surface, and I think, or hope I only imagined that I could smell the metallic odour of blood, the leaching away of Alice's life force.

At the next interchange I took a detour and headed back to Sierra Nevada by a different route. The forecast for today, because now it was today, was brilliant. The snow would be fabulous as it was yesterday. On this day I would spare no expense. I would seek out the best hotel and catch three hours sleep waking to the most lavish breakfast. I would spend the entire day skiing, stopping only to eat and drink, again nothing but the best available. Today I would satiate my desire for perfection. Every piste would be taken in a delight of ice crystals and sunshine. I would enjoy every moment in my last attempt at the garnering perfection.

I would then go to the terrace bar and have something exquisite from the menu. The drink would be selected from the very pinnacle of the list. Nothing would spoil the experience because I wouldn't need to worry about tomorrow or future miseries. On this, my second day at the slopes, there wouldn't be two of us sitting together, only me, the killer, broken on a wheel of sorrowful truth… This life wasn't going to end as the light slowly fades to a dying dullness. My life was going to end after a day of taking pleasures in the sunshine.

There would be no tomorrow to spoil my perfect day…

The End?

EPILOGUE

My amazing day, by Alice Jennings.

Alice never thought she'd find love again. Like so many others she'd spent a short time on an Internet dating site, eventually forcing herself out to date people she knew she wouldn't like after ten minutes. This only lasted five dates and she closed her account.

Now, in the bright white sunshine of the Sierra Nevada, unexpected love had come to Alice in the form of a man called Peter Robert Jackson. She couldn't believe that they just clicked from the first moment they set eyes on each other. The short hours they skied together was the most satisfying time she'd had in years. She knew within minutes of their first encounter this man was "the one". An instant connection as if they'd known each other intimately in another life, and she knew in her heart Peter felt the same about her.

Everything had gone well until she walked to the car. Alice had stopped to talk to Peter on the phone for no reason other than to hear his voice. Their car was parked a fair distance away and illuminated under bright lights; it was standing in glassy water. The others were making their way towards it. She had to stop walking to talk with Peter because with the car park was icing over and she feared falling on the slick surface. Alice talked for a few minutes holding the others up.

The car horn sounded and Alice made quick sincere promises to Peter. They would be together again within a matter of days. She knew it was their fate. The car horn sounded again and she rushed to climb into its warmth, the engine now running.

She never made it. Slipping on the ice she went down hard on the edge of a kerb. As she hit the ground with a terrible force and Alice heard a cracking sound, her femur was broken. She didn't know if it was audible or she'd heard it inside her head, but it was loud! It was hurting like hell but at least it wasn't a compound fracture. "A straight break", as the doctor told her later. Her friends crowded round the bed wishing her well before they rushed off to the airport, only four in the car instead of five.

After everyone had gone Alice looked for her phone. It was only then she realised that during the fall she'd landed heavily on her smart phone, shattering the screen. She couldn't contact the first person she thought of. This wasn't one of her sons, or her brother, or any of the party of twelve skiers over from England for a birthday celebration long weekend.

Alice only wanted to talk to Peter. Her SIM card would go in a spare phone in the next couple of days. Then she would contact him again, though she suspected he would attempt to contact her well before then. Peter had collected two or three phone numbers from the group so contact wouldn't be lost. Realising this Alice breathed a sigh of relief; he was already an essential part of her life.

Everything would turn out to be amazing in the end. Breaking a leg! What a way to end a perfect day.

GOLIATH'S EYE

Available soon

Do you want to save the world? David Spencer certainly didn't think this was his destiny.

He sees himself as very ordinary, an average teenager, not physically strong, and shy. His broken family move to a distant coastal town. Downcast by the move his spirits improve as he becomes closer to his brother Richard, and encounters the iridescent Daisy. With his new friends David becomes involved in a protest to stop a bypass destroying the magical and ancient woodland protected by a Giant. All around that ancient place a strange madness is developing; a slow creeping insanity.

His new home close to the woodland has a history of strange happenings. Things become disturbing when his brother goes missing. Half strangled voices demand retribution against a mysterious figure for the return of Richard. The quiet teenager discovers he's been elected as the only one who can help. At first David doesn't realise he's slowly absorbing the madness – becoming ever more savage in his efforts to free his brother from alien abduction.

Digging deep into it twisted pit of violence after more people are abducted David fights back – he faces a life or death showdown with help from his onetime adversary the Giant.

Both face death second by second in the final battle against the strange force that inhabits the woodland. Not everyone would survive…

ALL THE DEVIL'S PRAY

Available later this year

Mortimer Sands has spent most of his thirty seven years cloistered away on his mother's large estate. He knows little of the world, only understanding what his mother – who claims to be a virgin – has told him. Determined to meet others he embarks on a pilgrimage to Santiago De Campostilla. An innocent abroad – Mortimer could almost be the reincarnation of Christ himself. Early in the walk he is befriended by a small dog who watches over him, keeping him safe?

Daily, as he walks, he relives his strange formative years – bathing in black tulip petals, creatures with snakes in his garden, strange thoughts that enslave him. And at night he is tormented by the physical and the non-physical. He encounters a couple who take terrible advantage of his innocence, treating him almost like their slave. With the help of Gladys U Plymsoul he escapes their clutches. His jolly bubbly friend is not all she seems – she wants Mortimer in a very personal way. She wants to drag him towards Satan himself.

Naked and with her physical lust unsatisfied she attempts to murder Mortimer. She thinks he's dead… On awakening he seeks out Gladys to show her the truth. And reveals his true self…